Stone Temples

Chronicles of the First Twelve

Book One

Meagan Le Riche

Acknowledgements

I would like to thank my friends who have supported me during the long process that was this book – Pauline, Naomi, Alex, Teresa and Andrew. Without your support and belief this book would never have made it to this stage.

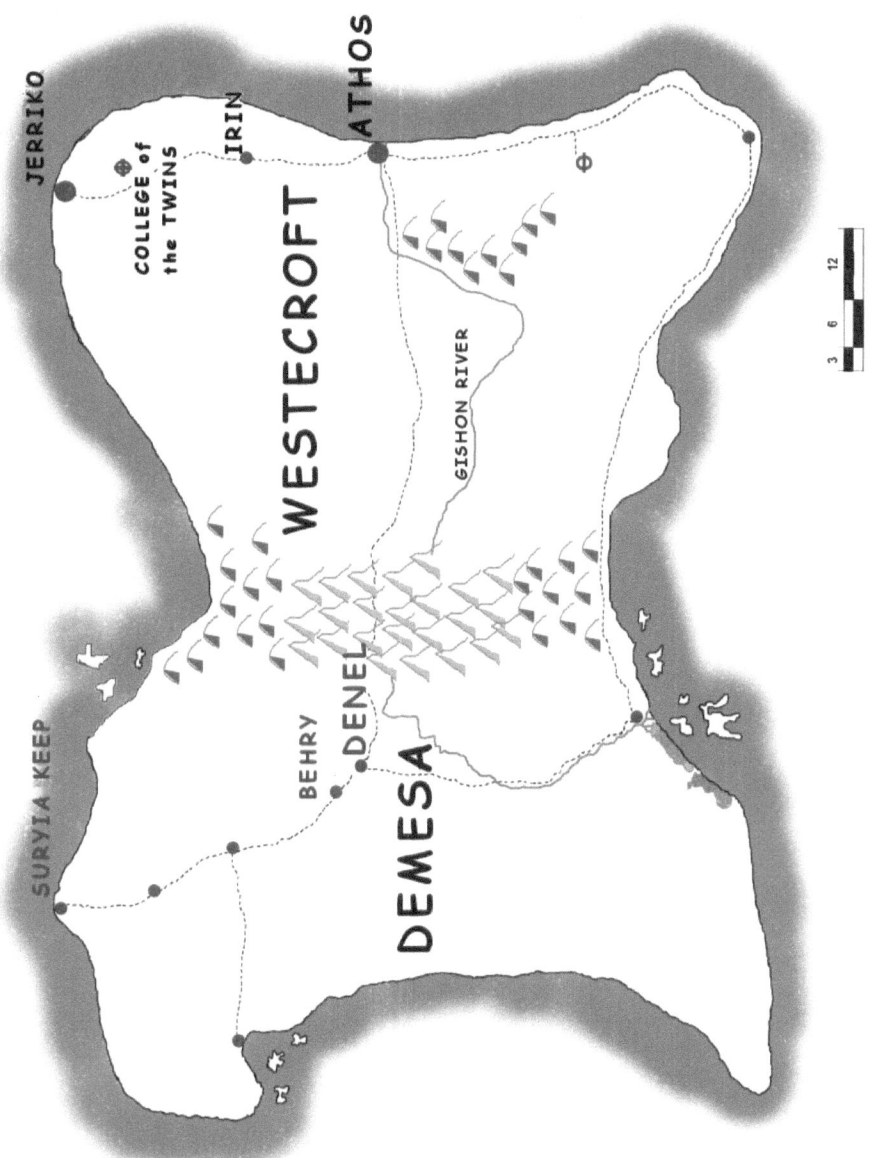

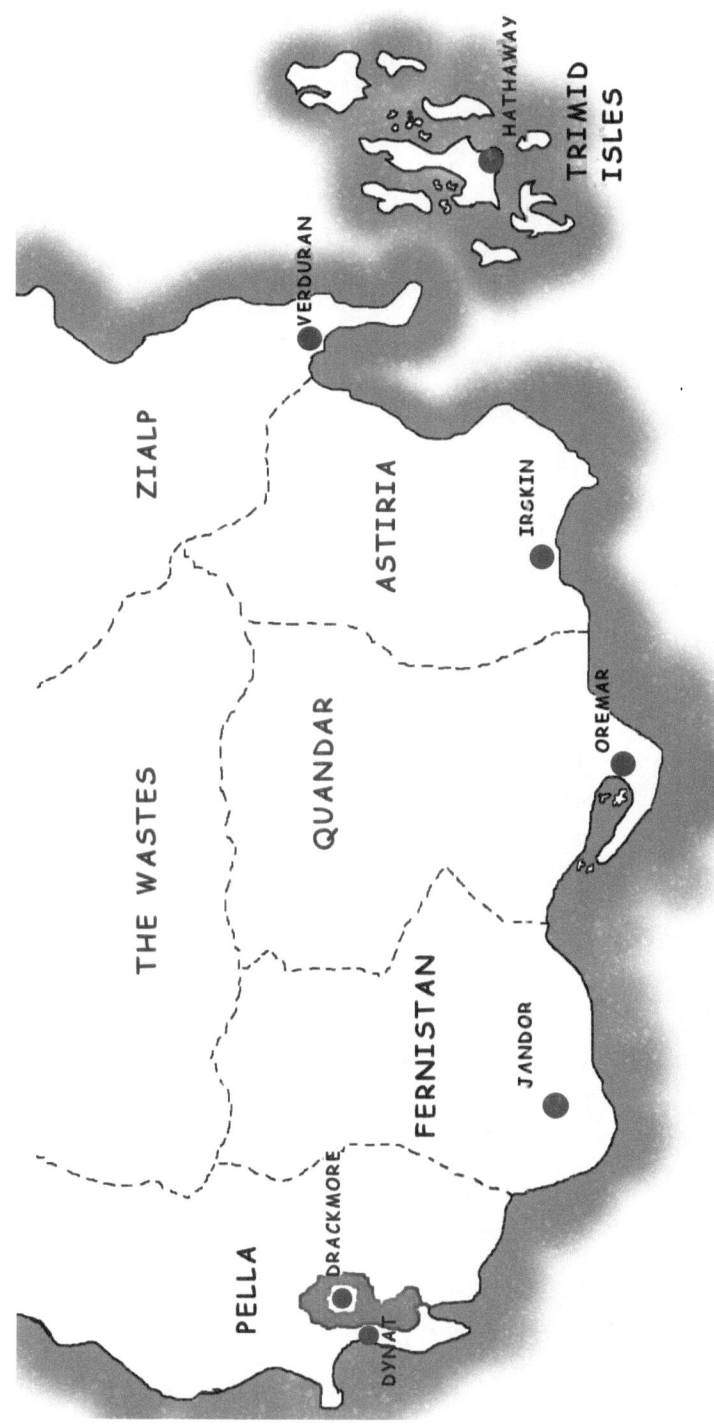

Calender

Each month is based on the time from one full moon to the next. As a result all the months are twenty eight days long, with the exception of Opal which has twenty nine days and is considered a sacred month.

Month	*Moon*	*Season North*	*Season South*
First	Opal	Summer	Winter
Second	Citrine		
Third	Topaz		
Fourth	Amber		
Fifth	Jasper	Autumn	Spring
Sixth	Carnelian		
Seventh	Garnet		
Eighth	Amethyst	Winter	Summer
Ninth	Turquoise		
Tenth	Lapis		
Eleventh	Jade	Spring	Autumn
Twelfth	Beryl		
Thirteenth	Peridot		

Chapter One

The First day, Opal Moon, year 2974
College of the Twins, Westecroft

Oriana, apprentice to the Wuhern Aneurin of Westecroft, was bored. In an attempt to alleviate her boredom, she was taking a nice long bath. "Ahhhh! The convenience of civilization and technology rolled into one," she sighed blissfully as she sank into the steaming pool. Sliding lower, long lashes brushed her cheeks as her lids closed over emerald green eyes. Long copper hair spread in waves covering her slender body all the way to the waist.

: Don't rest for too long Oriana. I have a job for you: The Wuhern's mental voice jolted her out of her reverie.

"Damn!"

: Don't swear Oriana:

: Couldn't you have told me about this job before I took my bath?: she asked her mentor.

: I suppose I could have· replied Aneurin *:However, I didn't think of it until after you had settled yourself. I told you not to swear:* he added as Oriana expressed her dissatisfaction at his reply.

Ten minutes later she walked into Aneurin's office slightly damp and still seething. Standing at a tall 5 foot, 8 inches she made an impressive sight with long hair hanging in damp ringlets around her face and green eyes flashing. Most people would cringe at the anger written there, but not the Wuhern.

At eighty years of age, Aneurin of Mendox was used to the sometimes flammable temper of his apprentice. No matter what Oriana said or did, the Wuhern, through long years and much experience in his position, was neither surprised nor cowled by anything she came up with. It did help that he, along with over half the other Masters of the Order of the Twins, had raised her from the age of ten, but only he could remain totally unmoved by any of her antics.

"Please have a seat my dear. I will be finished in a moment," Aneurin urged as he wrote something down. Oriana glanced around the room as she sat, noting the sudden lack of certain books from the veritable library that covered the walls of his office. "I am afraid that I will not be able to attend the blessing of Princess Oriel. Something has come up, so I have notified King Chrystopher that you will be attending in my place," the Wuhern announced, glancing up from his writing. "It will be good practice for you. One never knows when one's time is up."

"Master!" Oriana cried indignantly. "You've got a long way to go before you leave us!"

Aneurin raised a brow at her tone. "Maybe so my dear. However, one must be prepared. Therefore you shall go to Demesa on my behalf, whilst I do that which I must – and *no*, you may not ask me what it is." Oriana grimaced as her master stopped her curiosity dead in its tracks. "It is none of your business, and you will not need anything to distract you as you prepare for the blessing." Aneurin looked thoughtfully at his pupil.

"What?"

"Oh, nothing my dear," he replied, a smile twitching the corner of his mouth.

"Master?" She asked whilst sending an inquiring tendril of thought in his direction.

"Forget it Oriana. My thoughts are my own. Go prepare yourself for the journey to Denel. King Carlyle and Queen Demetria have kindly volunteered for you to travel with them. Their emissary will be here within the hour to escort you to Athos."

"The hour? But-" Oriana looked at the Wuhern in disbelief as she stood to leave.

"No 'buts' Oriana. Out! How many times have I told you – DO NOT SWEAR!!!!!" he added as the door slammed shut behind her. *There are some very interesting times headed this way, and I fear that Oriana will see the worst of it,* Aneurin thought to himself. *Yet I do not See her having a major part in them. How strange!* He let his mind flow, collecting thoughts and images from his students. *:Oriana! Stop swearing!:*

:It's my room, I'll swear if I want to!: was her reply.

In her rooms Oriana was going through her wardrobe, tossing various pieces of clothing over her shoulder. "He shouldn't lead people on and then refuse to tell them what he sees. Just because *he* can see the future doesn't give him the right to be mysterious," she muttered angrily. "Neither does being the Wuhern!" There was a knock on the door. "*WHAT?*"

A short, tousled blonde head popped into the gap of the now partly opened door. "Hey Ori? Is it safe to come in?" asked Michaela Debranny. At Oriana's grunt she entered the room. Spying the mess created by Oriana's packing technique, she asked, "What are you doing?"

Oriana looked up briefly from loading her trunk before answering. "*Lord* Aneurin is sending me to Denel for the blessing of Princess Oriel in his stead," she all but growled.

"You? Amongst royalty?" Michaela looked dubious. "Has he lost his mind?"

Oriana snorted. "It gets worse. I'm leaving for Athos today. I'll be travelling to Denel with their Majesties. King Carlyle has sent an escort for me. They're arriving within the hour."

"But the blessing is like, two months away," disbelief showed clearly on Michaela's face. "And why isn't the Wuhern going anyway?"

"Something has come up," Oriana imitated the Wuhern's tone. "And he thinks it will be good practice for me," she said. "After all, I will be Wuhern one day – if I last that long!"

"But still – you amongst royalty. I really think it's a recipe for disaster."

"Thanks for the vote of confidence Mick!" Oriana scowled at her friend.

"Hey! I have nothing against you, but you grew up on the streets, remember?" Michaela shrugged, "Not exactly the kind of person that the members of our Royal family mix with."

"Neither are you." Oriana threw another gown into the bag on her bed.

"I'm not the one who's going to be spending the next month or so with them."

"Don't remind me."

"On a completely different subject – do you have time to spare for lunch? I'm starving!" Michaela rubbed her stomach for emphasis.

"You would." Oriana shook her head. "No one would think you grew up on the streets, the way you eat."

"There's an insult there somewhere, I'm sure of it, but for the life of me, I can't find it!"

❧

"Lady Oriana?"

Oriana looked up from closing her bag to find an unfamiliar young man in her doorway. "Yes?"

"I'm Sir Liam, your escort to Athos. Lord Aneurin told me I could find you here. Your carriage is waiting in the courtyard when you are ready." Liam bowed in her direction.

"Thank you Sir Liam. I shall be with you shortly."

He bowed again, and left the room.

"What a dishy young man!" said Michaela entering the room. "If you don't want him, I'll have him."

"Dishy? Have you been reading Zialpan romances again?" Oriana raised an eyebrow at her friend. "He's from the aristocracy Mick."

"How do you know that?" She asked, throwing herself onto the bed. "And no, I haven't." Michaela glanced guiltily at her friend. "It was an Astirian."

Oriana rolled her eyes. "Because he's a knight. Only the aristocracy can become knights in Westecroft, remember."

"I'll take my chances," said Michaela. "Besides, there is a distinct lack of good looking males here."

Oriana laughed. "Shall I ask Lord Aneurin to transfer you to Pella? I hear that they are overflowing with good looking males!"

"Of course not!" replied Michaela. She looked sharply at her friend. "How do you know?" she asked, a suspicious expression on her face.

Oriana grinned. "I got talking to Lady Etheline's apprentice Moneta when they were here last year." Her grin widened. "She was *very* forthcoming about their best attributes."

"Oh *really*?" Michaela gave her friend an arch look.

"Yes really!" replied Oriana with a wide grin.

Michaela shook her head at her friend. "Shall I help you with your bags?"

"You just want to look at the dishy knight again."

Michaela squirmed. "You're going to be gone for three or more months Ori. I have to see you off. We haven't been apart since before we were novices. You're the only family I have."

Oriana laughed. "Oh please! I'm not family. At least, not as far as we can determine. Just pick up a bag."

"You're too kind."

As they trudged down the hall Oriana looked at her friend. "You were right you know."

"Of course I'm right," replied Michaela ignoring Oriana's snicker. "What am I right about this time though?"

"This will be the first time that we've been apart since we lived in Jerriko."

Michaela shuddered. "Am I glad we don't live there anymore."

"True, but we'd never survive if we went back. We're too spoilt now. All these creature comforts. I'm pretty sure we'd never be able to go back to sleeping on the street."

This time Michaela shrugged. "Why'd we want to? Go back, that is. And I beg to differ-"

"Yeah right!"

"As I was *saying* – I beg to differ. I think we are probably better able to survive now. We've learnt a few more tricks."

: *She's right Oriana. If you had to go back to the streets you are more capable of surviving than when I found you*: The Wuhern's voice echoed in both their heads.

Oriana scowled as Michaela grinned at their master's comment. : *How long have you been eavesdropping?*:

: *Long enough. I just called to say – No that is not what I was thinking Michaela! – What I was going to say was - hurry up! Young Liam can't wait all day for you!*:

: *We'll be there in a minute*: Oriana replied as they turned left, heading down the last hallway to the front doors.

"Ah. Here she is at last." The Wuhern glanced over as Oriana and Michaela walked through the college doors. "Michaela please pass those bags to the groomsman. He'll get them settled for us." He turned to Oriana. "Have a good trip my dear. I expect regular reports." :*And not the kind that say all's well, either:* He added for only Oriana to hear.

Trying hard not to grin at his silent remark, Oriana gave him a chaste hug before turning to Michaela to give her an affectionate one. "Yes my Lord," she said as she climbed into the carriage. "I shall report as soon as we reach Athos my Lord."

Aneurin shook his head. "See that you do." He turned to the young knight at his side. "Keep an eye on her Sir Liam. Try to keep her out of too much mischief."

"Mischief my Lord? Me my Lord?" called Oriana out of the carriage window.

"Yes you." He looked at the confused young man. "Be thankful that you aren't saddled with the two of them." He waved to indicate Michaela as well.

Liam fought a grin as he took in the expressions of the two young women. "My prayers to the Twins will be of thanksgiving then my Lord," he said. "I'm sure however that Lady Oriana will be on her best behaviour."

"I hope so," was Aneurin's only reply.

"We'll be off then," said Liam before mounting his horse.

"Have fun Ori!" Michaela called as the carriage pulled out. "And bring me home some souvenirs," :*of the dishy kind if you can:* she sent with a mental grin.

Oriana laughed. "I'll see if I can find anything to suit your tastes!" she called back before they were out of earshot.

"I take it you and Athenan Michaela are close," said Liam as he rode beside the carriage.

"Yes," replied Oriana. "You could say that we grew up together."

"Oh?"

"We lived on the streets until Lord Aneurin discovered us."

Liam blinked. "I wasn't aware of that."

"Not many people are. Not that it matters. Once you enter your novitiate it is of no consequence if you are a street urchin or the heir to a throne. Everyone is equal." Oriana shrugged. "That's not to say that some of the noble folk who enter don't try to pull rank, but it doesn't last for long."

"I see." Liam shook his head at the evil grin that had appeared on her face. "No I don't, but then it is a completely different environment to what I grew up in." He looked at his charge. "What age were you when you became a novice?" he asked.

Oriana sighed. "Ten." She looked out at the countryside, a feeling of unease that had nothing to do with his question coming over her. "How long will it take to get to Athos?" she asked.

Taking her question as a hint that she wished to change the subject, Liam answered her. "Two days. We'll stop the night at Irin. I booked us rooms on my way to the Wuhern's residence."

"Okay. Thank you."

She looked at the men that made up her escort. There were ten of them besides Liam. All were burly men, the sort that would have been bodyguards to The Dog back in Jerriko. The Dog, short for 'That Rabid Dog' as an enemy once named him, had run the streets when Oriana had lived there. Cross the Dog and you would disappear without a trace.

As she studied them she thought she sensed something familiar about the guard in front of Liam. Sensing her gaze he turned his head in her direction and winked at her. Oriana blinked in surprise. He knew her. Quickly she glanced at Liam to see if he had noticed the exchange, fortunately his attention was elsewhere. When Liam headed to the front of the carriage to talk to the head guard, the one who had winked at her took his place at her side.

"Now there's a face I never thought I'd see again." He grinned, "How've ya been Ori?" He looked her over, taking in her clothes and the carriage in which she sat. "Seems you've done good, little girl."

"Do I know you?" She asked, raising an eyebrow as she attempted to look unaffected by his comments.

"Come now Ori, don't tell me you've forgotten me?" His grin changed to a slightly evil one. "What will I tell The Dog next time I see him? Little Ori thinks she's above us all? He won't like that."

"I don't know what you are talking about," she told him, her mind working at a million miles an hour. If this man had worked for The Dog, she was either extremely lucky or in extremely big trouble.

She was fairly certain that the trouble she was sensing was not coming from him. Knowing who he had worked for meant he was good in a fight. However, if he was still working for The Dog and mentioned that he thought she had no respect for The Dog, the trouble that she sensed would be nothing compared to what would follow once The Dog found out.

His grin softened toward cheeky. "Don't worry Oriana. I'm not here to harm you. Just the opposite." He lifted one sleeve of his tunic slightly, revealing a tattoo. Oriana stared at the tattoo. She knew that design and she had been right when she thought her guards looked like The Dog's bodyguards. The man beside her was, or had been, one of them, even if the rest of the men weren't.

The tattoo was of a dog on a crate. On the crate was the name of the man on whom the tattoo was inscribed. The name of the man in front of her was one she had known very well as a child and had hoped to never hear of again. "The Dog has been keeping his eye on you for a long time ,Ori," he told her. "Fact is, he organised for you and young Mick to go to the Twins in the first place."

Oriana's jaw dropped open in shocked disbelief. "What!" she exclaimed in a whisper, so as to not catch Liam's attention.

His grin widened. "I didn't think you had forgotten me."

She scowled, realising that she had just given herself away. "What do you mean?" she asked. "Why had the Dog been keeping an eye on me?"

"Well now, that's not for me to say." He shook his head when she would have pressed him. "I wasn't given that information Oriana.

All I can tell you is that he has been watching you and Michaela since well before you left Jerriko. Some of the servants at the College are his people," he told her. "And I was told to join the guards a year or two ago, in preparation for this." He spread his hands to indicate the carriage and its guards.

"Since when had The Dog had the gift of Foresight?" she hissed at him. "I only found out four hours ago that I was going on this trip."

The guard shrugged. "I only know what my instructions are, and I must say, I'm enjoying being an honest man."

"Honest my foot." Oriana mumbled under her breath. "If you are here, you must have some idea about what is going to happen." Before the guard could reply, Liam returned. Nodding to the man, Liam returned to his place at Oriana's side. "Damn," she muttered, as the man returned to his place several paces in front of the knight.

"Did you say something, my Lady?" Liam asked, looking at her questioningly.

"No. Just have a bit of dust in my throat from the travel," she told him, trying to ignore the guard who was doubled over in laughter.

He didn't look convinced. "There is a flagon of wine in the cabinet in front of you, if you need it," he informed her.

"Thank you, Sir Liam." Oriana retrieved the flagon and helped herself to a small mouthful. Settling herself back against the cushions of the carriage, she closed her eyes and considered all that had occurred since she had embarked on this journey. There was still that niggling feeling of foreboding. Trouble was on its way, and she silently cursed that she had no real gift at foresight. The presence of The Dog's man was of small comfort, now that she knew he was here for her benefit. However, the information that he had given her was baffling to say the least. Sir Liam's reaction to her past had not been as derogatory as she had expected. This, on top of everything else, gave her pause for thought. As her brain ran all the information over and over she slipped quietly into sleep, hoping that when she woke she would have some idea of what was going on.

Chapter Two

The First day, Citrine Moon, year 2974
Royal Palace, Irskin Astiria

Water, still as glass, glistened in the sunlight. Short-cropped chestnut hair appeared on the mirrored surface, followed by the impish face of a four-year-old boy. Freckles, chasing each other across the bridge of his nose, bunched together as he concentrated on something beneath the surface. Carefully he raised one small hand, readying it to strike. Lower lip pinched between teeth as the hand dove into the -

"VARIAN ROBERT GAMALIEL XAVIER, GET IN HERE THIS INSTANT!"

"Fiddlesticks!" he muttered as his prey slipped away and his hand splashed into the water - returning empty.

"It's going to be more than fiddlesticks before Ria is done with you, young man," answered a much quieter male voice. "Mother wants to spend some time with you Var, and she can't do that when you are out here trying to catch fish like a bear." Varian looked up to find his brother Binjaymen standing behind him.

"But *Jay*!"

"Don't 'but Jay' me Var. You know how little time Mother gets to spend with us, and it is your birthday after all, so you should have expected that she would spend some time with you. You are her baby after all."

"I no baby!" Varian cried indignantly. "I is four!" and he stuck up four fingers as if to prove it.

"I know that, twit, but to Mother you are still her baby. You *are* the youngest." His brother took his hand, turning toward the house. "Come on, before Ria gets really angry, with both of us." He headed toward the path that would lead them back to the house. The term house was something of a misnomer for the building in question. With three long wings, two huge gardens and a very large set of stables, it was the main residence of the royal family of Astiria. Built by King Montrose the First in the year 1224, it was a marvel of the egotistical madness. The building itself was designed in a stylistic shape of the letter M which could be seen from several miles out at sea as it resided on the side of a hill.

It wasn't a long walk, despite the size of the gardens, and as they neared the house a slightly harried woman of middle years raced out of one of the doors toward them.

"Oh! Prince Binjaymen! You found him! Thank you so much," she exclaimed breathlessly before turning to the young man at his side. "As for you! What on earth possessed you to go wondering in the gardens so close to your party?" At that point she caught sight of Varian's soggy sleeve. "Look at this! What will her Majesty think! Come on you little scoundrel, now I'll have to bath you again."

"No bath! No bath!" the boy cried vehemently, trying to squirm his way out of the woman's grasp.

Binjaymen, watching from the sidelines, laughed. "Good luck bro," he said. "Uriahl's never been one to back down. See you at the party," and with that he headed into the house.

"NO BATH!!!" Varian continued to protest as Uriahl dragged him into the house behind his brother.

"Give me one *good* reason why you don't need a bath," she demanded as she closed the door to his room behind her.

"All's clean," said Varian. "Clothes wet, Me's all clean."

"Is that so?" she replied, arms crossed at her bosom.

"Yep!" He nodded, an impish grin on his face.

Uriahl laughed, gathering him into her arms. "Scamp! Let's get you into clean clothing then".

Varian nodded again, very pleased. "Okay!"

S

"My! Don't we look smart today," said Queen Claire of Astiria, entering the rooms of her youngest son. "What have you been up to on such an important and wondrous day?" she asked lifting him into her arms.

"Fishing," stated Varian, hugging his mother fiercely.

"Catch anything?"

"Nup." He scowled.

Claire laughed. "Better luck next time sweetie. So tell me," she said settling him onto her lap. "What did you get for your birthday?"

Varian's brow furrowed in concentration. "Jo gave me a puzzle. Jay gave me a toy horsy. Relley gave me a book – Me very own." A pleased expression came over his face before his brow furrowed again. "Mari gave me's somes building blocks. Shally gave me some clothes and Ria gived me a drum!" he told his mother excitedly.

"Oh No! Not a drum!" she exclaimed in mock horror.

"Yup!" Her youngest son nodded happily.

"Well then. It sounds like you don't need any more presents. You've already been given lots of them, so you don't really need one from your Father and Me." She looked at him slyly.

"Yes Me does! Yes me does!" Varian bounced up and down on her lap, causing her to wince slightly.

"Oh. All right then. Come and see what we bought you," she said, setting him on to the floor.

"YES! Yes! Yes! Yes! Yes!" Varian cried, racing out of the room.

"Slow down Varian," the Queen called after him. "You don't know where we are going yet."

Varian skidded to a halt. "Oops!" he said, looking as beguilingly embarrassed as only a four-year-old can.

"Give me your hand, Varian," Claire instructed as she caught up with him. He did as he was told, but danced up and down all the way to the bottom of the stairs.

"Where's we going?" Varian asked as they passed the kitchens on their way toward the back of the house.

"You will soon see," was his mother's only reply before she stopped suddenly.

"We here?" Varian asked, a perplexed expression on his small face.

"Nope," replied Claire, shaking her head. Quickly, before he could escape, she bent down and blindfolded him, then lifted him into her arms, holding him so as to prevent him from removing the blindfold.

"MAMA!!!" he screeched.

"Hush Varian! We'll be there shortly." In a matter of moments she was proven correct as they left the Palace and made their way to the Royal stables. "See. Here we are." She set him down and removed the blindfold.

Varian found himself standing on a box looking over the door of one of the stable stalls. Inside was a pure black Zialpan mountain horse. It might have seemed unwise to give a horse to a four year-old, however the Zialpan mountain horses never reached a height of more than ten hands. It was an advantage to be smaller in the mountains, where the snow and rocks made travel difficult, and where the altitudes meant that the air was thinner. It had been observed that even the people who lived in the higher climes of Zialp were small and slight of build.

"Mama! Mama! Tanko! Tanko! Tanko!" He screeched, jumping up and down with joy and almost toppling the box on which he was standing.

"Your welcome, love. So what are you going to name him?" she asked as she steadied him.

Varian paused just long enough to actually consider the question, before answering. "Shadow-walker."

What he actually said was 'thado-walker', but Claire, who had six children and many years understanding infantile speech, understood exactly what he was trying to say.

"Shadow-walker. A noble name for a noble beast."

"Me ride! Me ride!" cried Varian excitedly.

The Queen shook her head in amusement. "Not now love, we have to go to your party, and you need to thank your Father."

"Me ride! Me ride now!" The child pouted, stubbornly hanging on to the stable door.

"Now ye listen t' yer Mother, young Master Varian," said the stable master Gefram, appearing at Claire's side. "Ye canna go t' yer party smellin' o' horses. An' ye've plenty o' time t' spend with master Shadow-walker 'ere. I promise ye, ye'll 'ave a good an' long ride of 'im before ye go t' bed t'nite!" Both Gefram and Varian turned to the Queen for confirmation of the promise.

"You will indeed," she agreed.

"Okay's! Me goes to party now," stated Varian, getting down from the box. He headed for the stable door. When he got there he stopped and turned back toward where his mother and the stable master stood.

"Well?" he asked "Are youse coming?"

Claire laughed and headed toward him. "Yes dear. We are coming."

S

"So. Var, did you have fun today?" asked Josep. The two of them, as well as their other siblings, Binjaymen, Shrialla, Marriam and Jirrelle, were in Varian's rooms, relaxing, as was the after party ritual. Josep had accidentally established the ritual as a two-year-old, after Jirrelle's Blessing. All he had wanted to do was escape all the noise, and he had ended up in her room. However, it had continued and had grown into a private party for the sibs after they left the 'adult' party.

"Hmm". Varian chewed on his lip. "Yep! Lot's an' lot's of fun!"

"We're glad," said Shrialla. "Can you imagine what we'd have done if you *hadn't* had fun?"

"SHREE!!" exclaimed the others.

"Well?" She shrugged her shoulders. At the age of 12, Shrialla was just entering womanhood, and was doing so with a vengeance. Forgetting that she had an elder sister and was technically fifth in line to the throne behind her brothers and older sister, Shrialla had a tendency to put the airs of someone ten years her senior.

"Forget it Shree," said Jirrelle. As the eldest daughter, Jirrelle often took on the role of mother to her siblings, as Josep did the role of father. It was something that had occurred due to both the closeness of the siblings and the demands on the time of their parents, which came from running a kingdom.

Binjaymen turned to Marriam, who was sitting on the window sill behind him. "Do you think she might have been dropped on her head as a baby?" he whispered to her.

Keeping her eye on her sister, she replied, "Who knows. I suppose it would explain a few things." As the youngest daughter of Jaymes and Claire of Astiria, Marriam was something of a tomboy with the attitude to match. At the age of ten, she still had a couple of years before she had to worry about womanhood, but she was always insisting that she was not going to be like Shrialla. The two were like day and night in personality. So totally different, that their mother sometimes wondered if she had actually given birth to them or not.

"Stop whispering you two," Jirrelle told them.

"Yes mother," replied Marriam sarcastically, before turning to Varian. "What have you got planned for tomorrow, baby brother?"

"Ride thado-walker!" he told, bouncing on his bed in excitement.

"You can't spend all day on him Varian!" she protested laughing.

"I's can!" he insisted.

"Leave be Marriam." Binjaymen silenced her with a look when she opened her mouth to argue further. "He can if he wants to."

"You're certainly one very lucky four year old, Var," commented Jirrelle, ensuring that the argument stopped dead in its tracks. "I didn't get my own horse until I was six," she informed him.

"Same here," Josep chimed in, determined that Marriam would not get another opportunity to make a snide comment.

"Me special," said Varian, nose in the air and an impish grin on his face.

"Get your head out of the clouds kid. You're not that special," scoffed Marriam.

"Me is special!"

"Psst! Var!" Binjaymen covered his mouth with one hand as though telling a confidence. "Hush up. It's meant to be a secret, remember?"

Varian put on a face of artfully contrived innocence. "Me remembers."

Binjaymen laughed. "Scamp," he said, ruffling his brother's hair, before pouncing on him in a mock fight. Marriam and Josep quickly joined the melee, whilst Jirrelle and Shrialla looked on in amusement.

Before things could get too out of control, Uriahl, Varian's nurse, entered the room. "Alright you lot, scatter. Its way beyond your bed time and you've all got school tomorrow."

"But Ria!!" they groaned.

"Get!" She hustled them out before turning to Varian. "Now then birthday boy. Bedtime for you too."

"Yes Ria," he replied meekly. She looked at him, suspicious of his acquiescence. He yawned. "Me is tired," he told her, crawling into his bed. Still suspicious, she tucked him in and left.

Closing the door behind her, she shook her head in disbelief. "I'll be damned if he's actually tired. That kid's got more energy than the rest of them put together," she muttered to herself. "I'll check on him in an hour or so, just to be sure."

Inside the room, Varian was quickly and quietly removing the screws from his window. His favourite brother, Jay, had an annoying little habit of picking locks. Despite an age difference of ten years, Varian adored Jay, and had quickly tried to copy him. When Jay had found out, he had taught Varian the proper way to do it, but had refused to give him any real lock picks until he was six.

Unbeknownst to Varian, it was Jay's hope that he would forget, or that Jay would be able to push the time frame back a year or two without his brother noticing. This refusal frustrated Varian, and he had searched for all sorts of different pieces of metal, so that he too could pick locks. Unfortunately, he had actually ruined more than a few of the locks he had tried to pick, baffling the Palace guards in the process.

He had, however, discovered that one of the pieces of metal was perfect for removing the screws in his window, therefore allowing him to remove the window itself and get out, which is exactly what he began to do once Uriahl had left.

Once it was removed, he climbed out and into the apple tree, which grew outside. Moving quickly, and surprisingly, quietly for a four year old, he jumped down from the tree and scampered toward the stables. Minutes later he slipped inside and headed directly for Shadow-walker's stall. "'Night Walker," he whispered, patting the horse on the nose, then just as quietly he slipped back out of the stables and returned to his rooms with Uriahl none the wiser.

Gefram, about to go to sleep in the stable loft, smiled happily to himself as Varian left.

S

Chapter Three

The First day, Opal Moon, year 2974
Royal Palace, Denel, Demesa

"Oriel!!" cried Crown Princess Haileigh of Demesa, walking into the nursery. "Stop that at once!!!" Her black eyed daughter looked up at her and giggled.

"She is quite alright, Haileigh."

"ALRIGHT!!" Haileigh spun around and looked at her husband, who was leaning comfortably against a wall watching their daughter with sharp coal black eyes. "She is juggling balls of fire and you say she's alright?"

Mathew nodded. "She is half Pyrial. It is to be expected." He pushed off of the wall and started towards her, his red hair glinting in the sunlight, leaving one with the impression of flames.

"She is not even one yet. She shouldn't be capable of such magic."

"Love, a Pyrial of her age would *be* a ball of fire. Most Pyrials don't manage the change to solid for long periods until they are fifteen at least." Haileigh looked at her husband, horrified. "She is the first half Pyrial in history. We aren't sure what she is capable of, or what she is likely to do as she grows."

"But what if she spontaneously combusts in public. The Blessing is only two months away?"

Mathew laughed. "Don't worry love. She won't spontaneously combust in public or in private. I have a very firm grip on the situation, and I know what to look for. I have several nieces and nephews that I have watched grow. I can rein her in at any point. Most infant Pyrials aren't strong enough to go against me. Our half Pyrial daughter certainly isn't." He hugged her. "As for the Blessing, I'll make sure she doesn't do any fireworks on the day."

Haileigh sighed. "Thank you my love," she said, sinking into his embrace.

"Oh, by the way. Your father asked me to tell you, we received a message from Lord Aneurin in Westecroft. He is unable to make it, however he is sending his apprentice Oriana."

Haileigh raised an eyebrow. "Not able to make it? Well Oriana is certainly up for the job, but I don't understand why he can't make it." She shrugged. "Oh well. I'll give him a call later today and find out what is going on."

Mathew shook his head. "If anyone can get something out of that wily old coot, it's you."

Haileigh smiled. "Why thank you."

He grinned, and ruffled her ebony hair. "You're welcome."

R

"Aneurin, why are you sending Oriana?"

Aneurin jumped at the sound of Haileigh's voice. "It is most unfortunate that Ramolleana passed away so suddenly. You have yet to learn the courtesies of Wuhern's, Haileigh," Aneurin told her as he turned to the mirror which was situated on the other side of his desk, and met her golden eyes.

"No one is more aware of those facts than me Aneurin. So answer the question," she replied, sadness creeping into her expression.

"You are pert Haileigh of Demesa. Don't they teach the young anything these days?"

She ignored his question. "I'm waiting." In the silence that followed, the impatient tapping of a foot could be clearly heard.

Aneurin sighed. "Very well. I sent Oriana because she needs to see more of the outside world."

"That's a fairly paltry answer Aneurin," Haileigh told him, crossing her arms over her chest and tipping her head to one side. "Particularly as she grew up on the streets."

"Street wise she may be, however she has not seen any of the aristocratic world or the merchant world. To be a good Wuhern, she is going to have to be able to live in those worlds as well. She has been sheltered since she came to us. She needs to learn, and I have taught her all I can here," Aneurin explained.

Haileigh raised a brow. "So why aren't you coming?"

"I'm presently involved in some very important research," he informed her aloofly. "I'll update you and the other Wuherns when I have more information, but if I am right, what I am investigating will involve all of us, and may change the very fabric of our Order."

"Don't give me that Aneurin. I'm sure that you could take time out from your studies for the Blessing, no matter how important they are," she insisted.

Aneurin sighed again. Haileigh was like a dog with a bone when she was after information, she wouldn't give up. "Oriana is not to be told," he ordered her.

Haileigh gave him a look of surprise, but nodded in acceptance of the demand.

"I would not survive the trip."

"WHAT?!!!"

Aneurin winced. "Must you be so loud?" he asked, rubbing his ear.

"Yes!" Haileigh scowled at him. "What do you mean you would not survive the trip?"

"Look at me. I am *old* Haileigh. Very old. It is almost time for me to pass over and Oriana is not quite ready for me to go yet. As much as I want to be at your daughter's Blessing, were I to attend I would probably not return to Westecroft, and as lovely as Demesa is, I don't wish to be buried there."

"What is wrong?" Concern was evident in the princess' gaze.

"Nothing." He sighed. "I'm just worn out. I will live to see Oriana marry. That much I do know. Had she any inkling of my demise she would not have gone and there *must* be a Westecroftan at the Blessing."

"She deserves to know Aneurin," Haileigh told him, not hearing the warning in his last sentence.

"She will know once she returns. Nothing can prevent that, but she mustn't know before. She needs to enjoy this trip."

Haileigh looked at him sceptically. "Enjoy? She's an ex-street kid in an aristocratic environment. I don't know that she'll enjoy much."

Aneurin grinned. "Well, as much as she can then."

Haileigh smiled. "Take care of yourself, Aneurin."

"You too, Your Highness. And take care of that daughter of yours. She is very special."

"That she is." Haileigh sighed as the mirror in front of her went black again before showing only her reflection. She shook herself and went to stand by the window, her gaze taking in the golden sands outside the city and the colourful roofs that covered the buildings which made the city of Denel the sight that it was. Below her window thousands of people moved through the streets. Some on their way to work, others to socialize. It was a beautiful, if very different city. Built around several small oasis', Denel had grown from a trade town to the capital city of the driest Kingdom in the world. Its history was as colourful as the city itself, but despite her love for it, Haileigh could understand why Aneurin would wish to die elsewhere.

Before she took up the reigns of Wuhern of the Order of the Twins in Demesa, Haileigh had travelled the world extensively. From the deserts of her homeland to the icy wastes above Zialp. From the marshlands in the west of Pella, to the islands of the Empire of Trimid. She had seen it all. When she thought of her daughter's future, she hoped that she too would be able to experience all that Haileigh had, and more. She knew that there was more outside of Demesa than could be read about in books, and she knew that not many people born outside it found a home in this dry land.

As she continued to gaze out the window she sent a prayer to the Twins that Oriel's life be happy and that she too would know true love. Where it not for her travels she would not have met Mathew, as she stumbled across the home of the Pyrial's deep in the desert of her homeland. Thinking back to that day, when a sand storm had separated her from her escort and literally flung her into the ruins of Dezeal and into Mathew's arms, she smiled. What had seemed like the worst day of her life, had turn out to be the best. As she returned to the work on her desk, Haileigh sent a quick prayer of thanksgiving winging its way to the Twins.

R

"Haileigh! Just the person I was looking for," exclaimed King Chrystopher as he stepped out of the hall and into her office. The King was a large man. At six foot high, he tended to tower over most of his subjects, and years of eating palace food had given him a solid build. Between that and his regal stance, he was a very imposing man. Grey was starting to pepper his midnight hair, adding distinction to his looks.

"Father. What can I do for you?" Haileigh said getting up from her desk and giving him a hug.

"Mathew told you about Aneurin?" he asked, settling himself into a chair as his daughter returned to her desk.

Haileigh nodded. "I have just finished speaking to him now," she informed him as she sat back down.

"Oh?" Chrystopher leant back into the chair.

Haileigh grimaced. "He told me why he isn't coming."

"And?"

Now she sighed. "He said that if he attended the Blessing, he wouldn't leave alive."

"WHAT?!!!" the King was incredulous. "He didn't really say that did he?" he asked, sitting upright in the chair.

"Well, maybe not quite that way, but that was the general gist of the conversation. He is an old man and apparently he is not up to the trip, as much as he would love to be."

The King sighed and relaxed back into the chair. "True. He was here for your Blessing all those years ago. One often forgets the passing of time when one doesn't see a person for many years."

"He has asked that we don't let on about his condition to Oriana," she told him. "Apparently he hasn't told her and wishes it to stay that way."

Chrystopher looked at his daughter in surprise. "What ever for?" he asked, gold eyes so like his daughter's piercing her with a look that said 'you can not be serious'.

Haileigh shook her head in frustration. "I don't really understand his reasoning, and I'm sure that there is more to it than he was telling me, but I told him we would abide by his wishes."

"Then we shall do so. On a completely different subject, and the whole reason why I was looking for you – have you been speaking with the servants about the Blessing? I told Esta and Yaran that no matter what your Mother says, you are in charge of this and all changes must get approval from you."

Haileigh sighed. "Gee thanks."

Chrystopher looked at her. "Do you really want your Mother organizing this?" he asked. "You know what she is like. Just remember Edmett's coming of age."

Haileigh shuddered as she remembered the event in question. "Good Gods no! Alright, I can do this. Mathew is going to help me though. He may not like it and I'm sure that he won't appreciate it, but he *is* going to help!" Haileigh was adamant.

The King laughed. "I'll leave you to it then, my dear." He stood and kissed her on the head. "Have fun," he said. Chuckling, he left the room.

R

"Your Highness?"

Haileigh looked up from the page she was writing to find her housekeeper Esta at the door. "Yes?"

"Highness, her Majesty has asked for the ballroom to be decorated with buntings," Esta told her. Esta was a pretty young woman, close in age to Haileigh. Her northern ancestry was evident in her blonde hair and blue eyes, and though young, she was well capable of running a palace due to a childhood living in a tavern. They had met as novices in the Order of the Twins, and become friends. When Haileigh had returned to the Palace on completion of her training, she had brought Esta with her. In her role of housekeeper, Esta was able to bring Haileigh all sorts of information that as the heir to the throne, she was unlikely to come across daily.

"And?" Haileigh asked, knowing that the buntings were not the problem.

Esta grimaced. "Her Majesty wishes for pink buntings, your Highness." She waited for the immanent explosion. Haileigh was not your typical royal princess. Even before she entered the Order of the Twins, she had been different. Royal observers had been known to state that she was more like her Father than her Mother in both looks and personality, for which the entire kingdom was very grateful.

"No. Absolutely not." The Princess shook her head for emphasis as Esta sighed with relief. "I have no objections to buntings. This is a celebration after all. However I will not have *pink* buntings. Everyone knows that Oriel is female. She doesn't need to be saddled with the stereotypical pink to inform anyone of that fact."

"Thank you, your Highness. What colour would you prefer?"

"Hmmm. My preference would be blue, however people would consider it strange, so what about green? Perhaps a nice mint green? Or even a pale lavender?" She looked at Esta. "What do you think?" she asked.

"I think that lavender would be lovely, your Highness. It is still feminine without the inference that you dislike."

Haileigh nodded. "Indeed. Now then, do you have enough time to pull this all together?" She asked the woman. "I know my Mother can be a bit of a pest when it comes to entertaining, so I'm sure you have had to work around her, which cannot have helped with the time constraints."

"We'll be fine, your Highness. Yaran has been of infinite help and her Majesty hasn't had too many changes for us to worry about."

"Really?" Haileigh was slightly sceptical at that. She knew her mother too well.

"Well, most of her ideas were just not practical." Esta amended her statement. "We have been able to make it look as though we had fulfilled her requests without actually doing so," she said, thinking back over some of the more nonsensical of the Queen's demands, and smiling over how she and Yaran, the head Steward, had worked around them.

Haileigh laughed. "Good. If there are any other problems, feel free to interrupt me at any time. For everyone's peace of mind, this thing must go off without a hitch. I don't think anyone wants to have my Mother upset."

Esta shuddered at the image that came to mind. "No your Highness. No one wants that!" Esta agreed with her. "Unless there is anything else?" Haileigh shook her head. "Then I shall go and order those buntings."

"Thank you Esta."

"You're welcome, your Highness."

R

Chapter Four

The First day, Opal Moon, year 2974
Five miles out of Irin, Westecroft

Sir Liam glanced at the woman sleeping in the carriage beside him. She was like nothing he had ever encountered before. When Lady Oriana had informed him that she was originally a street kid he had almost fallen out of his saddle. To look at her one would think that she came from one of Westecroft's finest families. She held herself straight and tall, with the poise of someone who knew that they were entitled to be respected. Whilst her clothing clearly signified her religious background, it was still stylish, indicating someone who paid attention to the world around her, and when one was conversing with her, it was clear that she was a highly intelligent and opinionated woman.

When he had first beheld her in her rooms at the College, he had been left breathless. He smiled as he thought of at least a dozen women at court who were going to take an instant disliking to her because of her looks alone. The smile quickly changed to a frown as his thoughts turned to the number of knights and courtiers that were going to hound her like lovesick puppies. The smile returned as he considered her reaction to them. It quickly became an evil grin. He was going to enjoy sitting back and watching the spectacle.

Liam let his gaze roam over the trees surrounding the road. To his left he spotted a road marker, alerting him to the fact that they were five miles out of Irin. He was grateful to his monarch for having created the system of markers that covered the Kingdom. For the inexperienced traveller they were just sticks in the ground with a number and a letter carved into them, but for those who travelled the realm, dispensing the King's orders and keeping the law, they were a welcome sight. After a long day on the road it was a great relief to know that you were only a short distance from a dry bed and a warm meal. He looked back at Oriana and sighed. It was probably a good idea for her to wake up now. He had a sneaking suspicion that she had an equally flammable temper to go with the flame like hair.

"Lady Oriana?" Someone was shaking her gently. "Lady Oriana?"

"Yes?" she replied groggily as she awoke. She looked up to find Sir Liam looking at her.

"We are almost at Irin, my Lady," he told her. "I thought that you would like to know."

Oriana gave herself a little shake as the sensation of danger increased ten-fold. "Thank you – what the?" The carriage jerked to a sudden stop.

Out of the surrounding woods poured masked men. Their leader stopped at the side of the carriage. "Well, well, well, what have we here?" he said surveying Oriana, Liam and their bodyguards. "Hand over your valuables and there won't be any trouble."

Oriana gave an unladylike snort. "Highway robbery is illegal," she informed him as one of his men held a knife to Liam's throat. She glanced at The Dog's man. Like Liam he had a knife at his throat. Unlike Liam, she knew that he was quite capable of disarming his captor, as long as he had a distraction to cover what he was up to. She decided to provide it for him. All she needed was for the leader of the band to provide her with an opening.

The man laughed. "And who is going to stop us?" he asked.

Oriana almost laughed herself. He had just given her exactly what she wanted. Quickly she gathered herself and drew on the power she felt flowing around her. "Me," she replied making him laugh harder. With a quick thought she grabbed a gust of wind and threw the man at Liam's neck into the leader, grabbing his knife before it did any damage to the knight. Before the lesder could react she grabbed a handful of gusts and lifted the men who held the guards into the air before dropping them onto their comrades, allowing the guards a more likely chance of winning. As the guards attacked the robbers, rope appeared and tied up those Oriana had already dealt with.

Although they were still slightly outnumbered, Liam and the guards made quick work of their attackers. Oriana took care of tying them up, allowing the guards to continue fighting those who remained. Just when Liam thought they had caught all the men, he saw one head toward the carriage. There was no way he could get there in time, but before he could even sound Oriana a warning, he saw her arm move. Within seconds the bandit fell to the ground.

When Liam returned to the carriage after dispatching one of his men to Irin to alert the local constabulary, he saw a throwing knife in the man's chest. Oriana stepped out of the carriage and removed the knife, quickly cleaning it on a lace handkerchief. Liam looked at her, bemused. "You are very handy in a fight my Lady," he told her.

"What did you expect me to do, faint?" she asked, returning the blade to its hiding place.

"No. But I almost did when you confronted the leader."

Oriana grimaced. "Okay. That probably wasn't the smartest thing to do, but it did distract him enough so that I could use magic to free you and the guards."

"Indeed it did," Liam agreed. "I certainly didn't expect the throwing knife, though."

Oriana smiled. "A woman must have a few little tricks," she said.

Now Liam laughed. "Remind me never to offend you," he said. "I don't know what other little surprises you have up your sleeves, but I'm pretty sure that they are most likely to be lethal."

Deciding not to answer him, Oriana wiped her hands on her dress and took in the scene before them. "What are we going to do with these men?" she asked, looking at the pile of attackers.

Liam followed her look. "I've sent Sergent Osjan into Irin to get the local constabulary," he told her. "We'll wait here until they arrive, then we will head into town."

"I wonder who they are?" said Oriana still looking at them. "Their leader was certainly well spoken, which suggests that he has or had a good position in life." She sighed. "It would take a lot to turn a man to highway robbery."

"Yes." Liam also looked at the men. The guards were removing their masks. "I find it curious also, that there has been no reports of this happening here recently, yet there were enough men to over run us. It was almost as if they were waiting for us."

Oriana turned to look at him. "But why?"

Now Liam sighed. "I have no idea."

✍

"How many of our people are injured?" Oriana asked as the Inn Keeper lead them to their rooms. It had taken half an hour for Sergent Osjan to return with a detachment of guards from Irin. Liam had insisted that Oriana remain in the carriage while they waited. He and the remaining guards had stood watch over the highway men. By the time they had made it to Irin and the inn that they were staying at, Oriana was not only rather peeved at being treated like a delicate and breakable doll, but was also annoyed that she had not been able to question the attackers herself. In fact, Liam had quite purposely made sure that she couldn't even find out what information had already been extracted from the prisoners whilst they were waiting for their escort.

"One or two," Liam answered with reluctance as they climbed the stairs to the second floor of the inn. "But only a few cuts or bruises."

"Have they been seen to?"

"No." He shrugged. "There are no serious injuries, so they are looking after themselves."

Oriana gave Liam a pointed look. "Serious or not, they should still be looked at. Even a small cut can get infected," she told him, as they followed their guide down a long hall. "Bring them to see me as soon as everyone is settled."

"It is nothing to worry about," Liam insisted, as Oriana entered her room. The maid who had been assigned to her, followed with her luggage.

"Bring them to me." There was steel in her voice as Oriana repeated the command.

"Yes my Lady," Liam sighed as she shut the door on him, then followed the Inn Keeper to his room.

In her own rooms, Oriana was unpacking with the help of her maid. After the maid had left, she quickly undressed and gave herself a sponge bath from the wash basin that had been provided. Once done, she changed into a clean dress and set about restyling her hair. Having cleaned herself up, she strolled to her bags and retrieved the hand mirror she had brought with her. Gathering power to her, she gave a quick swipe of her hand over the face and Michaela's image appeared. "How's it going, gorgeous?" she asked.

"Don't tell the boss, but we were hit by bandits on the way here," Oriana told her friend.

"*What?!*" Michaela was flabbergasted. "You're joking, right. Please tell me you are joking!"

"I wish I was." Oriana released a small gust of breath in frustration. "We were less than an hour's ride out of Irin when they hit us. They out numbered us by three to one. A little bit of magical help from me evened up the numbers. But Mick. They weren't unlettered commoners. They were well educated, or at least the leader was."

Michaela looked at her. "You think they were waiting for you?" she asked.

"I don't know... Sir Liam seemed to think so. Something funny is definitely going on though."

"So, speaking of Sir Liam, how is the dashing knight?" Michaela grinned suggestively at her.

"Get your mind out of the gutter." Oriana rolled her eyes at her friend.

"I just asked a simple question." Michaela was the picture of innocence.

"Yeah right."

"I did!" Michaela tried desperately to defend herself, despite the fact that she was anything but innocent.

"Humpf." Oriana was plainly disbelieving of her friend. "He's fine. He came out of the fight unscathed, and should be in his room at the moment." Her expression said that she was not exactly impressed by this fact. "Look, I'd better go. I need to report to the boss."

"But -" Michaela pouted, not wanting to let her friend go quite so soon.

"Bye." Oriana swiped her hand over the mirror again. This time Aneurin appeared. "My Lord."

"Oriana! This is unexpected. Is everything alright?" Aneurin gave her a puzzled look.

She smiled brightly at him. "Everything is fine. You did say you wanted regular reports. So I thought I would be a dutiful student and get in touch whilst we are in Irin," she told him faceaciously.

"You are too kind, my dear. How has the journey been so far?"

"Uneventful. The countryside is lovely of course. Liam is a wonderful conversationalist, and the inn we are staying at hasn't got any bed bugs – that I can see anyway." Oriana grinned at him.

He looked at her suspiciously. "Why don't I believe you?" he asked.

"You wound me," said Oriana, bringing a hand to her forehead. "Oh how you wound me."

"Must you be so dramatic?" Aneurin sighed.

"You still love me, don't you?" Oriana gave him a sad little puppy dog look.

"*Oriana.*"

There was a knock at her door. "Must fly, my Lord. I think that Sir Liam is at the door. I'll report in again tomorrow." She swiped the mirror before he could get another word in.

"Are you ready to leave, Lady Oriana?" asked Liam, standing at her door the next morning.

Oriana looked up. "Yes. Has there been any word on who those bandits were, and why they attacked us?" she queried as she snapped the lid of her bag down with a bit more force than was intended.

Liam shook his head. "I am afraid not. Apparently they aren't talking and the local Sergent must wait until the district Captain can bring a truthseeker down."

"A pity." Oriana followed him down the hall.

"I have instructed that we be notified when they discovered anything," Liam told her, opening the inn door. "If I haven't heard anything within the week, I shall send a messenger."

"Good."

"Did you tell Lord Aneurin about the attack?" he asked, helping her into the coach.

"No. He doesn't need that kind of worry added to his already overflowing plate." She looked at her escort as he mounted his horse. "And you are not to mention anything either." The coach jerked as it took off down the road. "I have notified someone at the residence and they'll do what is necessary."

Liam raised a brow, surprised. "He has the right to know."

"I want you to swear that you won't tell him," Oriana insisted. "I have some very nasty little tricks up my sleeve to ensure your cooperation," she warned him. "I would hate to use them, but I will if necessary."

Liam held up his hands in surrender. "I swear. But I have to report to their Majesties. How do you expect to get around them?"

Oriana shrugged. "I'll worry about that when it happens." She looked at the countryside for a few moments before turning back to him. "Will we stop for lunch, or will we continue on to Athos?" she asked.

Liam grinned. "You seem to be very protective of your stomach," he commented.

"Of course. The stomach is one of the most important parts of our body," she said, primly. "Without it we wouldn't survive. I have seen people die of hunger. It's not a pretty sight." She tried not to shudder at the memories.

"No, I suppose it is not."

"So?" Oriana gave him an arch look. "You didn't answer my question?"

The smile which had slid off of Liam's face at Oriana's statement crept back. "I asked the inn keeper for a basket of food," he told her. "We won't stop, but you will get to eat." The smile widened. "However, you are going to have to play waitress for us."

"*Oh?*" Another arch look was sent in his direction.

"The basket is in there with you. When we start to feel hungry, the guards and I will require you to pass some food to us," Liam replied, the smile widening to a grin.

"And what if I don't?" she queried slyly.

"Then you will just have to walk to Athos," Liam suggested. "Because no one here will be capable of escorting you, my Lady."

Now Oriana grinned. "Don't worry, Sir knight. I'm not so heartless that I would refuse to feed my gracious escorts."

"I'm so glad to here that." Liam's expression was wry.

"When do you expect to get to Athos, if we aren't stopping to have lunch?"

Liam gave the countryside a quick, cursory glance before answering. "Late afternoon," he replied. "You will have plenty of time to bathe and recover from the journey before dinner."

"I see." Oriana also made a quick glance of the countryside. "What is the dining custom in Athos?" she asked.

"The Royal family generally dines alone, however as you are Lord Aneurin's chosen representative, they are having a formal dinner with all the noble families who are in residence, in your honour," the knight informed her.

Oriana rolled her eyes. "Wonderful," she said. "Just what I need." :*What have you gotten me into?*: she screamed silently back at Aneurin.

"You may as well get used to it, my Lady." Liam grinned at her obvious discomfort. "You are going to succeed Lord Aneurin I'm told, and therefore any time you visit Athos this will happen."

:*You may as well get used to it, Oriana*: Aneurin's reply echoed Liam's. :*Sir Liam knows what he is talking about*:

"Aargh! Why did I ever agree to this?"

"I can not answer that," said Liam, desperately trying to not laugh.

ℒ

"I see you haven't lost all your old skills, Ori."

Oriana glanced up sharply at the statement. The guard who worked for the Dog was riding beside her window. A quick look told her that Liam was at the head of the column and so could not overhear their conversation. She relaxed slightly. "Did you set that up?" she asked.

"Me?" he asked surprised. "Why would I want to do something like that?"

"You told me that you were instructed to join the guards 'in preparation for this'" she reminded him. "Why wouldn't I think that you were responsible."

He gave her a look of disbelief. "You know me better than that Oriana. I would never let a man put a knife to my throat willingly. The 'this' that I was preparing for? That was you leaving the College of the Twins to take on your responsibilities." Now he gave her a slightly pitying look. "I'm here to protect you." She gaped at him as he continued. "I have been assigned as your bodyguard." He leaned over and gently lifted her chin, closing her mouth. "The Dog wants you alive, little girl, and I'm here to make sure you stay that way."

Chapter Five

The Fifth day, Citrine Moon, year 2974
Royal Palace, Denel, Demesa

"Prince Varian! Her Majesty wants to see you!" the servant called out to the boy on the horse. "Their Highnesses are already with her," he continued when Varian pouted.

"Off with ye then," said Gefram, stopping the horse. "This time I'll clean 'im for ye, but then 'es all yours to keep clean an' 'ealthy."

Varian sighed. "Yeth Gefram," he said, dismounting with the stable master's help. "Bye Thado-walker." He gave the horse a final pat and followed after the servant back to the House. They entered through the central wing, and to Varian's surprise, headed towards his father's study.

"Ah! Here he is," said Queen Claire as the boy entered the room.

"Now that the whole family is here, let's get started." King Jaymes sat at his desk with his wife at his side. His eldest sons lounged on the floor while his three daughters shared a settee. Varian crawled onto his mother's lap. "The reason we called you all here is because we are going on a holiday of sorts," Jaymes informed his assembled family.

"Oh?" said Josep. "Where?"

"Why?" enquired Jirrelle.

"King Chrystopher of Demesa has invited us to the Blessing of his granddaughter Oriel," Claire told her children. "When the Westecroftan twins, Rhawn and Tarianne, were Blessed, only your Father attended. We were all invited but Varian was too young to travel and the rest of you were either sick, injured or had just recovered from being sick or injured, so I stayed home."

"This time however, everyone is hale and healthy. Your Mother and I feel that Varian is old enough to handle the trip, so we have sent a message informing Chrystopher and Illissa that we are honoured to be able to attend." Jaymes took over the commentary. "You have two days to pack what you want. You will also attend fittings for a new set of clothes for the Blessing." He gave his children a stern look. "We leave in three days."

"What!"

"That's so soon!"

"I can't pack in that short amount of time!" wailed Jirrelle, Shrialla and Marryam.

Josep looked at Binjaymen and Varian. "Women!" was his only comment.

"Watch your-self young man," said his mother, a mock scowl on her face. She turned to her daughters. "You have plenty of time, ladies. Get to it".

They bowed their heads. "Yes mother".

S

The Eighth day, Citrine Moon, year 2974
Irskin Harbour, Astiria

"We's going on a ship! We's going on a ship!" Varian sang as they headed to the wharf. He bounced up and down on the seat of their carriage. "We's going on a ship!"

Binjaymen looked over at Josep who was sitting beside their father. "What's the bet that he changes his tune once the sea sickness hits?"

Josep scowled. "It's more likely that he won't suffer sea sickness."

Jay grinned. "Have you got your lollies?" he asked his brother. Josep's first trip on a ship had ended in a very bad case of sea sickness. Subsequent trips had not improved his susceptibility to the affliction.

"Of course." Josep grimaced. "Alimaj had to up the dose of peppermint in them." He glanced at Jay. "And I brought plenty just in case other members of the family need any." Now he grinned. "I know for a fact that Mother ordered a large quantity of peppermint for tea, be brought aboard."

"Ah! So that's where you got it from." Jay's expression suggested sudden enlightenment.

"I don't think you can inherit something like sea sickness."

At that moment Varian's head swung toward his brothers as he tuned into the conversation for the first time. "What's sea sickneth?" he asked curiously.

Jay grinned. "It's where you get sick while you are on a boat or ship," he informed his younger brother. He sent an impish look in Josep's direction. "Jo suffers from it really badly."

"You didn't have to tell him that, Jay." Josep was clearly unimpressed and turned to look out the window at the passing city.

"Boys, be quiet." King Jaymes looked at his sons. "We are almost there. If you must insult each other, the least you can do is wait until you are out of my earshot to do it."

"Yes Father," they said in chorus.

"Time to disembark your Majesty, Your Highnesses," called the driver from the front of the carriage.

"Thank you Arol." King Jaymes watched his sons climb out. Before Binjaymen could take off after his brothers, Jaymes grabbed his arm and pulled him aside. "You will keep an eye on Varian, won't you?" he said.

"Of course, Father." Jay nodded. "I promise he won't get into too many scrapes whilst on board. Although since we will be on ship for a good two weeks, I'm not sure what he could get up to in his boredom."

The King nodded. "That's why I want you to look out for him He seems to look up to you. I don't know why, but he could do a lot worse."

Jay grinned at his father. "I know. Imagine what he would be like if he looked up to Shrialla!" Jaymes considered the possibility and shuddered. Before he could respond, Shrialla called to them impatiently. "Are you two coming or what?"

Jay fought to hide his laughter as they turned to see the rest of the family waiting at the gang plank for them. "I couldn't have asked for a better reply," he sniggered.

"Hush, Binjaymen." The King turned his attention to the Captain of their vessel. "May we have permission to come aboard, Captain?" asked Jaymes.

"Permission granted, your Majesty."

S

"Wheeeeeeeeeee!!!!!!!!" cried Varian, hanging over the prow of the ship.

"I told you he probably wouldn't suffer from sea sickness," commented Josep to Binjaymen, as they came upon their little brother. "Varian! Come away from there!" Josep was looking a little green around the gills, but was otherwise okay. Their mother was not doing so well, although the girls did not appear to be having any problems.

"But is fun!" Varian pouted at his brothers, still hanging on to the edge. "Pleeeaassee!!!"

"No Var," Jay was adamant. "I know you are bored, but that is a dangerous way of having fun. You don't see me doing that do you?" He asked, pulling his brother away from the edge.

"But Jay!!"

"Cut the whining Var," said Jo, picking up his brother and throwing him over his shoulder. At eighteen, and having spent a year working on a ship, Josep was taller than his father and with broad shoulders that were perfect for carrying cargo or younger brothers. "You are four years old and you keep telling us that you are *not* a baby so stop behaving like one." With Varian thumping his back and protesting loudly, Josep headed back along the deck to where the captain stood, Jay in tow. "Captain," he said bowing slightly so as not to over balance or let Varian escape. "My younger brother here," he pointed at the feet dangling from his shoulder, "Is complaining of boredom. I was wondering if you might see fit to give him a small amount of training in the way of seafarers. It might just keep him out of trouble for the rest of the trip."

The Captain gave the princes an appraising look. "Aye your Highness, it might at that." He turned toward the stern of the ship. "RECHAIRD!!!!!! Get yer butt over 'ere!" he hollered.

A young man of Josep's age came running down the deck. "Aye Captain?" he asked, skidding to a halt.

"Ye see this 'ere young scamp?" The Captain pointed at Varian who was still struggling on his brother's shoulder. The youth nodded. "Ye're t'teach him what ye can. Knot's an' stuff. Keep 'im outta trouble." The youth scowled. "'im is one o' the princes, so as there is t'be no hitting or cussing." He glared at the boy. "Ye get me?"

"Aye Captain" he replied sullenly.

The Captain turned back to Josep. "This 'ere is Rechaird. He'll show 'is Highness t'ropes, yer Highness."

"Thank you, Captain. Binjaymen or I will be around to keep an eye on our brother. He is most certainly a scamp." Jo set Varian on the ground. Before he could get away Jay grabbed his collar. "Varian, you said you were bored, so Rechaird here is going to teach you about ships," Josep told his brother, who was struggling to get away from Jay. "I want to hear no complaints. Jay hasn't even done his ship training and you are getting some preliminary training earlier than either of us."

"Me don't wants to learn!" Varian protested loudly, to the amusement of the Captain and the ship hand.

"Look Var, you keep telling us how special you are, so here is another chance to prove it," Binjaymen told him.

"Me is special!!! Me just don't wants to learns about ships yet." He looked up at Jay with sad little eyes.

Jay sighed. "I'll tell you what. I'll stick around and learn with you," he offered as Josep muttered "Sucker," in his ear.

"Okay!" agreed Varian brightening, whilst Jay glared at Jo.

Rechaird hid a grin. He couldn't really complain too much as the new assignment kept him away from some of the worse chores required on a ship. "Come then, your Highnesses," he said. "We'll start with knots." He led them away as the Captain and Josep looked after them.

"Rechaird know's what 'e is about, your Highness," the Captain told Josep. "He is a bright lad. The brightest I've seen in a long while." He gave Jo a conspiring grin. "But don' tell 'im I said so." He turned back to where the boys had settled on the foredeck. "If he stays out o' trouble, I reckon he could Captain his own ship, no problem."

Josep followed his look. "If he can keep Varian out of trouble, Captain, I'll buy him his own ship, if ever I have the opportunity."

"I'll let him know, your Highness. When the timing is right."

S

"So, Varian." King Jaymes addressed his youngest son as they sat down for dinner that night. "What did you get up to today?"

"Me and Jay learns about knots," he replied before tucking into the soup a servant had just placed in front of him.

Jaymes looked at Binjaymen and Josep, as the servants placed their soup in front of them. "Translation please."

The brothers looked at each other. "You tell him," said Jay. "It was your idea." He said as Josep picked up his spoon and gingerly lifted a spoonful of soup to his mouth.

"Gee, thanks Jay." Josep turned to his father. "Jay and Varian are beginning to learn shipcraft. They spent the afternoon learning about the different knots used."

"Excuse me?" Jaymes' tone was deadly quiet as his spoon clattered to the table. Silence reigned as the girls looked at their father in surprise. None of the children had ever heard Jaymes use that tone.

"What Jo didn't mention, Father," said Jay, placatingly. "Was that he decided that this was the best way of keeping Varian out of trouble, after we found him hanging over the prow of the ship."

The King's head spun in the direction of Varian. "You did what, young man?" he asked.

His youngest son looked up from his meal to reply, "It was fun!" before tucking back in, unconcerned.

"The idea was actually to have Varian learn a few things, just to keep him out of trouble." Josep informed his father. "He protested of course, so Jay volunteered to learn with him." He shrugged. "It is probably better this way, as Jay can keep him out of trouble whilst learning at the same time, and the ship hand who is teaching them obviously can't thump Varian the way he would if Varian was a new ship hand, so Jay can thump him instead."

"I see." Jaymes looked at his sons, disapproval on his face. "I can not say that I like this."

"I think it's a good idea, Father," said Jirelle. "Varian is a very active boy. He needs things to keep him occupied. Jay is the only one of us who actually gets any manner of respect from Varian, so it is only natural that Jay should learn with Var, as it is probably the only way that he will learn."

Jo and Jay shared an exasperated look. Jaymes just looked at his eldest daughter before replying, "Thank you, Jirelle. Your opinion is noted."

"She's actually right, Jaymes." Queen Claire stood in the doorway to the cabin, looking slightly green.

Jaymes stood quickly and went to her. "How are you feeling, love?"

She smiled slightly. "I've been better." She sat at the table. "Just some soup for me, please," she told the servant, before turning to her husband. "I couldn't help but overhear what was going on in here. While I don't really like the idea of Varian learning ship craft at the age of four, I know that it is probably the only thing that will keep him occupied enough during this trip." She sighed. "Mind you, the sooner we get to Demesa the better."

"If you have no problems with this, then I won't complain. Well, not too loudly anyway," said Jaymes, returning to his meal, as the servants handed out the second course. "But that doesn't mean that I won't check up on both of you." He looked at Binjaymen and Varian. "You are both too young for this, as far as I am concerned."

Binjaymen nodded, whilst Varian remained oblivious to the threat in his father's words.

S

"Father?"

Jaymes turned to find Josep standing behind him on the stairs. Indicating for his son to join him, Jaymes turned back to his contemplation, gazing over the ocean. In the distance he could see a colony of merfolk relaxing in the pale light of the new moon.

Josep stepped up to his father's side. "If you truly do not want them to, I can stop the lessons," he told him. "It's just.... I thought that it was the best option available." He gazed out over the water. "Jirelle is right, as much as I hate to admit it. You even told Jay that Varian looks up to him, and he is a *really* active kid." Josep sighed. "Maybe my memories of Jay are incorrect, but I don't recall him having as much energy. Varian tires me out sometimes. I don't know how Jay keeps up with him." When there was still no response from Jaymes, Josep continued. "The Captain highly recommends the ship hand he assigned Jay and Var, and you know how rare that is." He paused for a second, gathering his thoughts. "You've tried to teach me to make decisions based on what is best for all involved. I would hope that I have at least half of your good sense. You have ensured that all of us have had the best upbringing available. I know more about the running of a kingdom, from my time spent on a farm and on a ship, than any of my contemporaries. You have also seen to it that I had a thorough education in matters unrelated to governing, but related to my knowledge of the people who populate the land which will one day be my responsibility. Trust me to know how best to deal with my brothers."

"It's not that I don't trust you, Josep." Jaymes turned to his son, leaning on the rail. "I do. You are right when you say that you are better capable of running a kingdom than your contemporaries. You are." The King sighed. "I'm just having a bit of difficulty coming to terms with the fact that my children are growing up." He turned back to the water. "Jirelle has started looking at potential husbands! She's sixteen! I keep forgetting that your mother and I were married when she was Jirelle's age." Around them the crew were changing shift for the night. "Soon Shrialla will be looking for a husband."

"If she isn't already," Jo interceded.

Jaymes grimaced slightly. "True. But again, she's twelve! In a year or two I'll be sending Binjaymen to the country. Just because he is second in line doesn't mean he shouldn't still understand the concepts, and after that he'll go sailing. Before long it will be Varian, and I'll be dealing with Marryam getting married too. Time flies so fast." He looked at his son again. "You did the right thing, made the right decision. Varian needs the discipline, as does Jay, though not as much, and I'm sure they will both enjoy it." He snorted. "It will definitely keep Varian out of trouble for a while." Now he smiled. "But you still have to come up with a way to keep him occupied for the travel across Demesa to Denel."

Josep blinked at Jaymes in surprise. "Me?"

The smile became a grin. "You. You took on the responsibility to provide guidance to both of your brothers. You can't back out now."

"Lovely. If you'll excuse me then, I'm going to bed. I'm going to need all the rest I can get just to formulate ideas." Josep headed back downstairs, his father's quiet laughter following in his wake.

S

Chapter Six

The Fourth day, Citrine Moon, year 2974
Royal Palace, Denel, Demesa

"Haileigh!!"

"Yes?" Haileigh turned from her survey of the desert to find Mathew climbing the stairs, their daughter in his arms. She was standing on one of the few parapets the palace had, gazing out at the setting sun.

"Word has come from Astiria," he told her as he joined her, setting their daughter down so that she could roam and they could talk in peace. A palace guard had followed them up and was now stationed at the head of the stairs. He was perfectly positioned to prevent the young princess from trying to climb down them.

"Oh?"

Mathew grinned evilly. "The whole royal family is coming!"

Haileigh stared at him in disbelief. "You're joking."

He shook his head, taking her in his arms. "Sorry. But don't worry too much. Esta and Yaran have everything under control. They are putting them in the West Wing."

"The West Wing?" Haileigh raised a brow at her husband. "But that hasn't been used for three decades at least. Esta will be having fits over the dust," she said.

Mathew grinned, sliding around so that he was behind her. "Not quite. The Astirian's were the last to use it – at your Blessing." Haileigh's eyes widened. "And don't worry about Esta. She complained to your Mother about the dust, who awarded her the use of servants from all the noble houses to help."

Haileigh blinked. "Well," she said, slightly bemused. "She will need the help, certainly. After all, the entire Westecroftan family is going into the East Wing. Oriana will be housed at the College, along with Quenmir, Oren and Etheline." She tilted her head to look at her husband. "Have we heard from the Emperors of Pella and Trimid yet?" she asked.

Mathew shook his head. "I don't expect either of them to attend, but they may send one of their children as representatives."

"Oh?" Haileigh stepped out of his arms and stooped to pick up their daughter who was trying to climb her mother's leg.

The Prince shrugged. "The Emperor of Pella has a few too many problems on the home front to allow him to attend, and the Emperor of Trimid is… well…. how can I put this….more interested in his own pleasures?"

Haileigh looked at her husband. "And you know this how?"

Mathew looked at the floor. "I travelled extensively before I met you." Oriel chose that particular moment to try and fling herself into her father's arms. Haileigh clutched at her but was too late. Mathew managed to catch her before she hit the floor. Oriel giggled. Mathew sighed and looked at his wife. "I'd be more worried about her doing that at the Blessing, than the possibility of her spontaneously combusting," he commented, silently thanking his daughter for the distraction. "By the way, I've taken the liberty of calling in one of my cousins to act as nanny to our daughter."

"Not so sure of your abilities are we?" Haileigh asked archly, as she allowed her husband to change the subject, but remembering the details so as to question him further later.

"It's not that. I can't be everywhere, and I thought for your peace of mind it might be better if our daughter had a Pyrial as her nanny. Catryn is a very capable young girl. I trained her myself." Mathew defended his actions.

"I'd like to meet this young woman, if I may. After all, she will be looking after my daughter." Haileigh was unconvinced. "Maybe after all this mayhem is over we should visit your family. I'm sure it would be very educational for all of us, don't you?"

"Hmmmm"

R

"Eeeesssstttttaaa!!!"

Esta looked up from the conversation she was holding with another maid to see the Queen coming down the hall. "Best get on with it," she told the girl, who scurried away determined to stay out of the Queen's way. "Yes your Majesty?" She curtsied as the Queen stopped in front of her.

"I understand that you ordered lavender buntings." Queen Illissa was quite indignant, although only her tone of voice gave that away.

Esta suppressed a sigh. She had been expecting this moment to arrive, but had hoped it wouldn't be too soon. "Yes your Majesty, I did."

"I thought I told you to order pink buntings." The Queen looked down her nose at the housekeeper.

Esta bit her tongue. "You did, your Majesty."

"Then *why* did you order lavender buntings?" On anyone else the Queen's expression would have been called a scowl, however, the Queen, ever cautious of wrinkles, never let enough of an expression onto her face to allow it to do any damage.

"Her Highness requested lavender buntings, your Majesty." Esta curtsied an apology. "And I was given to understand that Princess Haileigh was in charge of the preparations for Princess Oriel's Blessing, your Majesty." She curtsied again.

"I see." If the Queen could have flounced, she would have, as she turned on her heel and went in search of her daughter. Esta let out a sigh as soon as the Queen was out of earshot.

"That didn't go too badly," said Yaran, appearing behind her.

Esta jumped. "Don't scare me like that! How long have you been listening?" she asked, turning to face him.

"I was just about to speak to you when her Majesty appeared."

"So you stuck to the shadows and eavesdropped?" Esta scowled at him. "It's not polite to eavesdrop," she admonished him.

"Come on Esta. You know as well as I do that you can't learn anything in a place like this if you don't eavesdrop or listen to gossip." He looked at her. "You've been spending too much time with the princess. Don't be fooled Esta. Princess Haileigh frequently eavesdrops." He shrugged. "I've seen her."

"Yaran!" Esta was aghast. "You haven't been spying on her Highness have you?"

"What do you take me for Esta?" asked Yaran, clearly offended. "I would never spy on the princess or the prince for that matter. If you must know, I've been with her when she was eavesdropping." He looked at her. "I can not believe you of all people would consider me capable of such a thing. You disappoint me Esta." He turned and walked off, leaving her standing staring at his retreating back.

R

"HAAIILEEIIGHH!"

Haileigh and Mathew looked up from the game they were playing with Oriel. Mathew looked at his wife. "I think the buntings have arrived," he said as they heard the click of her mother's heels in the hallway.

Haileigh sighed and looked at the floor before shaking her head. "I think you are right," she agreed just before the door burst open to reveal an obviously displeased Queen.

"Would you mind telling me why you told Esta to order lavender buntings instead of pink ones?" she asked before she had even finished shutting the door.

"Because I didn't want pink ones Mother," replied Haileigh patiently, causing Mathew to choke on a laugh.

"But *I* wanted pink," said her mother petulantly.

"Mother, what you want has nothing to do with it. Oriel is my daughter, I will have the buntings the colour that I want, and there is nothing that you can say about it."

Illisa's eyes widened in shock. No one beside her husband and her parents had ever spoken to her that way. "Haileigh, I am your Mother and your Queen. You will have pink buntings!" She insisted.

"Mother you may be the Queen, but there is one person who out ranks you and I have his permission to do anything I want," Haileigh's tone clearly said 'so there'.

The Queen looked at her daughter in disbelief. "Who?"

"Your husband, my father – the King."

The Queen blinked. "Oh!"

Haileigh raised an eyebrow at her mother. "Indeed! Father said that this is my daughter's Blessing, and I can have anything that *I* want, and I want lavender buntings, so I am going to have lavender buntings, and there is nothing that you can say about it. Now if you will excuse me I wish to spend some quality time with my husband and my daughter." With that, Haileigh turned her back on her mother to be confronted with a very red looking husband who was quite obviously trying to not laugh at the two women.

"Well then." The Queen, a mildly indignant expression on her face, turned and left the room, flinging the door open so hard that it hit the wall before rebounding and slamming behind her.

The minute the door was shut, Mathew let flow with a bellow of laughter. Haileigh just looked at her husband. "It wasn't funny," she said.

Mathew tried desperately to reign in his laughter. "Yes it was," he managed between guffaws. "Your mother looked like a child who hadn't gotten her own way, and you...." He was overtaken by another fit of laughter. "You looked like a mother or nanny taking the child to task."

Haileigh picked up their daughter and swept from the room. "Come on Oriel, let's leave your father to get control of himself." She looked back at him over her shoulder. "We shall see if everything is in order at the College." With that she left her husband trying to regain his composure.

R

"Your Highness!" exclaimed Aylena. "We weren't expecting you. What with the preparations for the Blessing and all." Aylena was an older woman, with graying black hair. Her doe-like eyes belied the intelligence of her mind, and many were surprised at just how quick she could be when the situation demanded it. Aylena had been close friends with Haileigh's predecessor, Ramolleana, and whilst Haileigh was the Wuhern of Demesa, it was Aylena who ran the College of Twins and kept her eyes on all the dedicates and acolytes of the Order of the Twins. At the time when Haileigh decided to escape the palace and make an appearance at the College, Aylena was busy processing the latest batch of novices, piles of papers filled her desk to the point where it was almost impossible to see her.

Haileigh grimaced. "I had to get out of there," she said as Aylena nodded in sympathy. "Mother was being difficult and Mathew was no help whatsoever. I realized that I had neglected the Order a bit too much, so I thought I might come and see if you needed any help." She looked at the pile of papers. "It looks like I arrived just in time. What do we have here?" she asked, placing Oriel in the small pen, which had been erected for use when Haileigh was working.

Now it was Aylena's turn to grimace. "The latest batch of novices, your Highness. Forty in all, coming from all over the country. We have also had a handful of transfers from the other Colleges. That's the stack over there," she said, waving a hand at the smallest pile.

"Right then." Haileigh pulled up a chair and gathered some papers. "Let's get to it."

R

"Excuse me? Your Highness?"

Haileigh looked up from the pile of papers she was reading to find a palace page in the doorway. "Yes?"

"His Majesty asked me to give you this." The page handed her a note, sealed with her father's personal seal.

"Thank you." The page bowed and left.

"What is it?" asked Aylena, looking up from the papers in her hands, as the Wuhern scanned the note.

Haileigh scrunched up her nose. "My father has just reminded me that, as a Royal Princess, it is my duty to invite the Lavens of the Order of Wyman to the Blessing of my daughter." She scowled. "And unfortunately he is right. In this situation I can not be Wuhern of the Order of the Twins. The Royal Family of Demesa favours no religion, particularly in the matter of a Blessing." She sighed. "Dammit! I hate it when he is right!" Haileigh crumpled up the note at threw it into the bin before she looked at her aide. "There is nothing to be done about it. I shall have to invite the Lavens." Now she shuddered. "Just the thought of those three anywhere near Oriel gives me the creeps."

"They don't have to participate do they?" asked Aylena. "In the actual Blessing, I mean." She took some more papers from one of the piles in front of her.

Haileigh shook her head. "No. Mother and Father will call on the Gods to bless the child, and four of Mathew and my friends will stand at the quarter points to represent the elements. Father suggested that I choose people not generally associated with religion for those positions."

"Who have you asked?" Aylena was curious.

"One of Mathew's sisters, Raina. Galatea of Maelyn. Uncle Auberon and Edmett," replied Haileigh, throwing another piece of paper into the bin.

Aylena nodded. "Certainly no one would associate any of them with either us or the Order of Wyman." She gave Haileigh a sly look as she made a note about one of the novices. "Raina for Fire and Galatea for water. Auberon for Earth and your brother for Air? He's certainly flighty enough for it."

"Aylena!" exclaimed Haileigh before bursting into laughter. "Show a little bit of respect for your prince, please," she said between giggles.

"Sorry," said Aylena, also laughing. "But he is, and you know it. We're just lucky that unlike some of the other kingdoms the succession here goes to the first born child not the first born male."

She slid a look at her future Queen. "Can you imaging Edmett as King?"

Haileigh shook her head. "No, I can't," she said, recovering. "But don't ever let my father hear you say that," she warned, a grin still on her face.

"As if I would."

✧

Chapter Seven

The Second day, Opal Moon, year 2974
Crown road to Athos, Westecroft

Oriana glanced at Liam as they rode toward Athos. :*You were right Mick*: she sent her friend. He had returned to her side before she could get her wits back and ask the Dog's man exactly what he meant. She hadn't had the opportunity to talk to the man since and as she couldn't really do anything about that, she had taken the time to gather a better picture of her escort.

:*I'm always right, Ori. Haven't you learnt this yet*: replied Michaela. :*What am I right about this time?* Her mental voice was not quite as strong as usual, but Oriana put that down to the distance at which they were conversing.

: *Sir Liam. He really is quite good looking*: Oriana looked back at her escort. In the fading sunlight his hair had taken on a bronze hue, making it look almost the same colour as her own. His eyes were an intelligent sky blue and his lips –

: *I may be right, but I don't need the poetic descriptions thank you very much*: Michaela huffed.

:*Then you shouldn't be eavesdropping!* Ignoring her friend, Oriana turned to the young knight. "Sir Liam? Is Athos much further?" she asked.

Liam moved his horse closer to the carriage. "No, my Lady," he replied. "As soon as we clear the forest, the city will come into view. Once we reach the city gates the palace is only a half hour ride to the south."

"I see." Oriana looked down the road before returning her gaze to Liam. "What is the city like?" she queried. "I have only been to the towns north of the College, and I wish to be as prepared as possible."

"I don't know that one can be prepared for somewhere like Athos," he said, a thoughtful expression on his face. "If I remember my history lessons correctly, the city started at the edge of the sea, atop a bluff. When the palace was built it was at the outer edge of the city, however it now lies in the centre of the city. The harbour is actually built at the bottom of the bluff at the mouth of the river Gishon." Liam's gaze turned introspective as though he was sifting through his memory. "The palace itself encompasses an area of about two square miles, that's with the gardens as well as the buildings. It started out as a watch tower cum lighthouse, but now the old city walls form the edge of the palace on the western side. Over the centuries the city has encroached on the desert. Slowly, the desert people who used to be raiders have either moved into the city or become traders." Liam smiled. "I think they realized that it was more profitable than raiding."

"I see," said Oriana again studying the road ahead. "Wow!" exclaimed she as the carriage suddenly exited the forest. The city of Athos lay before them, curling down toward the desert and the ocean.

Liam grinned. "I did warn you," was all he said.

❧

"Lady Oriana, allow me to welcome you to Athos." Oriana looked up as Liam helped her from the carriage to see an older man with the badge of the Lord Seneschal on his dark green tunic. "I am Yorick, Seneschal to their Majesties King Carlyle and Queen Demetria of Westecroft," he said, introducing himself. The seneschal was a small man. Years of palace life had given him only a slight belly, as he was often seen running all over the palace and the city. Whilst having a huge staff who worked for him, he believed in having a hands-on approach to his position.

"Thank you my Lord," replied Oriana, curtseying. "It is truly an honour to be here."

The seneschal turned to Liam. "Will you accompany us as I show her Ladyship to her rooms Sir Liam?" he asked.

Liam nodded. "Indeed my Lord." He flashed a glance of warning to Oriana before continuing. "There is a matter I need to discuss with you and Lord Willard once Lady Oriana is settled in."

Oriana stifled a 'humph' at his look. She was not happy about being left out of the discussion, particularly given her involvement in the matter. However, she understood that this was, at the moment, a matter for the proper authorities, of which she was not a member. That didn't mean she had to like it though.

"I see." Yorick's perplexed expression showed that he really didn't see but it was obvious that he wasn't going to ask questions – yet. "If you would both follow me." He motioned to the servants who had collected Oriana's bags to follow, whilst the palace grooms took charge of the carriage and horses.

The seneschal led them into the palace, down several corridors, up a few staircases and along several more passage ways, giving Oriana a tour as they went. "Don't worry if you have no idea where to go," he told her when they finally stopped in front of a door. "Each suite has a pull cord for servants, and they are more than happy to help where ever they can." He opened the door. "Here we are, Lady Oriana – your new home. I do hope everything is to your satisfaction." He turned to Liam. "I shall see you in my office when you are ready, Sir Liam."

Liam bowed. "Thank you my Lord," he said as the seneschal turned and left. "Well? What do you think?" he asked Oriana as they entered her suite, the servants following in their wake.

Oriana glanced around the room they had entered. "So far so good," she said before turning to him. She waited for the servants to leave her bags before asking. "Who is Lord Willard and why do you need to see him and Lord Yorick? You gave me a warning glance when you told Yorick you needed to see him, so I didn't say anything then, but I want to know now." She returned his look with interest.

Liam rolled his eyes and sighed. "Lord Willard is the Commander of the Army and the Guards," he told her. "I need to see them about the incident on the road to Irin. Lord Yorick, in his position as Seneschal, insists on knowing everything that is going on in the Kingdom. It is best to discuss something with him present, even if he has nothing to do with the matter."

"Oh. I suppose I will not be permitted to be part of this conversation?"

The knight grimaced. "As much as I understand your desire to be there. You don't know these men. The Commander is rather old fashioned. The idea that a woman help to capture robbers will set him on edge as it is. Were you to be present, I hesitate to consider the possibilities."

Oriana glared at him. It was as she had suspected but it still grated on her.

"I'll leave you to settle in." Liam grinned at her discomfort. "And have that bath you were talking about. I shall see you at the dinner then." He bowed and turned to leave, but turned back just before he reached the door. "I have requested one of the guards from the journey to stay outside your door until we know what is going on," he told her. He quickly stepped out, shutting the door behind him, leaving her no opportunity for argument.

♌

"Now, what did you want to see us about young Liam?" asked the grizzled Lord Willard as Liam entered the Lord Seneschal's office. He shut the door, indicating a need for privacy and earning him a raised eyebrow from the Commander "You've got Yorick and me puzzled."

"Indeed," agreed the seneschal, reclining in his chair. "The trip from the College of the Twins should have been most uneventful."

Liam bowed, before taking a chair. "If only it was, my Lords," he told them. "We were set upon by bandits not five miles from Irin." The Lords looked at him in disbelief. "The bandits out-numbered us by three to one. If it were not for the help of Lady Oriana, I would not be sitting here telling you about it."

Willard gave him a look of appraisal. He was sceptical about the role the Wuhern's apprentice had played, but he could sense that there was more to the story. "What are you not telling us Liam? If it were only bandits, even with those numbers, I doubt that you would concern us with it."

Liam nodded. "Indeed my Lord," he agreed. "If it were only bandits, I would probably not concern you with the matter. However, whilst they acted like bandits, I doubt that they actually were." At Willard's raised eyebrow he continued. "Their leader was a bit too well educated to be a bandit leader. And I find it most unusual that a band of over thirty bandits would be operating that close to Irin without coming to the attention of the local Captain."

"You think they were waiting for you and Lady Oriana?" The Lord Seneschal asked Liam's unvoiced question.

"Yes my Lord. But I don't know why. I also have no clue as to who they were, which makes the why even harder to work out." Liam looked at the Lord Commander. "I am waiting for the Irin Captain to send me his report. He was calling in the district truthseeker when we left," he told Willard. "The thing is… I got the distinct impression that they, whilst expecting us, were surprised at the makeup of our party. They claimed they want our jewels and money, but I think that it was just an excuse made at the drop of a hat when they realised the person or persons they were told would be part of the group, were not."

Willard looked at Yorick before turning back to Liam. "We shall certainly look into it," he told the young man. "If we uncover anything interesting we will let you know. Their Majesties have nominated you as Lady Oriana's protector whilst she is under their roof. That includes the trip to Demesa, by the way."

"I see. Thank you my Lords." Liam stood and bowed toward each of the gentlemen. "I knew it was best if you were told. You both have better resources available to you than I have. I will await your findings." He turned and left them, closing the door quietly behind him.

Once he was gone, Yorick turned to Willard. "Why on earth would anyone want to attack Aneurin's apprentice, be it Lady Oriana or someone else?" he asked. "It makes no sense whatsoever. And surely they wouldn't be trying to attack Aneurin, would they?"

Willard shook his head. "I've no idea. But we had better investigate it, because if their Majesties find out, they will have our heads, and if they don't, Lord Aneurin certainly will."

✄

"Michaela? You there?" Oriana asked, holding her scrying mirror in front of her.

Michaela's face appeared in the mirror. "What's up Oriana?" she asked drowsily.

Oriana grinned. "Did I wake you?" Oriana's tone was suggestive.

"Yes! But not for the reasons running around that dirty little brain of yours. *I* was up late last night working with Master Aneurin since you are off gallivanting around the countryside." Michaela scowled at her sleepily. "What do you want anyway?"

"We have arrived." She gave a little flourish with one hand. "I am now ensconced in the Palace," Oriana told her friend. She turned the mirror around so as to give Michaela a view of the suite she was in.

"Ah. I see. How was the rest of the trip." Michaela ran a hand through her mop of hair, trying to get the sleep out of her system.

Oriana sighed." Uneventful. Have you found out anything?"

Michaela shook her head. "Nothing. I even went and had a look in the Book of Prophecy – or should I say books." She grimaced. "The title is deceptive as there are actually ten of them, all as thick as my arm. But I digress. I didn't find anything."

"Darn. As we speak Liam should be with the Lords Seneschal and Commander, informing them of what happened." Oriana sighed again. "We are still awaiting the report by the Captain at Irin." She closed her eyes for a moment, considering. "You'll never believe who was part of the guards assigned to trip!"

Michaela gave her a suspicious look. "Why do I get the feeling that I don't want to know?"

"He was the roughest of the Dog's bodyguards!" Oriana told her friend.

Michaela gasped. "Isorren? You're joking, right?"

Oriana shook her head. "Something really weird is going on. He told me that he had been instructed to take up a position with the Guards for the time when I left the College." Michaela looked at her friend in disbelief. "According to him, the Dog has been watching us since we entered our novitiate."

"US!" Michaela was stunned.

"Yep. Isorren reckons that the Dog was responsible for us joining the Order in the first place," Oriana continued.

"But…but…but... that's impossible." Michaela was not dealing well with the revelation being given her. "How was he to know that we would want to join… that we would want to stay?"

"That's sort of what I said." Oriana grimaced. "I wasn't given a helpful reply. Look, I had better let you go, because Master Aneurin will be wanting my report." She grinned. "I'll keep my eyes open for any good looking men for you."

"Thanks. I think I'll try going back to bed." Michaela gave her friend a disgruntled look. "I am going to go back to those books, and others to see if I can find anything out. I'll ransack the entire library if I have too!"

As Michaela's face was fading from the mirror, Oriana was already calling the image of the Wuhern. "Master? You told me to report when we reached Athos."

"How kind of you to follow orders, Oriana." Aneurin was looking a little wearier than usual as he answered his apprentice's summons. "Anything interesting happen along the way?"

Oriana smiled sweetly, putting her recent conversation with Michaela to the very back of her mind, lest her teacher sense it. "Of course not, Master. We arrived earlier this evening. At present I am getting ready for dinner. Sir Liam has informed me that their Majesties have decided to have a formal dinner to welcome me." She looked at her master. "Isn't that so nice of them?"

"There is no need to be sarcastic Oriana." Aneurin gave his apprentice a disciplinary look.

"Me? Sarcastic? Never!" Oriana put on her most innocent expression.

Aneurin shook his head. "What am I to do with you?"

Oriana shrugged. "I don't know."

"No. Neither do I." He sighed. "I have spoken with Princess Haileigh. You are going to be housed at the College in Denel, along with Oren, Quenmir and Etheline. Their Majesties and the rest of the Royal family are will reside at the palace, so you need not worry about formal state dinners and the like," Aneurin told her.

"Thanks be for small mercies." Oriana glanced at the time candle on the table. "I had best leave you. I have to finish dressing for this blasted dinner."

Aneurin grinned. "Have fun."

"Gee, thanks."

⌇

"My Lady?"

Oriana turned to find Sir Liam standing behind her. He looked quite dashing in a burgundy tunic trimmed in gold over a cream silk shirt and black trousers.

"I thought you might like a bit of support," he explained at the question in her eyes. "You look stunning, by the way," he told her.

"Don't you mean stunned?" Oriana had left her room to find Isorren at her door. Not impressed to find out that he was the guard that Liam had assigned, she was further displeased to have him guide her to the anteroom outside the Royal Dining room. It appeared that his instructions were to make sure she was safe at all times, which unfortunately meant that she had had to wait with him standing at the doorway, and she had the sneaking suspicion that he would also be inside the dining room. Having a bodyguard was something that she was not happy about and really did not see the point of, but there had been no opportunity to discuss the matter with Sir Liam. She also doubted that she would have that opportunity tonight.

Liam shook his head, a smile on his face. "No, Lady Oriana. I meant what I said – stunning. The courtiers won't know what has hit them when you walk into that room."

Oriana was dressed in forest green velvet. Her gown had a fitted bodice with a square neckline which was edged in fine gold lace. The skirt of the dress was full and fell away from the waist in a pool of material, its hem embroidered with a floral pattern in gold thread as were the hems of the sleeves which widened from the elbow to hang almost to the ground. Her hair finished the picture. Gleaming in the candlelight, it was half piled on top of her head with gold strings of emeralds threaded through it, and a couple of ringlets framing her face. "Thank you for your words, Sir Knight." She grinned at him, purposely putting her irritation to the back of her mind, it had no place at a formal dinner with people that she did not know.

He returned the grin. "You're welcome, my Lady." Just then a servant motioned to them. "It would appear that their Majesties are ready for us." Liam held out his arm. "Shall we go?"

Oriana inclined her head and accepted his arm. "We shall." They stepped toward the door which opened to show them the banquet hall.

"Lady Oriana, of the Order of the Twins," announced the herald. "And Sir Liam of Carmichael."

Chapter Eight

The Nineteenth day, Citrine Moon, year 2974
His Majesties ship, Suriya Harbour, Demesa

Jaymes shielded his eyes and looked up at his youngest sons and their tutor. "Are you sure it is safe?" he asked the Captain, as he joined the King on deck.

"Rechaird may be young, but 'e 'as a good 'ead on 'is shoulders," replied the Captain, also looking up at the boys.

"Captain!" called Rechaird from the crow's-nest. "The pilot is coming up on the port bow!"

"Right then!" The Captain turned to look for a convenient crewman. "You there – take the pilot in charge and keep 'im out of my 'air!"

"Aye aye sir!" came the disgruntled reply from somewhere behind the King.

"And you." The Captain spotted another idle sailor. "Replace Rechaird in t'nest and send those young hellions back 'ere too!" Jaymes raised a brow at the Captain. "Well they are," the Captain defended his choice of description.

"I wouldn't have thought to describe them that way." The King did not discipline the Captain. He understood that the Captain was the ruler of the ship, and the fact that Jaymes was royalty meant almost nothing when it came to the running of the ship.

"You 'aven't 'ad them running around your ship deck for the past three days," complained the Captain.

"True. And it certainly is a more accurate description than I had managed to come up with," agreed the King, as the boys jumped off the ladder in front of the two men.

"That was funs!!" exclaimed Varian, running up to his father. Rechaird and Jay arrived at a more sedate pace.

"No offence your Highness," Rechaird murmured to Jay. "But I will be glad when you two depart."

"None taken, Rechaird," Jay responded softly. "Varian would try the patience of a dragon."

"You don't look like a dragon." Rechaird shot a bemused look at Jay.

"I think that was a compliment, but I'm not at all sure," replied Jay as they halted in front of King and Captain.

S

"Solid ground! At LAST!" Queen Claire exclaimed as she stepped off of the gang plank and onto the wharf.

"Mother? Promise me that you are not going to kneel down and kiss the ground," pleaded Jirrelle, as she stepped down behind her mother.

"Or anything equally embarrassing," added Marryam, waiting for the rest of the family to disembark.

"Can I do it then?" asked Josep, wistfully looking at the earth in front of him. His sisters just glared at him.

"Welcome to Demesa, your Majesties." A dignified elderly gentleman appeared in front of them preventing any scathing replies from Jirelle or Marryam. "I am Admiral Lord Cahirs, the Lord Warden of Suriya." He bowed stiffly to Claire and Jaymes. "Their Majesties, King Chrystopher and Queen Illissa send greetings. They apologize for not meeting you in person, unfortunately they are somewhat occupied at the present moment with the preparations for Princess Oriel's Blessing."

Jaymes nodded. "We understand."

The Admiral smiled. "I am sure you wish to rest from your journey, so I have arranged lodgings for you." He bowed again. "If you would care to step this way, I have carriages waiting for us."

"With all due respect, my Lord, are our accommodations far?" asked Jaymes, looking at Claire.

"No your Majesty," replied the man.

"Good. I have the feeling that my wife would prefer to walk," the King told him.

The Admiral looked at Jaymes, somewhat shocked. "Ah...um...Perhaps you should follow me then," he said, confusion evident in his expression. He quickly arranged for their luggage and servants to be taken by carriage to his residence at Suriya Keep, before leading them toward his home.

The family followed the Admiral through the streets of Suriya. It made quite a spectacle for the townsfolk to see a King and his family walking through their town. Children ran out of doorways and elderly people stuck their heads out of windows to get a glimpse of the Royal Family of Astiria. Jay, knowing what Varian was like, kept a tight grip on his shirt collar whilst the rest of their sibs formed an honour guard around them to prevent him from escaping as they climbed the hill.

Twenty minutes or so later they arrived. "Welcome to Suriya Keep, your Majesty," proclaimed the Admiral for the benefit of the staff who awaited them. He turned to his steward. "Please show their Majesties to their rooms so that they may freshen up." He turned back to the King. "Would your Majesty like to dine formally or would you prefer to have trays sent up to your rooms?" he asked.

Jaymes looked at Claire. "Our rooms perhaps?" he suggested, concern for his wife evident in his expression.

Claire nodded. "Our rooms," she said. "And the children can join us."

The King turned to the Admiral. "We will dine formally tomorrow night," he informed him. "Her Majesty will require an extra day's rest after our journey," he explained.

"Of course, your Majesty. I shall arrange it at once." He turned to one of the servants, giving him the instructions, before turning back to the King. "If your Majesties and Highnesses would like to follow my steward, he will show you to your rooms." With a nod from Jaymes, Lord Cahirs lead the way inside.

S

The Twenty-first day, Citrine Moon, year 2974

Varian sat on the window seat and stared morosely out of the window at the storm which was raging outside. For three days he had been stuck inside Suriya Keep. The harsh weather had set in late afternoon the day before and showed no signs of passing on. The ferocity of the storm had kept his sisters awake during the night, resulting in three young women about whom great care needed to be taken, particularly as Varian and his brothers had slept soundly.

Since their arrival in Demesa Josep and Binjaymen had stuck close to Varian, always keeping him in sight and, where necessary, keeping him in hand – literally! After discovering him scaring the wits out of a couple of maids on the first day of their stay, Jo and Jay had been resigned to the fact that they were most definitely going to spend their time in Demesa on 'Varian watch'. Subsequently, the boy was now chafing at the bit.

They had arrived at Suriya Keep late in the day, and after the incident with the maids, Varian's punishment had been to spend their first full day in Demesa with his mother, who was still recovering from the sea travel. Had the weather been better the following day, King Jaymes may have allowed Varian to join his siblings and spend some time out of doors, but it was not to be.

Queen Claire opened the door to the study where her children had ensconced themselves for the day. She took in the expressions on each of their faces, taking a gauge of their moods. Jirelle and Shrialla were engrossed in their embroidery, no sign of their irritability evident, but Claire knew her girls well. Marryam was busy reading, occasionally making a snide or sarcastic remark toward her elder brothers. Josep and Binjaymen were playing chess and from the look of it, Jay was winning.

She looked at her youngest child. "Varian, stop sulking," she admonished him. "It is unbecoming of a prince to sulk." He scowled at her. She ignored him and clapped her hands to gain the attention of the others. "Children, we have been informed that the weather will clear overnight," she told them. "We are, therefore, planning to leave shortly after breakfast." She looked at them sternly. "You are, as a result, expected to be packed and ready before breakfast."

The news that they were leaving had buoyed Varian's spirit and brought a smile to his face, the others groaned. Varian, being so much younger was not responsible for his own things, his nurse saw to them, while his sibs were required to pack their own belongings. After three days inhabiting Suriya Keep, a lot of their things required repacking.

S

The sun had chosen to shine for their departure. As the two carriages carrying the Royal family, and their entourage of wagons and riders wound down from the Keep and through the village, the inhabitants of Suriya village lined the road to catch a glimpse of the departing royalty. At the head of the column was a detachment of the Demesan army, resplendent in their gold and bronze tabards. Another brought up the rear of the column, assigned to keep the Astirians safe on their journey to the capital. Along with the army, the King had assigned a unit of the communications corps.

Where the army had gold tabards emblazoned with a bronze sun, the communications corps was identified by their red tabards with a golden phoenix rising from flames on the front. The comms corps, as they were known, was a relatively new group founded by Prince Mathew after he had married Princess Haileigh. Their role was to provide clear and accurate information about what was going on in Demesa at any one time. All information was correlated in the offices in Denel, and a report was provided to Mathew hourly during the day. A nightly report was given first thing in the morning unless an emergency occurred during the night. The King was provided with reports three times daily, and any information relevant to Haileigh was passed on by her husband.

Also assigned to the Astirian party was a member of the Heralds. The Heralds were under the control of the Lord Seneschal and were responsible for any official visitor from other kingdoms. They also collected statistical information about the various aspects of the realm, sending them back to Denel where they could be collated and used to benefit the Kingdom.

The herald travelling with the Astirians was Anatha, a young woman who had been with the heralds for five years. She was also an Athenan and had received information about the Royal family from both the Lord Seneschal and her Wuhern before arriving in Suriya for her assignment. As a result she was rather enjoying the banter that was going on in the carriage of the King and Queen.

Before heading out of Suriya, Jaymes and Claire had decided to change the travelling arrangements for the carriages. Instead of having all the males in one carriage and the females in the other, Claire had insisted on travelling with her husband, and as a precaution had included Varian in their carriage. Jaymes, knowing how close Varian and Binjaymen were, had sent Josep to the other carriage where much to his disgust he was left to deal with all of his sisters. His only consolation was that he was accompanying Jeson, the son of Lord Admiral Cahirs, who was travelling to Denel to join the army, and so had the opportunity to gather information about Demesa from him.

S

"Please stop that Varian," said his mother from across the carriage. Claire had been trying to have a conversation with the herald Anatha but it had become difficult once Varian had started drumming his hands on the window sill. He had been at it for fifteen minutes before his mother had finally said something. His father and brother were sound asleep, so were unaffected by his antics.

"Me bored," he complained, continuing to drum.

Claire sighed. "Try to get some sleep," she suggested. "Like your father and Jay." She pointed to their sleeping forms.

"Me no want to sleep," he told her, pouting.

"Then read a book."

When he shook his head at that suggestion, Anatha pulled something out of her bag and handed it to him. "This is a book to draw in," she told him. "I often draw pictures when I am bored." She gave him a small pile of charcoals. "Why don't you draw me a picture?" He gave her a slightly suspicious look, but accepted the gifts. "I am really looking forward to seeing something about your journey here, or about your home." She smiled at him. "But you can choose to draw whatever you like."

"Varian, what do you say?" Claire gave her son a stern look.

He smiled sheepishly. "Thank you."

As Varian began the task of drawing, Claire turned to Anatha. "Thank you so much Anatha," she said. "I am beginning to run out of things to keep him occupied." Claire grimaced. "I never had this much trouble with any of his brothers or sisters."

Anatha smiled at the Queen. "I am amazed that you had so many, if you don't mind me saying so, your Majesty. Neither of the Royal families of Demesa or Westecroft have had more than three children for as many generations as have been recorded," she informed a slightly bemused Claire.

"I know. I am originally from Westecroft myself," she told the herald. "Astiria had a problem a few generations ago where they almost ran out of a royal family altogether. Jaymes was one of three himself, and never really expected to take the throne, however his older brother died in a carriage accident when Jaymes was nineteen, and as the inheritance goes to the eldest male first, Jaymes inherited the throne before his older sister." Now Claire smiled as she took in the shocked look on Anatha's face. "As I was an only child myself, we had already decided to have four children before the accident took place." She looked at her two sons sitting across from her with a slightly misty expression on her face. "We weren't planning on our youngest two though."

"I bet you wouldn't give them up if you had the choice, would you?" Anatha asked.

"Not for all the riches in the world." Claire's reply was adamant.

S

"Where is Varian?" Jaymes asked no one in particular. They had stopped for a short break to stretch their legs and get a bit of fresh air and sunlight. Their resting place was one of several oasis' that dotted the desert. This one also had a small community camped on its edge, who provided goods and supplies for weary travellers.

Josep and Binjaymen looked around at their father's question. "I don't know," said Josep.

"I haven't seen him for about ten minutes." Binjaymen looked slightly concerned.

"Claire!" Jaymes called to his wife who was in conversation with one of the traders. "Have you seen Varian?" She shook her head. "Jirelle? Shrialla?" His elder two daughters both shook their head.

Marryam, who had been sitting under a tree reading, looked up. "He headed in that direction, Father." She gestured in a westerly direction, before returning to her book.

Jay looked at her in disgust. "And you didn't try to stop him?" he asked as he walked past her in the direction that she had indicated.

"No." She gave a shrug. "I figured that he wouldn't go too far as there was only sand to see for miles."

"You are unbelievable Marryam. This is Varian we are talking about. When has something like that stopped him?" Jay looked back over his shoulder toward Jaymes. "I'll try to find him. If I haven't found him in twenty minutes, I'll come back." He gave Marryam another disgusted look before continuing. "If I'm not back in an hour, send a search party."

As Binjaymen left, Jaymes headed over to his wife, who was looking concerned, despite her attempts to hide it. He slid an arm around her shoulders. "Varian will be fine. Jay will find him and bring him back." He grinned, reminding her of her sons at their cheekiest. "And then you can have the pleasure of yelling at him."

Claire gave him a look which said 'not funny' before replying. "And you will not? Yell at him?" she asked patently disbelieving.

"Of course I'm going to yell at him. But you get first shot."

As they waited, Josep, Jirelle and Shrialla walked over and joined Marryam under her tree. Anatha joined the contingent of comms corps and began preparing a missive to Princess Haileigh and the Lord Seneschal. The maids and footmen wandered about, quietly conversing and occasionally stopping to look at the wares of the locals. The army stayed restlessly at their posts at the front and rear of the convoy.

After forty minutes Binjaymen appeared from between two sand hills. The camp stirred, waiting to see if he had Varian with him. Jaymes and Claire joined their children under the tree.

When he was in shouting distance, Jay called out. "I couldn't find him!" Claire clung to her husband, as they waited for Jay to join them. Josep passed his brother a water flagon which he accepted gratefully. "I looked as far as I could," Jay told them once he had had a drink. "Not just in one direction either. I canvassed a wide area. But no luck."

Jaymes looked down at his wife, before turning his gaze over their entourage. "I want volunteers. Groups of four people will head out searching in all directions," he told his people. "We will have two shifts. The first shift leaves as soon as we are organised and will go out for two hours in their direction before returning. The second shift is to take over when they return." He looked at his family before returning his gaze to the rest of the people. "We are not leaving here until Prince Varian has been found and brought back."

S

Chapter Nine

The Thirteenth day, Citrine Moon, year 2974
Royal Palace, Denel, Demesa

Haileigh sat at her desk, staring intently at the three invitations in front of her. She knew it was a vain hope, but she really wished that they would disappear.

"Staring at them is not going to help, Haileigh."

She looked up to find her father leaning against her doorway. "Must I send them? Really?" she asked him in a petulant tone reminiscent of her mother.

He grinned, walking into the room. "You sound just like your mother," Chrystopher informed her, knowing her reaction.

"Anything but that!" Haileigh looked at him. "Why must we be unbiased? Every generation of the Royal family, from the beginnings of the Kingdom, has had a member who was part of the Order of the Twins, and yet we give the impression that we are above religion." At her father's raised eyebrow she modified her statement. "Well, maybe not above religion, but that we do not favour any one religion over another. It's ridiculous, not to mention the fact that it is really lying."

Chrystopher sat on an arm chair by the fireplace and gave his daughter an assessing look. "The Royal family does not favour any one religion over another. That is in the laws of the Kingdom, set down long before either the Order of the Twins or the Order of Wyman became as prominent as they are now. That there has been a member of the family in the Order of the Twins in every generation is just happenstance. Had anyone wished to join the Order of Wyman –", Haileigh shuddered at the suggestion. "they would have. The family is non-religious as a rule, and you will note Haileigh," he gave her a stern look, "that you are the first heir to the throne in Demesa's history to be a member of any order."

She looked at him in dismay. "How am I meant to stay within the laws if I am the head of one of the two religious orders that are dominant in my Kingdom?" she asked as she suddenly understood the implications of the history lesson she had just received.

The King shrugged, standing up. "That is something you shall have to consider before you take the throne, my dear." He picked up the three invitations Haileigh had been trying to avoid sending. "I shall see to it that these find their way to the appropriate recipients," he said as he walked to the door.

R

"Your Highness?"

Mathew looked up from his desk to find a young man in the red livery of the communications corps in the doorway of his study. By the embroidery on his shoulder, Mathew knew him for one of the runners, a corporal unless he was mistaken, although he did not recognise the young man personally. "Yes?"

The runner walked in and placed a piece of paper on his desk. "We've had word from Lord Admiral Cahirs, your Highness," he told the Prince. "The Westecroftan Royal family have landed safely and are making their way south at the moment."

Knowing that there was more in the note than the runner had mentioned, Mathew thanked the young man, picking up the note to read it. After reading it through a second time, he stood and went looking for his wife to give her the news.

As he walked through the corridors of the palace his thoughts wandered back over the years. He had first met Haileigh some five years ago. She had been fleeing from a sand storm when she had stumbled across one of the many Pyrial communities that inhabited the land she called home. He smiled as he remembered the shock on her face when she had realised that there were more than just humans inhabiting the sands of Demesa. It hadn't taken long for them to both understand that there was more between them than the heat of the sands. He had been stunned when she asked him to share her life. It had been years since he had lived amongst humans and here she was, a human over half his age younger than him, asking him not only to marry her, but also to be her consort and rule by her side when her father passed on.

At the age of thirty-five he had left the community that he lived in to explore the world. Not many Pyrials chose to leave their home environment. It was necessary to learn to exist in human form, but only a few felt the need to experience life as it actually existed on the outside. Mathew had been one of those few. He travelled the world for thirty odd years, even living in Denel for a few, although that was at the beginning of his journey and well before Haileigh was born. From Denel to Athos, and on from there.

He returned home shortly prior to Haileigh's birth and had been trying for years to be happy there when a sand storm literally blew her into his life. When they returned to Denel he was further surprised when her father not only blessed the union, but expressed true joy that the Pyrials had decided to play an active part in the Kingdom as he saw it. Haileigh's mother, on the other hand, had been inconsolable. No one could convince her that Mathew wasn't a monster. It had only been a command from her husband that had made her keep her opinions to herself.

King Chrystopher had been unconcerned that there was the possibility that Haileigh and Mathew would be unable to have children due to their difference in race. He knew that if there were no children from the union, Haileigh still had an heir in her younger brother. However two years into the marriage Haileigh had discovered herself to be pregnant. It was only with the birth of Princess Oriel that Queen Illissa's opinion of Mathew changed, and now a year later they were about to celebrate the Blessing of what Mathew hoped would be the first of many children that he and Haileigh would have.

He looked up from his thoughts as he arrived at the door to his wife's study. He knocked once and entered at her call. "This just came in," he informed her, passing the note over. "The Astirians will be here in four days. Also, the Quandarans will reach our shores in two days and the Zialpans two days later again." He studied her expression before continuing. "Still no word from Trimid or Pella, and as the Westecroftans are coming overland, they will probably arrive on the heels of the Zialpans."

Haileigh sighed. "Expect to hear from the three Lavens of the Order of Wyman shortly," she told him.

"Oh?" Mathew was slightly surprised at her comment.

She scrunched up her nose in disgust. "Father reminded me that I have a duty to invite them, much as I loath doing so, and he took the invites off of my desk the other day. I can only assume that they have been sent."

Her husband gave her an amused but loving look. "I take it that you were stalling when he found you?"

Haileigh scowled at him. "Yes."

Mathew laughed, bent over her desk and kissed her on the forehead. "I'll leave you in peace," he told her. "I still have work sitting on my desk that really should be done before the Blessing."

R

Haileigh looked up from her reading and glanced at the time candle on her mantle piece. Two hours had passed since Mathew left, and she needed a break. Turning to look out of her window, the Princess decided to go for a walk through the streets of Denel. It had been a while since she had actually spent time there. She stood up and called to her palace aide. "Beynon?"

Beynon stuck his head inside the doorway connecting their offices. "Yes, your Highness?"

Haileigh threw on a cloak. "I'm going out into the city for a while," she told him. "I need a breath of fresh air. Let Tuki know that I am on my way down."

"Yes, your Highness," Beynon replied, departing instantly to alert the bodyguard Tuki of the princess' impending departure, via the palace postal system.

As she headed downstairs, Haileigh contemplated the postal system that her grandfather created. Involving a series of pipes that were interconnected and several 'swapping' rooms, they allowed notes to pass from floor to floor in a downward motion. At each different level of the palace were a series of rooms dedicated to the transfer of notes from the system to their intended recipient.

King Yevgeny invented the system as a way to send instructions to his servants without having them climb three levels. His idea was that if he wanted them to do something on the first level of the palace, why make them climb two sets of stairs to receive his instructions and then go back down to fulfil them.

Haileigh did not have any problems with the system itself, however she was aware that it had its drawbacks. A runner still needed to go upstairs with notes as they were still to find a way to send notes up the pipes. It was the same when it came to passing notes on a level, as no way had been found to propel the capsules that held the notes, in a horizontal manner. There was also the problem that whatever was in the note was bound to end up in the palace grapevine. Haileigh learnt very quickly that you can not stop gossip.

Waiting for her at the base on the stairs was her bodyguard, Tuki. He was a large man, originally from the desert, and one who looked like a solid brick wall. He was very effective as a bodyguard, as all he needed to do was be visible and no one even considered harming Haileigh because it was quite obvious that he would do much more damage than they ever could. "Your Highness," he said, bowing slightly.

"Tuki," Haileigh inclined her head. "Ready to do a bit of shopping?" she asked as they headed out into the streets.

He grinned, white teeth glistening. "Sounds good. The missus has been complaining that I haven't brought her home anything nice in a while." He shook his head. "I told her that you were busy getting ready for Princess Oriel's Blessing, but she wouldn't listen. Said that a woman always has time to shop, and that I should remind you of that."

Haileigh laughed. "Oh, Tuki, I am going to have to meet your missus one day. She sounds like a very interesting person."

Tuki looked slightly frightened by that suggestion. "Now then, your Highness, I don't think that is such a good idea," he said, trying to dissuade her.

"And why not?" Haileigh asked. "She is completely right about women always having time to shop, and on a day as beautiful as today," she gestured about her, indicating the sunshine and slight breeze, "who wouldn't want to shop? I will just have to make sure that she gets something extremely special today." She gave him a stern look. "And you make sure that she knows that it is from me – with thanks."

"Of course I'll tell her," Tuki gave a wounded look. "She'd roast me over hot coals if I tried taking the credit for something you bought her," he grimaced. "She can always tell the difference between my purchases and yours."

R

"What do you think of this?" Haileigh asked Tuki, picking up a silk scarf from one of the many market stalls. The bodyguard was loaded up with packages of various sizes and shapes, and they had already sent back two loads to the palace.

"I think," he said, raising an eyebrow, "that there had better be some money left in the royal treasury or you father is going to have something to say about this spending spree!"

Haileigh scowled at him. "Spoilsport! Besides, there is plenty of money in the treasury as you well know." She glanced back at the scarf in her hand. "Well? Will your missus like it?"

Tuki gave the scarf a proper look before answering. "She will love it. You are spoiling her, you know."

Haileigh handed the stall owner some coins. "Well, everyone else spoils Oriel and you don't have any children for me to spoil." She looked up just in time to see him blush. "What's this? Does this mean that there is a little Tuki on the way?"

Before he could answer a herald came racing up and skidded to a halt in front of Haileigh. "Your Highness," he puffed. "Message from his Majesty." He handed her a piece of parchment.

Tuki looked slightly relieved at the distraction, as it gave him a reprieve from answering her question. Once the herald caught his breath, Tuki handed him the load of packages in his arms. "Take these back to the palace when you go, will you?"

"Damn!"

Tuki and the herald turned to Haileigh in surprise as the expletive ruptured the air. "Princess Haileigh!" Tuki exclaimed.

"Yes, yes, I know, it's unladylike to swear." Haileigh scowled at the piece of parchment in her hand. "But I was so hoping that they would say they couldn't make it."

Tuki and the herald looked at each other in confusion. "Huh?" the bodyguard asked.

"Dalbert, Ignatz and Zephaniah," the Princess told them. "The Lavens of the Order of Wyman," she explained when they continued to look blankly at her.

"Oh." It was clear that neither man really understood, but were not going to mention that to their Crown Princess.

Haileigh sighed. "Tell my father that you found me, and I will make preparations for the accommodation of the Lavens for the Blessing if they require it," she instructed the herald. "Oh, and tell him I promise to actually make sure that they are comfortable, as is my duty," she added as he turned to leave.

"What is the problem with these three blokes?" Tuki asked when the herald was well out of earshot.

Haileigh moved away from the stall before answering. "They are the Lavens of the Order of Wyman. They are the heads of the Order for each of the northern and southern continents, and the Trimid Isles," she explained.

"And you don't like them because?" The bodyguard was still confused.

"I don't like the Order of Wyman. It comes with being a member of the Order of the Twins."

Tuki gave her a look that said 'say what?' before answering her comment. "That isn't really a good excuse, if you'll pardon me for saying so, your Highness. Aren't religious orders supposed to be tolerant of all?"

"Whatever gave you that idea? They hate us with a passion and we return the favour." Haileigh took time to consider the situation. "I suppose it falls back to our Gods."

"Oh?"

"Well, I know the Twins don't hate their brother, but I get the impression that they don't exactly care for him all that much," Haileigh explained. "I don't know how Wyman feels for his siblings, although all the evidence points to contempt at the very least. When you consider that these attitudes have been passed down their religious orders for several hundred years, you can expect the emotions involved to modify a bit over the years."

Tuki pondered her words for a few minutes as they travelled down a street, heading back toward the palace. "I suppose I never really gave any thought to how religious people consider each other," he said after awhile. "What of the followers of Leia, Oryien and Jei? How do you feel about them?" he asked, curious.

Haileigh blinked. "I've never really thought about them, to be completely honest." She paused for a moment to consider. "You know, I don't think I have ever come across a follower of Leia or Oryien in all my travels. I know of them of course. Everyone knows about the mother and the father of the Gods, but now that I think about it, I have never heard of Jei." She looked at her bodyguard. "Who is he?"

"She," Tuki corrected her. "Jei is the youngest of the Gods. I'm surprised that you have never heard of her. My mama used to tell me stories about when the world was new and the Gods were decorating it. Jei was always my favourite." He smiled as he remembered. "I thought about following her as I grew up, but I couldn't find any information about her." He shrugged. "In the end, I decided it was better not to follow anyone in particular and just respect them all." He grinned. "I learnt at a young age to respect anything that has the potential to fry you. It is a lesson you tend to pick up when you live in a village which is in close proximity to a Pyrial community."

By this time they had returned to the palace. Haileigh left Tuki at his barracks on the ground floor and headed back up to her office. Their conversation weighed on her mind. When she reached her office, she picked up the mirror she used to communicate with the College of the Twins. "Aylena," she said when her assistant appeared on the surface of the mirror. "I've got a task for you." She paused to reconsider the situation. "Or one of the other Masters. I want all the information you can find in the Library and the Archives about the Goddess Jei," she instructed.

"Do I have a time frame for completion of this task?" asked Aylena, bemused that something other than her daughter's Blessing was occupying the mind of her Wuhern.

"A preliminary report as soon as you can," replied Haileigh, "and the rest as soon as it is collated."

"As you wish, your Highness." Aylena faded from the mirror.

Haileigh strode to her window. "Now why don't I know anything about Jei?" she wondered, staring out into the growing dusk. "And what does it mean?"

R

Chapter Ten

The Seventh day, Opal Moon, year 2974
College of the Twins, Westecroft

Aneurin stood staring out of his window. It had been a week since Oriana had left and his studies had progressed no further than prior to her leaving.

"Hello Aneurin," came a voice from behind him.

At first he thought his mind was playing tricks on him. It was a voice he had not heard for ten years and one which he never thought to hear again. He turned around slowly. If his mind had been playing tricks on him before, his eyes were surely deceiving him now. The man before him must be a ghost, yet he looked to be solid.

The man smiled. "Yes Aneurin, it is me."

The Wuhern's jaw dropped. "But you died! There was a ship wreck."

"There was a ship wreck, yes, but I was the only survivor." The man took a seat in an armchair across from Aneurin's desk. "I was badly injured and it took months for me to recover fully, however, the people that found me are brilliant healers." He smiled again. "They could teach us a few tricks, to be certain." He was a man of middle years, no more that fifty, with gold brown eyes and long hair which increasing years streaked with white to give him a salt and pepper look. His skin was pale, as though he had not spent a lot of time in the sun and a few more worry lines had appeared on his face in the years since Aneurin last saw him.

Aneurin slowly walked back behind his desk and sat down, shock reverberating through him. He blinked, but his visitor remained sitting in the armchair. When he had finally gathered his scattered wits he spoke. "Quenmir must be informed. You are still the Wuhern of Trimid after all, Nimitz."

The man, Nimitz, shook his head. "Not any more, my friend. I have been reassigned. The Twins have another job for me to do." He sighed. "Which is why I am here."

"Oh?"

Nimitz shrugged his shoulders. "You already have an idea of the situation." Aneurin raised an eyebrow in inquiry. "You sent Oriana to Denel in your place," Nimitz told him.

"How did you know about that?" Aneurin was incredulous. "How do you know about her?" He had only taken on Oriana as his apprentice in the last two years. Nimitz had been presumed dead for five.

Another shrug from Nimitz, before he continued. "You'd be surprised at what I know, Aneurin." He gave the Westecroftan a piercing look. "What do you know of the founding of our Order? Or the founding of the Order of Wyman?" he asked.

Aneurin gave him a confused look but answered anyway. "Our Order was founded when Varan, the only survivor of a massacre, sought refuge in a Temple to the Goddess Thayis. Seeking sanctuary and a home for the treasures that he had managed to save from his home, Varan appealed to the Goddess. His pleas were heard and Thayis, after consultation with her twin brother Theron, struck a deal with Varan. He was to found an order in their honour, that would provide teaching and healing to all those who desired it."

"And the Order of Wyman?" Nimitz reiterated.

Now Aneurin gave him a blank look. "The Order of Wyman is descended of the original priests of Wyman. They evolved into their present form in response to the growing popularity of the Order of the Twins." He grimaced. "Like their fore-founders, the Order of Wyman are not known for their humanitarianism."

Nimitz nodded. "Just as I thought. You are only aware of the official teachings on both the Orders. There is more to it than that, as you would eventually find out through your studies," the former Wuhern of Trimid told him. "However, we no longer have time for you to find the answers in books and scrolls. Let me start by telling you where I have been for the last five years." He took a moment to gather his thoughts before proceeding. "Five years ago I took a ship from Trimid heading for here. I had just found an intriguing piece of text in an extremely old scroll, which I wanted your opinion and insights on. We were half way here when this incredible storm blew up out of nowhere. The crew tried their hardest to keep the ship in one piece, but in the end there was no way that it would survive and so those who were left decided to abandon ship and hope we would survive." Nimitz paused as the memories of those moments washed back over him. "I had put all the important things from my belongings into a leather satchel and strapped it on my back before jumping overboard. During the night the storm raged. Praying to the Twins I watched as, one by one the remainder of the crew lost their fight. Just before dawn I lost consciousness, not knowing that I had been pushed through the storm by the current and would wash up on an unfamiliar shore as the sun broke from the horizon." Taking a few moments, Nimitz stood and strode over to Aneurin's drink cabinet and helped himself to a glass of wine. He gestured at his friend, offering him a glass but was turned down. Taking a mouthful to wet his throat, he returned to his chair before continuing with his story. "I was found on the edge of the beach by a group of knomes, who were alerted to my presence by a dragon who resided close by."

"A dragon!" Aneurin interrupted in disbelief.

Nimitz nodded. "I have since learnt that there are quite a few dragons still in existence in our world. They just don't have much time for ignorant humans. But to continue – the knomes took me back to their city and nursed me back to full health. After I had been there for close on six months and was beginning to explore the knome city I came across a temple to a Goddess. At first I thought that it was Thayis, but I soon learned that I was wrong. When my saviours realised that I had found the temple they packed me up and sent me off to the dragon, who is called Arist by the way." He took another mouthful of wine. "I had been with Arist a month when Thayis paid me a visit. She informed me that I had been reassigned and was to help Arist with his studies. She told me of Quenmir's promotion and the impending death of Ramolleana. I also found out about Haileigh's marriage to the Pyrial Mathew. She also mentioned that the temple I had seen was not hers but that of her younger sister Jei. At first I thought that maybe Jei only had non-human followers like her parents Leia and Oryien, but Thayis quickly corrected me, and it was then that she told me the true origins of our Order." Nimitz brought the goblet to his lips and took another sip. "You know, this is a really wonderful wine. What vintage is it?"

Aneurin rolled his eyes. "A '64."

Nimitz sighed blissfully. "A brilliant year."

"Get on with it Nimitz!"

"Patience Aneurin. Now then, where was I? Oh yes. What we were told is correct, as far as it goes. Varan was the only survivor of a massacre and did appeal to Thayis for sanctuary. What isn't in the chronicles is that the priest of Wyman and their followers were the ones doing the massacring, at the behest of Wyman himself." Aneurin gaped at him. "With the exception of Varan, Wyman eradicated all the human followers of Jei. Then, as now, Wyman did not see the use of non-humans, and so did not bother to kill the knomes who were and are followers of Jei. Admittedly the humans were the majority of Jei's followers so their death weaken her considerably and Wyman, whilst unable to kill her, was able to imprison her."

"If he had killed the knomes also, would Wyman have been able to kill Jei?" asked Aneurin, thoughtfully.

Nimitz shook his head. "Apparently not. I did ask the question. Thayis told me had he tried to kill her, he would have been banished from this world. As I understand it, there is a symmetry that must no be destroyed. If Wyman had killed Jei, his banishment would have meant the birth of another God, and Wyman was not going to allow that."

"Hmmm."

"Varan had been visiting the knomes when the massacre took place," Nimitz continued. "He arrived back at the human temple of Jei just in time to witness Wyman imprisoning her and her unicorn companion Armella. Hiding in the shadows, he was able to receive instructions from Jei, who told him to seek out Thayis or Theron. Watching Wyman gloat at his victory over Jei was almost too much for Varan, but fortunately he held his position. In his glee, Wyman flung down the keys that unlocked Jei's prison, causing them to break. Thinking his massacre complete, he left the temple. Varan snuck out and stole the pieces of the keys and fled back into the bowels of the earth, using the knomes tunnels to get him to safety."

Aneurin blinked. "The treasures he brought with him were the keys," he said with understanding.

"Yes, but he didn't keep them with him."

"WHAT?! Why ever not? He could have regrouped and freed Jei when Wyman wasn't looking." Aneurin was baffled.

"He could have," Nimitz agreed. "But it would have taken a long time and sufficient followers to give Jei enough strength to maintain her freedom when faced with Wyman's minions," he explained. "Instead, Varan scattered the pieces across the face of the earth. Some of this was done prior to his seeking the help of Thayis and some after. Jei had given him a prophecy regarding the keys in the last few minutes before he left her presence for the last time. Thayis and Theron instructed Varan to start the Order of the Twins to provide a background from which they could maintain a vigil for those who would come, for in the time that Jei gave the prophecy, all the Gods became aware of it also. Wyman saw no need in the beginning to do anything about the prophecy as he believed he could prevent it coming to pass as surely the chosen ones would turn up fairly quickly and he could turn them to him. As time passed it became evident he was wrong, something that didn't go down well." Nimitz smiled at the thought. "He also became aware of the work of his siblings. In an effort to find the chosen ones first, he followed their example and set up an Order dedicated to the location and if need be elimination of the Key bearers. Somehow the keys have been able to pass through the generations since their split without detection, and over time both Orders have forgotten their assignments. But the time has come for the keys to be reunited. All the signs are pointing to the resurrection of the Goddess Jei, and Wyman will do anything to prevent it."

"Why?" Aneurin was slightly perplexed. "Why did Wyman go to all the trouble of exterminating Jei's followers in the first place?"

"Please, Aneurin, use your brain. Wyman and His followers have changed much in last thousand years or so. What do you think Jei's opinion would be of the things that they do?" Nimitz stood and refilled his goblet.

"Oh. But if that is the case, why didn't the Twins or Their Parents step in to prevent it?"

"You know the Twins as well as I do, they prefer not to meddle, and as for Leia and Oryien," Nimitz shrugged. "Your guess is as good as mine. All I do know is that so far at least four of the twelve who will bear the keys to Jei's prison have surfaced and according to all the signs, another is due shortly. Whether they have the keys already I don't know, but if I am aware of their existence, then someone in the Order of Wyman is aware of them also."

Aneurin considered all that Nimitz had told him. "Okay, I understand what you are saying, and it fills in a lot of blanks I have come across recently. But what has this to do with Oriana?"

"I'm not allowed to say, only that she has an important role in the upcoming events," was all Nimitz would tell him.

"How long have we got?" It was time to prepare a strategy, and Aneurin knew he had little time to do so. Given the importance of Oriana, it also needed to be one that would not necessarily give away too much.

"You have just over seven years before they are all born, after that, I can't say. Arist has been unable to locate anything to indicate the date of the final event. He has access to all the works of all of the non-human communities on the planet, but so far nothing has surfaced," Nimitz informed his colleague.

Aneurin sighed. "What will you do now?" He asked.

"I will go back to Arist, and continue helping him with his studies. Hopefully we will be able to find out more." Nimitz gave

Aneurin an assessing look. "Don't mention this to the other Wuherns. They will be alerted in due time. Haileigh is already on the path to finding out, as is Quenmir. Oh, and he doesn't need to know I am still alive."

Aneurin scowled at him. "How am I supposed to know who these key bearers are?"

"I'm told that there is a book in the possession of your brother which will give you the signs you will need in order to locate them."

"My brother? What has he to do with this?"

Nimitz' eyes widened slightly as the realisation hit him. "You don't know, do you?"

"Know what?" Frustration was evident in Aneurin's tone.

Nimitz put his hands up in surrender. "It isn't my place to tell you. When the Twins want you to know, then I'm sure they will inform you."

"Nimitz!"

"I'm sorry, my friend, but I can't help you. Besides, it is time for me to return home. Arist will be wondering where I am." He tipped his head to the side, considering what he had just said. "If he realises I have even left," he clarified his statement slightly, although not to the satisfaction of his friend. Nimitz stood. "It has been good seeing you Aneurin," he told the Wuhern. "I have missed the company of humans during the last five years." He headed to the door. "I won't see you again, I'm afraid. So, take care." With that, he stepped out of the room leaving Aneurin staring in his wake.

It took the Wuhern a few moments to realise what had happened. When he did he dashed for the door. Looking out he saw that Nimitz was no where to be found. The corridor was empty and given there was at least fifty yards before the next door, there was no way the former Wuhern of Trimid could have reach the end before Aneurin stepped into the open doorway. Baffled, Aneurin returned to his desk. "What on earth just happened?" he asked himself. He looked down at the papers on his desk. There before him was a scroll he had never seen before. Opening it he found a note

> *Aneurin, my friend,*
> *This is the scroll that started my adventure. I*
> *am sure you will find it interesting. It may*
> *give you a bit of help preparing Master*
> *Athenan Michaela for the future.*
> *All the best*
> *Nimitz.*

Aneurin stared at the note in disbelief. "Michaela?" he muttered. "What has she got to do with this?" He picked up the scroll and began to read.

{

Chapter Eleven

The ninth day, Citrine Moon, year 2974
Royal Palace, Athos, Westecroft

Oriana glanced up and down the table taking in the faces around her. So far dinner had been a relatively pleasant affair. Liam kept up a running commentary on the various personages at the table. The couple opposite her were both entertaining and informative when Liam's knowledge was lacking. During the space between soup and main course at dinner two nights before they had introduced themselves to Oriana. Both were widowed in the last five years and had returned to court from their country estates at the end of last winter. Tamsin was a Duchess from the Lake District, whilst Alasdair was a Duke from southern vales of the Gishon River.

Tamsin had married in her late teens to the Duke of Aran, before his death five years ago she had borne him two children, a son Gareth and a daughter Rohana. Now that her daughter was married and her son come of age and inherited the Dukedom, she had returned to the Capital to find him a wife.

Alasdair had lost his wife three years ago. All four of their children were grown and married, and his eldest son was gaining practice in running the Dukedom of Kearney whilst his father was enjoying a well earned rest in the city. They had met at the dinner of a mutual friend last year and had quickly formed a firm friendship. Much to the surprise of all their friends and family, the relationship had quickly changed and they were now sharing a house despite the scandal it had caused. When asked if they were planning to marry, their standard response was 'when the moon turns the colour blue'.

When Oriana had asked why they chose not to marry, Tamsin had answered "We've both been there, done that and it suits us not to." Alasdair had grinned before saying, "And it keeps the children happy, as they don't have to worry about possible succession arguments." They had both taken to Oriana, and Tamsin had taken her shopping the day before, making sure that her wardrobe was up to standard for the trip to Demesa.

Liam was feeling quite relaxed tonight. Oriana had been in Athos a month and so far had managed to keep from insulting anyone. The King and Queen loved her and had taken her under their wings from the first moment. The only fly in the ointment was the fact that he was no closer to knowing why the attack at Irin had taken place and neither was the Lord Commander or the Lord Seneschal. As a servant placed dessert in front of Liam he tuned into the conversation that Oriana had started with the Countess of Jazmein who was seated next to her.

"The lower classes should not be permitted to have more than two children," the Countess was telling Oriana. Liam winced. He had a feeling that this was not going to end well. Across the table, Tamsin and Alasdair were waiting with baited breath to see how Oriana would respond, as both were aware of the nature of Oriana's background.

"*Really*? And why is that?" asked Oriana in an arch tone, eyebrows raised.

"Because they are too ignorant to look after them properly. Really they should have none, however they do serve the needs of worthy people so they can be permitted to have one or two," the woman replied haughtily, nose in the air as though Oriana really should have known this already.

"*Ignorant?*" the disgusted tone in Oriana's voice was completely lost on the Countess.

"Indeed. After all, look at the amount crime that the King and Lord Commander are having to deal with at the moment. If there was a limit of two offspring per couple there would be less criminals as there would be more jobs available to keep the lower classes out of trouble." The condescending tone of the Countess rubbed at Oriana.

Unfortunately for the Countess, Oriana had a very good memory, and in preparation for an eventual visit to Athos she had studied up on the history of the various aristocratic families. There were a few skeletons in the Countess' family of which she was unaware but was about to be forcefully educated.

"I see," Oriana murmured as she gathered her words before striking. Liam held his breath as he waited to hear what would come out of her mouth. "If that were the case my Lady, then I would not be required to have this conversation with you," Oriana told her.

"Oh? And why is that?"

"Because Countess, you would not be here." At the Countess' blank look, Oriana continued. "Your grandfather's grandfather was a criminal mastermind who got his hands on a title by forcing the previous owner of the title into so much debt with your great, great grandfather that he couldn't pay and ended up handing over the title in exchange for the cancellation of those debts." Silence reigned in the room.

"*How dare you!*" the Countess was incensed.

Liam dropped his head into his hands, muttering "I knew it was too good to be true." Across the table Tamsin and Alasdair broke into silent cheers.

Before Oriana could reply the King broke in. "Lady Oriana is correct, Countess Jazmein. The fifth Viscount of Tryval achieved the title as a result of the debts of the fourth Viscount." The Countess sputtered indignantly. "If you don't believe me, my Lady, then I suggest that you look at your family bible. I recall our father's having a good laugh about it before your father's death." The King turned his attention to Oriana. "Lady Oriana, we are leaving for Denel in the morning. I trust you are ready?" he said, forcefully changing the subject.

"Yes your Majesty," Oriana bowed her head slightly in acceptance of both the subtle order and the obvious topic change.

"Not a moment too soon!" Liam muttered under his breath, earning himself a hard look from his dinner companion.

Ò

"Tell me, Lady Oriana, what did you think of the fair city of Athos?" asked Demetria, Queen of Westecroft. Oriana was travelling with her and her children, the twins Rhawn and Tarianne.

"It is lovely, your Majesty. Certainly unlike anything I have seen before," Oriana replied.

They had been on the road two days and had another week and a half to go at least before they reached Denel. At the moment they were following the Gishon River. They would continue along it for another day before crossing the plains of Vival for three days. From there came the mountains that separated Demesa and Westecroft before finally reaching the desert. The mountains would take two days depending on weather conditions, as would the desert. If luck was with them they would reach Denel two days before the Blessing, giving them just enough time to recover from the journey and to prepare for the Blessing itself.

King Carlyle had informed them that they would remain in Denel for two weeks after the celebration. He had not given a reason for this but Liam had suggested quietly to Oriana that the King was loath to get back on the road so soon. Rumour had it that his Majesty wanted a bit of a holiday, and Oriana couldn't fault him for that. It would give her the opportunity to get to know Princess Haileigh and acquire an idea how the Demesan branch of the Order of the Twins worked.

"You seemed to settle in well during your stay," the Queen observed. "I understand that you may stay in Athos for a while upon our return from the Blessing."

Oriana nodded. "Lord Aneurin suggests it might be worthwhile to spend some time with our School in Athos when I spoke to him prior to leaving for Denel. I haven't really been anywhere but the College since leaving home to begin my studies," Oriana told her. "As I will one day take over from Lord Aneurin, it is to my advantage to see as much of Westecroft as possible during the next few years." Just then she caught sight of Isorren out the window and grimaced. The bodyguard had joined them on the trip, ostensibly as a member of the King's guard, but Oriana knew differently. Liam had informed her prior to leaving Athos that he had assigned a guard to her after consultation with the Lords Commander and Seneschal.

"Is something wrong?" the Queen inquired, noticing Oriana's grimace.

She shook her head. "Not really. I just noticed my bodyguard out the window. He does his best to stay invisible but I still know that he is there."

Demetria nodded in understanding. "You will get used to it,' she promised the young woman across the carriage from her. "It may take a while, but eventually you will not even notice him any more. Even Lord Aneurin has one." She smiled at Oriana's look of surprise. "I take it you didn't know that?"

"No. I've never seen one around him."

Demetria grinned. "He's there, usually hiding in the shadows. He was originally my father's, however as I had a bodyguard of my own when my father died, and Lord Aneurin's had recently passed on, Blaine took on the assignment with Lord Aneurin."

Ò

The Twenty-third day, Citrine Moon, year 2974
Desert of Demesa

"Aaaaarrrrgggggghhhhhh!!!!!" Varian landed on a stone floor with a loud thud. "That was fun. Can I do that again?" he asked no one in particular. He looked around in the dim light, trying to get a grip on his surroundings. As his eyes adjusted to the gloom, he noted the stone walls, carved with some form of ancient writing.

Taking a few moments to recover from his slide through the sand, he tried to decipher the words. After a moment of frustration, compounded by the fact that he was only just beginning to learn to read his own language, he gave up and took in more of the room. Spotting a passage, he headed toward the doorway. Down the passage he came across another room. Inside was what seemed to Varian's childish eyes as hundreds of balls of fire. "Cool," he commented as he took in the sight of a dozen Pyrials in their elemental form.

One of the Pyrials changed form in front of Varian's eyes, becoming human in a matter of moments. "Well, well, well, what have we here?" asked the woman who had appeared before him. "And who are you young man?" she asked, crossing her arms over her chest.

"Who are you?" Varian returned. "What are you?"

The woman grinned. "I asked you first."

The boy pouted, before answering. "Prince Varian of Astiria."

"Ah. Well Prince Varian of Astiria, I am Catryn, cousin of Prince Mathew of Demesa, and a Pyrial of the Emeran community of Pyrials." She gave him a once over. "What are you doing here?"

Varian shrugged. "I fell down a hole," he informed her.

"Which hole would that be?" Catryn queried.

"That one," Varian said, pointing down the passage through which he had come.

One of the other balls of fire drifted down the passage into the other room, before heading back and drifting past Catryn, who turned her head as though in conversation with it. "Ah, so we are going to have to fix the roof." She smiled at him. "Do you have family who might be missing you?" she enquired.

"Yup," Varian nodded. "Mama, Papa, Jo, Jirelle, Jay, Shrialla and Marryam," he told her.

"That is quite a family you have there," Catryn commented in surprise. "We had better get you back to them, hadn't we?"

"I suppose so." He didn't really look all that happy with her suggestion.

She grinned. "Lucky for you, young man, I happen to be heading to Denel, so I can take you back to your family." She held out her hand. "Come on, I'll show you how to get out of here safely." He took her hand and let her lead him through the stone rooms and halls to a staircase which led to the surface.

Jaymes held his wife close. The sun was already high in the sky the day after Varian's disappearance and still he had not been located. Binjaymen was not talking to Marryam, as he held her responsible for Varian vanishing. It did not help that their father had refused to let either Josep or himself participate in the search. Josep was busy trying to keep Jay occupied and distracted. He knew it was pointless, but he was under orders. However he was succeeding in the other portion of his orders – keep Binjaymen away from Marryam. Jirelle and Shrialla had reverse orders, as their parents had already been forced to break up one fight.

Josep and Jay turned their heads to the highway as the sound of horses hooves could be heard coming from the direction of Suriya. The distance too great to discern who the incoming travellers were, and the blowing breeze was using the dust from the horses' hooves to obscure the flags billowing at the head of the column.

"I wonder who that could be?" Jay murmured.

"Probably the Quandarans," Josep replied equally as quiet. "Although they should still be a day behind us at least." Jay gave him a questioning look. "Jeson told me that they were due in at Suriya two days after we left." He shrugged. "Unless they caught favourable winds or chose not to stay overnight, or both, they should have only left Suriya yesterday."

Five minutes later Josep's theory was proven correct, as the dust settled and the flags were made out to be blue and gold of the Quandaran crest, and the yellow and bronze of the Demesan army. Jaymes came forward as the column drew to a halt beside the carriages assigned to the Astirians, bringing Claire with him.

Gamaliel, King of Quandar, stuck his head out of the window of his carriage, intrigue evident on his face. "Jaymes, Claire," he acknowledged them. "I didn't expect to see you until we were all in Denel. Taking a bit of a breather?" he asked.

"Not by choice," replied Jaymes.

"Oh?" Gamaliel raised an eyebrow. "Let me get out of this confounded carriage, and you can tell me all about it." He turned to someone else seated in the carriage. "Yes you may get out and have a walk too, just stay within the boundary of the oasis." One of the footmen came forward to open the door for the King. He stepped out and was followed by three children – two boys and a girl. "Let me introduce my sons Terrent." The eldest bowed, he was the same age as Josep, and clearly took after his father with straw coloured hair and blue eyes. "Warren." This one was closer to Shrialla in age and must have resembled his mother, with reddish hair and brown eyes. "And my daughter Caraleine." Close in age to Jirrelle, she curtsied. She was the perfect mix of both her parents, her hair a strawberry blonde and her eyes a beautiful shade of blue. "My wife is back in Quandar waiting on the arrival of our fourth." Gamaliel gave Jaymes a conspiratory look. "We decided that you had the right idea in having such a large family, so we are following suit." The children all groaned. "Now come, tell me what caused this unexpected delay in your travel plans."

"It may make you change you mind about more children," Claire informed him.

"Oh?"

"Our youngest has disappeared," Jaymes told him. "He went walking and just vanished. No one realized that he had gone until it was too late." He gave Binjaymen a pointed look, daring him to contradict his father.

Josep wasn't paying attention to the adults' conversation. Since she had stepped out of the carriage he had been enthralled with the vision that was Caraleine of Quandar. Binjaymen looked at his brother and sighed with disgust. "Pick your chin up off of the ground," he muttered just before their father decided to perform introductions. Josep glared at him.

"Let me introduce the rest on my children whilst we are waiting for the search parties to return," Jaymes suggested to Gamaliel as Claire called the children forward. "Josep you know."

"Your Majesty." Josep bowed. They had met two years previous when Jaymes had sent his son to Zialp on a diplomatic mission. Gamaliel had been on a state visit at the time for similar reasons.

"My daughters – Jirelle, Shrialla and Marryam." All three curtsied in concert. "And my middle son Binjaymen., otherwise known as Jay." Jay bowed.

"A pleasure," Gamaliel informed them. "Your youngest is something of a scamp, I take it?"

A commotion erupted on the other side of the oasis, interrupting Jaymes before he could reply. Claire cried in disbelief and began to sprint to the site of the disruption. The crowd parted to reveal a small boy standing next to a young woman with bright red hair. If the sun caught it at the right angle, it appeared as though it were on fire.

"Where have you been?!" cried the Queen of Astiria, gathering her son into a hug so strong it had him protesting. "You are in so much trouble young man!" She put him on the ground and shook him whilst the rest of the family tumbled into the clearing. "You are grounded until you are sixteen! Twenty-one if you ever do that to me again!"

"Well? What do you have to say for yourself?" asked his father when Varian failed to answer his mother.

"Exploring," he told them nonchalantly, as though he had done nothing wrong.

"EXPLORING!!!!" Jaymes roared, making everyone who had gathered around them wince. Josep and Binjaymen shook their heads in disbelief that their younger brother could be so unfazed. The girls, seeing that Varian was okay, started creeping out of the circle of people.

Varian nodded. "Yup," he said. "Me went for a walk and fell down a hole in the sand," he told them. Claire uttered a cry of dismay and began to inspect him for injuries, causing Varian to wriggle and squirm.

Before Jaymes could explode again, the young woman who had brought Varian back spoke up. "He is fine, your Majesty," she told them. "A little dusty, and his clothes are probably full of sand, but he is otherwise unhurt."

"And you are?" asked Jaymes.

She bowed, unable to curtsy as she was wearing a shirt, tunic and pants. "Catryn of the Emeran community of Pyrials," she introduced herself. "Young master Varian fell through the roof of our community. As I was about to leave for Denel, I thought it best to bring him back to you."

"What takes you to Denel?" asked Gamaliel, who had drifted to join the Astirians when the rest of the gathering had started to disperse, confident that the young prince was okay. Although the village was close to a Pyrial community, their exposure to Pyrials was limited and their presence made the villagers nervous. Gamaliel, having met Prince Mathew on several occasions, was not disturbed by the young woman in front of him.

Catryn smiled. "Prince Mathew is my cousin, your Majesty," she explained, causing him to start when she addressed him properly. "He has asked me to be nursemaid to Princess Oriel." She grinned cheekily. "Until the Blessing is over anyway."

Jaymes gave her an assessing look. He had met Prince Mathew before also, and had no qualms about Pyrials. The King looked at his youngest son. In Catryn's presence he appeared to be behaving, certainly better than when he was in his brothers company. "Perhaps you would care to join us for the rest of the journey?" he asked. "At the very least it would give us the opportunity to thank you properly for bringing our errant son back to us." He gave Varian a displeased look, which was promptly ignored by the boy.

Catryn inclined her head. "Thank you, your Majesty. I would be honoured to travel with you and your family," she accepted, though she didn't need to. In elemental form, a Pyrial could travel more swiftly than even the fastest horse.

S

Chapter Twelve

The First day, Topaz Moon, year 2974
Royal Palace, Denel, Demesa

Haileigh stood at her bedroom window. She hadn't slept well, and as the sun's pale rays graced the horizon she was feeling rather put out. The Blessing was a week away and the nerves were starting to interfere with her normal routines. There was nothing for her to worry about. Esta had everything under complete control, even the Queen, surprisingly, and the guests were starting to arrive. The only thing Haileigh had to worry about was herself.

"Darling, the sun has not even risen yet. What are you doing out of bed?" asked Mathew, groggily. He had rolled over and reached out, only to find the other side of the bed empty. He sat up, rubbing the sleep out of his eyes, and let his gaze travel over her form.

She shrugged. "I couldn't sleep," she told him, turning to face her husband. "The nerves are starting to really hit me." She moved to sit on the edge of the bed.

Mathew snaked an arm out to take her hand. "Whatever for? Esta has everything running smoothly. The Astirians and Quandarans will be here later today, and the Westecroftans a few days after that. Everyone else has arrived and are enjoying the pleasures of this delightful city." Haileigh raised an eyebrow at his description. "What is there to be nervous about?"

"Nothing, I'm sure, but you know what I am like," she sighed. "Remember how I was leading up to our wedding?"

Mathew groaned and dropped back against the pillows. "Must I?" His wife thumped him. "It's one of the few characteristics you picked up from your mother." Haileigh picked up a pillow and hit him with it. "Oi!" he cried. "You were almost as bad for your investiture as Wuhern, and that was only in front of the rest of the Demesan branch of the Order, plus the other Wuherns." He took the pillow from her. "Nothing will go wrong. I'm sure of it." He pulled her into his embrace. "If there was anything problematical likely to happen, your seers would have given you warning," Mathew reminded her.

"I know, I know, but that doesn't stop me being nervous any way." She snuggled into his arms.

Mathew grinned as an idea came to him. "I know the perfect way to cure your nerves," he told her, before pulling her down onto the bed.

R

The entire royal family of Demesa stood atop the steps to the palace. The King and Queen were in the centre, Princess Haileigh holding Princess Oriel, and Prince Mathew, were on their left. Prince Edmett stood at his parent's right. They were awaiting the arrival of the Astirian and Quandaran royal families. Word had come early that morning that they had left Behry and would arrive just after lunch.

A century ago one of Chrystopher's ancestors had had the wisdom to erect a canopy over the steps, thereby preventing those that waited there from getting sunstroke. As it was, the family were continuously being provided with cool drinks to ensure that they did not overheat and faint before their guests arrived.

A runner had arrived just before lunch with a note which said that the royal party had been spotted one league from the city. Haileigh and her family had scrambled to readiness, and had been on the steps for over half an hour, though fortunately not all that time had been spent standing. Until the column had entered the city, Haileigh and Mathew had been sitting on a couch that had been brought out for them. Haileigh's parents had sat on their outer thrones, which were used for special occasions, and Edmett had lounged on an armchair he had requested. At the approach of their royal visitors, the family had stood, whilst servants whisked all but the thrones, out of the way.

Just then the first contingent of the army assigned to the royal parties entered the square in front of the palace. Behind them came the carriage containing the King and Queen of Astiria and the King of Quandar. Behind their parents carriage was one containing the Princes of both families, and then another with the Princesses, and lastly, the final army battalion. The army parted to allow the rulers to exit their vehicle. The Kings and Queen waited until the children had joined them, before heading toward the stairs.

As Jaymes, Claire and Gamaliel walked toward the stairs, Chrystopher and Illissa made their way down to stop at the base. Haileigh and Edmett followed, but stopped two steps above them. Mathew, who now held the rather fussy Oriel, stood two steps above his wife. "Welcome, my friends, to Demesa," Chrystopher hailed them. "Thank you for joining us to celebrate the Blessing of my granddaughter."

Jaymes, Claire and Gamaliel inclined their heads by way of greeting, whilst their children curtsied or bowed. "Thank you for inviting us, Chrystopher," replied Jaymes.

"We are honoured to be here," added Gamaliel.

"Come," said Illissa. "Your journey has been long. I am sure you will need to rest. Let our people look after you, and we will talk again later." She signalled to Esta, who had been waiting in the shadows of the palace. With an army of servants she took charge of their belongings, while Chrystopher and Illissa showed the visitors into the palace.

R

Varian was bored. All the adults were busy, and his brothers were out training with Prince Edmett. His sisters had gone with Princess Haileigh on a shopping expedition in the city and he was bored. For the last two days, Catryn had entertained him and the baby Oriel, but Oriel was sleeping and Catryn had joined his sisters. He looked over at the woman who had been temporarily assigned to look after him and scoffed. She was sound asleep and snoring loudly.

Varian rested his head on one hand and stared out of the window. *What can I do?* He wondered. He was just itching to get out and explore the palace, but a firm eye had been kept on him at all times since his last adventure. *But not now*, he realized. "He, he, he," he laughed quietly. Silently, he picked up the sketch pad that the herald Anatha had given days ago, and grabbed a bag. Putting them in, he searched the room for a pencil. Spotting one by his makeshift nurse, he crept across the room to pick it up. He added it to his bag, along with a couple of candles and a piece of flint with which to light them. He then slipped the bag over one shoulder and crept from the room.

In the hallway he looked around. People scurried all over the place, taking no notice of him, too busy putting the final preparations in place for the Blessing to be held in four days time. Acting as though he had every right to be there, Varian found the stairs and headed down toward the kitchens. The last few months of exploring at home had given him the experience to realize that having food with him would be a good idea.

After successfully managing to swipe a couple of rolls and some fruit, Varian continued down the stairs that ran behind the kitchens. Over the centuries, as the sands had encroached on the city of Denel, the owners of the buildings had just added to the tops of the buildings. The result was an interesting array of layers that were perfect for young children to go exploring through.

After a few minutes travelling down, Varian came across a door that was partly open. Gathering a candle and the flint from his bag, he lit the candle and entered the room to being his exploration. The room was rather dusty with disuse, and there was no evidence of windows. Prior to the sands reaching this level, any windows would have been bricked up to prevent the sand from getting in but strangely, this room had none.

In one corner of the room was another door. Varian crossed the room, heading toward the door. He frowned. A draft was coming from the gap under the door. He kneeled on the ground to investigate, sniffing the air. It smelled fresh. His brow furrowed in confusion, he stood back up and proceeded to open the door. The candle in his hand flared slightly at the sudden influx of air to the room.

Behind the door was a passage. To Varian's inexperienced eyes it appeared to be fairly new in construction. Over the past two days Catryn had given him a condensed history of Denel and its palace. He knew that he was at least three levels below the present day kitchens, which meant that he was in an area that had not been inhabited for at least two hundred years, yet the passageway showed clear signs of having been built in the last decade. Curiosity got the better of him. After all, he was there to explore, so why not see where the passage went?

He followed the air, which flew passed him as a mild breeze. Somewhere ahead of him there had to be an exit to the surface, and Varian really wanted to find out where it was. After travelling for half an hour with no sign of the exit, he stopped to rest. Being underground he could not tell what time it was, but given the mild rumbling coming from his stomach and the time when he left the nursery, he figured it to be near lunch time.

Pulling a roll from his bag, he sat on the ground and took in his surroundings. The passage had been shored up with stone and wood. Whoever was responsible for it, they were experienced miners. Binjaymen had taken him on an excursion to a gold mine at the edge of Irstin, the Astirian capital. Jay had explained the reasons for why the mine looked like it did. Despite his young age, Varian was able to understand the concepts completely, even though his vocabulary was limited.

After consuming his roll and an apple, Varian continued on his way. The passage itself was not terribly interesting to look at, but after what seem to him like two or three hours, the passage opened into a large cavern. The walls were completely sheer rock, obviously carved to make the place bigger. In the centre of the cavern was a large structure, constructed from the stone removed from the walls. On the outside of the structure were carvings and large bowls had been set up as torches which lit up the entire cavern, albeit not as brightly as the palace from which he had come.

Creeping up to the structure, Varian realized that it was actually a temple, hewn from stone. His brain ticking over, he decided that the carvings must explain who the stone temple was for. He pulled out the sketch pad he had brought with him, and tearing out a page, he grabbed his pencil and traced the carvings onto the page. Varian thought that even though he could not understand them, one of his brothers could probably explain them to him when he caught up with them later.

Slowly he moved around the outside of the temple, tearing out page after page from the sketch pad, and patiently tracing all the carvings that he could reach. When he had circumnavigated the building, he stepped back and sketched a picture of the temple, before heading back to the entrance he had discovered whilst doing his tracing.

As with the cavern, inside the temple large stone bowls had been set up as torches. The centre of the building was open, exposing the roof of the cavern which glittered with precious and semi-precious stones. At the back of the temple stood a huge, opaque crystal. Inside a figure could just be made out. Varian thought that it looked female, but due to the density of the crystal, he couldn't be sure. The floor was tiled with beautiful mosaics. Varian could not work out what they represented, however he knew that they were pretty. On the walls were large tapestries. On one of them was a man who looked a lot like Varian's father. Varian tried to fix it in his mind so that he could tell his father about it later.

R

Haileigh, Claire, Catryn and the girls returned from their shopping expedition laden down with packages. They had spent the better part of the morning and early afternoon in the market district, having taken lunch at one of the fashionable eateries which had sprung up in recent years. Tuki, Haileigh's bodyguard, had been heard to murmur that he was surprised that the merchants still had goods to offer for sale as a result of the royal shoppers visit.

"Varian? I have some new clothes for you to try on," called Claire, entering her son's room. "Varian?" She looked around. Seeing no sign of her son, and his temporary nursemaid asleep in a chair, the Queen started to get concerned. Uriahl, Varian's normal nurse, had been given a few days off as reward for her agreeing to travel to Denel with them. Claire was now beginning to regret that decision. She shook the nurse awake. "Where is Prince Varian?" she asked, displeasure colouring her tone.

The nurse had woken with a start and was slightly disorientated. "He was sitting at the window, your Majesty. I must have dozed off for just a moment. I'm sure he is nearby," she tried to placate the Queen.

"What time is it?" Claire asked, knowing full well what time it was.

"Uh…." The woman glanced at the candle on the mantle piece. Her skin turned pale as she realized how much time had passed.

"Mother?" Jirelle stuck her head in the door. She took one look at Claire's face and winced. She knew what that expression meant. "I'll get Father," she said before her mother could say a word. Jirelle returned a few minutes later with not only the King of Astiria, but also the King and Queen of Demesa and Princess Haileigh and Prince Mathew in tow. Neither the Queen nor the nursemaid had moved since Jirelle had left. Moments later Josep, Binjaymen and Prince Edmett entered the room, having heard through the palace grapevine what had occurred. Marryam had decided to steer clear of the scene after Varian's last adventure, and Shrialla had thought it wise to keep her company.

Jaymes looked at his wife and sighed. "My dear?" it was more a statement than a question.

"This *woman*," Claire spat out the word, "fell asleep and left our son unattended," she told him. "It would *appear* that Varian decided to go exploring *again*." Josep and Binjaymen winced at their mother's words.

"Cousin," said Illissa, guiding Claire out of the room so that Chrystopher could discipline the servant without an audience. "You should not worry. He could not have gone far. We shall set the guards to finding him, and I am sure he will turn up at any moment."

Jaymes shook his head. "It is kind of you to say so, Illissa, however, you do not know our youngest son." Illissa raised an eyebrow at Jaymes' words, while his sons nodded furiously. "Varian could loose a whole battalion of guards without so much as a blink," he explained. "You have not heard what happened during our journey here."

Haileigh and Mathew guided the party to a lounge room down the hall. They sat, and whilst refreshments were ordered, Jaymes and his sons told the story. At one point Mathew called Catryn to join them and add her insights to the episode. Chrystopher joined them just as the refreshments arrived, although he did not disclose what had happened to the nursemaid.

"Claire, I have asked Haileigh's bodyguard, Tuki, to personally oversee the search," Chrystopher told the Queen of Astiria. "If anyone will find your son it is him."

"Thank you Chrystopher, but I don't see that it will make much difference," Claire was rather despondent.

It was Haileigh who replied. "Tuki is the best, your Majesty," she told her with determination. "He has been keeping me out of trouble for more years than I care to count. Father assigned him to me when I left to travel the world, and if he could keep up with me," Haileigh grinned, "He will find young Varian."

Before Claire could respond, a messenger appeared at the door. The whole room waited with expectation. "Your Majesties? I have a note from the guard Tuki."

Chrystopher signalled that he would receive the message. The messenger handed over the note he carried, and waited by the door to see if there was a reply. The King of Demesa read the note in a silence so thorough that the only noise was that of the people breathing. When he had finished he looked directly at the Queen of Astiria. "Tuki has found evidence of your sons' explorations," he told her. "He seems to have gone down into the old parts of the palace that has been abandoned due to the shifting sands. Tuki is following his path and hopes to find him shortly."

"What do we do now?" asked Edmett, as the room began to relax slightly.

Haileigh fixed her brother with a look of disbelief, before answering. "Now, we wait."

R

Chapter Thirteen

The Third day, Topaz Moon, year 2974
Royal Palace, Denel, Demesa

Tuki and his contingent of guards headed down the stairs behind the kitchens. The heir's bodyguard had questioned the cooks and servants to determine that a young child around the age of four had been in the kitchens earlier in the day. Given that there was only one child of this age in residence in the palace, it was a safe bet that the child was indeed Prince Varian. One of the servants who worked in the kitchens had told Tuki that she had seen the child go out the back door that led to the stores. Tuki hadn't expected to find much evidence of Varian's path, but had been pleasantly surprised when a grubby little hand print had appeared on a wall, providing an indication as to the direction Varian had gone after leaving the kitchens, and that direction had been down.

After going down one flight of stairs, childish footprints began to appear in the thickening dust that covered the floor. One flight became two, then three, four, five and finally, at the end of the sixth flight of stairs, the footsteps veered to the left and a door that was open. The guards followed the footsteps in. Tuki, in the lead, stopped dead in his tracks when he saw the open door on the far side of the room. "When did that get there?" he exclaimed in disbelief. "That should not be there!"

The commander of the detachment of guards with Tuki looked at him. "Sir?"

Tuki shook himself. "Sorry Brenth. I was in this room a few years back when one of cook Ayren's daughters got lost whilst visiting her mother. That door was not there." He stared at the door as though willing it to disappear. "Princess Haileigh gave me a copy of the history of the palace after that event, and it contained a copy of the original palace floor plans. Unless I am mistaken, this level was the third floor up from ground level when the palace was first built, and did not have a balcony or any windows, as it was an office of the then Lord commander of the Army." Tuki grinned as he remembered the story. "He was a rather paranoid individual, who thought that the common people were all out to get him."

Brenth returned his grin. "And who's to say that he was wrong?"

"True. Send word to their Majesties. Tell them only that we have a good idea of where he is, and that we hope to have him back in a short while. I'm going to follow the young rascal," Tuki informed the guard. "The rest of you follow, but drop off one by one every hundred meters or so. That way, if I come across any problems you will be within eclose reach and messages can be passed on easily."

Brenth bowed. "Yes, Sir." He turned to one of his guards to send off the message before following after Tuki as he headed through the door.

S

"Well, well, well, what have we here?" asked a voice from behind Varian as he picked up the crystal shard from the altar. The boy jumped and turned to find a man, only as high as Varian's waist, standing behind him. The child blinked in surprise at the sight.

"Who are you?" was the first thing that came out of Varian's mouth.

"I would ask you the same question, young human, but I shall relieve your curiosity." The knome bowed. "I am Jacobah, guardian of the temple and priest of the imprisoned Goddess," he said, introducing himself. "Would you care to return the favor and tell me your name?"

Varian looked at him. "Prince Varian of Astiria," the child replied.

"Ah… so you are the one," understanding was evident in the knome's tone. He smiled at the boy. "You may keep that," Jacobah told him, indicating the shard that Varian had taken from the altar. "My people have no need for it anymore."

"What is it?" asked Varian, looking at the crystal in his hand.

The knome smiled enigmatically. "You'll find out in time," was his only response. "Are you hungry?" Jacobah headed off Varian's curiosity with a deft change of direction.

Varian pulled a roll from his bag, slipping the crystal inside at the same time. "I have food," he replied. "But thank you any way," he added, remembering the manners that Ria had drummed into him. "Would you like some?" he offered.

Jacobah shook his head. "Thank *you*, but my people do not eat bread as humans make it." He gave Varian a conspiratorial wink. "It disagrees with us." Jacobah pondered the problem of the child in front of him. It was obvious that someone would be looking for him shortly if they were not already doing so.

"Another follows," said a quiet voice from behind him. Jacobah turned and saw his colleague Reymentha standing in the shadows of a pillar. "A human man comes in search of the child. He is expected," she told him.

Jacobah glanced at Varian to ensure that his attention was not on the knome before commenting. "Expected? Why?"

"You have read the scriptures too, Jacobah," she replied. "You know the signs. You know what is to come."

"Scriptures? Where in the scriptures are you talking about?" he whispered frantically, keeping one eye on the human child.

"'*The child shall come first and he will be the first, but the first man shall follow and find him, and through him shall come others to pave the path for the return of the Goddess.*' The third book, fourth chapter, final page," Reymentha said, quoting the scriptures. "There is more, but it isn't of relevance at the moment."

"I haven't read the scriptures recently, or at least, not that part of them," Jacobah hissed, peeved to be pulled up on a lack of scriptural lore. The priestess just raised an immaculately groomed eyebrow at him. He scowled at her, but was unable to make further comment when a shadow fell over them and the altar. The two knomes looked up to find an adult human male blocking the doorway.

Tuki stood in the doorway and looked into the temple. At the altar sat Prince Varian. Halfway to the altar were two small humanoid creatures, one male, one female. It was obvious, although surprising to Tuki, that they were knomes. The temple was large enough to fit a congregation of humans as well as knomes. Tuki looked back to the knomes, who were in a slight state of shock. "To whom is this temple dedicated?" he asked them quietly, puzzlement colouring his tone as he felt for the first time as though he were coming home.

It was Reymentha who replied. "The Goddess Jei, she who was imprisoned, but who will one day see freedom again."

"Imprisoned? Jei? Why? And why am I only now finding her?" Though he was supposed to be collecting the errant young Prince, the discovery of a Temple to the one Goddess that he had ever considered serving was an opportunity that he could not pass up.

"It is not the time for this discussion, human," Jacobah told him in no uncertain terms, his voice changing slightly. "The child must return to his parents." He pointed at Tuki. "You will return here later for instruction. Then shall you know the truth." Reymentha looked at her colleague in surprise, but chose not to comment.

Tuki nodded and focused his attention on Varian. "Ÿour Highness!" he called. "Your parents are not pleased with you."

Varian had turned his head at Tuki's call. He grimaced at the body guards words. "I'm grounded," he muttered.

"That would probably be the least of your worries, young man, from what I hear." Tuki grinned at the child. "If we leave now, you might be able to soften their ire by just a little bit." He held out his hand to the prince. Varian sighed and walked up to the man. Giving him his hand, he allowed the body guard to lead him back toward the palace.

Once the two humans were out of sight, Reymentha turned to Jacobah. "That was not you speaking just then," she told him.

"I know." Jacobah was perplexed. "And it wasn't the Lady either. I have spoken with her before, as have we all. It was another of the Gods, though I know not who."

Reymentha gave a little half smile. "It will be revealed in time. It always is." She walked to the doorway and looked out at the passage from which the humans had come. "We had best start preparing for his return."

"The man? Or the boy?" asked Jacobah, following her gaze.

"The man. The boy shall not return here. He has other places that he must go before the prophecy is fulfilled." She blinked. "Aargh! I wish They would stop doing that!" Reymentha stamped her feet in frustration.

The priest grinned. "You too?"

S

"So, your Highness," said Tuki, as he and Varian headed back toward the palace, "I think we shall keep some of the details of your trip to ourselves, shall we?"

Varian looked up at the man. "What you mean?" he asked.

Tuki gave him a conspiratorial wink. "We didn't see the knomes. You didn't leave the palace, and you never saw the temple."

"Why?" the little prince was perplexed.

"It will be our secret." Tuki paused a moment to consider how to put what was going through his mind in a way that the boy would understand. "I don't think many people will believe us if we tried to tell them anyway."

"Oh." Varian thought about it for a while as they walked, leaving Tuki on tender hooks whilst he waited to see if the child understood. "Okay's, it's our secret." The Prince grinned at his tall partner. "Cool!"

Just then they came across the first of the guards who had followed Tuki into the passage. "Good to see you safe and sound, your Highness," said the man as they joined him. The scene was to repeat all the way back to the room in the palace from which the passage left.

When they returned to the room, Tuki called all the guards to him. "I want you all to forget about that passage," he told them. "I am going to close that door, and when we leave this room I will lock the door to this one behind us." He gave the assemblage a stern look. "If I hear one word of what happened here today, I will hunt down the perpetrator and silence them myself. Is that understood?" They all nodded. None of them understood what was going on but they were not willing to cross the Heir's bodyguard either. "Good. Now let's get this young man back to his parents before his mother has a nervous breakdown."

"I'm afraid it's too late," said a voice from behind Tuki, causing the bodyguard to turn around in surprise. "She had the nervous breakdown hours ago," said Prince Binjaymen as he leant against the doorframe. "You are in so much trouble young man," he commented as he spotted his younger brother.

"Your Highness, we weren't expecting you." Tuki was flabbergasted. "I anticipated that all of your family would be waiting together."

Jay grinned. "It's alright, Master Tuki. Your secret is safe with me." He leaned down and picked up his brother, who protested at the indignity. "I don't know why you want the door locked, but then I don't really care." Jay headed out of the room. "Oh, and just so that you are aware – I followed the guard you sent with the note when he returned here."

The guards all looked at Tuki. The bodyguard fell into step with the Astirian Prince, whilst the rest fell in behind him.

S

"Here he is Mother," said Binjaymen, walking into the room with the contingent of guards following him as far as the doorway. Varian was still under his arm and complaining bitterly about it. "I'm told that he is a bit hungry but otherwise fine."

Claire jumped up from her seat and raced over to her sons. Jay relinquished his brother to their mother happily. Claire was so emotional over getting Varian back that she couldn't form any words to express both her joy and her anger. Jaymes was not so overcome. "Right. From now on young man, you will not only have your nurse but also three guards looking after you day and night," the King of Astiria told his youngest child. "I have had *enough* of this wandering off at the first chance. If you must explore, you will be taking guards with you. Then at least I will know that you are safe." He turned to Binjaymen. "As for you....when did you disappear? Hmmmm?"

Jay gave his father a sheepish look. "I slipped out after we received the note from Master Tuki." He shrugged. "I figured it might be a good idea if a member of the family was close by when Varian was found, so I followed the guard."

"I see. You and I shall have a little talk about that later. For now, I think perhaps," Jaymes looked over at Chrystopher. "We should all have something to eat?"

Chrystopher nodded. "I'll inform the cooks that we are ready for dinner." He looked at his wife and daughter. "A group meal would probably be beneficial to all at this point."

"Indeed," agreed Illissa. "I shall speak with Gamaliel and see if he and his family would like to join us."

"Perhaps an informal dinner, Father? Mother?" Haileigh suggested, as the Queen headed towards the door. "There will be few opportunities in the future for such a gathering, and I am sure that a formal dinner is going to be a bit pointless at this time." She motioned in the direction of Claire, who had yet to untangle herself from her son.

Illissa paused in the doorway. "I shall inform the maids after I have spoken with Gamaliel," she said, indicating her approval of the suggestion.

"Then we should go and change before dinner." Catryn, who had been sitting quietly in the corner, looked at her cousin. "I'm sure that Master Varian with need a wash after his escapades," she commented.

Before Mathew could reply, Claire held her son at arms length and answered for him. "Yes, *Master Varian*," her tone indicating her annoyance with her son. "You do need a bath. You are covered in dust!" Varian pouted, but wisely refrained from complaint.

S

Knome kingdom of Deyenth

"So, Priest Jacobah, to what do I owe the honour of your visit?" asked Gerafer, King of Deyenth. "It is most unusual for the Keeper to leave the Temple." Gerafer was not a young knome. As the youngest son of Abaranth of Essoter he had jumped at the chance to start a new kingdom when the time had arisen. Now some twenty years later, he had at times wished that he could change his decision.

Jacobah bowed before his king. "Your Majesty, I bring important news for the Twelve Kingdoms. The First has arrived," he said, shocking the knome he was addressing

Gerafer blinked. "You are sure?"

"Yes, Majesty." The priest was adamant. "I discovered him not two hours gone. He retrieved the Key," he informed the King.

The King of Deyenth closed his eyes and pondered the information the priest had given him. He ran the prophecy over in his head. It was something that all knomes were required to know by heart. "And the first man?" he asked.

Jacobah nodded. "He followed, and he shall return shortly for instruction. As we speak, Priestess Reymentha is preparing for his return."

"My brother must be informed." Gerafer turned to look at the fresco that covered the walls of his throne room. It contained the most important story in the history of the knomes. "We suspected that they would arrive soon," he told the priest. "When the human mage Nimitz came to live with the dragon Arist, Quenton told me that we would live to see the Return, but I did not truly believe him." The king scowled. "I hate it when he is right." He sighed. "Have you sent word to High Priest Dethicon?" Gerafer asked.

"Yes, your Majesty. I suspect that he already knows, however I thought it best to notify him anyway," Jacobah informed him.

"Very well. Thank you, Priest Jacobah." The King returned his gaze to the fresco for a moment. "I suppose we had best start preparations."

S

Chapter Fourteen

The First day, Topaz Moon, year 2974
Beside Gishon River, Westecroft

"Lady Oriana?"

Oriana turned to face the Queen at the sound of her name. She had been gazing out the window at the scenery. "Yes your Majesty?"

Demetria gave her a sly look. "What do you think of Sir Liam?" she asked innocently.

The apprentice Wuhern raised an eyebrow at her queen. "Are you match making by any chance, your Majesty?"

"Match making is beneath a queen," Demetria informed her, as she adjusted her sleeping son on her lap. His twin sister had fallen asleep on their nurse. "It's just that you happened to be staring in his direction, that's all."

Oriana snorted under her breath in disbelief. "He is a fine gentleman," she told her. "A man worthy of the title he carries." Her gaze wandered back in the direction of the man in question.

Liam was riding alongside the King, who had decided that he wanted a bit of fresh air. They were on the edge of the Demesan desert so it was deemed safe by his guards.

"How are you faring young Liam?" Carlyle asked as they rode.

Liam shifted in his saddle. Since being assigned to Oriana he'd had more exposure to his rulers than he had ever wanted. "Quite well, your Majesty," he replied. "The ride to and from the College of the Twins was preparation, I think."

The King nodded. "Good, good." He scanned the horizon. "And Lady Oriana? She has been of no trouble to you?"

"Not at all, sire." Liam phrased his reply very carefully, knowing of the favor that Oriana had received since her arrival in Athos. "Lady Oriana has been very easy to look after." *Not*, he thought but refrained from saying.

"Wonderful." Carlyle looked quite pleased with himself. "And how is your father? His presence has been missed at court."

Liam gave the King a sideways glance at the sudden change of topic. It made him feel most uneasy. "His arthritis is getting worse, but he has my sisters to look after him." The knight grinned at the thought.

"He is getting his enjoyment by complaining about their attentions to their husbands, and spoiling their children behind their backs."

Ò

The Fifth day, Topaz Moon, year 2974
Royal Palace, Denel, Demesa

Aylena, Master Athenan and assistant to Wuhern of the Order of the Twins in Demesa hurried down the palace hall toward the office of Haileigh, heir to the throne of Demesa and Wuhern of the Order of the Twins. Puffing slightly she knocked on the doorframe of her Wuhern's office. When Beynon looked up, Aylena asked, "Is her Highness in?"

Beynon nodded. "Go on in, Master Aylena. I have orders to let you interrupt at any time."

Aylena raised an eyebrow at that, but said nothing as she walked over to the connecting door to the Princess' office, knocked, and at the affirmative sound from behind it, went in. "You wanted this as soon as possible, your Highness," she said, handing a package to the Wuhern when she looked up.

Haileigh took the package, looking at the cover. "This is the preliminary report?" she asked. There were only a dozen or so pages in her hand.

Her assistant shook her head. "That is the lot. The archivists have written you a note. I think it is at the end of the report. They told me that there may be more information with the other Colleges or Temples, however as the other Wuherns were coming here for the Blessing, it might be appropriate to inquire on the topic when they are all here."

Haileigh flip the pages for a few seconds before responding, "Thank you, Aylena."

"Will there be anything else, your Highness?" asked her aide.

"Not at the moment." The Wuhern smiled. "But thank you for asking."

Aylena sighed under her breath in mild relief. "You're welcome, your Highness," she said before leaving the princess to her reading.

Once Aylena had left, Haileigh called out to her secretary. "Beynon!"

He stuck his head in the door. "Yes, your Highness?"

"I don't want any interruptions for the next hour," she informed him. "Not even my parents or my husband," Haileigh insisted to her secretary's shock. "I don't expect any of them to need to see me," she said, "But if they should, take a note and tell them I will get back to them."

"Yes, your Highness," replied the stunned man, before he shut the door and headed back to his desk, praying fervently that his boss' parents stayed far away during the next hour. The idea of telling his King or Queen that they couldn't see their daughter filled him with dread.

Once Beynon had shut the door, Haileigh locked the door and put a locking spell on it for reinforcement. The last thing she wanted as she examined the report in her hand was an interruption. Sitting in her favorite armchair, Haileigh began to read. After a few minutes a frown creased her brow.

"There is nothing here!" Haileigh cried in disgust as she finished reading it. "Youngest of the Gods. Got that. But why don't we know anything about her? What happened to her? Surely there has to be something around." She threw the report onto the ground, dislodging the note from the archivists. Haileigh started to pace across the room. "The Gods Oryien and Leia prefer not to meddle with their creatures, but they still have the odd follower." She took a moment to stare out her window before continuing her pacing. "Okay, so I haven't met one that I know of, but Mathew has, and Father has. Neither one of them has mentioned meeting any followers of Jei. It's like she ceased to exist, and that is not possible, because she is a God." Just then she noticed the piece of paper stick out of the report. Haileigh picked it up. "What's this? *Dear Wuhern Haileigh*," she read under her breath. "*It is the humble opinion of the archivists that, on the topic of the Goddess Jei, certain books and parchments have been removed from both the Library and the Archives. No logical explanation can be given for this removal. Nor can we give a current location for the missing volumes as their date of removal is also unknown. Investigations were made into the log books of previous archivists with the hope that they would provide some answers. This hope was in vain. It is the suggestion of the archivists that inquiries be made to the other Colleges and Temples. This may result in the acquisition of the information that you require. Sincerely, Masters Wajid, Cosima and Clio.*" Haileigh stared at the piece of paper in disbelief. "Removed? Why? What could they have in them that was so important or damaging that they had to be removed?"

College of Wyman, Denel, Demesa

"Really Ignatz, is this the best you can do?" Dalbert, Laven of the Order of Wyman for the kingdoms of the northern continents, swept into his counterpart's Demesan office in a flurry of robes.

"So good to see you too, Dalbert. Is Zephaniah with you?" Ignatz, Laven for the southern continent, looked up from the report he was reading.

"Yes. He will join us shortly." Dalbert sank into a chair. "I believe he was having some trouble getting his luggage properly seen too." He glanced around the room. "Can't you do something about this?" he asked, waving his hands at the walls. "There is no sense of your importance here."

"Not all of us require reminders of our status, Dalbert," commented Zephaniah as he slid in the door. He helped himself to a glass of wine before sitting in a chair across from Dalbert.

"How is Trimid?" Ignatz asked him, pointedly ignore Dalbert's disparaging remarks about his office décor.

The Trimidian Laven took a sip of his wine before answering. "Hot, sticky and wet," he replied. "It is also a touch on the unsafe side, being as we are in the middle of the typhoon season." He took another sip of his wine. "It is actually a pleasure to be here," Zephaniah remarked. "Despite the heat, it is nice to be dry at the moment."

Dalbert stood and also helped himself to some of Ignatz' wine. "I must say, I was rather surprised to get the invitation from Princess Haileigh for the Blessing," he commented as he returned to his seat. "Given her religious preferences, after all."

Ignatz sighed and gave up on the report that he was trying to read. "Are you? You obviously don't know much about Demesan law then," he observed.

"Why would I know anything about Demesan law? Astirian, yes; Pellan, certainly; Quandaran, definitely, but Demesan? Not something I really need to know," replied Dalbert.

"Under Demesan law, the royal family must not show favour to any one religion," Ignatz told his colleagues. "Therefore, under law, Princess Haileigh must invite us to the Blessing of her daughter."

Rather than joining Dalbert and Zephaniah in a glass of wine, Ignatz poured himself a shot of whisky. "She may not wish to invite us, but by law she must. And my spies in the palace tell me that her royal Highness had to be reminded by her father of this fact."

Zephaniah raised an eyebrow. "If the royal family must not show favour to any one religion, then how can the heir to the throne the head of a religious order?" he asked, mildly perplexed.

Ignatz shrugged. "It's a quirk of the law," he replied. "There is nothing to say that a member of the royal family cannot belong to a religious order, just that the family itself cannot show favour to any particular order. Theoretically, at any given time a member of the family can belong to our Order if they so wished. It's just never happened yet."

"So how does that allow Princess Haileigh to be the head of the Order of the Twins? She will be the Queen of the Demesa when her father passes on. How can the royal family remain neutral if the head of the family is also the head of a religion?" Dalbert inquired, reclining comfortably in the chair.

"That is up to her Highness to work out." Ignatz took a sip of his whisky. "If she doesn't then the council of lords will probably force her to abdicate." He contemplated the idea for a moment. "If they do, it will put the kingdom in a precarious position. Do they put Prince Edmett on the throne, or Princess Oriel, quite probably with a regent?" He took another sip, rolling it around his mouth to enjoy the flavour a moment longer. "The only thing of importance to *me*, would be how I could benefit from the situation, and at the moment, there is no point in bothering to worry about it." Ignatz met the eyes of each of his colleagues. "We have bigger concerns at the present time."

"Oh?" the other Lavens provided a reply in stereo.

"Indeed." He looked down his nose at them. "Have either of you located the four that we are needing?"

"What do you mean?" asked Dalbert. "We really only *need* one. Of course having four or all twelve would of course be advantageous."

"I'll take that as a no from Dalbert. Zephaniah?" Ignatz turned his gaze to the Trimidian.

"Ah, no." Zephaniah sighed. "If one has appeared in Trimid, they have done so away from any of my people."

Ignatz smiled smugly. "Well then, isn't it a good thing that I know where two of them are?"

"Haileigh?" Mathew stuck his head in the door.

"Hmm?" His wife glanced up. "Yes?"

"The Westecroftans are almost here," he told her. "Are you all right?"

"What? Oh, sorry." Haileigh stood up. "Yes, I'm fine, just a bit distracted, that's all." She gave him a kiss on the cheek. "How long until they get here?"

Mathew studied his wife as they left her office. "Half an hour. Your father decided that after the Astirian arrival, he would wait until the Westecroftan's had been sighted from the city walls before bothering to go outside."

"A smart man, my father." Haileigh looked down at what she was wearing. "Do you think anyone will notice that I am wearing work clothes?" she asked.

"Yes." Mathew laughed at her. "I know for a fact that your mother will most definitely notice."

"Rats." Haileigh had an unladylike scowl on her face. "Why must she be so......*girly*!" she complained as they reached their rooms.

"Girly?" Her husband raised an eyebrow as he pushed her behind her dressing screen.

"You know what I mean." She raised her arms to allow the maid to help her change. "Any other person would have no idea that what I wore as day wear was any different to what I wear for greeting guests, except my mother." She stepped out from behind the screen. "There. Better?" she asked her husband who had ensconced himself in a chair whilst she changed.

Mathew raised his arms in surrender. "I had no problem with what you were wearing before." He stood and joined her by the door. "But you look positively beautiful," he said, pulling her into a kiss, much to the embarrassment of the maid. "Let's go greet Carlyle, Demetria and company."

R

College of the Twins, Denel, Demesa

Oriana glanced up at the vaulted ceilings of the foyer in the Demesan College of the Twins. *Impressive* she thought.

"They are aren't they." Oriana turned at the comment, to find an older woman with graying, black hair standing before her, with two novices in tow. "Welcome to Demesa. Master Oriana, I am Master Aylena."

"Thank you. It is a pleasure to be here," responded Oriana.

Aylena smiled. "If you would give your bags to these novices, I will show you to your rooms." She motioned the pair forward. "I have given you the suite usually reserved for the Wuhern of Westecroft," the Master Athenan informed her guest as they walked. "Princess Haileigh has notified me of the situation and I felt that you would not mind."

"No, not at all. That is fine by me." Oriana grinned cheekily. "I should probably get used to them anyway."

Aylena smiled but refrained from commenting. They travelled for a few minutes down a long corridor. When they reached the end, Aylena opened a door. She instructed the novices where they could relinquish their loads, before turning back to Oriana. "I know that you will wish to wash the grit and grime of the road off, however the Wuherns will be dining shortly and they have invited you to join them," she informed the younger woman.

"That's fine. If there is a wash basin I can rinse enough to feel clean," Oriana replied. "Just send someone to show me where dinner is and I will be fine." She picked up one of her bags and pulled out a clean dress as she spoke, giving it a quick shake before draping it over a chair.

"Of course." The Master motioned the novices out of the room. "I'll leave you to it then." Aylena smiled. "If you need anything, the gold cord by the fireplace calls a servant." She headed to the door. "I look forward to getting to know you whilst you are here," she said before leaving and closing the door behind her.

Oriana investigated the suite, quickly finding the bathing room. Taking a few moments, she wet a cloth, stripped off and quickly washed of the dirt she had managed to acquire between the township of Behry and the capital. She had just finished changing into her clean dress when there was a knock on the door. Answering it, Oriana found a servant who showed her to the dining room down the hall.

The Demesan College of the Twins had assigned an entire floor to visiting Wuherns. Each of the eight who lead the Order were given suites. The eight suites were split in half, with the library, dining room, conference room and private temple separating them.

As Oriana slipped into the dining room, one of the women at the table rose. "Oriana, my dear! So good to see you!" she cried. "Where is that old rascal? Too busy for the likes of us?" she grinned as she said it, taking the edge of the words. "Come, sit between me and Rochelle." The woman indicated a spot next to her and a younger woman close in age to Oriana.

"Thank you Etheline." Oriana smiled and walked toward her. Etheline was not a small woman. The best description Oriana had ever heard for the Pellan Wuhern was well rounded. In her fifties, Etheline was the mother of ten, and her years of parenting showed on her face and in the now mostly grey hair. A cheeky woman, she constantly had a smile and her eyes always sparkled with life.

"Now then, let's get the introductions out of the way. That way we can spend the rest of the evening enjoying this wonderful spread" Etheline said once Oriana had sat down, waving her arms to indicate the food gracing the table. "To your left is Rochelle. She is the Wuhern of Fernistan." Rochelle dipped her head in recognition. With chocolate brown hair and startling gold eyes, Rochelle reminded Oriana of a wolf. "Then we have Belalie from Zialp." The Zialpan was a stark contrast to her neighbor white hair and pale grey eyes that showed incredible intelligence. Belalie raised her hand in acknowledgement. "Opposite me is Oren of Quandar." Etheline lean over. "He's a bit of a reprobate," she whispered in Oriana's ear.

"I heard that Etheline," commented the man in question. "And coming from you, I'll take that as a compliment." He turned his attention to the Master Athenan. "If you believe anything she says, then there is no hope for you." Now he grinned, showing glistening white teeth that would normally be hidden by his sand and white beard. "However, as you are Aneurin's chosen successor, I think you know how to handle her."

Etheline ignored his jibes and moved on. "Last but not least is Quenmir from Trimid." She pierced him with a look. "Are you actually going to speak tonight?" the Wuhern of Pella asked.

"Etheline, why would I need to speak when you do such an admirable job of it?" enquired the man. In his early forties, Quenmir was regarded as quite a catch. Fulfilling the cliché 'tall, dark and handsome' perfectly, he had found, in his youth, that he rarely needed to look for women, as they generally flocked to him. Now happily married, he was aging so well that he was generally described by his wife as 'like a fine wine'. Oren laughed out loud at Quenmir's comment. Belalie rolled her eyes and Rochelle hid a snigger. "A pleasure to meet you Oriana," said Quenmir, ignoring his colleagues. "I have heard many good things about you."

"Right! Now that that's over. Let's eat!" Etheline prevented Oriana from finding a response to the Trimidian's statement. "I'm famished!"

Chapter Fifteen

The Seventh day, Topaz Moon, year 2974
Denel, Demesa

The day dawned clear and bright. Throughout the city banners and flags fluttered in the breeze. Flowers had been shipped in from the agricultural edges of the country to help bring more colour to the city and make it look more festive. A fleet of cleaners were roaming the city, ensuring that the streets were kept clean.

The army itself, in conjunction with the city guards, had a clearly visible presence to ensure that the peace was kept and to prevent anything interrupting the ceremony. During the celebrations after, it was their job to keep the drunken brawls to a minimum.

Across the length and breadth of the city people were preparing themselves for the event of the year. In the palace the visiting royalty were being helped into their finest clothing by their own servants, and those borrowed from Chrystopher and Illissa. The King and Queen were enjoying a quiet breakfast in their rooms, glad that the focus was off of them to a degree. They were leading the Blessing, but the child involved was the grandchild, not their own. This took some of the pressure off and allowed them to enjoy the morning.

The aristocrats of the kingdom were also busy in their preparations. Some had returned to the city from their estates on outer edges of the realm only days before. In the temple district of the city, the various heads of the Order of the Twins and of the Order of Wyman were also getting ready.

The Lavens of the Order of Wyman met over a full and greasy breakfast. They all agreed there would be no opportunity to influence the royal family in any way during the next couple of days. Whilst enjoying a glass of wine at the end of their meal, they decided to enjoy the day by irritating as many of their opposition as possible.

The Wuherns of the Order of the Twins met in the College temple for a session of meditation and reflection. Afterwards they sat down to a light breakfast of fruit and yogurt, with water or juice as their beverage of choice. Quenmir, Oren, Belalie and Etheline attempted to give Oriana and Rochelle an idea of what was going to happen at the ceremony. Whilst she was aware of the theory behind the ritual, Oriana had never participated in, or witnessed the formalities during her time in the Order. Rochelle had guided several Blessings before her investiture as Wuhern, but had never witnessed a royal one.

Felasia, the Wuhern of Zialp, was too old and ill to travel to this Blessing. Added to this was the fact that her apprentice Stephas had been killed recently in a skiing accident and she was in the process of locating and training a new one. As a result, the Zialpan branch of the Order of the Twins was unrepresented at Oriel's Blessing, although Rochelle had brought greetings and a gift for the infant princess.

Back in the palace, Haileigh was a slight mess. Mathew, in order to make sure that his wife had some sleep, had drugged her wine the night before. Waking in the morning had been slightly difficult for Haileigh as a result, and Mathew had refused to let her have the antidote that would have allowed her to recover quicker and get stressed out earlier. Subsequently, at the fourth hour after dawn, with the effects of the drug finally completely worn off, Haileigh was fretting about almost every aspect of the ceremony that would take place in two hours.

On the streets of Denel people were slowly leaving their homes, campsites or inns, and drifting toward the open amphitheatre in the centre of the city, slowly filling it with an audience eager for the show to begin.

The city of Denel had been built around several oasis' that had formed around the shell of an extinct volcano. The volcano had been worn away over the millennia since it had died, and now provided the perfect site for an amphitheatre. The original kings of Demesa had realized its potential and had built seating into the inner walls. Stairs had been built up to the rim, which had been shorn off to provide a large platform for people to stand on. The floor of the volcano had been levelled resulting in a perfect stadium for concerts and other important events.

In the centre of the amphitheatre a large stage had been erected. It was a double circle, with the outer circle raised slightly. The Blessing party would stand in the centre with the witnesses on the raised section. The total diameter of the stage was thirty metres, with the outer circle five metres wide, providing enough room to stand and not fall off.

✧

As midday approached, the amphitheatre was almost full. The royal families and visitors arrived to take their places on the lowest seats in the stadium. The nine witnesses filed in and took their places on the edge of the stage. The five Wuherns and Oriana spread themselves over one half of the circle whilst the three Lavens stood on the other half. A gap formed on either side of the Lavens, separating them from the Wuherns. Next onto the stage came the representatives of the four elements. Edmett stood in the east for Air, Raina in the north for Fire, Galatea in the west for Water and Auberon in the south for Earth. Chrystopher and Illissa took their place in the centre and waited for Haileigh and Mathew to arrive with their daughter. The stadium hushed as the Crown Princess of Demesa and her husband entered and walked up onto the stage.

"Who brings this child to be blessed by the Gods?" asked Chrystopher in a voice which could be heard in the topmost parts of the amphitheatre.

"We do," replied Haileigh and Mathew, equally as loud.

"Why should the Gods grant this child their blessings?" inquired Illissa.

"Because this child is a gift from the Gods and is pure of heart," was the response from Oriel's parents. They handed their child over to her grandparents.

Oriel in his arms, Chrystopher turned to face Auberon. "What is the advice of Earth? Should the Gods grant their Blessings?"

"The child is made of Earth, and to Earth it shall return when it's time is over. Earth recommends that it be Blessed," replied Auberon.

Illissa turned to Galatea. "What is the opinion of Water? By what right does this child claim the Blessings of the Gods?"

"The body of the child consists of Water. Throughout its life it will consume Water and wash itself with Water. When overcome by emotion it will shed tears. Water advocates that this child be Blessed," was Galatea's response.

Chrystopher looked at Edmett. "What say Air? Is this child worthy of the Blessings of the Gods?"

"This child requires Air to breathe in order to remain alive. Even as we speak, it breathes. Air believes that the child should be Blessed," Edmett answered.

Illissa approached Raina. "What is the counsel of Fire? Is it fitting that the child should receive the Blessings of the Gods?"

"Fire is the creative source of all life. Through the fires of love this child was created, and through those same fires it shall continue the cycle of life. Fire endorses the Blessing of this child," said Raina in reply.

The King and Queen looked at each other. "The elements are agreed," said Chrystopher.

Illissa nodded. "There is no reason for the child not to be Blessed." She took Oriel from her husband and returned the child to her mother before returning to Chrystopher's side.

They raised their arms toward the sky. "Great Gods! We, your earthly people, call on you to Bless this child. Grant her a long and prosperous life, in which she may experience all the joys that this world has to offer. Show her the wisdom of your people. May she fulfill the potential she was granted at birth. This we ask, so mote it be."

The stadium waited in silence for some sign of the Gods Blessing. No sound came from the masses, as, from a cloudless sky, with the sun just past its zenith, a beam of pure light bathed Oriel and her parents, rising from the depths of the earth far into the sky. A gasp rose from the crowd at this obvious sign of approval. The witnesses all blinked in surprise, as none had ever seen such a sight before.

After a moment the ray of light faded before disappearing completely. Chrystopher was the first to recover. "By the will of the Gods, and by Their sign, this child, Oriel, daughter of Haileigh and Mathew, is Blessed."

As if the King's regained composure was that of his people, the crowd suddenly burst into cheers. Clapping, hollers and singing erupted, filling the amphitheatre with sound. The rest of the people on the stage were slower to regain momentum. Haileigh and Mathew looked at each other and then their child in mild disbelief. The Wuherns silently expressed their surprise, whilst the Lavens grinned openly in evil glee, as though they new what such a sign might mean. Illissa was the last to recover, shaking herself and glancing at her husband as though to say 'what just happened?'

"Our daughter has come to us from the elements. With joy and love we greeted her birth. We welcome you here and now and we ask you to come and see our Blessed child. As we will, so mote it be," said Haileigh and Mathew, closing the ceremony as they came out of their shock.

Chrystopher just took his wife's hand and lead her down the steps and onto the floor of the stadium. His movement provided the initiative for the rest of those gathered on the stage.

Varian, seated on the lower tier of the amphitheatre with his parents, glanced over at the stage as the participants left. Standing by one of the struts which supported the outer rim of the stage was a knome. Varian was just about to tug on the sleeve of his brother Binjaymen when he caught a signal from the knome. Quite clearly, although only if you had been looking at the knome, it raised a finger to its lips as though to say 'it's our little secret'. Varian grinned, and just so that the knome knew that he had received the message, Varian raised his finger and returned the signal with a grin and a wink. Just then his brother grabbed his hand and pulled him after their parents who were proceeding to return to the palace for the celebrations.

R

Ignatz turned to his colleagues, an evil grin on his face. "Our God has handed us a plate full of fun," he said happily. "Did you see their faces? They had no idea what that sign meant! It was beautiful. It was wonderful. It was so perfect an opening for us to have lots of gloriously evil fun at their expense!"

Dalbert and Zephaniah gave him identical looks of disgust. "Really Ignatz, don't you think you are going overboard a bit?" asked Zephaniah. "After all, Princess Oriel is completely out of our reach. I mean, her mother is the Wuhern here."

"Zephaniah, have you no faith?" The Laven in charge of the Order of Wyman in Demesa and Westecroft gave his Trimid counterpart a pitying look. "So we can not convert the infant princess to our cause. So what? Those hapless Wuhern's have no idea what is going on. You could see it in their faces. That means that we are at least three steps ahead of them."

Dalbert shook his head. "You are being overly enthusiastic, brother. We may know what the sign meant, but that is only one and there are twelve in all to locate. Oren is not so stupid as I would like to imagine, and will most certainly work it out quickly. Just because we are three steps ahead now does not mean that it shall always be so." He looked over at the group of Wuhern's who were presently getting to know the young princess before turning back to his comrades. "The Twins sat on the fence once. All indications are that this time they won't be so accommodating to the plans of Wyman."

In the group with Princesses Haileigh and Oriel, Oren, Wuhern of Quandar, turned his attention to the group of Lavens. He frowned as he caught the gaze of Dalbert. Something in his expression said 'I know something you don't' and it was a feeling that Oren had had since the ceremony. He turned his focus back to cluster of Wuhern's. Seeing Princess Oriel in the arms of young Oriana, he touched Haileigh's arm and gestured to a spot a few steps away.

"What can I do for you Oren?" Haileigh asked, intrigued, when they had removed themselves from the group.

"They are up to something," he said, indicating the gathering of Lavens.

Haileigh shrugged. "Aren't they always? I swear it is written in their scriptures that the Laven must at all times conspire to cause trouble for the Order of the Twins."

Oren grimaced. "Not quite," he told her. "However, Aylena mentioned to us that you had ordered the archives to research the Goddess Jei. It occurred to me that she may have come across something in her studies that could give us a hint as to what the Laven's could be trying to do," he said, avoiding the question in her eyes at his earlier statement.

"I don't see how. There was almost nothing in the information that she gave me." Haileigh was quite disgusted by the fact.

"Do you mind if I have a look? Quenmir's predecessor was investigating the same topic at the time that he was lost at sea. I am curious to see what caught his interest so much." Oren glanced back at the Trimid Wuhern. "It seems to be a bit more than coincidence that Nimitz disappeared after studying the topic of Jei." He looked at the young woman in front of him. "You aren't planning any trips in the future are you?"

Haileigh rolled her eyes at him. "Really Oren, you are making mountains out of mole hills. But no," she assured him, "I am not planning on going anywhere."

R

Merfolk kingdom of Mayarasta

Brayamine, King of Mayarasta, was nervous. He had just received word that his cousin's wife was pregnant with their first child. This in and of itself was not cause for concern. It was the fact that both his cousin and his wife were living as humans that was making him nervous. No mermaid had ever given birth as a human or, more to the point, spent her pregnancy in human form.

His cousin made a successful living as a merchant on the Trimidian island of Ascu. Being a merman was a distinct advantage to him, as he was able to sell goods that most humans had great difficulty getting their hands on. None of his clientele were aware of his merfolk status, although they probably would not have had a problem with it anyway, as the Trimidian's lived in close proximity to seventy-five percent of the merfolk population.

Brayamine sighed as he stared out at the expanse of ocean before him. There really was nothing he could do about the situation. Perhaps he would, ask Galatea to drop in on them once she returned from the Blessing of the Demesan Princess.

"Darling? What are you doing out here?" Kerelia swam up to her husband. "Tosca has been searching for you for hours."

"He had only to ask Mesran where I was," replied Brayamine, turning from his perusal of his kingdom.

"You know that Tosca doesn't like Mesran," the Queen admonished him.

The King grinned. "The thought did cross my mind." He gave his wife a hug. "Why is Tosca so frantic to find me?" Brayamine asked.

"Dessi, your ambassador to Essoter, has sent a messenger. They are quite insistent that they can not return until you have received the message," Kerelia told him.

"And of course, they have to deliver it to me in person, don't they?" Brayamine shook his head as they swam back to the palace. "I knew there was a reason I sent Dessi all the way to Essoter. He is so dramatic."

Kerelia swatted him. "Dramatic or not, that poor mermaid cannot return home until you have heard her message. Be nice to the poor girl. I swear she can't be more than a day over twenty, and it is quite obvious that she is a shy little thing too."

They entered the palace to a fanfare of trumpets and a seneschal who was looking most displeased with his king.

"Your Majesty! I - " the merman began.

"Yes, yes, Tosca, I know. I must remember to inform you of my whereabouts at all times," said the King, brushing past his seneschal and heading toward the audience chamber. "Queen Kerelia informs me that there is a messenger from Essoter waiting to see me. Do send her in." Brayamine settled himself into his throne.

"Your Majesty?" the mermaid swam in hesitantly, sliding to a halt a couple of metres from the throne. "I bear a message from Ambassador Dessi." She waited for the King to nod his consent for her to continue. "Word has come from Deyenth. The First has arrived."

Brayamine, who had been lounging in his throne, sat bolt upright. "The First?" The messenger nodded timidly. "Good grief! Kerelia!" He turned, searching for signs of his wife, whom he knew to be hiding somewhere nearby, listening.

"I'm here, Brayamine," she said, stepping out of the shadows to his left.

"You heard?" he asked. She raised a perfectly curved eyebrow. "You heard." He turned back to the messenger. "Have you spent much time in Mayarasta before, child?" he enquired. When she shook her head, he continued. "I'm going to ask you to stay for a few days, as I may have a message for you to take back to Ambassador Dessi and King Quenton." The king smiled encouragingly at the girl. "We will put you up here at the palace, and I shall ask my Prime Minister, Mesran, to show you the city." Brayamine turned to his seneschal. "Tosca, please take this young lady to Mesran and ask him to show her the city." He gave the man a hard look. "Tell him that I will catch up with him shortly. Oh, and send Xeniala to me."

"Yes your Majesty." The seneschal bowed, and took the girl in hand.

Once they had left, Brayamine slipped over to his wife. "The First! I cannot believe it!"

"What I can not believe is that you want Mesran to look after that poor girl," commented Kerelia. "We're not matchmaking are we?"

"Me? Never," replied her husband. "But he does really need to settle down."

"Brayamine! He is at least twice her age," protested the Queen.

The King shrugged. "Not quite, but it worked for your parents, didn't it?" Before Kerelia could answer, Xeniala, High Priestess of Leia, arrived. "Ah, Xeniala, prompt as always," said Brayamine, taking advantage of the interruption.

"Your Majesties." The mermaid bowed. "What can I do for you?"

"Word has just come from Essoter that the First has arrived," Kerelia informed her.

"We were wondering if the Lady had seen fit to provide you with any other information," said Brayamine when the Priestess did no more than raise her brow at the Queen's statement.

"Not on the topic of the First, your Majesties," replied Xeniala. "Although I was aware of the existence of the First." The Priestess gave her rulers an enigmatic smile. "The Lady did, however, ask me to pass on something to you, your Majesty," she said, looking directly at Brayamine. When he raised a brow, she continued. "She asked me to tell you that you need not worry about your cousins on Ascu. *The birth shall go well. A boy it will be, and a major part in our future he shall play. Although you will not meet him until the prophecy is almost complete.* With that, the High Priestess of Leia bowed to a stunned King and Queen, before sweeping regally from the room.

✿

Chapter Sixteen

The First day, Amethyst Moon, year 2974
Order of the Twins, Athos, Westecroft

"That looks positively enthralling," drawled a voice from the doorway.

Oriana looked up from her studies to find Liam leaning against the door frame. "Oh absolutely. Would you like to borrow it?" she asked sweetly in reply. In the six months since their return from Demesa Oriana and Liam had become rather close. It began innocently enough when he offered to show her more of the city after she settled in to the Temple of the Twins in Athos. Within a few short weeks what began as a friendship, with mutual attraction hiding in the shadows, became something more.

He walked over. Making sure her page was marked, he then lifted it from her hands. Turning it over, he appeared to be seriously considering it. "Hmm, thank you but no." He shook his head. "It's not quite big enough to stabilize my desk."

Oriana laughed, standing and taking the book from him, she placed it on the desk before responding. "Are you sure? I guarantee you will find it most educational."

Liam grinned. "Only if I needed a cure for insomnia which, fortunately, I don't, after all, I have you – OI!" He jumped as she thumped his arm. "That wasn't meant as an insult, but as a compliment," he told her.

She scowled at him. "How on earth do you figure that for a compliment?" Oriana inquired as she made a note on a scrap of paper on the desk.

Liam wrapped his arms around her waist and rested his chin on top of her head. "Well, you always make sure I get plenty of exercise."

Unseen by Liam, Oriana raised an eyebrow. "Well," she said turning to face him, "Are you sure you want to go out to dinner?"

"Hmmmm,....You or food? It's a tough decision," he mulled over the idea. "No, I think I have to go for the food," he decided.

"Hey! You prefer food over me?" Oriana was indignant. She pushed against him, but it was like pushing a rock wall. He was immovable.

He grabbed her hand and pulled her toward the door. "Haven't you heard the theory about fuelling up before exercising?" He grinned as he dragged her down the hall. "And besides, Tamsin and Alasdair will be most upset if we miss our weekly date with them."

✍

"So, Liam, when are you going to pop the question?" asked Alaisdair, causing the young knight to choke on his brandy. They were sitting at the table while their ladies had momentarily retired to the powder room of the restaurant. Through his association with Oriana, Liam had become close friends with both Alasdair and Tamsin. The four of them had been meeting weekly for dinner at Tamsin's favourite restaurant for months. It gave Oriana, who due to her studies was not at court much, a chance to find out what was going on in the capital. Along with considering Oriana as their daughter, Alasdair and Tamsin now thought of Liam as a son.

"Ug...um," Liam spluttered, before recovering enough to respond. "What makes you think that I am going to?"

Alasdair laughed. "Spoken like a man. Deny it 'til the last moment." He sipped his brandy. "I'd get a move on if I were you," he advised. "I know of several young upstarts who think she is single and are ready to make a move."

"What!?" Only the control he learnt as a page prevented Liam from dropping the snifter of brandy he had been in the middle of lifting to his lips.

"That got your attention." The Duke glanced toward the powder room before continuing. "I didn't think you had noticed. You've been rather circumspect about your relationship with our young Athenan."

"It's not something anyone really needs to know about," replied Liam. "You, of all people, know what the gossips are like around here." He finally managed to take a sip of the brandy without worrying that he would spit it up again.

"True, but – blast!" Alasdair was prevented from finishing his sentence by the return of Oriana and Tamsin. "All right now, love?" He asked Tamsin as she and Oriana returned to their seats.

"Of course. We were just catching up on some girl talk whilst we had the chance." Oriana blushed slightly at Tamsin's reply. "I'm sure you two were doing the same thing while we were gone," the Duchess commented to her partner, causing Liam to choke again on his brandy. He put it on the table, pushing it away from him as he came to the conclusion that it really wasn't safe for him to drink the stuff tonight.

Alasdair raised an eyebrow at the woman he loved. "Girl talk? I hope not."

"You know what I mean," Tamsin said, exasperation clearly evident in her voice. "Advice and/ or gossip that should only be heard by members of ones own sex."

"Oh that. Of course we did. We knew you would expect nothing less, and want a full report later." He grinned at her. "It is our duty as men to cater to the whims of our women."

"Riiiiggghhhttt," said Oriana in disbelief. "And we will believe that one when pigs sprout wings and learn to fly."

"Your lack of faith in me is so hurtful, Oriana." Alasdair tried to give her a wounded look, but didn't succeed very well, causing the rest of the table to burst into laughter.

Tamsin shook her head. "Leave the acting to the professionals, my dear," she advised him. "They know what they are doing. Oh, which reminds me." She turned her attention back to the young couple across from her. "The Royal Theatre Company is performing a new play called 'In the wind'. It starts next week and I was wondering if you wanted to go?" she asked them.

Oriana looked at Liam, who shrugged. "It sounds interesting. I've never seen a performance of the Royal Theatre Company," she replied.

"Well then, of course you must go," Alasdair insisted. "Everyone must see the Royal Theatre Company at least once in their life."

"I'll organize the tickets tomorrow then." Tamsin glanced at the restaurant's time candle. "Oh, my, it is getting rather late." She looked at her partner. "You have a meeting with the King in the morning, so we should be off," she told him.

Alasdair sighed by didn't argue with her. They all rose and headed to the door, paying their bill before leaving. As the couples prepared to separate, he turned to Liam. "Remember what I said," he told the younger man, before he and Tamsin headed home.

"What was that about?" asked Oriana as they walked back to the Temple.

"Nothing," denied Liam. "Just some advice about an investment I made recently."

"Uh huh." Oriana was sceptical, but with no evidence to contradict his statement, she refrained from further comment. They walked the rest of the way is comfortable silence.

"What are your plans for the weekend?" Liam enquired as they reached the gate to the private quarters of the Temple.

"Nothing much," replied Oriana, thinking. "I have service in the morning, but I am free to spend the rest of the day with you, both days. Why?" she asked as she turned to wrap her arms around his waist.

"Oh, I thought we might have a picnic, as the weather watchers are predicting fine days for the weekend," he said, returning her embrace. "There is a little place I found down the coast I think you will love."

"*Really?*"

Liam placed a kiss on her forehead. "Yes, *really.*" He gave her a thorough kiss on the mouth before releasing her. "Sleep well."

"You're not coming in?" Oriana asked, miffed. There had been very few nights in the last month or so that Liam had not spent at the Temple with her.

"Sorry, can't tonight, as much as I really want to." He grimaced. "I have a meeting with Lord Commander Willard first thing and so had best sleep in my own bed at the palace." Liam grinned slyly as a sudden thought occurred to him. "I should probably borrow that book from you after all. I am likely to need a cure for insomnia tonight." He shied away from her as she attempted to hit him. Giving her an exaggerated bow, he departed, leaving his lady love bemused and slightly depressed that she would be sleeping alone tonight.

℗

"So, what did she say?" asked Alasdair, as he settled into a chair beside the fireplace in Tamsin's room.

"And they say women are the worst gossips!" the lady complained from behind her dressing screen.

"Well?"

"Oh, all right!" Tamsin shrugged out of her dress. "She said she can't see herself marrying Liam."

"Why ever not?"

"She says it's because she doesn't know who she is."

"Huh?"

Tamsin slipped into her nightwear. "Well, she is a street brat after all."

Alasdair gave her a blank look as she stepped out from the behind the screen to join him. "She really thinks that that makes a difference?" He was flabbergasted. "She is apprentice to the Wuhern of Westecroft. In a few short years she will be the Wuhern. What happened before she entered the Order is a non-issue. She is a Priestess and as such holds as much rank as any peer of the realm. More when she becomes Wuhern, as only the King and Queen will out rank her. This is just ridiculous!"

"Calm down Alasdair."

"Calm down? Calm down! How can I calm down when I just told Liam to pull his finger out and ask her, for crying out loud, before someone else did, and the silly girl is going to turn him down because of her insecurities!" He stood up and started pacing.

"Alasdair, stop that," snapped Tamsin. "You're making me dizzy. And besides, it's not up to either of us. They'll sort it out, I'm sure." He turned to her, disbelief written on his face. "They are adults, Alasdair. If they can't sort it out then they don't belong together. It's as simple as that." She gave him a pitying look. "Besides, if Liam can't convince her then he isn't the man I thought he was." Tamsin looked down her nose at him, which was quite a feat given that he was standing and she was seated. "What did you and Liam talk about?"

Alasdair returned to his seat by the fire. "I asked him when he was going to pop the question. He denied it of course, and so I told him about the young upstarts who have an interest in Oriana. I'm sure it will have the desired effect. If he wasn't already planning on asking her, he will now."

Tamsin left her chair and sat on Alasdair's lap. "Then we leave them to it. We are not them. They are perfectly capable of working it out. As I said, they are adults. We have both been in a similar situation and it worked out just fine, didn't it?"

"I suppose so." He wrapped his arms around her waist, supporting her.

✍

The fourth day, Amethyst Moon, year 2974
Athos, Westecroft

Oriana looked up at the sky, inspecting the clear blue colour that was dotted slightly with white clouds, as she led her horse to the edge of the city. "It would appear the weather watchers were right," she commented as she halted the beast in front of the man who waited for her.

"I am constantly impressed by how often they get it right," he replied as she drew up beside him. Liam took her hand and brought it to his lips. "You are looking lovely today, Oriana." Dressed in what she considered good, but not formal clothing, Oriana looked like something from a painting. She wore a light cotton lawn gown of pale green under a darker dress made of a heavier cotton twill. The colours highlighted the colour of her eyes, and made her hair look bronze. The recent bout of sunshine had given her nose a spattering of freckles, and as she had ridden up to him, the picture she presented had taken Liam's breath away.

The seriousness of his expression prevented the apprentice Wuhern from making a joke in reply. Instead she nudged her horse closer to his and leaned over, kissing him full on the lips. "Thank you," she said when she released him. "Now then. Where are we going?"

The young knight grinned. "That is for me to know and you to find out," he stated as he quelled the passion that had filled him at Oriana's kiss. Taking her hands in one of his, he pulled a blind fold from his belt and deftly covered her eyes with it. "I will take this off when we get there," he said when she protested, trying in vain to pull her hands from his. "Promise me you won't try to take it off."

"But how will I ride if I can't see?"

"I've tied your mare's reigns to my horse. She will follow happily along, I promise you. Well? Don't make me tie your hands up too."

"Oh, all right," Oriana promised rather sulkily.

Liam leant over and kissed her. "You won't regret it."

As they rode, Oriana tried to use her other senses to work out where they were. Sharpening her hearing she made out the sounds of various birds, some of which she knew, but could not identify any that were particular to a certain area. Even the calls of the insects in the area were not helpful. The Master Athenan began to focus on her sense of smell, but it too failed her. All she could detect was the smell of the ocean, mingled with the scent of the pine trees lining the road.

Finally Oriana gathered her other sense, honed during her years at the College, and let it sink into the earth, trying to detect facets of the geology of the area that could help her to identify where she was, but to no avail. The soil below the road was the same as the soil on which half the city of Athos was built. It was a loose loam mixed with sea sand that had migrated up from the sand dunes. In some parts she detected a slab of granite, however this did not help her either, as the palace was built on a granite cliff and there was a granite quarry to the south of the city.

Just as Oriana gave up trying to work out where she was being taken, her horse halted and she found herself being lifted down from the bay mare. Liam removed the blind fold and waited for a reaction as Oriana took in the scene before her. "Oh...my...goodness...." she breathed, stunned by the vista.

She was looking at a cove, walled on each side by small granite cliffs, and a beach of pure white sand that led to a pool of crystal clear water. It was separated from the ocean by a small natural breakwater that had formed when the cliffs had broken apart a millennia or so ago. Looking back at the way they had come, the path to the main road was hidden by a forest of old pines. At the edge of the trees, leading toward the ocean, was a small field scattered with wild flowers in a variety of bright colours. Overhead eagles and other seabirds soared, and in the forest could be heard the calls of jays and other smaller birds.

"It is incredible, just incredible," Oriana murmured. Looking around, she found Liam setting up a picnic. "How did you find this?" she asked as she wandered over to join him, sinking down onto the blanket.

He passed her a glass of wine. "By sheer accident," was his sheepish reply. "I was out this way searching for some smugglers who were thought to be in operation nearby, when I stumbled across the cove." He smiled at her expression. Oriana was shocked at the thought someone would use such a beautiful place for smuggling. "Fortunately the smugglers hadn't found this cove and were using one a mile or so down the road." Liam raised an eyebrow at her and gave her a quirky grin. "You like?"

"I like. Oh yes, I definitely like." Reverting to the speech of her childhood, she added, "You done good, real good."

For the next couple of hours they enjoyed the food Liam had the kitchens at the palace pack for them. The sun continued to shine, although as the afternoon progressed more and more clouds began to fill the sky. After a short dip in the ocean they returned to the blanket to dry off and redress, before consuming the last of the wine and the fruit they had left.

"I have a question to ask you, if I may?" Liam requested as they enjoyed the wine. Oriana gave him an inquiring look but nodded her consent. She was puzzled by the way her lover had phased his request. Liam sat up slightly and slid onto one knee. Pulling something out from one of the bags he had brought the food in. "Will you, Master Athenan Oriana, do me the honour of marrying me?" He opened his hand to reveal a ring.

Oriana gaped at him in shock. "You are joking, right?" she insisted when she had recovered sufficiently to speak.

"No," he said, shaking his head. "I'm serious. I want to marry you." He held the ring out for her to take.

Oriana put her hands up as though fending off the ring. "You can't marry me," she told him in no uncertain terms.

"Why not?"

"Because I am a street kid."

Liam looked at the woman he loved in disbelief. "What has that got to do with the price of fish in Trimid? You are a Master Athenan and heir to the Wuhern of Westecroft."

"You can't marry a street kid. You are going to be a duke. Duke's don't marry street kids," Oriana insisted, her eyes wide and almost unseeing. The shock of the proposal was still with her.

"You aren't listening to me. You aren't a street kid any more. You are a priestess of the Twins and as such have as much rank as any duke in the kingdom." He took her by the shoulders and shook her slightly. "I…want…to…marry…you." Liam punctuated each word with a little shake of the woman he held.

"I'm still a street kid, Liam." She pulled herself from his grasp and stood. "Why do you think Lord Aneurin wanted me to stay here for a while? Because he wanted me to acclimatise myself to the world of the aristocracy." She gave him a sad little look as he stood to join her. "How can I marry you when I don't even know who my parents are? Your parents will never accept me." She shook her head. "I can't do that to you."

"Oriana. It doesn't matter where you came from, or if you don't know who your parents are," Liam insisted, incredulous that they were even having this conversation. "My mother passed away several years ago, and my father will love you. Yes he will," he said when she shook her head again, this time in denial. "For two reasons. The first is that you are an intelligent, interesting individual who has a fine sense of humour and a distinct dislike of most of the higher families of the kingdom, which is something you have in common with him. The second is that I love you." Oriana blinked at him in surprise. "My father is an old man. I am the youngest of his children and the only male. He has been hounding me for a few years to get married and provide him with grandchildren. He has even gone so far as to suggest an arranged marriage, which, I might add, I turned down rather vehemently." Liam took her hands in his. "I love you, and I want to marry you. Please."

"I can't. I just can't. It's not fair to you or your family." She strode away and mounted her horse, not giving him a chance to stop her. "I'm sorry. I love you, but it would be wrong for me to do so," she said, tears streaming down her face. She nudged her horse into a trot and headed for the trees.

"ORIANA!" Liam called after her to no avail. He quickly repacked the picnic, mounted his horse and took off after her. Just before he reached the trees rain began to fall. He looked up in surprise to see that as they had been discussing his proposal the clouds had completely filled the sky and turned a nasty shade of grey.

Sighing with dismay, Liam returned his attention to the fleeing figure of Oriana. He pushed his horse into a gallop, and put his head down to duck the tree branches that got in his way as he raced after her.

∽

"So much for the fine weather," Liam commented sourly, as they reached the Temple gates. He had caught up with her at the road and they had ridden home in silence, rain falling on them the whole way. Oriana had refused point blank to discuss the matter, saying there was nothing to discuss. Liam disagreed. He couldn't believe she could be so narrow-minded over the topic. He knew what his father's opinion of Oriana would be, but she refused to accept it. Given that she had never met the man, and had these opinions based on things she had been told about the nobility whilst living on the streets, frustrated him no end. Liam sighed. It was as if the weather was responding to their moods.

As the pair approached the stable, an Athenan came racing out from the school quarters. "Master Oriana," he cried, skidding to a halt in front of her as she dismounted from her horse, handing the mare over to a groom to be looked after. "A messenger arrived from the College whilst you were out," the man panted slightly as he tried to catch his breath. "Lord Aneurin has recalled you to the College," he told her when she raised an eyebrow, indicating for him to continue. "You are to leave immediately. Master Valeigh has arranged for your belongings to be packed, and has sent word to the palace asking for a contingent of guards to travel with your carriage."

"Immediately? Can't I even change into some dry clothes?" Oriana asked, somewhat surprised at the implied urgency of her return. She wondered what caused her master to change his mind and drag her back to the College. When she returned from Denel there had been word waiting for her that Lord Aneurin wanted her to remain in Athos for a while to study and become familiar with the ruling families of the Kingdom. His note had also said she was to pay particular attention to the goings on of the Order of Wyman and discreetly familiarise herself with the various members of importance in Westecroft, most of whom resided in Athos. The timeframe her boss had given her for these assignments had been a couple of years. Now, not quite six months later, he suddenly changed his mind. As soon as she returned, she was going to have a word with him about that.

Liam, still sitting in his saddle, looked disgusted. "Why am I not surprised that you managed to arrange to leave the city as soon as you turned me down," he said, anger colouring his tone.

Wet through to the skin and resembling a drowned rat, Oriana was not in the best of moods. She hadn't wanted to say no when he asked her to marry him, but felt she had no choice. Standing in the middle of the courtyard of the Temple of the Twins, dripping wet and with her life suddenly thrown upside down, her temper had already started to fray. This was the last straw. "You think I *arranged* this?" she asked in disbelief, her voice rising slightly. "When, pray tell, did I get the chance? I've been with you all afternoon."

The knight scoffed. "Like that would be a problem for you. You are the apprentice to the Wuhern of Westecroft. Everyone knows the priests of the two Orders have the ability to perform magic. It wouldn't surprise me if the shock you showed when I asked you to marry me was all an act, and you knew before we left that this was going to happen. It is not beyond you, I am sure, to prearrange all this," he said, snidely, waving an arm to indicate the weather and the Athenan standing somewhat forgotten beside Oriana.

"You...you..." Oriana was so flabbergasted at the accusation that she had difficulty responding to it.

"Cat got your tongue?" Liam asked smugly. "Surprised to be caught out?"

"How *dare* you?!" Oriana clenched her fists at her side, wishing he was standing on the ground so she could slap him. "You don't know anything about me or my Order. You are an ignorant, egotistical, stuck up brat! I want nothing more to do with you!" she cried as she started to turn red with anger. "I am so glad I turned you down now. At least now I know what you are really like. I am glad I found out before I made the mistake of actually marrying you! And to think that I actually wanted to marry you. What a mistake that would have been!" Determined to have the last word, she turned on her heel and stalked across the courtyard to the private quarters, intent on having a warm bath and finding some dry clothes before she left.

"This is not over, Oriana! I promise you!" Liam yelled across the courtyard, startling the Athenans and acolytes that were hurrying around in the rain. "You mark my words, woman! This is *NOT* over!"

Chapter Seventeen

The Twelfth day, Amethyst Moon, year 2974
College of the Twins, Westecroft

"WHY WON'T YOU TALK TO ME!!!!!" Oriana screamed in frustration. Her anger was directed at her master, the Wuhern Aneurin, who had been avoiding her since she returned to the College of the Twins, at his insistence, six days before hand. The Wuhern had been 'unavailable' when Oriana arrived.

She had attempted to see him or speak to him mentally every day since then, but he blocked her at each turn. He had not left his rooms once in the time she had been back and as he had a lazy waiter linked to his office, the only people to enter his rooms were those he summoned.

Whenever Oriana became aware of such a summons to one of her colleagues, she had asked them to take Aneurin a note from her, but still she had no reply. It had gone so far that the other Athenans in residence had taken to avoiding her for fear of her temper. Even Michaela was treading carefully around her friend.

"You call me back here with no explanation and then you ignore me. *WHY?*" She yelled the question both verbally and mentally at the Wuhern. "No 'sorry to bring you home', no debriefing, no anything. It's not *fair!*"

"'*Life isn't fair, Oriana*'" paraphrased Michaela, standing in the doorway with a wary expression on her face. She wasn't sure it was a good idea to visit the other Athenan, particularly when the apprentice Wuhern was in such a mood. However, as they were friends, Mick felt it was her duty to look after Oriana as she knew the other woman would look after her if their positions were reversed. "Isn't that what Lord Aneurin would say in reply to your comment?"

"Don't mention his name in this room," Oriana growled.

"And how would he complete the sentence?" asked Michaela, ignoring Oriana's comment. "Oh, that's right. '*You of all people should know that Oriana.*" The Master Athenan grinned at her friend. "That's what he would say, isn't it? Or words to that effect, anyway." She walked over and gave Oriana a sympathetic hug. "Think of it this way – you don't have to worry about scurrying around after useless bits of paper, or burying your head in a book that is more likely to put you to sleep than provide any useful information because the boss said to. You have your days to yourself at the moment, and the minute he decides to talk to you again, you know that that is going to end." Michaela's expression clearly said 'am I right, or am I right?' although Oriana continued to glare at her. "Think of it as a....holiday. Yes, think of it as a holiday. You should be resting, relaxing and recuperating from your time in the 'big city'." She grinned cheekily at her friend.

"Why are you here Michaela?" Oriana did not sound impressed.

"I feel so loved," Michaela said expansively, but continued at her friends deepening glare. "I thought you could do with an outing. You've been couped up inside since you got home, because you were." She stopped, looked at her friend and changed what she was about to say. "Are hunting the Wuhern, and I decided you need a break." Mick gave Oriana an artificially sad look. "We haven't caught up and gossiped since you left. We can head into the village and enjoy a few hours of good company, good food, good gossip and good beer. What do you say?"

Oriana did not look happy, but she did consider the idea, seriously even. "All right," she replied, surprising them both.

Michaela blinked. "Well, let's go then." She stepped behind her friend and pushed her toward the door. "That beer is calling to me," she said as they headed out.

Whilst the Order of the Twins did not prevent its priests and priestesses from partaking of any of the 'joys' of life, they tended to live a rather quiet life. Meals at the Colleges and Temples were a fairly plain affair. With so many to feed, the cooks usually prepared whatever was easiest and sufficient enough for the numbers that inhabited each place. If there was a major festival or celebration, then there would be fancier fare.

Most of the food eaten at any time at the College was grown on the grounds. This meant it was always fresh. Some Athenans returned to the College just for the food, as they had not found anything that tasted as good in the outside world.

Most Athenans very rarely drank anything stronger than fruit juice. No alcohol was served with meals, although it was permitted on the grounds of the Colleges and Temples. Its consumption was permitted to Athenans of any level, but not to acolytes, and the Athenans usually kept wine or spirits in their offices or personal rooms. Like the food, the grapes that produced most of the wine consumed at the College were grown on the grounds.

The grapes had been planted in the early years of the College in Westecroft and now provided income to the Order of the Twins as they sold wine, along with spare fruit and vegetables, clothing and other items created by some of their members, at the local village of Caar. The money was then used to update pieces of equipment used, or purchase any material needed which the College could not produce. Any left over was sent to other Temples to be used for charity works around the country.

Michaela and Oriana, having been raised on the streets of Jerriko, had been introduced to alcohol at an early age as it had often been safer to drink beer than water. As a result, they had no worries about consuming the various alcoholic beverages available both at the College and at the local inn.

After a short walk they arrived in Caar and made their way to the inn, taking a seat in one of the booths that could be found in the front bar.

Michaela placed her elbows on the table between them and rested her chin on her hands. "You are planning on filling me in on your time in Athos, aren't you?" she inquired after the waitress had taken their orders. "It was too far away for mental communications and your letters *apparently* failed to make it to the College." She gave Oriana a rather pointed look. "You must have been *rather* busy, because I could never raise you when I tried to get you in the mirror."

"Point taken," Oriana grumbled. She was glad when they were interrupted by the waitress returning with their drinks. "I had a lot of other things on my mind at the time," she informed her friend.

"Such as?"

"I started seeing Liam Carmichael," Oriana muttered before taking a sip of her beer.

Michaela blinked. "You what?" she sputtered, almost showering the other Athenan with a mouthful of beer.

Oriana studied the pint of beer as though it were the most fascinating object in the world. "You heard me."

"I know, but I was sure my ears were deceiving me." Mick looked at her colleague in disbelief. "We are talking about *Sir* Liam, aren't we? The knight that escorted you to Athos? The one I called dishy?"

Oriana sighed despondently. "Yep. That's the one."

"Wow. Way to go Oriana!" Michaela grinned. "Although, I must say that while I am happy for you, I am also extremely envious of you. Is he as good as he looks?"

"*MICHAELA!*" Oriana shrieked, flabbergasted, her raised voice causing the attention of the other patrons to focus on their booth.

"Well? Is he?" Michaela looked unrepentant as she took a mouthful of her drink.

"That is none of your business, Athenan," replied Oriana, haughtily. Before Michaela could push her friend any further, the waitress returned with their meals. A few minutes of silence ensued whilst they consumed the food and the rest of their drinks.

After the waitress returned to clear away the empty plates and take another order of drinks, Michaela returned to their previous conversation, albeit not exactly where they had finished. "So. You said you started seeing Sir Liam. What happened?" she asked, putting her elbows on the table and resting her chin on her hands.

"Nothing," was the reply.

A snort came from the opposite side of the table as their second round arrived. "Yeah, right."

"I mean it. Nothing happened." Oriana didn't appear very convincing in her attempts to dissuade her old friend from the topic.

"Oriana. Really. We have been friends for how long?" Michaela asked. Oriana shrugged. "Right, too long. I know you too well. Spit it out, because I am going to keep nagging you until I find out."

"Grrrrr!"

"That won't stop me."

Oriana threw up her hands in surrender. "All right, all ready!" She took a sip of the beer to help her courage levels a bit. "He asked me to marry him," she told Michaela, grateful that her friend had finished her own mouthful before hearing the news.

The Athenan gaped at her friend. She blinked a few times and then finally managed to scrape her jaw of the floor. It was a few minutes before her stunned brain could form enough words to make a sentence. "Congratulations. I will be your bridesmaid, won't I?"

Oriana shook her head. "There isn't going to be a wedding."

"But you just said…. Oh Oriana, you didn't."

Oriana nodded. "I turned him down."

"Why?" Michaela's tone was incredulous.

"He's an aristocrat, Mick. I can't marry him, no matter how much I may love him." Oriana was vehement in her belief.

Her friend gave her a look of disbelief. "You are the apprentice to the Wuhern of the Order of the Twins in Westecroft, and a Master Athenan in your own right. Whatever came before we entered the Order no longer exists." Michaela gave her a stern look. "You could marry Crown Prince Rhawn if he was old enough. It is your right as a priestess of the Twins to marry whomever you wish, should you choose to do so."

"That is just about what he said," replied Oriana.

"Let me guess, you didn't believe him." Michaela's voice was filled with scorn.

"You don't understand."

"You are right. I don't. I don't know what it is like to be in love with a gorgeous man who loves me in return. Oh, and who just so happens to be heir to a duchy too. But hopefully, one day I will." The Athenan was patently disgusted with her friend.

"Look, it doesn't matter if I love him and he loves me. If his family doesn't accept me then there is no future for us." Oriana's expression suggested she was close to tears, but holding them back with considerable effort.

"Oh, for crying out loud, Oriana." Michaela shook her head in disbelief. "How can you say that, when you don't even know what they would say if they knew you were marrying him? I mean, given you were both in Athos and they are all here, I am presuming they don't know." She looked at Oriana for conformation of the statement. At her nod, Michaela continued. "Considering you know all of his sisters and most of their families, I can't see why they would object."

"I do?" Oriana was stunned by this little piece of information.

Michaela nodded. "You witnessed the Blessings of three of his nieces and two of his nephews. You were also at the wedding of the youngest of his sisters, which Lord Aneurin presided over."

"I did? I was?"

The Athenan gave her friend an appraising look. "Two drinks? Someone is a bit stressed over there, isn't she?" Before Oriana could comment, Michaela continued with her lecture. "His father was at the elevation ceremony when you received Master status and was the first person to congratulate you." She scowled. "He even beat me to the punch." She took a mouthful of her beer before snagging a passing waitress to order more. "I can't see why you think they would not accept you," Michaela continued once the waitress was on her way back to the bar. "You could be born of two unmarried Athenans and you would be accepted, whether you were an Athenan or not, so why you're past should matter now that you are an Athenan, I don't know." The waitress returned, temporarily interrupting the monologue. "Besides, Duke Ostin is desperate for his son to marry and produce another heir to the Duchy. He'd accept a whore into the family if his son chose her. I would think he would be overjoyed Liam had chosen you."

"Are you calling me a whore?!" Despite her inebriation, Oriana was indignant at what she saw as an insult.

"Oh for crying out loud!" Michaela shook her head in disbelief. "No. I am not calling you a whore. You know me better than that." She took a sip of her drink. "What I am saying is – why on earth did you say no. There are no barriers in the way for you to marry the man you obviously love, because you have been in a bear of a mood since you got home. The only barriers that I can see are those in your mind."

Oriana shook her head drunkenly. "It wouldn't work."

"There is no point arguing with you when you are in this state," said Michaela before raising her glass again. They sat in silence for a few minutes, drinking their beers. On the other side of the room a band started up. Made up of local lads, they provided some lively entertainment.

Oriana and Michaela enjoyed the music for a while, before Michaela filled her friend in on the most recent gossip from the college and village. Various friends dropped by as the girls drank, Oriana getting drunker by the glass. Amongst the visitors were Liam's sisters and their partners, although the Athenan was unaware of who they were related to.

As a break occurred in the music, Michaela looked up from her conversation with the local blacksmith to find Sir Liam heading toward their table. Ending her conversation with the man, she raised an eyebrow in greeting as he reached the table. Liam nodded in return. He glanced at the woman he loved and blinked as he realized that she was totally drunk. "I think she has had enough, don't you?" he asked Michaela.

At his words Oriana registered his presence. "Liam!" she cried, standing up and attempting to wrap herself around him. "He asked me to marry 'im, ya know? Hic," she informed the people around them.

Michaela looked at her friend before responding to Liam's earlier comment. "I think you are right. I'd hate to be her in the morning. She isn't usually like this." She paused to reflect on their previous drinking attempts. "You know, I don't think I have ever seen her like this." Michaela sighed. "Come on Oriana." She stood up and pulled her friend off of the young knight.

"Want some help?" Liam asked her.

"Yes please."

"What are you doin' 'ere?" Oriana asked Liam as he helped Michaela guide the Athenan out of the Inn. "I left you in Athos."

"Yes you did," he replied. "But I did tell you it this wasn't over."

It took a while to get the women home as Oriana was lacking her usual coordination and even Michaela was a little unsteady on her feet. When they reached the College, Michaela lead the small group to Oriana's rooms. On the door was pinned a note. Michaela removed it as she opened the door and let Liam guide Oriana to her bed. Reading it she snorted. Liam looked up. "I'd hate to be her tomorrow," said Michaela, causing the knight to raise an eyebrow. "Lord Aneurin has finally decided to see her." She laughed quietly. "He has refused to see her since he called her back, and now that he wants to see her, she will be suffering from a hangover." The Athenan looked over at her friend, almost comatose on the bed. "Don't bother about undressing her. I doubt she will notice."

Liam glanced at the woman on the bed and nodded. "True," he said as Michaela placed the note on to Oriana's desk. "She probably won't remember me even being here." They both headed toward the door. "Let her know I was here and I will be back." He grinned slightly evilly as they reached the front door of the College. "I have no intention of leaving until I have her word she will marry me."

"Good," replied Michaela, causing the knight to blink. "You have my full support."

"I do?"

Michaela raised a brow. "You are supposed to say that to Oriana – in front of witnesses." She grinned at his expression. "But yes, you do. She does love you. I gave her a haranguing earlier this evening. I can only hope it will sink into that thick skull of hers. A word of advice?" Liam nodded. "Nag. Nag as much as you can. She will eventually give in." Michaela opened the door. "She'll complain and bitch and moan, but she will give in, in the end," she said as he stepped out and onto the steps.

"Thank you."

Michaela smiled with sympathy. "You're welcome. And I am sure I will be seeing you frequently over the next few weeks."

Liam returned the smile with a grin. "You can count on it." He turned and headed down the steps, leaving Michaela to close the door behind him.

Chapter Eighteen

The Thirteenth day, Amethyst Moon, year 2974
College of the Twins, Westecroft

"Urgh!" moaned Oriana as she woke. She felt horrible and would have sworn something had died in her mouth. Groping for the cup of water she kept at the side of her bed, she opened her eyes, winced at the light filtering in from behind the curtains, and surveyed her room. After emptying the cup Oriana sat up slowly and gingerly. "What was I thinking?" She asked as she refilled the cup from the jug that sat next to it.

It was then she noticed the letter sitting on her desk. She emptied the cup again before attempting to stand. Upon successful completion of this task with only a slight bit of dizziness and nausea, Oriana walked to her desk and tried to focus on the letter resting there. "Blast him!" she swore as she read it. "He avoids me for a week, won't even reply to written notes and *now* he decides to see me."

Putting the note down, she headed toward her bathing room, stripping off last nights clothing as she went. Pulling the red chain that hung at the foot of the bath she dumped hot water into it. When enough water to satisfy her had filled the bath, she released the red chain and pulled the blue, adding just enough cold water to make sure she did not burn herself. She grabbed a jar of salts from the collection on the window sill and dumped a handful into the bath before stepping in and stretching out in the hot water. Just as she settled herself there was a knock on the door to her suite.

"Yo! O-r-i-a-n-a? Are you awake in there?" called a familiar voice. Michaela opened the door and stepped into the main room.

Having half sat up with the intention of leaving her bath, Oriana slid back down when she realised who her visitor was. "If I wasn't before, I would be now Mick," she grumbled just loud enough for her friend to hear.

"Where are you?" asked the Athenan, resting a tray on the desk. She waited for Oriana's reply before she moved again.

"I'm in the bath."

"Ah." Michaela took a seat in one of the arm chairs to wait for her friend. "I brought you some breakfast, if you can keep it down."

Oriana's stomach rebelled slightly at the thought. "I hate you sometimes," she told Michaela. "How is it that you do not suffer from hangovers?"

In the main room, Michaela grinned. "I would say it has to do with the fact that I don't drink as much as you." Oriana snorted. "But, we both know that is not true," Michaela continued, ignoring her friend. "So there must be something in my family line which prevents me."

"So instead, you enjoy watching me suffer?"

"Oh my yes! It is the only time I ever get to really pay you out. You got the letter from Lord Aneurin, I see," she said, spying the piece of paper she had removed from Oriana's door the previous evening.

"Yes," was the grumpy reply from the other room.

Michaela let her gaze drift toward the door of the bathing room. "Do you recall Sir Liam helping us home last night?" she enquired cheekily, before sitting back to watch the explosion she was sure would occur.

"WHAT!" Oriana sat bolt upright in the bath. "Oh, bugger. Note to self – do not sit up fast when suffering from a hangover." She slid back down into the water slowly as she tried to gain control over her suddenly spinning head and stomach. "You are lying aren't you?" she asked when she had recovered enough. "Please tell me you are lying."

"Sorry," said Michaela, shaking her head. "He showed up at the inn and when we decided you had consumed enough, he helped me get you home." She stood, deciding now might be a good time to leave, and headed for the door. "He left a message for you with me."

"Oh?" was the piteous comment from the bath.

"Yes. He said to tell you he will be back to see you and that he has no intention of leaving the area again until he has your agreement to marry him." She grinned as she imagined her friend's expression. "Your breakfast is on your desk. I'll see you later." With that, Michaela dived out the door and shut it before Oriana could make a protest.

In the bath, Oriana closed her eyes as if trying to hide from the world. "What have I gotten myself into?" she asked, before sliding down the bath until she was fully submerged.

✍

Oriana stood before the door of her superior, wincing slightly at the light shining through the open windows behind her. She raised her fist and knocked lightly on the door. Despite the fact she really wanted to bash on it, the delicate feeling in her head prevented her from doing so.

"Enter!" called the Wuhern, making her wince again.

She turned the handle and pushed the door open. "You summoned me, my Lord," said Oriana, a slight inflection in her voice indicating displeasure. She closed the door behind her and waited for his acknowledgement.

Aneurin sat at his desk. Several piles of books lined its edges and a couple of stacks of paper in the centre showed the potential to hide him completely if they were to grow any taller. "Indeed," replied the Wuhern without looking up from a paper he was engrossed in. "Have a seat."

Oriana scowled but obey. She sat there in silence for several minutes as Aneurin continued to read. "Stop fidgeting Oriana! Patience is a virtue you should learn to cultivate," he snapped, finally looking up and fixing her with a glare.

"I am patient!" she retorted. "I am probably one of the most patient people in Westecroft!"

The Wuhern gave an un-gentlemanly snort of disbelief. He was echoed by an eavesdropping Michaela.

:*Bugger off Mick!*: Oriana sent her.

:*Indeed, Michaela*: added Aneurin. :*I will speak to you later*:

:*Aw but!*:

:*No buts!*: Oriana and Aneurin replied in concert.

The Wuhern and his apprentice both ignored the grumbles of Michaela and focused their attention back on each other.

"I called you back as a result of your report on the Blessing of Princess Oriel," the Wuhern explained. "However, since I sent your notice of recall I have been inundated with important information both regarding the Blessing itself, and of a matter connected to but independent of it."

Oriana blinked and looked at him with a vague expression on her face. "You've lost me."

Aneurin sighed. "If you must insist on over-indulging in alcohol, would you at least try to engage your brain and pay attention to what I am telling you?"

"Well excuse me, but you're the one who has ignored me for the last week!"

"And if you had listened to me just now you would have heard why that was."

"All I heard was a bunch of words running around in circles!"

Aneurin smacked the palm of one hand against his forehead. "Do you see the piles of paper and books in front of me?" he asked, clearly enunciating each word.

Oriana scowled at him. "I am not blind!" she responded acidly.

"This is what I have been dealing with for the last week and a half," the Wuhern told her. "Some of these result from your report. Some are courtesy of Oren, Etheline and the other Wuherns," he said, pointing to the stacks. "This pile is as a result of a visitor I had not long after your departure for Athos." Now he pointed to a stack of books and scrolls that stood beside his desk.

"Oh?" Oriana could not see the importance of one visitor.

"Nimitz of Trimid," she was informed.

Oriana blinked in surprise. She had never met the former Wuhern of Trimid, but she knew of him and was well aware of the circumstances of his death. "You were visited by a ghost?" The existence of a ghost of the man did not surprise her. She had met a couple of ghosts herself since she joined the Order. It was the fact the man had disappeared at sea which caused her some scepticism about his ghost.

Aneurin shook his head. "It appears he survived the shipwreck which caused his disappearance and presumed death," he revealed to her. "And in light of the information he provided me with, when coupled with your report and the messages I have received from my fellow Wuherns, I have been rather busy."

"Uh huh." Oriana was non-plussed. "Is Nimitz going to return to Trimid?" she enquired.

"No. The Twins have given him a new assignment, apparently."

Oriana pondered the Wuhern's words for a moment before replying. "So what has all this to do with me?" she asked.

"I am given to understand that you have received a marriage proposal," the Wuhern said, suddenly changing the tack of the conversation.

"WHAT?" Oriana yelped. "Where did you hear that?" The sharp right-hand turn in the conversation knocking her off balance. The fact her boss knew of the proposal shocking all the other news she had just received out of her mind completely.

Aneurin gave her a pitying look. "Young Liam came to see me yesterday," he informed her. "He asked for my consent."

Oriana's eyes bulged. "He *what?!*"

"I gave it, of course." Aneurin gave her a look of fatherly indulgence. "I was quite flattered to be asked, I must say. It has been years since anyone came to me for such a reason." Now he gave her a look of mild disapproval. "I am disappointed however, that you turned him down. You will reconsider, of course."

"Do I get any say in this?" Oriana was indignant at the way the two men were intent on taking things out of her hands.

Aneurin raised a brow at her. "You mean to say you don't want to marry him?"

"I didn't say that."

"Good, because Liam will be here shortly." There was a knock on the door. "In fact, that should be him now. Come!"

The door opened to reveal Liam of Carmichael.

"I do not believe this!" Oriana gave her master a look of complete disgust.

"Welcome Sir Liam. How are you today?" enquired Aneurin, ignoring Oriana.

"I am well, my Lord. And you?" Liam bowed slightly.

"Quite well, thank you." The Wuhern nodded to indicate his apprentice who had stood at the arrival of Sir Liam. "Oriana is ready for your excursion."

The woman in question spun to look angrily at the knight before turning her attention back on the Wuhern. "*WHAT*?! What are you talking about?" she demanded of her boss.

"Liam is taking you on a tour of the Carmichael lands," Aneurin told her. Oriana gaped at him in disbelief. "Now be a good girl and go and enjoy yourself." He took a moment to consider her. "And don't give young Liam any grief," he added sternly.

Oriana was so flabbergasted at the outrageous manoeuvrings of the Wuhern and the man who apparently loved her that she could only open and close her mouth as she struggled to come up with a response.

Aneurin stood and walked around his desk to stand by Oriana. He put his hands on her shoulders and gave her a slight shove in Liam's direction. "Off you go," he said as Liam caught her hand.

"I'll have her back before dark," the knight told him cheekily as he dragged a bewildered Oriana out the door.

"Don't cut short your outing on my behalf," responded the Wuhern, a large grin on his face, as he shut his door behind them.

"Right. Now I can get back to work without any interruptions," he said, returning to his desk. :*Michaela? My office, pronto*:

ʂ

"It's a conspiracy! That's what it is," Oriana insisted when she could speak again. By this time she was seated on her horse and halfway to the village of Carmichael, with Liam riding by her side. She turned to glare at the man beside her. "Can't you accept my wishes and just leave me alone? Why did you have to go to the Wuhern?" she demanded of him.

"Please Oriana. It's not your wish to be left alone," said Liam. "If it was, you wouldn't have been in tears when you turned me down." He shrugged. "We both know you want to marry me, and I definitely want to marry you or I wouldn't be willing to make a fool of myself and keep asking until you agree." He took a moment to survey the countryside, considering how to phrase his next statement. "Your previous comments about my family have absolutely no substance, as you proved beautifully last night when you were reacquainted with them at the Inn."

Oriana went white. "I didn't, did I?" Her memories of the previous evening were vague at best and the thought that she had met his family whilst obviously rather drunk terrified her.

Liam grinned mischievously. "Yep. Everyone, except Father and my nieces and nephews. My sisters were all very happy to see you again." Oriana groaned and covered her face in dismay at this news. "You seemed to have a great time catching up on the local gossip with them," Liam said, clearly enjoying Oriana's discomfort. "And I promise you they are looking forward to you becoming one of them – so to speak."

"This is not fair!" Oriana moaned. "Why is everyone ganging up on me?" she asked no one in particular.

"We only want what is best for you," replied Liam, an innocent expression on his face.

"Oh no. I don't think so. Michaela might be looking out for me, but not you and not Lord Aneurin." Oriana was adamant. "You want what is best for you, and Lord Aneurin is most definitely not looking out for my best interests."

"How can you say that, when the man is the closest thing to a father you have known?" asked Liam, stunned that she would say such a thing about a man she clearly respected.

"Don't get me wrong, I think the world of the man, but he has his own agenda and plans based on what he sees with his precognitive abilities." Oriana sighed. "I learnt very early on in my apprenticeship that Aneurin does what is best by the Order of the Twins and, to some extent, the world at large, not what is best for his students, or even himself."

"Oh?" Liam was mystified.

Oriana quirked a brow at him. "Do you know why I was selected as Lord Aneurin's apprentice? Why he hadn't selected one before I made Master Athenan?"

Liam shook his head. "No."

"It was not because I am the smartest person, or due to my skills as a diplomat." She ignored the snort of derision from her companion. "It certainly wasn't as a result of my background. Nor was I chosen because I was the best person for the job." Oriana looked at the sky as if to say 'why me?' "To be honest, I don't even understand the true reason, but when confronted by some of the other Masters over the decision, Lord Aneurin replied 'because she has a job to do that can only be done if she is the Wuhern of Westecroft.'"

Liam thought it over before responding. "It seems fairly self-explanatory to me."

Oriana scowled at him. "Yeah, but he hasn't told me what that job is," she complained.

"Maybe you are not supposed to know." He gave her a puzzled look. "How do you know that much anyway?"

She blushed. "I overheard the conversation – well, argument."

Now Liam raised an eyebrow at her. "You were eavesdropping," he accused her.

"A product of my misspent youth, you could say," she replied, shrugging.

Liam just rolled his eyes and turned his attention back to the road.

⌆

Chapter Nineteen

The Thirteenth day, Amethyst Moon, year 2974
Duchy of Carmichael, Westecroft

"Well. That is the Duchy of Carmichael," said Liam as he and Oriana headed back up the main road.

"I have seen most of it before," commented Oriana.

"Oh? When?" Liam was curious.

"When we first got here, Michaela and I did a bit of exploring," she told him. "We had never seen forests or pasture lands, and the outcome being we were rather curious about the place we were now going to call home."

Liam was rather intrigued by this information. "What were your impressions – if I may ask?"

Oriana let her mind wander back to those first few months at the College, no longer paying attention to where Liam was leading her. "Michaela was a bit bored. She missed the ocean and the bustle of the city. It was better for her when we were allowed to visit the village on market days, as it reminded her of the markets back home." She smiled, reminiscing. "I loved it. For me it was so beautiful and peaceful. All I wanted to do was climb a tree and sit there for hours. You know, I think I actually had to be fished out of a tree a time or two by one of the Masters who were in charge of the novices."

"I can just image that too," said Liam. He pulled his horse to a stop, Oriana's following suit. "This is Carmichael Hall," he told her as she regained her sense of where she was. "Home of the Carmichael family for twelve generations." Oriana blinked bewilderedly at him as he dismounted. "Come. My father is waiting to see us."

"*WHAT?!*" Oriana screeched. Liam rubbed his ear in an attempt to get some hearing back. "NO! No, I am not meeting your father! This is unfair! Underhanded! Rude, even! Let me go!" she cried as Liam ignored her ranting and lifted her easily from her saddle and placed her on the ground.

"Thank you, Ryks." Liam acknowledged the stable hand who had come to claim their horses. He turned his attention back to Oriana. "For crying out loud! You've met him before. It is not like you are meeting him for the first time. In fact, you have had several conversations with him over the last three years at various times and different occasions." Liam grabbed hold of her hand before she could escape, and dragged her toward the front doors of the Hall. "Stop being such a coward!"

"*Coward?*" Oriana stopped dead still. "Did I just hear correctly? You called me a coward?"

"Yes, I did. You are being a coward right now and you are being a coward with regards to marrying me." Liam gave her a look of disdain. "You are afraid I don't really love you and that you may not fit in – both of which are ridiculous – and as a result, you are digging you heals in and refusing to let yourself be happy. I call that being a coward."

Oriana glared at him. "I'll show you who's a coward," she exclaimed before storming off toward the Hall, leaving Liam to follow in her wake, a sly grin on his face.

Carmichael Hall had once been the winter residence for the Royal family of Westecroft. The first Duke of Carmichael had received it as reward for saving the then King from an assassination attempt. It was built of solid stone with large windows to let the weaker winter sun in. Across the top was a parapet, left over from the time the building spent as home to the king, and at each corner of the rectangular building was a small watch tower previous used by royal guards.

The ground level windows had been enlarged at some stage after the exchange of owners, and in one case were actually a set of glass doors. The first floor of the building was devoid of balconies, but the second floor had some at the rear of the building, overlooking the well manicured gardens.

In front of the building was a circular driveway which lay at the end of the entrance road. This provided the lord with a view of all those who approached the great Hall. The centre of the circle contained a lawn which bordered a small lake. Just before the entrance road met the driveway there was a bridge over what was ostensibly a small river. Originally there had been a large fortified gate after the bridge but this had been removed and the stones used to provide building material for later extensions to the Hall.

The front doors were set inside an archway, and were themselves arched. They were made of six inch thick hard wood, reinforced with a steel cover overlaid with ornately embossed copper. A counterweight required to help the average person to actually open. This was added to the doors by the first Duke of Carmichael who couldn't afford the six men required to the job.

Liam caught up with Oriana as she mounted the steps. "Does this mean you are going to marry me?" he asked cheekily.

"It means I am thinking about it. Nothing more." Before she could say anything else the doors opened to reveal a liveried servant.

"Master Liam, Lady Oriana." The man bowed. "His Grace is waiting for you in the throne room."

"Thank you, Cathal." Liam took Oriana's hand and led her forward into the house.

"Throne room?" Oriana raised a brow in inquiry.

"It's the Duke's study," Liam explained. "When the house belonged to the Kings of Westecroft it was their throne room when they were in residence." He grimaced. "When my father's great grandfather was Duke, he turned it into his study but insisted that the name remain." Now Liam sighed. "The Carmichael stubbornness is a gift from him."

"Uh huh." Just then they stopped before an ornate door. It was carved timber of the same variety as the front door, though only three inches thick, and was inlaid with embossed gold panels. "The throne room, I take it." Oriana gave Liam a slightly sarcastic look.

He flushed with mild embarrassment. "Indeed." Beside the door was a blue cord with a gold tassel at its end. Liam pulled on the cord.

"Enter!" called a voice from inside the room.

Liam pushed open the door to reveal an older version of himself behind a large desk, seated on what was clearly a throne. Oriana raised her brow again, but Liam just gave a small shake of his head as if to say 'don't ask'.

"Liam. You have finally returned," said the man, addressing his only son. "And Lady Oriana, Master Athenan and apprentice to Wuhern Lord Aneurin." Liam bowed as Oriana curtseyed. "When are you going to make an honest man of my son and marry him?" the Duke asked her.

"*FATHER!*" Liam exclaimed.

The man gave his son a baleful look. "What? You want to marry her. The whole village wants her to marry you. Quite probably the entire Order of the Twins wants her to marry you. What is the problem, young woman?" he asked a stunned, and bright pink, Oriana.

"Father! If she doesn't want to marry me, I am not going to force her to," said Liam, jumping to Oriana's defence and giving her a bit of time to formulate an answer. "She has to make the decision. None of us have to right to make it for her."

Oriana gave him a look of gratitude before turning her attention back to his father. "I am honoured that you have such a high opinion of me as to want me to marry your only son and heir, your grace," she said, a placating tone infusing her voice.

The Duke snorted. "Honoured doesn't give me grandchildren, young woman. A marriage does. As does a bit of mattress dancing." He ignored the squeak of embarrassment from Liam. "I want at least one of each sex before I hand over the reigns to this young rascal, and at the rate you're going, I'll be dead in the grave before he's even married!" The Duke pinned her with a look. "What incentive do you need in order to get the deed done?" he asked.

Oriana quirked an eyebrow at him. "Did you just offer me a bribe, your Grace? You would bribe me to marry your son?" she inquired, a deadly stillness in her tone.

"So? What of it?" The Duke shrugged, nonchalantly.

"I am not a whore to be bought, your Grace." Liam winced at her response.

Now the Duke raised a brow at her. "Did I say that you were? No."

"I don't need to be bribed in order to marry your son, or anyone else for that matter." Oriana was defiant. Standing behind her, Liam winked at his father as he realised exactly what the man was up to.

The Duke fought to prevent a grin. "Then prove it."

"Fine." Oriana squared her shoulders. "Name the time and the place, and I will marry your son. No bribes, no incentives."

"Right then." A satisfied smirk fought to be released. "A week from today. Here at the Hall. Middle of the afternoon. Your boss can preside."

Oriana nodded her agreement. "Fine." She turned on her heels and strode from the room.

Liam turned to his father. "You wily old coot!" he said with admiration.

Now the Duke allowed the grin he had been fighting to appear. "Got what you were after, didn't I? You'd better catch her before she leaves."

Liam bowed slightly and then sprinted after Oriana. He caught up with her just before she reached the front doors. "Look, you don't have to go through with this if you don't want to," he said, offering her an out if she needed it.

"No. He wants a wedding, he'll get it. No one is going to think they can bribe me and get away with it." With that, she stormed down the front steps and vaulted onto her horse, not even wondering why it was waiting for her, and dashed back to the College as though there was a fire on her tail.

♌

"Well, old friend? Are you happy now?" The Duke asked a tapestry on the wall to his left.

"Of course," replied Aneurin, stepping out from behind the tapestry. "Aren't you?"

The man grinned, a mildly evil expression on his face. "I do believe so," was his slightly pompous response.

The Wuhern returned his grin. "I must say, I am in awe of the way you manipulated her into the marriage without her suspecting a thing."

"I do believe it was one of my better pieces of work," the Duke agreed, congratulating himself on a job well done.

"Although, you do realise that when she works it out, you could very well be a dead man," said Aneurin, deflating the Duke's ego just a bit.

"I think I can handle myself against a young woman such as your apprentice, Aneurin," scoffed the Duke.

"You underestimate Oriana considerably if that is the case, Ostin," commented the Wuhern. "I have had reports from their Majesties that she has verbally taken down several high ranking and rather pompous individuals at court," he told the man next to him. "Any number of Master Athenans refuse to go near her for fear of being disassembled – literally."

"I'm sure you are exaggerating," remarked Ostin.

"If you don't believe me, ask your son. I am given to understand he was present at each and every one of her verbal disassemblies whilst she was in Athos." The Wuhern gave an envious sigh. "I do wish I could have been there to watch."

"Why weren't you?" enquired the Duke. "It's not like you to miss a party and the one missive I had from Liam told me Oriana went to the Demesan Blessing, not you."

"Other things to worry about," said Aneurin, shrugging. "You know, like saving the world and feeding the multitudes."

Duke Ostin glared at him. "If you do not want to tell me – say so – don't string me along. We have known each other too long to play games."

"It is not that I don't want to tell you, my friend. It is just that you do not need to know." Aneurin glanced at the time candle on the mantelpiece. "I really must go if I am to make it back to the College before Oriana."

"How did you get here anyway?" asked the Duke. "It is not often that I have guests appearing out of nowhere."

"I found out recently that there is an underground passage between here and the College," the Wuhern informed him. "I believe it is a leftover from the days when Carmichael Hall belonged to the King and the College was used for visiting royalty." He looked at the family portrait hanging above the mantle. "It will probably come in handy for Oriana once she and Liam are married. I will have to tell her of it as a wedding present."

"Where does it come out?" Ostin was rather curious that there was a secret passage in his home neither he nor his children had managed to locate.

"In the lower kitchens, behind one of the fireplaces," Aneurin related to the man. "I have set one of my Master Athenans in Athos to the task of finding out who was actually responsible for the tunnels."

The Duke blinked. "Tunnels? As in plural? More than one?"

"Oh, yes." The Wuhern nodded. "There are several leading out from the College. Two to different spots here at the Hall. One to the village and I have yet to discover the destinations of the others." He looked at the time candle again. "Blast! I really must dash. Oriana will have almost reached the College."

"Let me know what you find out about those tunnels," the Duke said to Aneurin's back as he flipped up the tapestry and slipped into the passage behind it.

"Will do!" the Wuhern's response echoed back out of the wall.

✍

Aneurin had just made it back to his desk when there was a knock at the door. "Enter!" he called, trying to not sound completely out of breath.

"Sir?" said the young man who popped his head inside the door. He was a few years older than Oriana, and wore the purple sash at his waist that indicated to those in the Order of the Twins that he worked in the communications section of the order.

"Yes, Master Venci?" Aneurin had lifted a piece of parchment from his desk to hide the fact that he was in the process of taking a few deep breaths.

Venci entered the room and bowed slightly. "There has been a communication from Trimid, sir," he told the Wuhern. "It came by land and sea, arriving yesterday," he said, knowing that this information alone was of importance to his leader. The Wuhern blinked and lowered his paper, a slight nod indicating that the Master could continue. "There was a large earthquake just off the coast of the island of Ascu. It hit just over two months ago, on the first day of Carnelian. Hundreds of homes were destroyed and hundreds more by the tidal wave which followed. All the islands of Trimid were affected by the upheaval. It was responsible for the destruction of all the communication mirrors of the Order, requiring the message to be sent by sea and land." The young Master laid a sealed scroll on the Wuhern's desk. "This was sent along with the general communiqué. It bears the seal of Wuhern Quenmir."

The Wuhern glanced at the scroll, then back at the young man in front of him. "Thank you, Master Venci. You have the written communiqué in the mail room, I take it?"

"Yes sir. A copy is presently being made for your perusal, as is another for the archives," replied Venci.

Aneurin picked up the scroll. "Good, good. Thank you again, Master Venci," said the Wuhern in dismissal. The Master Athenan bowed and left the room, closing the door behind him.

Aneurin broke the seal on the scroll and read

Dear Aneurin,

Sorry I haven't been in touch during the last few months, but we have had a bit of a crisis here in Trimid. There was an earthquake off of one of the lower islands which has disrupted things quite a bit.

Since the quake, I have come across an interesting piece of paper that might help you on the quest you told me about. It was discovered after the quake, when it fell from a book that was dislodge. It appears to be a prophecy of some kind.

I have made copies and sent them to the other Wuherns. I know that both Haileigh and Oren will be interested, as it seems to cover a topic we were discussing at Oriel's Blessing.

If you have any insights, I would look forward to hearing them. Oh, and by the way, since the quake, the local Randons have been going crazy. I am not sure what Zephaniah is up to, but I would keep an eye on Ignatz if I were you.

All the best,

Quenmir.

Aneurin stared hard at the letter for several minutes before looking at the piece of paper that had accompanied it. He was almost afraid of what it might contain. The last few months since he sent Oriana to Athos and Denel, had been ones of constant surprises. He was beginning to wish he had actually gone to Denel with her. Then, at least, he would not have to deal with all the dramas that had occurred since she had left.

He sighed and picked up the paper, unfolding it as he brought it within reading distance. There was no point in procrastinating, especially when he was continually remonstrating Oriana for doing just that.

The child shall come first
and he will be the first,
but the first man shall follow
and find him,
and through him shall come others
to pave the path
for the return of the Goddess.

Twelve in all there shall be
to retrieve the keys from their keepers,
and twelve with each of them shall go,
to release the Goddess from her prison.

The First Twelve will be the ones
on whom her freedom rests.
For should even one
not desire her release to be,
then her prison shall remain
until eternity.

Born apart each,
by fourteen moons,
the chosen Twelve will be.

By night, day, sun and moon,
By earth, air, fire and sea,
A sign shall be seen,
To identify them to thee

The first shall be born with a storm that ends
The second is half of a whole
The third is removed from the sun
The fourth shows her face with a column of light

Fifth shall bring the ocean to the land
Sixth shall veil the face of the moon
Seventh by blood and dark be born
Eighth is more than is seen

The ninth is born as day and night reverse
The tenth shall follow the steps of the eleventh
The eleventh is sent by the spring
And Last shall enter with a stars fire

By these signs thee
shall know the twelve
And twelve years thus
From the last sign shall be
The end of the beginning
Or the beginning of the end

When at the height of the equinox
When night and day are equal
Shall the Goddess see freedom or
eternal imprisonment face

Let the children of the Gods
Show their wisdom and might
And the Gods themselves
Will finally do what is right.

Chapter Twenty

The Fifteenth day, Amethyst Moon, year 2974
College of the Twins, Westecroft

"That conniving, manipulating, underhanded, scheming, piece of rabbit dung!" Oriana swore. She was standing on a box in the middle of the workroom of Opi, Master Athenan and seamstress of the College of the Twins, and had just realized what the Duke of Carmichael had done.

"Oriana! Stand still and don't swear," Opi reprimanded her, as she tried to pin together the pieces of material which would form Oriana's wedding dress.

"He duped me!" the apprentice Wuhern complained in her defence.

"Which he are we talking about?" asked Michaela from her seat by the door. She was there to witness the transformation of Oriana-the-street-kid to Oriana-the-Marchioness, or so she had said when she joined her old friend at the seamstress'. Little did she know Oriana had a surprise in store for her colleague.

"Take your pick, but mainly the he that is the Duke of Carmichael." Oriana stifled a shriek as the seamstress accidentally pricked her with a pin. "He tricked me into agreeing to marry his son."

Michaela shrugged and tried unsuccessfully to hide a grin. "Well, you did want to marry him didn't you?" she asked.

Oriana scowled at her. "You are not being helpful!"

"Whoever said I was supposed to be?" her friend enquired. "Last I checked it wasn't part of the job description."

"Since when did being a friend have a job description attached to it anyway?" Oriana snarled.

Michaela put her hands up in mock surrender. "You still didn't answer my question," she said, trying to change the subject.

"Stand still Oriana!" insisted Opi. "How on earth do you expect me to finish this if you keep fidgeting?"

"Sorry Opi," Oriana apologized, before focusing her attention back on Michaela. "That is beside the point Michaela, and you know it. I do not like to be forced into doing things and you know it."

"As I see it, *Oriana*, you were not forced." Michaela made a point of inspecting her fingernails before returning her gaze to the frowning face of her friend. "You were masterfully played. Duke Ostin manipulated you, yes, but he did so by using your pride against you."

"Well, excuse *me*!"

Michaela smirked at her. "Darling, I love you like a sister – I think – but you have one of the largest streaks of pride I have ever seen. It is not something to be ashamed of. It is just an integral part of what makes you, you."

Before Oriana could respond there was a knock at the door. Michaela stood and opened it to reveal a man in the livery of the Duke of Carmichael. "Lady Oriana," he said bowing, "I come bearing a gift from the Marquis of Sayzer and the Duke of Carmichael." He handed Michaela a velvet covered box and an accompanying note, before bowing again and leaving the room. The three women in the room looked at each other, before Michaela regained enough wits to close the door. She held out the note to Oriana, who shook her head. "Opi will kill me if I move. You read it."

Michaela shrugged, but after a glance at the seamstress revealed her agreement with Oriana's statement, did as she was told. *"Dear Oriana, thank you for accepting my hand in marriage. As a token of my gratitude and my love, I offer you this small gift with the hope that you like it. Inside the box you will find the rings my father gave my mother when she agreed to marry him. It is my hope you will wear them, and our marriage may last as long, if not longer than, theirs. Yours always, Liam, Marquis of Sayzer and Knight of the Realm of Westecroft."* Michaela looked at her friend. "I am not going to open that box," she insisted. "That is for you to do."

Opi looked up from her pinning. "That's fine," she said, surprising the other women. "I have finished with Oriana for the moment. It's your turn now Michaela."

The Master Athenan gaped at her colleague. "What?!" she spun her head to face her friend. "What is this all about Oriana?" she asked suspiciously.

Oriana carefully removed the pinned dress before answering. "You didn't think you could get away with being my maid of honour without getting all dressed up did you?" she said as she laid the dress on the work table and changed back into her own work clothes. "You have been my friend for as long as I can remember and there is no way known I would get married without you being at my side. Opi is going to make sure you look the part on the day, is all."

"That is not fair, Oriana," Michaela complained.

"Oh, do quit whining and get up on the box, Michaela," Opi instructed her. "Here, put this on." She shoved a dress into the woman's hands.

"'Life wasn't meant to be fair, Michaela'" said Oriana, paraphrasing the Wuhern.

"Shut up Oriana," responded Michaela as she did what the seamstress asked. "Open the box and let us see the goodies."

Oriana smirked at her friend, knowing that she had the upper hand at the moment, and did as requested. She gasped as she lifted the lid to reveal what was inside.

"Be a good girl, Oriana, and show us what you got," said Master Opi around a mouthful of pins.

Oriana turned the open box around to face the other women, causing them both to gasp as well. Inside the box were two rings. Both were made of white gold.

The first was a band of filigree, about half a centimetre wide, interlaid with emeralds and rubies. The emeralds were small marquis cut chips, designed to look like leaves, whilst the rubies were circular chips, designed to look like the buds of flowers.

The second ring was of solid yellow gold. It had a large solitaire diamond mounted on it, and more diamond chips embedded in it. Carved into the ring was a flowing line and small leaves which connected the chips in a pattern matching the filigree on the other band.

"Yikes, Oriana," Michaela exclaimed, her eyes wide. "I don't know that I would feel safe with those on my finger. Just think how much they must be worth." When Oriana failed to respond, Michaela added. "Put them on, you dunce."

Oriana took a deep breath and gingerly removed the first ring from the box. She slid it onto her left ring finger and retrieved the second ring which she also slid onto that finger. "Great Gods above," she breathed as she looked at the effect they made on her finger.

"You did good girl," said Opi, taking a moment out of her work to look at the rings. "I don't think even her Majesty has so beautiful or expensive a set of rings as that." She paused to consider the set for a moment. "And you still have the wedding band to come."

Oriana looked up at Michaela, a mildly alarmed expression in her eyes. "What have I gotten myself into?"

∂

Haileigh stared at the piece of paper in front of her. She closed her eyes, hoping that when she opened them she would read something different. "Blast it!" she cried as she opened her eyes to find the piece of paper unchanged. "Well, I did want information, but this wasn't exactly what I was thinking I would get." She sighed and rested her head in her hands.

After a few moments she lifted her head and stood. Walking over to the mirror she said the incantation that would allow her to speak to her colleague Aneurin in Westecroft. The face of the mirror cleared to show the Westecroftan Wuhern deeply involved in a pile of papers, with Athenans scurrying in and out of the room. When there was finally no one but Aneurin in the room, Haileigh spoke. "Have you received a communiqué from Quenmir, Aneurin?" she asked, causing the man to look up in surprise.

"It is most unfortunate that Ramolleana passed away so suddenly. You have yet to learn the courtesies of Wuhern's Haileigh", Aneurin told her as he shut his office door, before turning to the mirror.

"We've been through this before, Aneurin. No one is more aware of those facts than me. So answer the question". Having read said communiqué, Haileigh was *not* in the best of moods.

"Haileigh, I don't have time for this," the Westecroftan complained. "Oriana is getting married in a few days. As a result, I am swamped with details, not to mention my own studies."

"Oriana is getting married?" Haileigh was surprised. "Give her my congratulations. I'll organize a gift later." She growled slightly. "Don't try to change the subject. Have you heard from Quenmir?"

Aneurin sighed. "Yes. I received word from Quenmir. What of it?"

"Did he send you the copy of the prophecy?" Haileigh asked, insistent on an answer.

"Yes." He gave her a puzzled look. "Where are you going with this, Haileigh?"

"Oriana told you of what happened at the Blessing?"

Aneurin gave an exasperated sigh. "Yes, Haileigh. She gave me a full report, as did Oren and Etheline, though I am not sure why." He took in her agitation. "What is going on?"

"Read the prophecy, Aneurin. It will explain everything," Haileigh persisted, almost bouncing.

"Haileigh, I have." The Westecroftan was nonplussed at the behaviour of the young woman in front of him. "Quenmir wasn't even sure if it was a prophecy."

"It is a prophecy, Aneurin, trust me." Haileigh felt her frustration levels rising. "Read the fourth line of the sixth stanza."

"Fine," he said, humouring her. He fossicked on his desk for the piece of paper in question. Picking it up, he read the line in question. Suddenly the colour drained from his face as he realized what had Haileigh so antsy.

"That is right, Aneurin," she said, smugly. "That is my daughter that they are referring to."

He looked up at her. "But ... No, I understand." He gave her a sympathetic look. "I had a visit from Nimitz of Trimid not long before your daughter's Blessing," he told her.

"But he's dead!"

Aneurin shook his head. "No, he's not, but that is another story." He sat down on a chair by the mirror. "He told me about the imprisonment of the goddess Jei, and her impending release. He didn't tell me everything, however, he did mention four of the twelve had surfaced, although he didn't know how long we have until the final event." He looked at the piece of paper in his hand. "At least we now have a better idea of what is going on."

"You could have told me a bit sooner about Nimitz's visit, Aneurin," Haileigh complained. "I have been trying to unearth information about Jei since before the Blessing, and hadn't been able to find anything." She scowled at the mirror. "Anything pertaining to her has vanished from our archives here."

"Please don't whine, Haileigh. It is unladylike," Aneurin admonished her. "I didn't know you were interested in her until after Oriana returned to Westecroft, and by that time I was busy trying to follow all the leads Nimitz had given me." He glanced back down at the prophecy. "Oh, dear."

The tone of his voice caused Haileigh to look up suddenly, worried. "What?"

"The first line of the seventh stanza," he said.

Haileigh looked at the line in question. "What of it?" she asked.

"'*Fifth shall bring the ocean to the land*'" Aneurin looked at her. "There was an earthquake in Trimid. It caused a tidal wave."

Haileigh's eyes widened as the full import of his words hit her. "Five of the twelve are in the world. No wonder that Zephaniah and his Randons have been going crazy. They are trying to locate the fifth member of the prophecy."

"Why?" Haileigh asked slightly perplexed.

Aneurin lifted the prophecy, and read from it. "'*The First Twelve will be the ones on whom her freedom rests. For should even one not desire her release to be, then her prison shall remain until eternity.*' If one of the prophesied twelve does not want Jei freed, then she will remain imprisoned until the end of time. Wyman would not want his sister released. After all, He was the one who imprisoned Her in the first place," Aneurin explained. "He will have set his servants to locating the Twelve and subverting them to His cause."

"But if He only needs one, why attempt to subvert all of them?" queried Haileigh, uncertainty evident in her voice.

Aneurin thought about her question for a moment. "Just to be certain that His plans work, would be my guess." He shrugged. "Who knows how His mind works."

"So what do we do now?" Haileigh asked, thoughtfully.

"You take great care with your daughter," Aneurin advised. "And we search out the other four of the twelve who have already appeared. I shall advise Quennir to investigate the island of Ascu. In the mean time, we must all be diligent for signs announcing the rest of the twelve." He studied the prophecy for a moment. "If one was born in the last two months, then we have almost a year before the next one is due." Now Aneurin looked at Haileigh. "Will you notify the other Wuherns? With Oriana's marriage happening in three days time, I am bound to forget."

Haileigh nodded. "Of course I will." A smile finally appeared on her face. "Give Oriana my best." She paused as a thought occurred to her. "You will tell Oriana about the situation, won't you?"

Aneurin shook his head. "Not yet. She has enough on her plate at the moment." He smiled. "I'll let her know when she has settled into life as a married woman."

Haileigh snickered. "Be well, Aneurin."

"And you, Haileigh," he replied as she began to fade from the mirror. "Great. This is just what I needed now, ...not."

ℒ

The Eighteenth day, Amethyst Moon, year 2974

Aneurin looked up as someone knocked on his office door. "Yes?" He had been in the process of looking over the details of the latest group of students.

A young novice opened the Wuhern's door. "My Lord? There is a gentleman here to see you," he informed Aneurin. "He says that he is your brother, my Lord."

Aneurin's eyebrows shot up. "My brother?"

The novice nodded. "Yes, my Lord."

The Wuhern returned the paper to his desk. "Send him in, Davo."

The novice bowed. "Yes, my Lord." He stepped out into the hallway.

A few minutes later, a man of the same age as Aneurin appeared in the doorway. "Thank you, lad," he told the novice. "You can shut the door now. Make sure no one disturbs us." The novice looked at the Wuhern for confirmation of the order. When Aneurin nodded, the boy left, closing the door behind him. "Hello Aneurin. How have you been?" asked the man as he seated himself on one of Aneurin's arm chairs.

"Andrion," the Wuhern acknowledged him. "Well, as you should know considering that we are twins. What brings you here?"

"The wedding of my grand daughter. Great-grand daughter, really," Andrion told him.

Aneurin sat down in the other armchair. "Oh? I wasn't aware that you had any children."

"Oh yes. Several." He shrugged. "Most of them have passed on, but they have all been fruitful over the years."

"So where is this wedding that you are attending?" Aneurin was curious. He had not seen his twin since before he had entered the Order of the Twins. Andrion had always been the black sheep of the family, and had been thrown out of home when he was twelve. Had it not been for their bond as twins, Aneurin would have presumed his brother was dead.

Andrion grinned. "Why here, brother dear. Are you not presiding over the wedding of your apprentice in two days time?" he enquired, cheekily. He sat back and watched with glee as Aneurin realized what he meant.

"*ORIANA?!*" the Wuhern gasped in disbelief. "Oriana is your great granddaughter?" Aneurin fell back into his chair, one hand clasping his chest. "How?"

"I am not going to answer such a silly question, when I know you understand the process of having children," remarked his brother, archly.

"But….. She was a street kid in Jerriko." Aneurin was flabbergasted by the news.

"I know. He father was a sailor from Trimid who knocked up one of my granddaughters," Andrion said, matter-of-factly. "Not many of my children or grandchildren actually married." A proud smile creased his sun browned face. "Took after me, they did."

"Does she know?" Aneurin asked as his faculties returned.

Andrion shook his head. "No, and I would rather you didn't tell her either."

"Why on earth not? It would mean she had a family." The Wuhern was stunned at what he saw as his brother's callousness.

"She doesn't need to know just yet," Andrion was adamant.

Something in the other man's tone alerted Aneurin to the fact that something interesting was going on. "What are you up to, Andrion?" he asked. "What is going on? First Nimitz turns up alive, and now you pay me a visit." He glared at his twin. "Nimitz said you have a book I need. It is supposed to tell me what some signs are, but I now have my hands on the prophecy they refer to. Why would I need that book?"

"Smooth change of topic there, my brother," said Andrion, impressed. "I'll pass on the book shortly, but now is not the time. You may have the prophecy, but the signs it mentions are rather obscured. The book I have will clarify things for you."

"Who are you working for, Andrion?" Aneurin asked, suddenly suspicious. His brother was being extremely frustrating. This was not an unusual thing, as he had always been like that. However, he was being rather cagey about the information he was giving over.

"The world, my brother, the world." The man stood. "It has been so nice seeing you again, Aneurin, but I must go." He gave his brother a sardonic bow. "I must book into my accommodation, but I will see you at the wedding." Before Aneurin could respond, Andrion had opened the door and left, leaving his twin in a state of mild shock.

The Wuhern of Westecroft looked at the ceiling of his office. "Why me?" he asked. "Why me?"

Chapter Twenty One

Twentieth day, Amethyst Moon, year 2974
College of the Twins, Westecroft

Oriana stood at her window, staring out over the vineyards of the College. Usually the sight would bring her peace and tranquillity. Today, however, even the beauty of the vines in full leaf could not ease her tension. "What have I gotten myself into?" she asked the air, not expecting a reply.

Today was her wedding day. It was a day she had never actually considered would happen. Having been brought up on the streets of Jerriko, with no idea who her father was, and only vague recollections of her mother, the idea of getting married had been a foreign one. In little over an hour she would admit to the world she loved a man and she was committed to spending the rest of her natural life with him. Not only that, but she would become Marchioness of Sayzer and, one day, Duchess of Carmichael. It was not exactly something she was looking forward to.

There was no doubt that she loved Liam, but she wished, not for the first time, that he was just a commoner. It would have been so much easier. She grimaced. Complaining would do her no good. Lord Aneurin would just tell her it was good training for her, for when she took over as Wuhern. It would give her experience dealing with the aristocracy, something which she lacked.

A knock on the door interrupt her thoughts. Michaela, her best friend from before they entered the Order of the Twins, stuck her head around the door. "Are you ready?" she asked.

"You can't be serious?" Oriana scoffed. "How can anyone be ready for something like this?" Michaela stepped inside the room. "Wow," said Oriana as her friend's gown was revealed. "You look fantastic."

Michaela rolled her eyes. "It's all your fault." She was wearing a dress made from a rich bronze silk. A fitted bodice with a heart-shaped neckline was edged with a fine green silk ribbon which had gold vines embroidered on it. The skirt of the dress was full and fell away from the waist in a pool of material, its hem edged with the same ribbon as the neck. The hems of the sleeves were also edged with the ribbon and widened from the elbow to hang almost to the ground. The chemise she wore under the dress was made of gold chiffon and its sleeves were visible from the elbow to the wrist. Around her waist she wore a belt of plaited gold thread which rested on her hips, and when she walked, rust coloured leather half boots could be seen peaking from beneath her skirt. "You don't look too bad yourself," she commented, giving her friend the once over.

"Thank you." Oriana's dress was identical in design to Michaela's. The material was white silk, over a shimmering white chiffon chemise. Where Michaela's dress had green ribbon, Oriana's had gold, embroidered with silver, and instead of vines, it had roses with diamond chips sewn on where the flowers were. Her belt was plaited gold, silver and copper threads and on her feet she wore white leather half boots.

"There is just one thing missing from the beautiful picture you make, and Lord Aneurin has sent me to give it to you." From behind her back Michaela removed a white and yellow gold coronet and a square of the same shimmering white chiffon as Oriana's chemise. The coronet looked like a circlet of roses. Each leaf and petal was intricately carved. Only a centimetre and a half in height, it came to a point at the middle of the forehead where a teardrop shaped diamond hung to rest over the third eye. The veil was embroidered at the edge with silver thread and diamond chips, in the same rose pattern as the ribbon of the dress. "Opi made the veil. The coronet comes from Antica and Sofru," Michaela informed her friend. "Sit down and let me put it on you."

Oriana did as she was told, stunned at the beauty and intricacy of the gifts. "I can't wait until you get married," she told Michaela as the veil was secured under the coronet.

"What makes you think I am ever going to get married?" the other Master Athenan asked.

"Look at me. I never thought I would ever get married, but here I am on my wedding day." Oriana smirked at her friend. "It will happen to you too."

"We'll see," replied Michaela, unconvinced. "All done. Now, let's get you to that hunk of a husband-to-be of yours." She stepped away from Oriana and opened the door wider so her friend could leave the safe confines of her rooms. The women stepped out into the hallway and made their way down to the front door of the College. "Where are you going to live once you and Liam are married?" Michaela asked as they walked.

"At Carmichael Hall," Oriana told her. "I will be keeping my rooms here, but living at the hall. Lord Aneurin told me there is a secret passage leading from the hall to the College. Apparently it is a lot quicker to travel by the passage than by horse along the roads."

"Cool." Michaela was impressed. "Are you going to show me where it is?" she enquired.

"I don't think so," said Oriana, a smile on her face. "I would hate to have you interrupt anything."

"Oriana!" Before Michaela could say anything more they reached the front door. Two novices bowed to them and opened the doors to reveal an ornate carriage, bedecked with flowers, which neither woman had ever seen waiting for them. Another novice was holding the door to the carriage open, whilst two Athenans were positioned at each end of the vehicle.

The women looked at each other and took a deep, fortifying breath, before heading down the steps to the waiting carriage. The novice helped first Oriana, and then Michaela into the cushioned interior before shutting the door. Within minutes they were away and heading toward Carmichael Hall and Oriana's date with destiny.

The drive took about ten minutes, and when they arrived an army of servants were waiting for them at the front of the hall. Michaela looked over at her long time friend. "This is it. In a few more minutes you will no longer be a footloose, fancy free, single woman, but a married lady with responsibilities."

"Gee thanks, Mick." Oriana shook her head in disbelief at her friend's lack of tact. "Such a wonderful and inspiring speech, that."

One of the footmen stepped down and opened the door to the carriage. He set some stairs into place and held a hand out to assist the two women down to the ground.

"It's true," Michaela said defensively as she accepted the hand of the footman and descended to the driveway.

"I'm not denying that," Oriana responded as she followed her friend. "But you *really* didn't have to verbalize it." She rearranged her skirt as she settled herself on the driveway. "I'm nervous enough as it is."

"And so you should be," said a voice from behind the lines of servants who had bowed or curtseyed when the bride had stepped out of the carriage. Oriana and Michaela spun in that direction as the lines of servants parted to reveal an older couple who were very familiar to Oriana.

"Alasdair! Tamsin!" the bride cried, picking up her skirts and running toward them in a very unladylike way. "What are you doing here?" she asked as she skidded to a halt in front of them.

"Liam invited us," Tamsin managed to tell her as Oriana wrapped her in a hug. "He thought that as you didn't have any parents to represent you on the day, Alasdair and I could fill in for them," she continued as Oriana released her to hug Alasdair. Tamsin turned her attention to Michaela. "I'm Tamsin, Duchess of Aran," she introduced herself. "And this is my partner, Alasdair, Duke of Kearney. You must be Michaela." Tamsin smiled. "We have heard so much about you."

Michaela winced as she curtseyed. "Some of it good, I hope." She looked at her friend as the Duke and Duchess laughed. "Oriana get you head up from his Grace's shoulder, wipe your tears and let's get this show on the road," she ordered her friend.

"Must we?" Oriana raised her tearstained face. "Are we sure that this is a good idea?"

"It's too late to back out now," Alasdair said to her as he disentangled himself. "There are six hundred people waiting in the courtyard including Liam, who is looking rather anxious at this point."

Oriana blanched. "*Six hundred?!* Who are they? I don't know that many people!"

Michaela snickered. "Sure you do," she told her. "Over half of them are from the Order, and the rest are from the village."

"Indeed," agreed Tamsin. "Alasdair and I are the only people Liam invited from Court." She paused to think before she continued. "I don't believe he even notified their Majesties of his impending nuptials."

Alasdair took Oriana's arm. "We had best get you to Liam before he has a nervous breakdown," he said as he led her toward the stairs. "Tamsin, Athenan Michaela, if you would be so good as to lead the way?"

Michaela grinned mischievously at him, before curtseying. Tamsin smiled and took the lead, taking them up the stairs and into the main hall before turning down the passage that would lead to the back of the house.

When they arrived at the door to the inner courtyard they were met by one of Liam's sisters who was holding a bunch of flowers. "Oh Oriana! We are so thrilled to have you join the family!" she gushed as they drew to a halt in front of her.

"Ah... thank you Caileigh," replied Oriana, somewhat nonplussed. Michaela hid a grin behind her hand as she watched her friend's discomfort. It was almost too good an opportunity to say 'I told you so'. She held her tongue, it would have been just too easy.

"Here." Caileigh handed her the bunch of flowers. "These are from my sisters and I. Mother gave us a bunch each on our wedding day, so we thought you should have one too," she explained. "Duchess Tamsin, if you would like to come with me, I shall see that you are seated in the spot reserved for the mother of the bride." She curtseyed as she said this. "Athenan Michaela, please wait for the music to start before stepping into the outer courtyard," she instructed the other woman as she lead them to the edge of the inner courtyard. "Duke Alasdair, please wait ten seconds before following the Athenan." With that she led the Duchess into the outer courtyard, disappearing as they stepped through the archway.

Michaela and Alasdair waited patiently for the music to start. Oriana was not so patient, almost bouncing with nervous energy. After what seemed to her like hours, but were only a few minutes, the music started. Michaela stepped through the arch, and walked slowly down the aisle which appeared before her.

Alasdair silently counted to ten. Smiling benevolently, he turned and gave Oriana a light kiss on the brow. "Time to go," he said before guiding her toward the arch and following in Michaela's wake.

Oriana almost baulked as they stepped through the arch and she saw all the people waiting to witness her marriage to Liam. The courtyard was octagonal in shape and had been divided in quarters by the chairs on which the guests sat. At the top of the courtyard was a half circle with a dais where Liam and Aneurin waited for her.

As they walked down the aisle Oriana glanced at the faces of those who occupied the chairs. Blinking, she paled as she noticed the old man seated beside her bodyguard. If it had not been for the man waiting for her at the top of the courtyard she would probably have stopped to query why 'The Dog' was there.

Within moments she was at the side of the man she loved. Alasdair calmly handed her over to Liam and stepped back to join Tamsin in the front row of seats. Michaela waited to the left of Oriana. When Oriana placed her hand in Liam's she handed Michaela the bunch of flowers.

"Greetings friends," said Aneurin formally. "I welcome you all to witness the dedication of these two people to each other. Before us stand Oriana, Master Athenan of the Order of the Twins and Liam, Marquis of Sayzer and knight of the kingdom of Westecroft." The Wuhern indicated to each as he introduced them to those assembled.

"They stand here today to formally acknowledge their love for each other and their desire to spend the rest of their natural lives together."

Aneurin turned and picked up a piece of rope from the table which was behind him. He lifted their joined hands to a horizontal position and wrapped the rope around their wrists. "This rope symbolizes the joining of this couple, that their lives are about to become one," he said as he tied a knot in the rope. Now the Wuhern took a cup from the table. "This cup symbolizes the sharing that will now be part of the lives of these two people." He offered the cup to first Liam and then to Oriana, holding it as they sipped the wine. When they were done he returned the cup to the table.

Aneurin picked up two rings from the table. He returned to the couple and lifted them above his head for the gathering of people to see. "These rings symbolize the circle of life. Unbroken they represent the continuation of life from infant to child, child to adult, and then the cycle begins again. These rings also represent the combination of these two people into one." The Wuhern flashed the rings showing the design which, like all Westecroftan rings was made of two different rings of gold entwined so they made one. "With these rings this man and woman become husband and wife in the eyes of the law." He turned to Liam, handing him one of the rings. "Do you agree to make this woman you wife?" he asked. "Will you love and cherish her until the end of your life?"

Liam looked over at Oriana, before returning his attention to the Wuhern. "I do so agree."

"Place the ring on her finger," instructed Aneurin. He then handed the other ring to Oriana. "Do you agree to make this man you husband?" he asked. "Will you love and cherish him until the end of your life?"

"I do so agree," replied Oriana without pause. She didn't even wait for the Wuhern to tell her to put the ring on Liam's finger.

Aneurin looked at the sea of people. "Will the witnesses step forward?" A distant cousin of Liam's and a Master Athenan stepped forward. The cousin was carrying an ornate box. Aneurin removed the rope from the hands of the couple and placed it into the box. Once this was done, the Wuhern invited the witnesses to sign the official document. When this had been completed, Aneurin raised the document for all to see, before placing this in the box also. He closed the box and locked it with a spell. He bowed to the witnesses before turning back to the wedding guests. "Friends, may I now present to you Liam and Oriana Carmichael, the Marquis and Marchioness of

Sayzer," Aneurin said, turning the couple to face their family and friends. A large cheer rose from the gathering. Oriana and Liam stepped down from the dais and into the welcoming arms of their friend who had stood up when the Wuhern had announced them man and wife.

Several hours and a few glasses of wine later most of the guest were looking a little worse for wear. Oriana was doing her best to not get too drunk. She spotted Michaela hiding in a corner. Several steps away from her friend, was Isorren. Oriana searched frantically for 'The Dog'. Seeing Isorren had reminded Oriana that 'The Dog' had been at the wedding. She headed directly for Michaela. "Did you see him?" she asked her friend as she halted in front of the other Master Athenan.

"See who?" Michaela was confused. Oriana's attention should have been on her husband and her future life but it was clearly on something else.

"'The Dog'" Oriana hissed, her eyes flitting frantically about to make sure that Isorren wasn't in listening range.

Michaela shook her head in disbelief. "Oriana, what are you talking about? 'The Dog'? He never leaves Jerriko."

"Michaela…He was here. I swear it." Oriana was adamant. "He was sitting next to Isorren at the wedding."

"Why would he be here? Really Oriana." Michaela rolled here eyes. "Give me one good reason why 'The Dog' would be at your wedding?"

"I don't know." Oriana had no answer to her friend's question. "I told you what Isorren said when we first left here for Athos. Isorren still works for 'The Dog', even if he is my bodyguard."

Michaela shook her head. "Even if he was here, my recommendation to you is to forget about it." She turned to look over at Isorren, before looking back at her friend. "You just married a gorgeous man, who is rich and well placed at court. You have a whole new chapter of your life to read. I suggest that you concentrate on that and not wonder about what 'The Dog' is or isn't doing." She looked up to find Liam making his way toward them. "Look, here comes your husband now." Michaela grinned. "I think it must be time for you to leave the party."

"*Michaela!*" Oriana turned bright red at the hidden meaning in her friend's words.

"I don't know, Oriana. I think Michaela has the right idea," said Liam, grinning suggestively. "Let us take her idea and run with it." He took his wife's hand and pulled her toward the bushes she had been standing in front of. Liam grinned at Michaela. "Give everyone our apologies," he said as he stepped into the bushes and pulled her into a secret passage hidden there.

Chapter Twenty Two

Twenty-eighth day, Carnelian moon, Year 2975.
Royal Palace, Isrkin, Astiria

"Your Majesty?"

Jaymes looked up to find his assistant in the doorway. "Yes, Mostyn?" He had been in the middle of going over reports on the recent harvests.

"Commander Penwick requests an audience, your Majesty," the assistant told him. Mostyn had been working for the royal family of Astiria since he was a teenage. Now in his fifties, he had watched the current king grow up and fully intended to be there when the current heir took the throne.

The King sighed. "Send him in, Mostyn," he said in resignation. Jaymes laid the pages he had been reading back onto the pile. He had his suspicions as to why the Commander of the Palace guards had to see him. It would mean some fast talking and aversions if he was right.

Penwick, Commander of the Palace Guard, bowed to the King when Mostyn had closed the door behind him. "Your Majesty." The Commander was a tall man with a solid build that was due to of muscles rather than fat. Despite the fact his position was predominantly an administrative one. Penwick insisted on staying fighting fit.

"Commander Penwick." The King acknowledged him with a nod of his head, and then waited for the commander to outline his reasons for the appointment.

"Your Majesty, I would like permission to double the size of the palace guard," the Commander asked almost apologetically. Penwick had grown up with Jaymes. They had studied together and, they had run amok together in their spare time. Penwick was well aware that Jaymes did not want guards in the palace at all, but for security reasons accepted a small contingent.

Jaymes winced inwardly. "For what reason do you wish to do this, Commander?" It appeared his suspicions were to be proven correct.

"With all due respect, your Majesty, we have a situation in the palace I really feel supports the need for extra guards," said the Commander, in explanation.

Jaymes gave Penwick a pointed look. "And what would this situation be?" he asked, knowing full well what it was before the Commander answered.

"Someone is damaging the Palace locks, your Majesty," Penwick informed his King. "We have yet to determine whether or not they are trying to break in or break out, but the culprit has been increasingly more frequent in his or her work, to the point that we are now having to replace some locks two or three times a week." Penwick looked rather uncomfortable as he continued. "The Chancellor of the Treasure is getting rather upset with the amount of money that is being spent on this, and I feel he would be happier if we used the money to increase the guard temporarily in order to catch the perpetrator."

Jaymes had to bite back a grin before he could respond. "You don't know whether this person trying to get in or out? Why would anyone try to get out of the palace?"

The Commander shifted from foot to foot. "I can't say, your Majesty."

"I must say I am uncomfortable with the idea of increasing the guard when you are unable to identify the person responsible for this baffling ….. well, crime really isn't the right word, but it will have to do," commented the King, hoping he could dissuade the man in front of him from the course he wanted to take. "Perhaps if you try to identify the culprit, then come back to me in two weeks time. If there has been no change in the situation, I will authorise the increasing of the guard," Jaymes allowed, a plan already forming in his mind to prevent the need for such action.

Penwick sighed. He had known that the King would respond like this. "I really feel leaving it another two weeks is not in your best interests, your Majesty. We have no idea what this person's agenda is."

Jaymes mentally frowned. He did not want to make his old friend feel stupid, but he was left with no choice. "You don't know the agenda of this person, nor do you know their identity, and yet you want me to increase the guard?"

"Uh… Yes, your Majesty. Although only temporarily, you understand." Penwick's tone was apologetic and placating.

"I will reconsider the situation in a fortnight's time, if you have either been able to discover the agenda or identity of this person," Jaymes informed the Commander, his tone indicated no arguments would be accepted.

Penwick bowed in acknowledgement of this decree. "Yes, your Majesty. Thank you for your time, your Majesty." He bowed again and left the room.

When Jaymes was sure the Commander was well out of earshot he called for his assistant. "Mostyn!"

The elder gentleman entered the room. "You called, sire?"

"Yes. Send for Prince Binjaymen," the King instructed. "I don't care where he is or what he is doing, but I want him here inside of half an hour."

"Yes, your Majesty." Without another word, Jaymes's assistant left the room and set about locating the second in line to the throne.

Jaymes picked up the report he had been reading before Penwick's arrival and tried to concentrate on it whilst he waited for his second son to arrive. He had just managed to complete the first page when Mostyn opened the door.

"Prince Binjaymen, your Majesty," the assistant announced. He closed the door behind him once the Prince was in the room.

"You sent for me, Father," Prince Binjaymen asked, settling himself into a chair. At the age of 16 Binjaymen had joined his brother Josep in height, now beating his father. His brown hair was the same shade as his younger brother Varian, but where Varian had their mother's blue eyes, Jay had their father's brown ones. As he had grown he had become rather gangly, all skin and bones. His father was hoping that the next year or two would put some muscle on him.

Jaymes looked up from his report. "Yes, I did. I want you to give Varian a proper set of lock picks before you return to the Laranson farm," he told him, as he placed the paperwork back onto his desk. "And make sure that he knows how to use them properly," the King added as his son gaped at him in surprise.

"But…but…You didn't teach Jo or me until we were ten!" Jay protested. He was home after having spent two months at a farm in the north of the kingdom where his brother Josep had been four years previous. He was due to go back at the end of the week, and was only visiting home because the owner of the farm had come to town with the harvest and was purchasing supplies and visiting relatives whilst he was in the capital.

"I am aware of this," conceded the King. "However, Varian has been destroying the palace locks, to the point where Commander Penwick has just asked me to increase the palace guard. Double it, in fact."

Jay winced. "He's doing that again?"

Jaymes shook his head. "He never stopped, Binjaymen," he informed the young man. "He has just become more determined. Since you have been gone, the guards are replacing up to ten locks a week, some of them two or three times." He rested his chin on his hands. "I am well aware of the fact that he learnt to pick locks from you in the first place, but as you would not give him any picks, he has made his own from scrape metal he managed to scavenge."

Binjaymen blushed slightly. "Um… well…" He tried to think of some form of defence.

"Don't bother to deny it." Jaymes found his son's embarrassment rather amusing. "I caught him at it once, and received a rather interesting dissertation as to why he was doing it." He looked down his formidable nose. "Therefore, you are going to do as instructed and give your younger brother a proper set of lock picks and educate him in the finer points of picking locks before you return to the farm."

"Yes, Father," Jay replied apologetically.

"Dismissed." With that, the King picked up his report and appeared to ignore his son.

Binjaymen stood up and left the room, his destination the slightly shadier sides of Irskin.

♦

Charlie, owner and Innkeeper of the Red Dragon was rather surprised to find himself enjoying the day. Despite owning an Inn in one of the poorer areas of Irskin, he was doing extremely good business today. The harvest had brought many folk to the capital and plenty of the wagoners had found their way to his little establishment. Most were enjoying an ale or two or four, but some were also actually eating. It was one of those times when he was grateful he had married a woman who knew how to cook for a crowd. He moved down to the other end of the bar to see if any of his patrons needed a refill and noticed a new one had turned up. "Can I get you anything, sir?" he asked, taking in the man's long black cloak which hid anything that could identify what the man did.

"Just a tankard of ale," replied the man. "But do you have a private room I could rent for an hour or so?" He slid two gold coins onto the bar as Charlie poured his beer.

Charlie blinked. "Yes sir!" he said in surprise. "Henri!" he called out over the din of noise the drinkers made.

"Yes, boss?" responded a busty, blonde woman from the other side of the room.

"Would you please show this gentleman to a room at the top of the stairs." Not waiting for a reply from her, Charlie returned his attention to his customer. "You can have it for as long as you like, sir." He handed the man his tankard of ale.

"Wonderful." The man smiled. "I am expecting three men to join me."

Charlie nodded. "I'll send them up to you as soon as they arrive. Will they ask for you?" Something about the man was giving him the creeps, and this was not something that often happened to a man who had lived in the underbelly of Irskin for all his life.

"Yes. They will ask to see the black merchant," the man informed him. "Can you send up some bread and cheese, now that I think about it?" he asked as Henri finally made it to the bar, having juggled several amorous drunks along the way.

"Of course, sir. No extra charge." Charlie headed to the kitchen as Henri showed the man to his room, leaving his son in charge of the bar. He had just collected the plate of bread and cheese when the other men arrived. Charlie showed them up to the room. He knocked on the door. "Sir? I have your bread and cheese, and your guests are with me."

The man opened the door. "Thank you, innkeeper. That will be all." He closed the door behind the innkeeper. "Welcome gentlemen, my name is Maklin, and I am a Randon of the Order of Wyman."

The biggest of the three stepped forward. "I'm Unwin, this 'ere is Parnell." He pointed to the man on his right. "An' this is Carr." He looked the Randon over. "We was told you 'ad a job for us that might pay well."

"Indeed. My master wants a certain boy taken from the palace," Maklin told the men. "You will each be paid three gold coins now, three when the child has been delivered to the building I have selected as a halfway house, and a final three when he has been safely delivered to my master."

"Wot's the kid, that he's so important?" asked Unwin.

"It is safer you don't know," said the Randon. "You will find his room on the second floor, eastern side of the first wing. His window is the third from the end of the wing."

"Where's this buildin' we're supposed to take 'im to, then?" demanded Parnell, hands on hips, feet spread and looking extremely menacing.

Maklin smiled, pleased with his selection of thugs. "It is a building on Seagull Street, at the docks. A red brick building, two doors down from the Golden Gull."

"Right then. When's you want this done?" It was Carr who asked the important question.

"Tonight," was Maklin's response.

"Tonight? Wot's if we 'as somethin' planned already?" argued Unwin.

The Randon gave them all a look which said 'I doubt it'. "If you had something on tonight, you would not be getting this offer," he told them.

"Oh."

Maklin pulled out three small bags from inside his cloak and placed them on the table. "Here is your first payment. I will meet you tonight at the designated location. I will wait until midnight. If you haven't arrived with the child before then, I will leave and take my gold with me." With that, the Randon stood and left the room.

♦

"Master Jay! Long time, no see!" exclaimed the merchant as Binjaymen entered his shop.

"Alas, yes, Master Featheringull. My father has seen fit to send me into the country for an apprenticeship," Jay told him, a smile on his face. "I managed to escape for a while when my master brought the harvest to town."

"Dear me, you poor thing." Featheringull took the prince by the arm. "Why don't you come back here with me? We can have a drink and catch up like old times," he suggested as he steered the young man into his back room. "Coen can look after things for me for a while." He sat Jay down at a table and poured him a glass of wine. "So what brings Prince Binjaymen to my door?" he asked as he sat down.

Jay grinned sheepishly. "I am kind of in trouble," he told the merchant.

"Oh? What have you been up to?" Featheringull was curious. He hadn't seen the boy for several months.

"It's not what I've been up to this time," Jay replied. "It's what Varian's been up to that has caused the problem."

"Prince Varian? How can your little brother get you in trouble?" The merchant sipped his wine as he waited for Binjaymen's explanation.

"He has been destroying the palace locks." Jay picked up a cake that Mistress Featheringull had placed on the table before continuing. "He is trying to pick them, but I haven't let him have a proper set of picks, so he went and tried to make his own. It is not funny," he complained as Featheringull burst into laughter.

"Oh, my dear boy, but it is," said the merchant when he had regained most of his control. "It is the funniest thing I have heard in ages." He took another sip of his wine. "What does this have to do with your visit? Wait... let me guess. You need a set of picks to give to him?"

Jay swallowed the mouthful of cake he had been nibbling on. "Yes. Father has instructed me to give him a set and educate him on the proper usage before I return to the farm." He took a mouthful of his wine to wash it down.

Featheringull smiled. "I'll have Coen bring a set over to you tomorrow."

"How much is this going to set me back?" Jay inquired. Not that he needed to watch his money, but he had been taught to be careful where money was concerned.

The merchant thought it over. "For you - one gold and two silver coins," he told the boy.

Binjaymen tried not to wince as he pulled his purse out from around his neck. He didn't bother to haggle down the price as he was well aware of the going rate for a decent set of picks, and Featheringull's picks were the best you could get. He knew he was getting a bargain, compared to what the merchant would normally charge.

"It is always a pleasure to do business with you Prince Binjaymen," said Featheringull as he pocketed the coins. "Can I interest you in a nice bolt of silk? I hear your sister is getting married shortly. You could have a lovely dress made up as a gift for her."

Jay smiled. "Thank you for the suggestion, but I think I will leave it for today."

"Be sure to pop in next time you make it back to town!" instructed the merchant as he showed Jay back into the warehouse.

"I'll do my best." With that Jay left, meandering back toward the palace.

♦

Chapter Twenty Three

Twenty-eighth day, Carnelian moon, Year 2975
College of the Twins, Westecroft

"Lord Aneurin?"

"Lord Aneurin?"

The Wuhern of Westecroft looked up to find two Athenans in his doorway. "Yes, Venci, Berringar? What can I do for you both?" He held up a hand as they both tried to speak. "One at a time please. Venci, you first."

Venci gave his comrade an apologetic smile. "Word has come from Carmichael Hall, my Lord. Lady Oriana is in childbirth," he told the Wuhern.

"Wonderful news, Venci. Thank you. I shall have to go over there shortly to see how she is doing." He turned to the other Athenan as Venci left. "Yes, Berringar?"

"My Lord, you may wish to delay your trip to Carmichael Hall for a while," the Athenan informed him. "There is a lunar eclipse occurring at the moment."

The Wuhern was puzzled. "This is a problem? I don't understand what has you so upset."

Berringar grimaced. "Well, my Lord... The next scheduled lunar eclipse, as far as the astrologers have been able to work out, is not due until the middle of next year."

Aneurin blinked as he tried to get his head around what the other man was saying. "This eclipse is not scheduled?" he asked.

"That is correct, my Lord. All the astrological records the Order has have allowed us to work out that the next eclipse is not due until next year." The Athenan was pleased the Wuhern seemed to understand what was being said.

"You are sure that this is an eclipse? There isn't a cloud or something going in front of the moon?" enquired Aneurin in order to make sure he was understanding things correctly.

"We are sure," said the astrologer, adamantly.

The Wuhern turned and stared out of his window. "I see. Thank you Berringar," he said, dismissing the Athenan as his mind began to sift through information. Something was niggling at the back of his mind.

"You're welcome, my Lord." The Athenan left, closing the door behind him.

Aneurin walked over to his desk and began to fossick among the papers there. In a matter of minutes he had the one he wanted in his hand. It was the prophecy Quenmir had sent him. He quickly scanned through the manuscript. "There!" he exclaimed in delight as he located the passage he was looking for. "*Sixth shall veil the face of the moon. Could it be?*" He hurried over to the mirror and said the spell that would call up the corresponding mirror in the office of Haileigh, Wuhern of Demesa. Unfortunately it was not Haileigh but one of her sub assistants who was waiting when the picture cleared.

"My Lord Aneurin," greeted the woman. "We were not expecting your call. Can I take a message?" she asked.

"No," replied the Westecroftan Wuhern. "I really must speak with Princess Haileigh. Could you please get her for me?" he insisted.

The woman curtseyed. "At once, my Lord." She knew better than to argue with a Wuhern, even if she was going to get her head chewed off when she woke the princess. She quickly left, heading toward the Princess' rooms.

Aneurin paced as he waited. Within a few moments a very dishevelled Haileigh appeared in the mirror.

"What is so important you had to wake me up in the middle of the night Aneurin?" she asked waspishly. She was not impressed that she had been woken from a sound sleep.

"How much of the prophecy do you remember, Haileigh?" the Westecroftan asked, not the least bit apologetic at having woken her.

The princess scowled at him. "All of it," she told him. "I memorized it."

Aneurin rolled his eyes. The news shouldn't have surprised him. "What is the second line after the one which identifies your daughter as one of the twelve?"

"The second line? *Sixth shall veil the face of the moon.* Why?" Haileigh enquired, perplexed at the line of questioning.

"I have just been informed that there is an unscheduled lunar eclipse in process at the moment.... And Oriana is in labour."

"Congratulations to her," said Haileigh, before the rest of what Aneurin had told her sunk in. "*WHAT?!*"

Aneurin winced, and rubbed his ear. "You heard me."

Haileigh blinked. "Oriana's child? Are you certain?"

"No, I am not certain, but it is a distinct possibility," replied the other Wuhern. "I am going to investigate whether any other children are born today or tomorrow in Westecroft, just to make sure."

Haileigh nodded. "I'll look into Demesa. I'll get back to you on that one." She paused to think for a moment. "You should probably get in touch with the others. We want to be certain of this before you tell Oriana," she suggested.

Aneurin shrugged. "I'm not sure that I am going to tell Oriana at all," he told his counterpart.

"Why ever not?" Haileigh was surprised.

"I keep getting these little pieces of information from different sources that suggest the less she knows the better, at least at this point," he informed her.

"I don't really understand that, but that is okay." Haileigh covered her mouth as she yawned. "Aneurin, I'm going back to bed. I am sure I will be able to think better in the morning."

Aneurin smiled. "Very well, your Highness. Sleep well." Once the mirror had returned to it's normal state, he rugged up and headed over to Carmichael Hall. There was a birth he wished to witness.

Irskin, Astiria

"Wot was it that Randon bloke said? Where was that window?" asked Carr in a whisper, staring up at the building in front of him.

"Second floor, third window from the end," replied Unwin, equally as quiet.

"Right then, that's the one," said Parnell, pointing up to the window in question. "An' ain't that good – someone planted a tree right next to it."

"Right. Carr, you go up first. Parnell, you follow, in case 'e needs 'elp, and I'll stay down 'ere an' keep watch," instructed Unwin.

"Oy! Why's you get to stay down 'ere?" asked Parnell. "Why don'ts one of us?"

Unwin looked uncomfortable. He was glad the dark sky kept the blush on his face from showing. "'Cos I don't like heights," he explained sheepishly.

"Oh. That's alright then," said Carr, satisfied with the explanation. He shimmied up the tree. "Cor! The gods is shining on us tonight!" he exclaimed once he had investigated the strength of the window.

"What's up?" asked Parnell as he joined him in the tree.

"The window ain't secured," Carr told him, as he removed the structure in question.

"Oy! Enough chit chat. Get on with the job!" Unwin called up the tree.

"Alright. Don't get your knickers in a knot." Carr climbed in the window. Spotting the child asleep in the bed, he quietly made his way over to him. Careful not to wake him, Carr lifted him over his shoulders and made his way back to the window. He handed the boy to Parnell, who then began to make his way back down the tree as Carr climbed back out the window, replacing it before following his colleague. When they had both reached the ground Carr helped Unwin put a sack over the child and they quickly and quietly made their way off the palace grounds, managing to avoid the roving guard patrols.

Thirty minutes later they arrived at the designated building on the docks. The Randon Maklin was waiting for them. "You got the boy. Good!" Maklin had to stop himself from rubbing his hands together with glee. Everything was going exactly to plan. He opened the door and ushered the men inside. Directing them where to place the boy, he motion to two other Randons to grab some rope. Once the men had removed the boy from the sack, the other Randons made quick work of tying his hands and feet. The gag would have to wait until the child was awake.

Maklin motioned for the three men to join him outside. He closed the door behind them, leaving the child in the care of the other two Randons. "Well done," Maklin said as he reached inside his cloak for three small purses. "Here is your second payment." He handed them their purses. "Meet me here in three days time to collect your final payment. By then the child should have been safely moved elsewhere." He gave them a stern look. "Be warned. If for any reason the child does not make it to his next destination, you will all be held personally responsible, and no further payment will be forthcoming. Therefore you are advised to keep your mouths shut and be discrete in your spending of your spoils. Do you understand me?"

All three men nodded. "Yes, sir." Something in the Randon's eye recommended against crossing him.

"Good. Off with you then." As the men left, Maklin returned to the warehouse. "Deena?"

One of the Randons looked up. "Yes, Maklin?"

"I'm leaving you in charge whilst I go notify Ludwig of the success of our endeavour," he told his colleague.

"Yes, Maklin."

◆

Carmichael Hall, Westecroft

"Where is he? Where is that bastard?!" Oriana screamed between puffs and pants. "Let me at him. I am going to kill him!"

"Now, now dear, that isn't the way to speak about your husband," admonished the midwife, trying to keep her patient calm.

"Who said I was talking about Liam," the Marchioness snarled at the woman. "It's his father I want to kill!" She went back to puffing and panting to try to relieve some of the pain she was experiencing.

"Oriana, she is only trying to help," said Michaela from the other side of the room. She had decided it was the safest place to be after she had walked into the room and had to duck to get out of the way of a flying mug.

"There is nothing – not a bloody thing – she can do to help me now," Oriana puffed. "Only the Gods and this child can help." The midwife wiped the perspiration off of Oriana's forehead. "Is anyone going to tell me where the manipulative, arrogant, son of a bitch is?" The Athenan demanded as the other woman checked her progress.

Michaela shrugged. "I believe that Duke Ostin, and Lord Aneurin are in the study plying Liam with alcohol to stop him from worrying too much about you," she informed her friend.

Before Oriana could make a snide comment the door to her chambers open to reveal Tamsin, Dowager Duchess of Aran. "Hello everyone," she said as she entered the room. She walked over to the head of Oriana's bed and kissed her on the brow. "Sorry I am late, my dear, but Alasdair had a bit of trouble coming up with a legitimate reason for us to leave Athos." The Duchess looked over at the midwife. "How is she going?" she asked.

The woman curtseyed. "Well my Lady, she is in the last stages. The baby should be here any time now."

"Good, good." Tamsin turned to Oriana. "Now just do your best to relax. When the baby is ready to come into the word you will know when to give it a helping hand."

"I wouldn't stand too close to her if I was you, your Grace," suggested Michaela.

"Oh? Why is that?" asked Tamsin, curious.

Michaela grinned. "Oriana has been contemplating high treason," she told the Duchess, ignoring Oriana's threats and curses.

Tamsin shook her head in amusement. "Who have you been considering killing, young lady? Liam? The father is usually the one."

It was Michaela who replied. "No. This time she wants to kill the grandfather."

"Ostin? Why ever for?" the older woman posed the question in shock.

"This is all *his* fault," Oriana managed to get in before Michaela could open her mouth. "If I get my hands on him – he is a dead man!"

Deciding that she wasn't likely to get the full details out of Oriana, Tamsin turned to Michaela for an explanation. "He tricked her into marrying Liam," said Michaela, an evil smirk on her face. "He used her pride against her and she didn't realise it until it was too late to back out."

Tamsin sighed. "I see."

On the other side of the Hall, unaware of his possible demise, Duke Ostin was busy welcoming Alasdair into the fold. "So glad you could make it," he told his peer as he handed him a snifter of whisky.

"Wouldn't have missed it for the world," replied the Duke of Kearney. "Tamsin was most insistent that we get here before the baby was born," he said as he took a seat. "As it was, it was a near thing. We would have been here two days ago, but I had problems getting the King to let us go."

Aneurin, who was seated opposite him, raised a brow. "Oh? Any particular reason?"

Alasdair shook his head. "Not that I could work out and not that he would articulate. In the end, here we are." He looked over at Liam. "You look a little peaked, boy," he commented.

Liam looked over at him, eyes wide, and his hands shaking slightly as they held his glass. "My wife is upstairs going through outrageous pain, and you lot expect me to sit here calmly?"

"Son, women are built for this," his father tried to explain to him. "She will be swearing and cursing at you, but in a few hours she will be so proud of herself that she will have forgotten all about it." Liam gave him a look of sheer disbelief.

"It's true," agreed Alasdair. "Each time my wife went through this she swore she would never have another child. She promptly forgot about it within minutes of holding our child in her arms. In the end we had three girls and four boys."

"I am not putting her through that!" exclaimed Liam, real fear covering his face.

Aneurin looked over at the time candle that resided on the mantelpiece. "My Lords, welcome to the month of the Garnet Moon," he told the other men. "It is now a quarter past midnight."

Liam went white. "She has been up there for twelve hours!"

"Relax boy," Ostin instructed his son. "Twelve hours is a rather short amount of time for a first child," he told him as he refilled his glass. "Your mother was in labour for thirty hours before your sister Radelia decided to grace us with her presence." The Duke of Carmichael couldn't help but enjoy his son's discomfort. "You took twenty hours before you put your mother out of her misery."

"Ostin!" admonished Aneurin. "I think the boy has heard enough. If you are not careful, he is likely to faint on you."

Ostin was saved from answering by a knock on the door. Alasdair stood up and opened it. In the doorway stood Michaela, a huge grin on her face. "Liam, congratulations, you are the proud father of a healthy baby girl. She was born five minutes ago and weighed in at a very nice 3 and a half kilograms and 48 centimetres in length."

"A girl?" Liam asked, stunned. Michaela nodded. "I have a daughter," he said to no one in particular. "I have a daughter!"

Ostin wrapped his arm around his son's shoulder. "You had better go and have a look at her, my boy."

They all trooped up to Oriana's chambers. As the others went in, Michaela pulled the Duke to one side. "I'm not sure that you should go in there, your Grace," she advised.

"And why might that be, Athenan?" he asked.

"It was not your son Oriana was considering killing during her worst moments," she told him. "She wanted to kill you."

The Duke chuckled. "I'm sure it was just the pain talking," he said, unfazed.

Michaela shook her head. "I'm not so sure about that, but at least you can't say I didn't warn you." She followed him in to find Liam sitting on the side of the bed watching as Oriana held their daughter. Tamsin, Alasdair and Aneurin were crowded around the bed. The midwife had left to go home.

Oriana looked up and spotted Ostin. "The only thing saving you from instant death is this little girl," she informed him in no uncertain terms.

"Then I shall be eternally grateful to her," he responded, unapologetic. "Have you decided on a name?"

Liam looked at Oriana, waiting for her to nod in agreement, before responding. "Yes. We thought we would name her after Lord Aneurin's mother, because he has been like a father to Oriana since she joined the Order of the Twins, and also after my grandmother." He looked down at his daughter, before looking back up at the people gathered around the bed. "Ladies and gentlemen, may I introduce you to our daughter – Althea Phoebe Carmichael."

Chapter Twenty Four

First day of Garnet Moon, Year 2975.
Royal Palace, Irskin, Astiria

"Rise and shine, sleepy head," called Uriahl, knocking on the door of her young charge. When there was no response she opened the door. "I don't believe this," she said as she spotted the empty bed. "Varian, king of the late sleepers is awake before I come to get him up? I do not believe it." The nurse looked around the room. "Varian? Where are you?" There was no response. "Hmm? I wonder where he could have gone?" She headed out of the room to search for the missing prince.

A couple of doors down, Uriahl came across one of the cleaning crew. "Ann? Have you seen Prince Varian?" she asked the woman, knowing that she had been at work since before dawn.

Ann shook her head. "No, Ria, I haven't. Isn't he still in bed?" Prince Varian's love of sleeping in was a well known palace fact.

The cleaner's response had Uriahl worried. "No," she told her.

"Maybe Gefram will know?" Ann suggested. "You know how much his Highness loves his horse."

Uriahl brightened at the idea. "Of course! Shadow-Walker is Prince Varian's pride and joy. He probably snuck out to go ride him." The nurse gave the other woman a grateful smile. "Thanks Ann. I'll go and check with Gefram now." She waved at the cleaner as she headed back toward the stairs that would lead her down to the ground floor.

A short walk took her through the gardens and up to the stables. Blinking, she stepped inside, her eyes trying to adjust to the gloom. "Gefram?"

"Mornin' Ria," said the stable master in reply as he stepped out from one of the stalls and causing the nursemaid to yelp. "Wot can I do for ye?" he asked.

"Gefram, good morning." Uriahl managed to regain her composure. "Have you seen Prince Varian this morning?" she enquired hopefully. Uriahl had the funny feeling that something wasn't right. Years of looking after the royal children had given her a sixth sense when it came to any one of them.

Gefram scratched his head as he thought about her question. "Nup," he replied. "I canna say that I 'ave." He glanced over at Shadow-Walker's stall. "Nup," he reinforced his previous statement. "Shadow-Walker is still in 'is stall, so Master Varian ain't been 'ere."

Uriahl went white at the news. "Th – thank you, Gefram," she managed to stutter. "I must go." She fairly flew back across the grounds to the palace, racing inside and up the stairs to the Queen's chambers. In a situation such as appeared to be occurring, the Queen had to be informed.

Skidding to a halt, Uriahl knocked on the door to the outer chamber. The Queen's maid opened it, and before she could say a word, was interrupted by the nurse. "I must see the Queen!" she insisted. "It is a matter of extreme urgency!" Not bothering to wait for a response, Uriahl pushed past the other woman and strode into the Queen's dressing room. She fell to her knees, hands on the floor, head almost touching the ground. "Your Majesty, Prince Varian is missing."

Claire looked at her son's nursemaid in surprise. Uriahl had never been one for dramatics was her first thought, before the nurse's words sunk in. "What?!" She half rose from her chair.

Uriahl looked up, expressions of fear and apology fighting for position on her face. "I went to wake him up as usual this morning and he wasn't in his bed," she explained, her words almost tripping over themselves. "I asked the cleaning crew if they had seen him, but they had not. I then went and asked Gefram – you know how much he loves that horse – but Gefram hadn't seen him either."

The Queen took a deep breath. "Calm down, Uriahl," she instructed, trying to follow her own advice as she slowly sat back down. "I'm sure he is somewhere here in the palace. Have you checked the kitchens or Binjaymen's room?"

The nurse shook her head. "No, your Majesty. I passed Prince Binjaymen on my way to Prince Varian. He was heading down to practice his archery and try to beat Prince Josep." She paused to try and calm herself. "I didn't think to check the kitchens as Prince Varian doesn't really eat breakfast at the moment. I often find myself having to force him to eat it."

Claire mulled over the other woman's words. "Before we panic too much, let's check every possibility," she suggested. "Pat?"

"Yes, your Majesty?" Claire's maid had been hovering just outside the room. When summoned, she quickly appeared at her mistress' side.

"I want you to organize a search party," the Queen told her. "I want every room and every square centimetre of the grounds covered. Prince Varian has done a vanishing act and I want him located. However, this is to be done discreetly. The King is not to find out, nor is Commander Penwick. Your people can ask questions but they must not be overt about what they are doing in any way."

Pat curtseyed. "Yes, your Majesty. I shall see to it at once." She left the room as swiftly and as silently as she had entered it.

Claire looked at Uriahl. "Now we sit back and wait." She smiled what she hoped was reassuringly. "I'm sure he will turn up. We both know what a scamp he is."

♦

Varian yawned. His sleep drenched mind barely registering that he was waking of his own accord. He wriggled his shoulders, wondering sleepily why his bed felt so hard, and slowly opened his eyes. The first properly formed thought that entered his mind was that this was not his room. He went to rub his hands across his face, in order to wipe the muck out of his eyes, but found they were tied behind his back. This brought him wide awake in an instant. Further investigation showed his feet were also tied up. "What on earth?" he asked, not expecting a reply.

"So, our little fish is awake," said a male voice from somewhere behind him.

Varian managed to push himself around so he faced the direction from which the voice had come. "Who is there?" He directed the question to the shadows.

One of the shadows detached itself from the walls. "No one you would know, your Highness." The shadow became a figure, covered from head to foot in a black woollen cape.

"Why am I being held prisoner?" Varian was never a happy person when he was first awake and finding himself in a strange place, tied up, was not helping to improve his mood. "You obviously know who I am, therefore I demand to know why I am here."

"Patience, little prince. You are not going to come to any harm," he was told. "In fact, we have very important plans for you." A smile appeared beneath the hood of the figure. "You are a very special person and we are going to make sure you live up to your full potential." Somewhere behind the figure a door opened. Another robed figure entered the room, bearing a tray. "You must be hungry. Here is your breakfast," said the first individual. "My colleague here will feed you. I advise against spitting it at her or refusing to eat it. You are going to need all your strength."

Varian scowled at them. He did not like it that they had figured out what his plans were. He was not happy he was being fed as though he was a baby. It was demeaning, even if he didn't have much choice because his hands were tied – literally.

♦

Pat re-entered her mistress' room to find the Queen and Uriahl sitting, staring out of the window in silence. "Your Majesty?" Claire looked up, expectantly. "I am afraid we found no sign of Prince Varian," she informed the older woman. "And one of the footmen discovered adult sized footprints leading away from the tree outside of his Highness' bedroom window."

The Queen went white. "What direction did they go?" she asked in a quiet voice.

The maid bit her lip before replying. "Toward the palace fence."

Claire turned to Uriahl, "Come with me," she told her. "You too," she instructed Pat as she stormed past her and out of the room, heading down the hall. The two women followed orders and trailed along behind her at breakneck speed.

They had traversed two staircases and three passageways when Josep and Binjaymen came into view. The boys raised their hands in greeting but were forced to jump apart and take refuge on either side of the wall as their mother ignored their presence and kept going as though a dragon was on her tail. Josep looked at his brother. Binjaymen returned his look. "Varian," they said in stereo. Neither one had to comment further, they just peeled themselves from the wall and hurried after their mother and her entourage.

Another three staircases and a dozen hallways later they caught up with her just as the door to their father's office slammed shut in their faces. Josep bent over, gasping for breath. "We are a good two decades younger than her," he managed. "How is it that she looked like she had just been on a stroll in the gardens and we look like we ran a four league race?"

Binjaymen slumped against the wall, puffing and panting as he tried to regain his equilibrium. "This is Mother," he responded. "And this is Varian, too. After six kids and his antics, she is a pro." He slid up to the door and pressed his ear against it. "Besides, she has the advantage of the adrenalin caused by the knowledge of whatever he is up too this time."

"True," agreed Josep, as he joined his brother at the door, both of them hoping they might hear enough to discover what scrape their kid brother had gotten himself into this time.

Jaymes looked up, startled as the door slammed behind his wife's maid. He took one look at Claire's face. "Varian?"

Claire nodded. "Not his fault this time." She caught her husband's questioning glance at the maid and nurse. "Presumably kidnapped."

Outside the door, Binjaymen yelped, only to be shushed by his brother. Unfortunately his reaction caused them both to miss Uriahl and Pat's explanations to the King. They jumped away from the door as their father hollered for his assistant, who responded immediately. Statue-like, the boys remained on either side of the door as Mostyn left, returning shortly with Commander Penwick. When the door shut behind them, the boys looked at each other, nodded and fell back against the door to eavesdrop on the conversation. This time they caught the explanation.

As the King began giving instructions for the search, Binjaymen peeled himself away from the door and began sliding out of the room. Josep caught him just as he headed down the hall in the direction of his rooms. "What are you planning, Jay?" he asked, suspicious. He was well aware his brothers had a special bond between them and he didn't want to see anything happen to either of them.

"Nothing," replied Jay, desperately hoping he could lose his brother before they reached his rooms.

"Right," scoffed Josep. "And a herd of pigs just flew past. Jay, you can't go after him. You don't even know who has him or why."

"What makes you think I will go after him?"

Josep rolled his eyes at the question. "You always go after him. It is always Jay to the rescue." He gave his little brother an assessing look. "if you try to go after him, you are just as likely to get yourself into trouble – and I don't mean with Mother and Father, either."

"You are going to make a wonderful king someday, Josep," said Binjaymen, trying to distract him. "I am quite sure you passed the worrying exam with flying colours." When Josep went to respond, Jay cut him off. "I am not stupid. I know my limitations. Go worry about something else like… oh I don't know… your impending betrothal to Caraleine of Quandar?" Before Josep could make a reply, Jay ducked into his rooms and shut the door with a resounding thud.

♦

Binjaymen stepped into the dim that was the warehouse. He had been forced to wait a bit longer than he had intended before leaving the palace. Josep had been skulking around outside Jay's rooms for an hour or more in order to make sure Jay didn't go after Varian. As he thought back on it, Jay snorted in disgust. Josep should have known better than to think anything would deter Jay.

"Master Jay!" The merchant Featheringull looked up in surprise. "I was just about to send your purchases to you." He took in the young man's expression. "Is there a problem?"

"May we talk in private?" inquired Jay, a slightly authorative tone to his voice. He rarely used his position as a means of getting something, but the situation warranted it.

Featheringull blinked. He had never personally heard that tone in the Prince's voice, although he was aware the young man had it in him. "Of course. Come with me. Coen! Look after the shop," he instructed when his son looked up. The man lead Jay into the familiar back room and through to another, smaller room which served as the merchant's office, closing the door behind them and making sure that it was locked. "Don't worry about what you say in this room. I have made sure that it is sound proof," Featheringull told the Prince. "Now what can I do for you?"

Jay glanced at the walls of the room. "I'm not going to ask how, but be sure that I may need the secret to it in the future," he said as he sat down. He caught the merchant's eye. "My brother Varian has been kidnapped."

The other man paled. "Who would do such a thing?" he asked. "The Royal family is dearly loved." He glanced at a picture on the wall of his children. It had been painted by one of the struggling artists in the area and given to him as a birthday gift, by his daughter. Seeing it made him think of what his King and Queen must be going through. "How are your parents taking it?"

"Mother is taking it remarkably well, and Father has already organised a search of the city." Jay sighed. "All caravans and carriages leaving the city are also being searched. However, the problem is that there has been no official notice from the kidnappers. No ransom demand or anything like that."

This shocked the merchant. "How can I help? I presume you are here because you want my help in some way."

Binjaymen nodded. "Yes. You have access to the city grapevine like no one else I know. If there is anything, any speck of information floating along it, I am positive that you can get your hands on it," he explained, leaning forward across the desk. "I'm after who has him, why and where. If there is anything about what they plan on doing to him, I want that too."

Featheringull considered the young man in front of him. The prince was right. He did have access to the gossip that flowed through the city like the wind. In all possibility he could get his hands on at least half of what the boy wanted, which would be a start for him at least. "I can't promise anything, but I shall do my best for you, although it may take a while. My advice to you is that you return to the palace," he told the prince. "Your father may get some information whilst I am fossicking through the gossip. What I will do is to send Coen with the lock picks when I have something for you. Once he has been, you can return here for the information and take action as is necessary," Featheringull advised.

The merchant had known Binjaymen for several years. The grapevine that Jay had spoken of was often filled with the escapades of the young Prince Varian and the subsequent rescues by the dashing Prince Jay, as the young women of Irskin called him. However, Featheringull knew what the young man was capable of and what he could do if pushed. The man actually liked the prince, considering him an equal, and hated the idea of him getting hurt. Looking at the boy in front of him, he began to feel sorry for whoever had taken Prince Varian. They were in for a nasty shock.

Jay nodded his acquiesce at the merchant's suggestion. "You are right. Father's spies may come across something, or the kidnappers may send a note. The best place for me to be at this point is at the palace." He stood up and held his hand across the table, waiting until Featheringull had clasped it. "Thank you, Master Featheringull, for your help. I shall await your message at the palace."

"I am just glad I can be of service to you, your Highness." The merchant bowed slightly as he held the door open for the young prince. "Hopefully we will have some news shortly, one way or the other."

Binjaymen sat on a window ledge in the library, staring out at the gardens impatiently waiting for the visit of Coen Feathingull. He had been back in the palace two hours and Josep was still unaware that he had even left. So far there had been no news of Varian's whereabouts, or why he had even been taken.

"Would you stop that?!"

Jay looked up to find Jirrelle staring at him, an irritated expression on her face. "Stop what?" he asked, perplexed. The rest of his siblings were also in the library. All of them were desperately waiting for their parents to provide them with some news, even a tiny scrap of information, about Varian.

"That!" she replied, pointing to his fingers which were drumming against a patch of ledge that his body was not inhabiting. "We are all worried about Varian, but there is nothing we can do except wait. I know it is frustrating. The rest of us are just as concerned as you are, however, that is not helping the situation."

Jay was about to respond when there was a knock on the door. All five siblings looked up, expectantly. A footman opened the door. "Prince Binjaymen, there is a merchant wanting to see you, your Highness."

Jay jumped up, trying not to look to enthusiastic as his sibs sighed their disappointment. "Thank you. Where is he?" he asked as he followed the man out of the room.

"The Lord Steward put him in the green Audience Chamber, your Highness," replied the footman, trying to keep up with the young prince as he half sprinted in the direction of the audience chambers.

They reached their destination in a matter of moments and Binjaymen dismissed the footman just outside the door. When the man had returned to his post, Jay entered the room and closed the door behind him. Sure enough, Coen Featheringull was waiting for him. "Your Highness," said the young man, bowing.

"Master Coen. Your father has information?" Jay couldn't keep the hope and excitement out of his voice.

"Yes, your Highness," replied the boy, handing over the small parcel he held as he spoke.

Jay smiled as he accepted the delivery. "Wonderful. Tell your father that I will be there within the hour. I just have to make sure my brother is not on my tail." The boy bowed again and Jay showed him out of the room. The footman returned to show the merchant out of the palace and Jay returned to his siblings, formulating a plan for his escape as he went.

"What was that all about?" asked Shrialla, as Binjaymen re-entered the library.

"None of your business," Jay told her.

Josep raised a brow, sceptically. "Keeping secrets from us, little brother?"

"Of course," responded Jay. "How else am I to make sure that any present that I buy you is a surprise?" He didn't wait for a reply. "I am going to try and take a nap."

"You? A nap?" Marryam scoffed in disbelief.

"Yes. Me, a nap," he insisted. "The waiting is getting to me. I hate having to sit around and do nothing." He turned and stomped out of the room, leaving his siblings staring in shock at his receding figure.

Josep looked at Jirrelle. "Why don't I trust him?" he asked.

Jirrelle shrugged. "Only you can answer that."

Well aware that he was probably the focus of any conversation currently being undertaken by his brother and sisters, Binjaymen raced back to his room and changed into clothing more appropriate for the city. Into a pack he stuffed a second set of clothes, these ones more suitable to sneaking around at night, and his lock picks. He lifted his mattress and retrieved the two knives he had been given by his present foster father, and slid them into his boots. Next he put the sheaths for the set of throwing knives he had also been given, into the bag. A quick glance around his bedroom to jog his brain, in case there was anything he had forgotten, and then he was out the window and on his way back to the warehouse of the merchant Featheringull.

It was Coen who spotted him, when Jay entered the warehouse for a second time that day. His father was busy with a customer, so the boy showed the prince back into his father's office. Jay paced as he waited for the merchant to finish and come back to give him the information that he had gathered. He was so absorbed in his pacing he didn't notice when Mistress Featheringull brought a tray with wine, cakes and pies on it, and left it on the desk.

Finally, Master Featheringull entered the room. He motioned for the prince to sit down and closed the door before he spoke. "I have two pieces of information that should help you," he told the boy. Jay looked at him expectantly. "The first comes from one of my men who was drinking at a local inn yesterday. Apparently a well, although interestingly dressed gentleman came in, paid for a room, and then met with three well known ruffians. After this person, who was dressed in a long black cape which my man thought was made of velvet, left, the three other men came down looking like they had just inherited a fortune. My man told me they each ordered a very expensive drink that they would normally have not been able to afford, and sat savouring it before they finally left."

Jay considered the information. "That definitely sounds like they had been hired to do a job like kidnapping my brother, I'd say." He gave the merchant a look that said 'and the rest please'.

Featheringull nodded his agreement at Jay's statement. "The other information I have comes from a most interesting source, and they want in if you find it useful," he told the prince, who raised a curious brow. "My informant is a street kid living down at the docks. He noticed quite a bit of activity at a warehouse that has been unoccupied for a couple of years. Until two days ago it was one of his sleeping places, but someone has placed magic on the locks and obscured the windows with, and I quote, 'expensive black material'. He also told me that late last night, three men matching the description of our ruffians were met at the door to this warehouse by a man in a 'rich' black cloak. They handed over a sack to the man, which they were paid for, and left."

"How do we know that Varian was in the sack?" asked Jay. "It could just have been some expensive artefact."

"True," agreed Featheringull. "But I had some men checkout this warehouse, and I find it interesting that there has been a steady stream of Randons going in and out of it."

Jay's head snapped up. "Randons?" Featheringull nodded. "What would they want with Varian? The Order of Wyman has been extremely generous to my family of late."

The merchant shook his head. "I can not say, your Highness, but I doubt they are interested in artefacts."

"This kid wants to help?" Jay asked, thinking.

"Yes."

"Set up a meeting." A look of grim determination came into Binjaymen's eyes. "Tonight I go get my brother."

♦

Chapter Twenty Five

First day of Garnet Moon, Year 2975.
A warehouse on the docks, Irskin, Astiria

Varian was bored, or that was the picture he presented to his captors. Apart from eating when instructed and demanding to be released, he had remained sullenly silent all day. He had also spent a good portion of his time appearing to sleep. He had actually fallen asleep shortly after his breakfast and woken to hear his guards talking. They had not realised he was awake and were discussing their assignment in front of him. Through this he had been able to glean the reason for his abduction, and he knew he was not going to fall in with their plans.

The young prince used his time 'awake' to thoroughly investigate every nook and cranny with his eyes. He also managed to move the mattress they had provided him to sleep on, closer to the wall. Unbeknownst to those guarding him, the spot where his bed now resided was close to a broken pipe. When the number of his guards lessened he hoped to use the pipe to cut through the rope binding his hands and in his 'sleep' undo those tied around his legs. Whilst he had not yet figured out his escape plan, he knew he needed to have free movement in order to get out.

Varian sighed. He had managed to watch the guards enter and leave the room several times. Each time they did he caught a flash of what he thought might be magic. It was a depressing discovery to realise this, as it meant there was little chance of him leaving through the front or back doors. The boy moved to a horizontal position, laying on his back and staring at the ceiling. Could he make it to the roof he wondered? He was just about to close his eyes again to see if he could get any more information out of his jailers, when a movement near the top of the wall caught his eyes. He quickly checked out what the adults were doing before returning his focus to that which had grabbed his attention.

At the top of the wall he had leaned his bed against, was a window. Further investigation showed the window had a broken pane. Whoever had placed the material over the window had not noticed the break, and those responsible for the security of the facility they were in had obviously not considered that a child would think to climb a wall and escape through a window, which was the thought running through the crafty mind of the six year old currently staring at the window. Behind his back, Varian tapped his hands together in glee. Hopefully he would only have one guard when night fell, and he could use this to his advantage. He closed his eyes, a feeling of bliss suffusing his mind as he formulated his escape plan and waited for the perfect moment to implement it.

♦

"Jay?" Binjaymen looked up to find Master Featheringull standing in the doorway. "It is time," the merchant told him. Binjaymen had told the merchant to drop both the 'Master' and 'your Highness'. He had thought it safer, given the circumstances. They decided it was best if Jay returned to the palace so as to not clue his family into what he was up to. It also made sense as there had been nothing he could do until night fell. "We are to meet Pip outside one of my storage warehouses," Featheringull said as the prince stepped out of the office to join him. "He will take you on from there."

"I'm ready." Jay followed the merchant out the back door of the building. "Have you been able to determine any reasons behind the act?" He asked the older man, couching his words in terms unlikely to cause suspicion, as they walked through the back streets of Irskin.

"Not really," replied Featheringull. "No one has been able to get into the building and very little is being said in the street. The only thing we have come across is a reference to something that has to happen in a dozen or so years."

"Oh?"

"A discussion was overheard saying they wanted to train the scamp up so that it would fix a mistake their boss made a long time ago." The merchant had a rather puzzled expression on his face as he passed on the information that his men garnered.

Jay frowned, assessing the words of his partner. "When this is all over, I think I may ask you to investigate that a bit further, but at the moment I have other things to worry about." They walked the rest of the way in silence.

"Hey mister!" came the whisper as they neared the storage warehouse. "Over 'ere!" In the shadows of the building was a boy, only a couple of years older than Varian.

"Jay, this is Pip," said Featheringull, introducing the prince to the street kid. "Pip, this is Jay. He is the one who is interested in the sack those men delivered last night."

"Wot's it worth to ya?" the boy asked, a sullen expression on his thin face.

Jay grinned, white teeth flashing in the night. "Featheringull has a bag of coins for you, most of them are silver and gold, which he will give you when the contents of the sack have been retrieved," the prince informed the urchin whose jaw dropped. "He will wait here for both of us to return before you get it. So… where is this building?"

Pip blinked and picked his jaw up from the ground. "Come wit' me," he instructed and took off. After a moment of delay caused by disbelief, Jay followed, sliding along the walls of the warehouses, keeping to the shadows so as not to be seen.

♦

"Darling, sit down!" Claire insisted as she watched her husband wear a hole in the carpet of his office as he paced from one side to the other. A faint smile creased her mouth as she realised what she had said. "That feels rather strange to be saying it to you, instead of the other way around."

Jaymes sighed. "I am impressed that you are so calm."

"I am just trying not to show my distress."

The king walked over to where his wife sat and wrapped his arms around her shoulders. "The others went to bed without a fuss?"

"Yes. Jay was rather distracted, but that is to be expected." She closed her eyes for a moment. "I am just glad he hasn't tried to do anything rash and go after Varian himself."

The King smiled. "I think that would be rather difficult, given we still don't know who has him, or why." The smile turned to a frown as he pondered the problem.

"Why wouldn't the kidnappers ask for a ransom?" the Queen enquired, bewildered that they hadn't heard from the perpetrators by this time.

Jaymes was interrupted before he could reply by Svendon, the Commander of the Army and Quay, the head of the intelligence arm entering the room.

"Your Majesties." Both men bowed. "We have some news with regards the whereabouts of Prince Varian," said Svendon. He motioned to Quay, indicating that he should give his report.

"We have an agent in the local college of the Order of Wyman, your Majesties," the chief of the spies told them. "They found out that they are responsible for the abduction of your youngest son."

"*What?!*"

"*Why?!*"

The man shrugged. "As far as the spy could determine, they want to convert him and make him into a Randon."

"Why didn't they just wait and invite him in when he had finished his schooling?" Claire was mystified. "Why resort to abduction? He is only six after all."

"We haven't been able to determine that, your Majesty," replied Svendon. "However, Quay's people have almost managed to locate where they are holding him at the moment."

Jaymes' eyes widened at the implication. "He is not at the college?"

"No, your Majesty," answered Quay, shaking his head. "They have apparently put him somewhere else at this stage and are planning to move him to the college later."

"Keep us informed," instructed Jaymes. "I want my son located, and when I have him back, Laven Dalbert is going to face my wrath."

♦

"That's it?" Jay looked at the boy at his side in surprise.

"Yup."

Binjaymen studied the building across the lane from where they stood. There were two men standing outside the front door. Another two were at a side door. Jay suspected there would be two more at the back door. He glanced up, hoping for some inspiration. It came so quickly it left him breathless. "Is there any way up there?" he asked Pip, pointing to a ledge that ran along the side of the building just below a set of windows.

Pip considered the place in question. "I think so. Follow me." He slid along the wall and around the corner of the building. Finding the door, he gave it a push. It refused to budge, causing the boy to swear vehemently.

Jay pulled his picks out of his pocket. "Here, let me." He moved the boy out of the way and went to work on the lock.

"Where'd a toff like you learn to do that?" Pip asked, impressed.

Jay grinned as the lock released and he opened the door to the ramshackle shed. "What makes you think that I am a toff?" he queried as they entered the building.

Pip snorted. "You may look like you ain't, but yer clothes is too nice and you speak funny," he told the older boy. He darted across the floor of the building, toward a set of stairs. "These lead to that door." He pointed to a spot near the top of the wall. "Once outside again, there is a bridge which crosses over to that ledge on the other side." That said, he ran up the stairs.

Jay followed. When they reached the top he looked at the younger boy in dismay. "You call this a bridge?"

"Yup." Pip began to cross. Jay shuddered, but followed. The bridge was little more than a collection of beams that had been assembled with some cables to work as a heavy lifting machine for goods. It had definitely seen better days.

Much to Jay's surprise, they both made it across safely, and holding the wall tightly they made their way to the closest window. The hastily constructed curtain on the window was slightly lopsided and they were able to find a spot where they could see into the main room of the warehouse. When he spotted Varian on a mattress against the wall to the left of the one they were on, he almost fell off as he bounced in joy. It was only Pip's quick reflexes that prevent him from making an unfortunate leap.

The two boys watched silently as Varian made sure his captors were not watching and used a piece of broken pipe to cut his bonds. Jay imagined himself clapping rather than giving in to the impulse in case it caused him to loose his balance. Watching his little brother he noticed him glancing up at a window above his present location. He motioned to Pip and they moved around to that side of the building. A few minutes later Jay had located the window and realised why Varian had been looking at it. Knowing his brother was unaware of his presence, Jay worked at the broken pane of glass. A few minutes later it was gone.

A sudden gust of cold air caused Varian to look up. The wind had blown the curtain further into the room and Varian could just make out the face of his brother Jay in the window. His hands formed fists in triumph. Keeping an eye on his guards, Varian watched as Jay and another boy removed all the panes of glass in the window.

Seeing that Varian had noticed him and Pip, Jay motioned to Varian, intimating he should remain where he was. They all waited with baited breath, hoping the guard would leave Varian alone for a few minutes. They had almost given up when the door opened and another person came in and spoke with the guard. The two people looked over at Varian, who was feigning sleep, then back at each other. They must have decided it was safe to leave the sleeping child alone as the guard left the room with the other person.

As soon as the door was shut, Varian sat up. He looked up at his brother, expectantly. Jay did not disappoint, throwing a rope into the room, which Varian caught as it swung back toward the wall. The boys at the window held on tight as Varian climbed up the wall the way he had been taught when he had travelled by ship to Demesa. In a matter of moments he was at the top of the wall and climbing out of the window.

Jay gave his brother a quick hug, but motioned for him to be silent. He indicated to Pip that he should go first, and then nudged Varian to follow, whilst he brought up the rear. They had just finished crossing the 'bridge' when a commotion erupted in the street. The boys looked down to find a detachment of the army and the guards surrounding the building Varian had just vacated. The men parted to show a richly dressed man who demanded entry to the building.

Jay looked at Varian. "We had better get down there quick," he said before dashing past Pip, dragging his brother with him.

"Do ya know 'im?" asked Pip as he struggled to follow the other two boys.

"Yeah," replied Jay. "That's our father." They raced down the stairs and across the floor of the building, not bothering to close the door as they left and headed toward where they had seen the King. They reached the back of the detachment of guards just in time to hear the guards at the door denying Varian was there. As one of a group of guards were sent in to investigate the building, a young corporal noticed the three boys. He gave one of his neighbours a prod and the two of them circled back, coming up behind the boys. When Jay realised they had been noticed, he motioned to the other two to follow him. The corporals lead them to the front of the group just as the guards returned to report there was no one inside.

Before Jaymes could react, the leader of the detachment of guards noticed the corporals and their detainees. "Uh, your Majesty?"

"Yes?" Jaymes snapped his head around in the direction of the query angrily. "What?" Then he saw his sons and their associate. "Why am I not surprised," he said before beginning to laugh in sheer relief. "Let's take them all home and make sure they are washed, fed and get a good night's sleep. Commander – take these people into custody." He indicated to the Randons. "I'll deal with all this tomorrow," he instructed once he had recovered his composure.

"Where are we going?" Pip asked as he tagged along behind Varian.

"Home," responded the younger boy.

"Where's home?"

"The palace," replied Jay as he brought up the rear. His stride was interrupted a moment later as Pip, wide eyed and pale, fainted dead at his feet.

♦

"What on *EARTH* did you think you were doing?" demanded Jaymes of his second son. They were in his office. Varian and Pip had been bathed and sent to bed, but Binjaymen was not so lucky. "Did you even consider the possibility of what they would have done to you if you had been caught?"

"Uh –" Jay tried to respond but was not given the chance.

"Bad enough your mother and I would have been mourning the loss of one son but your actions could have left us mourning two," Jaymes continued, incensed at his son's lack of consideration. "It was ill conceived, irresponsible and unacceptable behaviour, whether you are a prince of the realm or not! And to involve a minor! How would I explain to his parents if something happened to him?"

"Father, Pip doesn't have any parents – that he knows of, any way," Jay told him when he could get a word in. "He is a street kid. He was the one who showed me where to find Varian in the first place."

"Oh." Jaymes was at a loss for words.

"Just for the record, whilst I will concede that I did not consider my actions could affect you and Mother, I do not feel I was acting in an irresponsible manner. I investigated the situation thoroughly before I made any attempt at rescue and Varian was partially responsible for his escape as it was," Jay explained, unaware his father was not paying any attention to what he was saying. Several moments of silence followed the end of Jay's explanation.

"Young Master Pip is an orphan?" the King asked when he returned his attention to Binjaymen.

"Most likely," replied his son, perplexed at the change of topic, but still waiting for a response to his reasoning.

"I had been considering how to reward him," murmured Jaymes. "I believe it would be in his best interests if your mother and I were to foster him," he informed Jay, looking up to gage his son's reaction.

Jay's jaw dropped. "How do you think Mother will react to such a suggestion?" he inquired, shocked.

"She would probably suggest it if she was aware of his situation," remarked the king. "She appeared to be quite taken with him. It would also provide Varian with a friend closer in age to him, especially as you are about to return to the country," he reminded his son rather pointedly.

"Ah…yes, it would, however have you thought about how much work it is going to be? He is quite a bit rough around the edges," Jay commented. "You might want to give the tutors and Uriahl a pay rise as compensation."

Jaymes looked down his nose at his son. "I am sure that you are exaggerating the situation."

"We'll see. We will see."

♦

"Master Pip, I would like to properly show my gratitude for your help in releasing my son Varian from his abductors," said Jaymes formally, causing the boy in question to stare at him blankly. They were in his office. Claire stood behind her husband looking welcoming.

"He says thanks for helping to get Varian back," whispered Jay from his position behind him. Varian had not been permitted to attend and was busy sulking as he was being tutored.

"Oh. No problem, yer Majesty," replied Pip happily after Jay's translation.

Claire hid a grin behind her hand as Jaymes continued. "I would like to reward you for your efforts on behalf of the kingdom."

"Oh. Yeah, cool!" Pip brightened at the word 'reward'.

The King looked at his second son. "Perhaps you should explain it, Binjaymen," he suggested.

Jay looked pleadingly at his mother, but a slight shake of her head told him she agreed with her husband. He sighed and stepped to stand beside Pip. "What my Father would like to do as your reward is to foster you," he told the younger boy. The blank look returned to Pip's face. "What this means is that you would become a member of the family – sort of," Jay explained. "You would live here at the palace, be taught how to read and write, among other things, and never have to wonder where your next meal was coming from or where you would sleep at night."

Pip looked from father to son and back again. "You serious?"

Jaymes nodded. "In effect we would become your parents," he said, trying to reassure the boy. "Jay and Varian would become your brothers."

"You'd also pick up a bunch of sisters," Jay muttered, gaining a look of dismay from his mother.

"Would I have to talk funny like you guys?" Pip asked. He figured he would probably accept their offer, but he knew the way to get the best deal was to haggle. He wasn't good at it, but he would try.

Jay grinned outright. "Yes. It tends to be a result of learning to read and write." That comment caused him to receive another look from his mother, but he let it float over him.

Jaymes looked at the street urchin, considering. He could see the boy wanted to say yes but was trying to get as much as he could out of the deal. "As part of being fostered by us, you would also be required to become a peer of the realm," he told the child, knowing he would not understand the words. "There is a piece of property, which presently does not have an owner, which will be given to you if you accept our offer." Jaymes watched, satisfied, as the boy's jaw dropped. "However it has a title attached to it, and Duke Pip of Keegan just doesn't sound right. Do you want it?" he asked.

"Uh…I guess so," replied the boy, completely bamboozled by all that had been said.

Claire smiled beatifically. "Then we shall have to find a new name for you. Pip was the name from your old life." She considered the child. "Phillip," she said. "Yes, Phillip works, and you can keep Pip as a nickname." The Queen walked out from behind her husband's desk and went to wrap Pip in a big hug. "Duke Phillip of Keegan, welcome to the family."

♦

Chapter Twenty Six

Seventh day of Garnet Moon, year 2975,
College of the Twins, Irskin, Astiria

Felasia, Wuhern of Astiria stared at the letter from her king in dismay. She could not believe the stupidity of the Randons here in Astiria. The woman looked at the other pieces of paper that covered her normally neat desk and sighed. *I am getting too old for this*, she thought, but at least she had finally found a new replacement. The Wuhern sighed again. Should she fill him in now? Have him in the room as she discussed the matter with her colleagues? Perhaps not. Felasia would speak with Aneurin before she informed her apprentice of the situation. That decided she turned to the mirror next to her desk. As age had caught up with her, Felasia had found walking rather wearying. As a result, the mirror she used to talk to the other Wuherns had crept closer and closer to her desk, until all she had to do was turn in her seat to be able to use it.

Aneurin's image appeared in the mirror. "Felasia! How are you doing? My sincere condolences at the death of Stephas. Have you found a replacement?"

Felasia smiled. "I am well as can be for someone of my age. Thank you for your thoughts, they are appreciated and yes, I have found a replacement. His name is Andjo and he has been with the Order for almost as many years as you," she told him. "But this is not why I wished to speak with you." She paused, considering how she would frame her words. "I received your communiqué with regard to the prophecy Quenmir found, and I believe I have some information for you about it." She grinned somewhat evilly. "The local Randons gave it to me, actually."

"Oh?" Aneurin was intrigued.

"Yes. As we speak, that young Laven Dalbert should be up before King Jaymes and Queen Claire." There was a look of pure, unadulterated glee on her face. "His subordinates took it upon themselves to kidnap their youngest child, Varian. It is my guess he has a large part to play in the prophecy, or they would not have been so stupid."

"You are joking?!"

Felasia shook her head. "They apparently hired some thugs to abduct him out of the palace, with the intention that they would subvert him to their cause, but they didn't anticipate the brilliance of either young Varian or his elder brother Binjaymen, with whom he shares a deep bond. Between the two of them, the boys managed to affect Varian's escape before the King even managed to get to where the idiot Randons were holding him."

Aneurin blinked in disbelief. "Are you sure that this was not one of Dalbert's ideas? It is possible after all," he asked.

"No. Dalbert has more sense than to try something so stupid. He would not have been elevated to the position of Laven if he were," the Astirian Wuhern reminded her counterpart.

The Westecroftan considered her words. "True. I had not really thought about it that way. But what has all this to do with the prophecy?"

"The prophecy mentions the 'chosen twelve' will be born fourteen moons apart," Felasia informed him. "You told me your suspicions that Princess Oriel and the new born Althea are members of the twelve, and the earthquake and tidal wave that hit the Trimidian island of Ascu last year was due to the birth of another of the twelve – correct?"

"Yes."

"Then by my calculations, working back from Althea's birth, and taking into consideration the signs mentioned by the prophecy – Prince Varian of Astiria is the first of the twelve." Felasia sat back in her chair and waited for the information to sink in. She was rewarded with an expression of such utter astonishment that it was all she could do to not laugh out loud. "Unless I am mistaken, either Prince Rhawn or Princess Tarianne is also a member of the twelve."

"You are certain?" Aneurin asked, eyes wide as he considered the possible consequences.

Felasia shook her head. "No, I'm not. This is only based on my calculations, the information you sent me and that which was in the prophecy. Further investigation will need to be done to prove if I am correct or not."

Aneurin was in shock. "Do you realise what you are suggesting?"

"Yes Aneurin, I am well aware," she said, speaking slowly as though to an innocent. "I am also aware I do not personally have the time to do the investigations required. I am going to have to leave that up to you." Felasia sighed. "I can not leave something this important in the hands of my apprentice. He is having enough trouble dealing with his sudden promotion as it is." She closed her eyes momentarily as she let her thoughts follow those of her apprentice. "The Order here in Astiria expected me to select someone a bit younger," she said when she reopened them. "However there is not the time. We need someone who knows the Order and all the people in it. You know what it is like when one of us leaves this life. You have seen it several times now."

"Yes, I have," agreed Aneurin, sadness seeping into his voice. "You haven't informed Andjo of the situation then?"

"No, I haven't," she told him, Leaning back in her chair. "I was hoping for your insight. Given his present difficulties, I am loathed to place more on his plate. However, if you think it best I will."

Aneurin considered the situation. "Leave it with me. I will get back to you on that one," he said. "I will organise the investigation with Haileigh, as she has a vested interest in it. If you should leave us before we decide to reveal the situation to Andjo, I will ensure that he is informed at his investiture."

Felasia nodded. "Very well then, I shall leave it in your capable hands."

House of Wyman, Irskin, Astiria

"You *idiot*! You addle headed, imbecilic, brainless twit!" screeched Dalbert, Laven of the Order of Wyman for the northern kingdoms, as he slammed open the door of his sub-ordinate's, Archibald, Dean of the Order of Wyman in Astiria, office and stomped into the room. He placed his hands on the desk and leaned over it. "What under the skies of Wyman possessed you to even think about kidnapping Prince Varian?" he demanded, seething with fury at having to stand before the king of Astiria and apologise for the actions of one of his priests. "Do you have *any* idea of what your stupidity has cost this Order? Not only here, but in all the northern kingdoms? I am going to have to spend years, absolute *years* fixing this mess. The Astirian's will have nothing to do with us for centuries, and all the other kingdoms will be extremely wary of us." The Laven pushed himself off of the desk and started pacing around the room. "You have just ruined any chance of Varian's position in the prophecy remaining the knowledge of only our Order! Centuries of work have just gone down the drain and you are responsible!"

"But....I...thought -" Archibald tried to pull himself back up into his chair and explain, but Dalbert was not interested in explanations.

"I want you and any Priests involved in this debacle at the House in Oremar within two weeks," he commanded. "And if you involved any civilians..." he glared at the other man. "I want them there too!" Finished, he turned and stormed out of the room, slamming the door behind him and causing it to shatter into a thousand splinters. A series of slams could be heard as the Laven left the building. When silence finally reigned, the Dean let out a small breath and began the task of locating those involved in the abduction. He was not looking forward to his forthcoming time in the capital of Quandar.

Royal Palace, Denel, Demesa,

Haileigh sighed as she read the report in her hand. It was proof positive her daughter was one of the chosen twelve mentioned in the prophecy. Curtsey of her father's agents in the other kingdoms, and through a census conducted in Demesa shortly after Oriel's birth, Haileigh was now certain there could be no other possibility, as not one other child had been born on the planet the day that Oriel was born. The report also told her that so far no child had been reported as being born on the first day of the current month in Demesa. This increased the odds that Althea Carmichael was the fifth member of the twelve.

The Crown Princess of Demesa looked at the mirror beside her desk and winced. "I had better tell Aneurin," she murmured with a distinct lack of enthusiasm. There were times when she wished she had not been elevated to the position of Wuhern. She struggled as it was with the fact she would one day rule the kingdom. That she also was the leader of a religious order was sometimes too much to deal with.

Under her breath the Princess muttered the words that would show her counterpart in Westecroft. "Good afternoon Aneurin," she said when the mirror cleared and Aneurin of Mendox appeared before her.

"Good afternoon Haileigh," the other Wuhern responded in kind. "To what do I owe the pleasure of your conversation?"

Haileigh raised her brow. "You are in a strange mood, old friend."

Aneurin shrugged. "I have just been talking with Felasia in Astiria. She had some interesting information for me."

"Ah. Well I have some news for you too," she informed him. "All my sources confirm that Oriel is the fourth member of the 'first twelve', and so far the research suggests that Althea is the fifth."

"I see," he sighed. "Felasia had information that suggested the identity of the first member." A grin of childish delight settled on his face. "The Order of Wyman gave it to her."

"Voluntarily?" Haileigh was surprised.

Aneurin shook his head. "They had the audacity of kidnapping Varian of Astiria," he told her. "Felasia put all the pieces together with thanks to the prophecy Quenmir found and the information we had sent her."

"Oh?"

"The prophecy states the twelve will be born fourteen moons apart," he reiterated. "She realised what we should have, that this means one year and a month apart. Althea was born a year and a month after the quake and wave in Ascu," he informed the Demesan Wuhern. "That occurred a year and a month after your daughter was born. Working back by that timing, there is one other before we have Rhawn and Tarianne of Westecroft, and finally we have Varian of Astiria."

Haileigh deliberated over his words for several minutes. "You said Rhawn and Tarianne." She looked at Aneurin for confirmation. "Does that mean they are both members of the twelve?"

"No," replied the Westecroftan Wuhern. "I have yet to get a hold of their actual birth records, but I suspect only one of them was born on the day that would coincide with the prophecy."

"Ah!" She thought about it for a moment. "So who is the one we are missing so far? Have you been able to determine anything?"

"Haileigh! I only spoke with Felasia an hour or two ago," said Aneurin in frustration. "She was the one who told me how the pattern actually worked. Even you didn't figure it out!"

"Well. There is no need to be narky about it," the Princess replied, slightly insulted.

"Look, I don't have the time to start a slanging match with you." Aneurin sighed. "I am going to let Master Athenan Michaela in on all the details of what we are dealing with. She is going to be my right hand person, and will probably come and visit you in the next few months."

Haileigh blinked in surprise. "Why are you telling this to Michaela and not Oriana? Oriana has a vested interest in the whole situation after all."

Aneurin closed his eyes for a moment before replying. "Michaela also does, in a round about way," he informed the other Wuhern. "I will let her explain it to you when she arrives in Denel. Besides, Michaela will be Oriana's assistant as they have a sister-like relationship. Trust me when I say it will be better if it is this way." He gave Haileigh a look of pity. "I am sure you would be happier if you were not aware of your daughter's position in the future. If someone else was able to worry about that part of her life for you, whilst all you had to worry about was the normal mother worries, would it not be a load off of your shoulders?" he asked.

"I suppose so," Haileigh reluctantly agreed. "It would be easier. But Aneurin, life was never meant to be easy. Isn't that what everyone tells us as we are growing up?"

Aneurin nodded. "Yes, but I have foreseen enough of Oriana's future to know this is the way it should be."

Haileigh sighed. "Fine. I shall look forward to meeting this Master Athenan of yours. If she is anything like Oriana, then I am sure she is up to the task."

"Oh, she is like Oriana." The Westecroftan grinned. "Indeed, she is very much like Oriana."

⚘

College of the Twins, Westecroft

:Michaela, I need to see you right now: Aneurin called silently.

:I am on my way: replied the Athenan. A few moments later there was a knock on the Wuhern's door. It opened to reveal Michaela Debranny, Master Athenan and best friend of Oriana. "What can I do for you my Lord?" she enquired as she walked toward his desk.

"Have a seat and read this," instructed the Wuhern, handing her a small stack of papers.

"What is it?" Michaela asked as she did as she was told.

"A report I have prepared especially for you," Aneurin informed her. "The details of which are strictly confidential and you are not to tell anyone, particularly Oriana." The Wuhern's tone brooked no argument. Michaela raised an eyebrow in surprise. It was a habit she had picked up from the Athenan in question who used the little arch of hair to convey any of a thousand words and emotions. "You will understand why once you have read it." The Wuhern told her in response to the question asked by that brow.

As Michaela settled in to read, Aneurin looked at her in consideration. He was a little unsure if she was up to the job he was about to set her, despite what he had said to Haileigh an hour before. It was not that she wasn't capable of understanding the situation and its requirements, but rather she could have difficulty with the secrecy that was necessary. Michaela was a very open and personable individual, despite how she had spent the first years of her life. Aneurin was also curious to see her reaction to the background information that was mentioned in the report.

Twenty minutes later the Athenan looked up from the pages she had been reading. Her face was pale, almost transparent as she looked at the Wuhern in shock. "I don't know which emotion is more prevalent at the moment," she said when she finally found her voice. "Joy at actually having a family, that I am related to my best friend and to you, or horror that I am a descendant of 'The Dog' and I can not even let my cousin know we are related." Michaela blinked several times as she tried to get a hold of herself. "The other aspect of this report is having a bit of difficulty sinking in at the moment," she told her boss.

"I am going to help you out a bit," Aneurin mentioned in an effort to alleviate her fears. "I want you to go to Trimid and investigate things there for a while. It should help you to adjust to the information overload that you have just experienced."

Michaela shook her head in disbelief. "I am not so sure about that," she disagreed before glancing out the window to watch the setting sun send ribbons of golden light through the trees. "How many people are aware of the contents of that report?" she asked, turning her attention back to her great great uncle.

"All the Wuherns," he told her. "And probably all three Lavens."

"Will you be telling Oriana anything about what is in it?"

"No."

Michaela gaped. "Why not? Her daughter has an extremely important role to play in the future, if I am reading this correct. She has a right to know."

Aneurin shook his head. "She does not need the distraction. Her own future has enough in it without the added worry. Besides, by the time Althea begins to take an active part in the prophecy, Oriana will be aware of the situation." He looked at the time candle on the mantle piece. "I suggest you go and pack. You will be leaving for Trimid in the morning."

"May I say goodbye to Oriana?" the Athenan enquired.

"I think it best if you do not," replied Aneurin.

"Fine." Michaela was not happy with the response. "You get to deal with her temper when she finds out that I have gone without letting her know."

Aneurin just smiled. "I have been dealing with it for fifteen years, Michaela. Another bout is not going to hurt me, I assure you."

Ascu Island, Trimid

"Heinrich!"

Heinrich Aban, Master merchant of Erecol on the Trimidian island of Ascu, looked up from his paperwork to find his wife Deidre in the doorway. She was holding their son Michael in her arms and did not look happy. "Yes dear?"

Deidre scowled at her husband. "Your son has just done the impossible," she informed him.

"Oh?"

"He turned his tail into legs." It was clear by the expression on her face that Deidre was rather alarmed by this.

Heinrich blinked. "What?" he exclaimed. "He should not be able to do that until he hits ten at least!" The merchant could clearly understand his wife's alarm at this development. The normal development of a merfolk child was to spend the first ten years of their life in merfolk form. After this time they would begin to learn how to take the form of their human cousins and would slowly learn to walk on two legs. At the age of fifteen they would be able to spend days at a time in human form without the need to submerge themselves in water. Michael's sudden ability to turn his tail into legs defied all the common beliefs of his people.

"I know that!" responded Deidre. "Why do you think I am so upset?"

Her husband sprang out of his chair with the agility of someone with half his bulk. Years of living like a human had given him a slightly larger size than was normal for a merman. "We have to take him to Tain!" Heinrich insisted, dragging his wife and child out of the room. "He will know what to do!"

Mountain path, Central Zialp

"Papa?" called the little boy from his seat on the wagon. He had white blond hair and pale blue eyes and a cheeky grin that said he had been up to something, even if he hadn't.

The man at the head of the column looked back at his son. "What, Innis?" The column was a group of gypsies who had travelled the roads of Zialp and Astiria for centuries.

"Are you and Mama going to have another baby?" he asked.

The woman next to him laughed. "Darling," she said hugging him. "What makes you ask that?" She was constantly amazed at what her four year old son came out with.

The boy turned his attention back to his mother. "You're getting fat," he told her, pointing to her belly. "When Jeri got fat, she had a baby and then she got thin again."

Now his father laughed. "Out of the mouth of babes," he said, smiling at his wife. He was about to say something further when his attention was caught by a movement in the trees. In seconds the column was surrounded by men, all bearing arms. "Erin! Take the boy and run!" The leader of the column shouted as he drew a sword from his belt and began to fight.

Erin hesitated a moment before she followed her husband's orders. Awkwardly, she picked Innis up and dropped him over the side of the wagon, before following him down to the ground. She grabbed his hand and pulled him toward the trees. All around them men were fighting and the rest of the women from the column were following Erin's lead.

As gypsy after gyspy fell, the attackers turned their attention to the fleeing women and children. No boy was spared, and any woman or girl over the age of twelve were raped before they were killed.

Erin ran, pulling her son with her. She knew that there was an attacker on her tail and that her husband had most likely fallen.

Whoever their attackers were, they knew what they were doing. "Hurry Innis! We must hurry!" she panted as she ran.

"But, Mama, what about Papa?" the boy argued, trying to keep up with his mother.

"We have to forget about him," she told her son brutally. "We must get to safety!"

"Stop running, you bitch!" came a voice from behind. Erin yelped, picked up her son, and ran faster. She didn't bother looking back. She had no intention of letting the man catch her. "Nothing is going to save you. You may as well give up now, and maybe I will be a bit kinder to you."

Suddenly she tripped, throwing Innis to the ground several feet in front of her. When she looked up she noticed a small cave, just big enough for the child to fit into. "Innis!" he looked up at her voice. "There." She pointed to the mouth of the cave. "Get in there."

"But -"

"Don't argue with me, Innis! Just get in there." Erin knew she was done for. When she tripped she had twisted her ankle badly. There was no way it would support her weight, let alone her child's, as she tried to get away. Her only hope was that Innis, by hiding in the cave, would manage to escape the destruction of his family. "And stay away from the opening."

Scratched and bruised, Innis did as he was told. He sat back from the opening, just as his mother had said. Within moments the man who had been chasing them found his mother. Whilst he could not see what was going on, he could hear his mother's screams. Curled in a ball, he waited, tears falling silently down his face.

After an hour her screams finally stopped. Innis crept toward the cave mouth, but someone grabbed him from behind. He shrieked, but the sound was muffled by a small hand over his mouth. He looked up into the eyes of a man, no bigger in height than Innis' waist. "No child, it is best if you do not go out there," the man whispered. "There is nothing you can do for your mother now. Come with me and we shall see that you are looked after." With that the man led the injured child into the bowels of the earth.

❊

Chapter Twenty Seven

First day, Turquoise Moon, year 2981
Royal Palace, Denel, Demesa,

Oriel stood on the parapet of the palace and watched the sun set in a blaze of glory. She had finished all her school work, and whilst this was usually the time she spent with her parents, her Mother was presently distracted by some important work for the Order of the Twins and her Father was away on business.

She loved to come up here. You could see all the way out into the desert and at dawn and dusk, the sun's rays made the sand look like it was on fire. Her mother had often commented that she knew her daughter was half Pyrial by the simple fact that Oriel loved heat and anything to do with fire.

The girl sighed. Oriel sometimes wished that she was either fully human or fully Pyrial. Being half of each meant she only had half of the good and the bad of each race. She could play with fire and do all sorts of cool things with it. She was always in human form, but she had yet to learn how to take the Pyrial form. Her father had never even let her try to become a Pyrial. He said it was because he didn't have enough controls in case something went wrong, but Oriel suspected that it was because her mother was worried she might get stuck in fire form.

"Oriel!" The girl turned to find her mother behind her. "Your father has sent word that he will be back in the morning," Haileigh told her child as she wandered across the parapet to her. "He will require a day or so to rest, but has asked me to let you know he will be taking you to the Dragon's Tooth community in three days time." She smiled at her daughter. "It is time for you to meet the other side of your family and learn what it means to be a Pyrial."

"Really?" Oriel's face lit up with joy. She had been waiting for this moment for as long as she could remember. She had met various members of her father's family over the last couple of years, but they had not been able to teach her anything about her other side. "Truly?"

Haileigh nodded. "Really."

"Cool!" Oriel bounced up and down with excitement.

Haileigh's smile turned to a grin at the delight on her daughter's face. Mathew had warned her this would be Oriel's reaction, but she had not believed him. "I am so pleased to see you are happy about this," she remarked. "I wonder if I am going to get you back."

Oriel wrapped her arms around her mother's waist. "Of course I am going to come back! I live here. But I have so been wanting to visit the Pyrials. I want to learn more about myself," she told her mother.

"I am reassured by this," Haileigh said, the grin firmly in place. "I shall have to bury myself in work to prevent myself from becoming lonely in your absence."

"And you don't do that already?" asked a male voice from behind them. The two Princesses turned to find Mathew standing at the top of the stairs.

"Father!" Oriel released her mother and flew across to embrace her father. "Mother told me you weren't getting home until tomorrow!" She sent her mother a slightly accusing look.

Mathew laughed. "I wasn't, but we managed to make better time than I had anticipated."

"All right you two, break it up," said Haileigh as she joined her husband and daughter. "Dinner will be being served shortly. We had better go in."

✧

Third day, Turquoise Moon, year 2981
Sun Road, Demesa

"Father? How old are you?" asked Oriel as they rode along toward the area of desert that Mathew's family inhabited.

The Prince Consort looked over at his daughter. "Why the sudden curiosity?" They were half a day's ride south of Denel, with another day to travel in a westerly direction before reaching the home of Mathew's family.

The Dragon's Tooth nation of Pyrial's lived in a section of desert so hot that there were no human communities in close vicinity. Unlike most Pyrial communities, Oriel's relatives had taken up residence in the ruins of a human city that had been abandoned over a thousand years before. They had inhabited the area for centuries now.

The princess grinned cheekily at her father. "Because I want to know."

"What if I don't want to tell you?" He raised an enquiring eyebrow in her direction.

She shrugged. "I'll keep asking until you tell me."

Mathew shuddered at the thought. "I will tell you when you turn twenty-five," he told her.

"Why twenty-five?" Oriel asked, bemused.

"Because that was the age your mother was when she found out how old I am," she was informed.

Oriel gave her father a look of irritation. "What is to stop me from asking Mother how old you are?" she inquired.

Now Mathew shrugged. "Oh, about thirty or fourty leagues," he replied with and evil little grin. Oriel scowled at her father but had no comeback for his answer.

✿

Fifth day, Turquoise Moon, year 2981
Dragon Road, Demesa

"Are we there yet?"

Mathew sighed as he heard the question again. Oriel had been asking it on and off for the last three hours, ever since they left the oasis village of Morgan. "Do you see the black lump over there?" He pointed in a westerly direction.

Oriel squinted as she looked where he was indicating. "Yes."

"When we reach the base of that lump you will know we are there." Silence reigned in response to his comment.

As their horses ploughed through the sand, Oriel kept her eyes on the lump. After a while she noticed it was getting bigger. She kept watching, eventually it appeared to grow an extra bit. Both the lump and its baby, as Oriel had begun to call it, kept growing and soon she could identify it as rocks.

After two hours Mathew and his daughter stood at the base of the rocks. Oriel looked up in awe. "Wow!"

Mathew grinned, nudged his horse and began to move into the crevice between the two spires. Oriel followed. Ten minuted later they emerged, blinking, into a clearing surrounded by the ruins of stone buildings and filled with a crowd of beings.

"Welcome to Dragon's Tooth, Oriel," said Mathew, dismounting and coming to stand by her horse. He lifted her down and turned her to face the gathering in front of them. Half of the assembly were in human form; the others were balls of fire floating in the air at various heights. Oriel clung to her father, slightly unnerved by the sight.

One of the older women stepped forward. "Welcome, Granddaughter. It is wonderful to meet you at last." She glared at Mathew as she greeted the girl. "I am Faith, and this is Luke," she said as a man joined her. "We are your grandparents, and these," she waved a hand to indicate the crowd behind her, "are your cousins."

Oriel looked at her grandmother shyly. "All of them?"

Faith laughed. "No, I guess not. You have a few aunts and uncles amongst them too."

"Come," Luke interrupted. "You have both had a long journey. I am sure that you would like to rest and refresh yourselves." He looked at Mathew. "Your entourage?"

"Resting comfortably at Morgan."

The Pyrial nodded. "This way. We have organised lodgings for you." He led them toward the buildings.

As they walked, Luke entertained Oriel with stories of her cousins whilst Faith dropped back to Mathew. "Don't bother complaining that you haven't met her yet, Mother," he commented when she had joined him. "You could easily have made the journey to Denel."

"And who would have looked after the community?" she gave him a pointed look.

"Any one of the other members of the Council of Elders," replied her son just a touch sarcastically. "You and father may be the Chief Elders, but you are not the only members of the Council." He looked forward to his daughter and his father who were deep in conversation. Any reserve Oriel felt had melted in the warmth of her grandfather's aura. "You didn't even bother to come to her Blessing."

Faith scowled. "You know we don't do that sort of thing. Why would we have attended? I was not happy that Raina was there, and most displeased you had her in the ceremony."

"Mother, just because our people prefer not to live in the rest of the world doesn't mean those of us who break the mould should not be allowed to participate fully in that which goes on out there," he snarled at her. "I personally think it was beneficial to myself, Raina and Oriel to go through a Blessing. Raina enjoyed it." Oriel, hearing the anger in her father's voice, turned back toward them. Mathew gave her a reassuring smile. Placated, she returned her attention to her grandfather. "Your granddaughter is *half* Pyrial, Mother." Mathew looked back at his mother as he said this. "She has a major role to play in the outside world. Do *not* infect her with your prejudices or I promise you – you will regret it for the rest of your days!" With that said, Mathew picked up his pace and joined his father and daughter as they entered what would be their home for the coming weeks.

✿

Tenth day, Turquoise Moon, year 2981
Circle of Protection, North of Dragon's Tooth, Demesa

"Well," said Medhat when he had completed walking around the circle of stones. "I must say, this is as much a first for me as it is for you, young Oriel." He gave her an encouraging smile. "I have never taught anyone how to *become* a Pyrial, just the opposite in fact."

Oriel wasn't sure what she should say so she asked a question instead. "What did you just do? The air is tingling."

The Pyrial moved to the centre of the circle and laid a mat beside the stone slab which lay there. He considered the girl as he did so. "Yes, perhaps that is the best place to start." He nodded. "Have a seat." He waited until she had followed his instruction before he continued. "What I did was to initiate a circle of protection. It will protect us from anything outside and protect the outside from anything that we may do." He waited for the information to sink into her mind.

She tipped her head to one side as she mulled over his words. "How?"

Medhat suppressed a grin. Oriel reminded him of her mother at that moment in time. "You saw me lay my hands on the stones?" Oriel nodded. "I used the magical life energy I possess to open the magical gate which resides in the stone. My hands were the funnel for the energy. Once a gate is opened, the magic that is focused in that part of the circle is released and spreads over a defined area. When all the gates are open then the circle is complete."

"But it is not a circle," said Oriel, looking up. "It is a sphere."

Medhat could not help himself. He burst into laughter. Imperiously Oriel waited for him to recover. The expression of royal displeasure on her face did not help matters, but he eventually managed to regain control. "My apologies, Oriel. You sounded so like you mother when she was here…it was most amusing." He took a deep breath. "You are quite right. The circle of protection is not a circle but a sphere. It is called a circle because one must walk in a circular direction in order to activate it." The Pyrial stopped and considered his student. Oriel shifted restlessly under his gaze. "What has your mother taught you of magic?" he asked finally.

At the age of eight, Oriel had already begun to study magic. It was not something her mother was happy about, however Oriel, unlike her peers, was already capable of using magic because of her unusual parentage. Before her daughter had started schooling Haileigh had insisted she be taught to control her usage of fire, something Oriel readily created. Her studies had begun with simple meditation and quickly moved forwarded.

Medhat listened carefully to all the princess told him. Having spent some time in the outside world he was most impressed by her knowledge of human magic. It was giving him an idea as how to go about her Pyrial studies. "Very good," he said when she finished her dissertation. "Let us begin your new studies." He shifted his position to that which a human used for meditation. Oriel automatically copied him. "I want you to go into a deep trance," he told her. She closed her eyes and did as instructed.

Medhat watched and waited until he was sure she had accomplished the task then he switched his mode of communication to the mental form all Pyrials used in elemental form. *:go to your core:* He linked himself to her and watched as she did so. *:Find the essence that is you:* Slowly she located the pool of light that was her essence. She sunk into the pool. *:Let yourself dissolve into the essence:* Oriel did as instructed. It felt as if she were melting. *:Your essence is fire:* the Pyrial told her. *:Visualize yourself as a spark. Let the spark grow into a small flame:* He waited, watching as the physical shell that was the human Oriel dissolved slowly under his direction and was replaced by the Pyrial Oriel. *:Let the small flame grow to a large flame….Congratulations Oriel. Open your eyes:*

Oriel opened her eyes, not sure what she would see. Medhat held up a mirror. She looked into it and saw a blue/white ball of flame in it. The shock of the sight sent her quickly back into human form, causing her to fall to the ground as she had been floating when she was a Pyrial.

Her teacher grinned. "Well, we successfully taught you the transformation," he mused. "Now we just have to work on getting you to hold it."

✧

Twentith day, Turquoise Moon, year 2981
Dragon's Tooth, Demesa

:How is she going?: Mathew asked Medhat. The two Pyrials were watching Oriel mingle with her younger cousins. She had finally managed to hold the Pyrial form for a couple of hours at a time and was getting to spend time with her cousins who were too young to transform into human form.

:Quite well: replied Medhat. *:The more she practices, the more time she manages in Pyrial form:*

Mathew kept his gaze on his daughter. *:She is an interesting colour:* he remarked. *:I do not recall seeing anyone of us with that colouring:* Whenever Oriel was a Pyrial or studying with her teacher, Mathew also reverted to Pyrial form. He was an orangey red colour, as were most of the community varying only by shades. Oriel's blue/white was most unusual.

Medhat the Pyrial tipped forward in a nodding manner. *:Her colour is of a very hot fire. The white of hot coals and the blue that is seen at the very base of a flame:* He considered his student. *:I am not sure why that is. As a half Pyrial I would have expected her to be either redder or more yellow than her cousins:* He glanced over to the sundial. *:I had best collect my student. It is time for another lesson. Oriel!:* the young Pyrial stopped her forward movement and turned in the direction of the summons. *:Time for your lessons:* The girl did not bother to complain, but followed when her teacher headed out toward the circle of protection.

✧

:Mathew!: The thought sizzled across his consciousness.

:Yes?: The Pyrial Mathew responded.

:A pack of humans have just turned up looking for you: The herald of this news was his sire.

Mathew made a hiss before transforming himself back into a man. He headed out to the main clearing. The escort he had left at Morgan awaited him.

"Your Highness, I bring urgent news from Denel," said the sergeant in charge. He handed the Prince a scroll.

Mathew cracked the seal. It belonged to his deputy. As he read the colour drained from his face. "Someone find Oriel!" He snapped out the order before he had even finished absorbing the information the page contained.

"Mathew?"

He looked up to find his parents in human form in front of him. "Chrystopher is dead," he told them. "Long live Queen Haileigh." He turned to his escort. "Water your horses. We will be leaving for Denel within the hour."

Chapter Twenty Eight

Sixteenth day, Turquoise Moon, year 2981
Carmichael Hall, Westecroft

Oriana stood at the window of her home office and watched her children play. It was hard to believe seven years had passed since she first came to Carmichael Hall as Liam's wife.

Her eldest child, Althea was a feminine version of her father with chestnut brown hair and sapphire blue eyes. She was also rather spoilt by her grandfather who often used the excuse that his gifts were in thanks for his continued existence. Osten had never forgotten Oriana's comment when he first saw his granddaughter and utilized every opportunity to use it to give the young girl gifts.

At six, Althea was an extremely bright child. She also had more energy than most of her peers. Strangely, she used this excess energy to help others. Liam had commented that she was rather like her mother, that way.

Their second child was Caelan, four years old and constantly trying to keep up with his big sister whom he adored. Caelan took after his mother in looks but was blessed with his father's temperament.

Last was Edain. Oriana sometimes wondered who her youngest son took after as he was quite content to watch his elder siblings play. She had never come across such a placid child, particularly at the interesting age of two.

The apprentice Wuhern laid a hand across her swelling belly. Soon the group below would be joined by another. Oriana hoped it would be another girl, although she knew she would be happy with whatever the Gods granted her.

"Oriana?"

She looked over her shoulder to find her husband standing in the doorway. "Hi." She smiled as he walked toward her.

He stood behind her and wrapped his arms around her waist. "What are you up to?"

"Just watching the children," she replied. "To what do I owe the pleasure of your visit?" she asked, curious. Liam was usually locked in the ducal office with his father at this time of day, going over business.

"Father has asked me to go to Jerriko and check over our people there," he informed her cautiously. "It would only be for a few days."

"I see." Her eyes narrowed slightly at his words. "You are not expecting me to go with you, are you?"

He kissed the top of her head. "No," he reassured her. Despite the fact she had not lived there for over twenty years, Oriana had a distinct dislike of the city. "I thought I might take Althea with me."

Oriana turned in his arms. "Why?"

Liam shrugged. "She is old enough to travel the distance and I thought it might be a nice treat for her. She can see some of the rest of Westecroft, because if she is anything like either of us, she is going to travel anyway."

"But what about…" Her voice trailed off as she was unable to make herself say the words.

"'The Dog'?" Liam waited for her to nod. After seven years of marriage he was well aware of all aspects of his wife's background. "We don't know if he is still alive and if he is Althea will be with me at all times. If he isn't, no one who might have replaced him is likely to associate us with you anyway." Oriana looked unconvinced. "If it makes you feel better, I can take Isorren with us," he suggested.

"Uh…no…that's fine." Oriana paled slightly at the idea and hoped Liam would think it just part of her pregnancy. "I'd rather Isorren stayed here with me," she added before attempting to change the topic. "When do you leave?"

"Tomorrow," Liam replied. "I'll be back before the little one is due to make its appearance." He placed a hand on her belly.

⌀

Jerriko, Westecroft

"Did you enjoy the ride?" Liam asked his daughter as they settled into Carmichael House in Jerriko. They had been on the road all day, arriving as the sun went down in a spectacular display of red, orange and gold.

"Yep!" Althea nodded enthusiastically. They were in the family dining room, enjoying a light meal as the heat of the day began to fade. "Thank you for bringing me, Papa."

Liam smiled at her. "You are most welcome Althea." He took a sip of the iced tea their housekeeper had provided him. "Tomorrow we will go down to the markets. I have some people to meet with, but we can do some of the tourist walks afterward if you would like?"

Althea chewed thoughtfully on the food in her mouth. "Can we do some shopping?" she asked once she swallowed the mouthful.

Her father mentally winced. "Have you been spending time with your Aunts?" he inquired, dismayed. Oriana was not one for shopping which caused Liam to suspect his sisters had introduced Althea to this activity. His daughter gave him a puzzled look. "Never mind," he said, shaking his head in defeat. "Yes, we can do some shopping. I am curious as to why you would want to though." Liam gave her an enquiring look.

She shrugged. "I want to get something for Mama, Poppa, Caelan and Edain," Althea told him.

"With what money?" The knight was curious. He was not aware of his wife giving her any before they left, although, knowing Oriana, that didn't mean she hadn't.

"Aunty Micky gave me money for my birthday," the little girl informed her father. "And Poppa gives me pocket money each week."

Liam gave his daughter a penetrating look. "I may have to speak to your Poppa about that," he murmured under his breath. "What we will do tomorrow then, is visit my people first, have lunch and then do some shopping. Does that sound like a good plan?" he suggested.

Althea tipped her head to one side as she considered his words. "Yep. Sounds good!" She grinned happily at him.

He laughed at the expression on her face. It was very like one he often saw on his wife's face when she had managed to trick someone into doing what she wanted them to. "Off to bed with you, child. We have a big day ahead of us."

The little girl slid off of her chair and walked over to her father. He leaned down so she could kiss him on the cheek before she ran up to her temporary bedroom.

☙

Althea carefully picked up the silk wrap from the rack in front of her. It was a beautiful piece of work with many different shades of blue and green swirling together in a variety of patterns. Gold embroidery provided a wonderful highlight to the colours on the silk, lifting them. As she slid it over her hands, the little girl considered the possibility of giving it to her mother.

Her father was in the office of the silk merchant, going over the books and dealing with any concerns the man might have. His daughter was amusing herself under the watchful eye of the merchant's wife.

"That is a very pretty scarf," said a voice from behind her. Althea turned to find an old man behind her. He reminded her of Unca Ani as she called Wuhern Aneurin. "What are you planning on doing with it?" the man asked. The little girl glanced at the woman behind the counter. She was not sure if she should respond to the man. The merchant's wife nodded, indicating it was safe. "Don't worry. I know Mistress Jooli quite well," he reassured her, noticing her discomfort.

"I thought I might give it to my Mama," Althea told him shyly.

He smiled at her. "I am sure she will love it, but why don't you buy something for yourself?"

"I haven't found anything I like," she said, shifting slightly on one foot. Despite the assurances of both the adults, the girl did not feel entirely comfortable.

Sensing this, the man held out his hand. "My name is Andrion," he introduced himself. "I knew your Mama many years ago."

Wide eyes looked up at him in surprise. "You did?"

Andrion nodded. "Yes. She lived here when she was your age."

The information crept past Althea's guard. "Really?"

He inclined his head. "You remind me of her. True, you have your father's hair but your personality is very like your mother and her cousin Michaela." Andrion pulled something out of his pocket. He opened his palm to reveal a crystal shard on a silver chain. "This belonged to your mother's great, great grandmother," he told the child. "I knew her too, and she gave this into my keeping for you." Althea glanced at the pendant before returning her gaze to the man before her. "It's all right. You can take it. You are meant to have it."

She took the necklace from his hand. "Why didn't Mama have it?" the girl asked, curious.

"Your mother wasn't the person intended to have it," Andrion informed her. "Her mother's great grandmother was gifted with foresight. She foresaw your birth and entrusted me with the crystal. I was instructed to pass it on to you when the time was right." He glanced up as he heard footsteps on the stairs which led to the silk merchant's office. "It is time for me to go." He gave her an apologetic look. "It was lovely to meet you, Althea." Before she could respond Andrion had slipped out of the building.

The girl looked down at the pendant in her hand. As the back door of the room opened to reveal her father, she slipped it into her pocket.

જ

Twenty first day, Turquoise Moon, year 2981
Carmichael Hall, Westecroft

"MAMA!"

Oriana looked up from her discussion with Lord Aneurin just in time to see Althea barrelling into the room. With an apologetic glance in the direction of her boss, she turned her attention to her daughter. "You're back," she said, opening her arms to collect her daughter in an awkward hug. "Did you have fun?"

"Oh yes! Lot's and lot's of fun! We went shopping!" the girl told her mother as her father entered the room at a more sedate pace.

"Everything is sorted out?" Oriana enquired, looking up at her husband.

Liam nodded. "No problems. I will give Father a report after dinner. He is somewhere on the estate at the moment."

As Oriana and Liam had been talking, Aneurin had caught sight of the crystal hanging around Althea's neck. It was a piece he recognized from his childhood. "Althea? Where did you get that necklace?" he asked quietly, trying to not attract the attention of his apprentice. He failed.

"What necklace?" Oriana glanced down at her daughter trying to see what had intrigued the Wuhern. "She probably bought it, didn't you darling?"

Althea shook her head. "A man named Andrion gave it to me," she told the adults. "He said that it had belonged to…." She scrunched up her nose as she tried to remember the words he had used. "My Mama's great, great grandmother." A triumphant grin creased her face as her memory provided the answer.

"When was this?" Liam asked. He had noticed Aneurin paling at the little girl's words, although Oriana was busy concentrating on their daughter. The knight decided to speak with the Wuhern later if an explanation was not forthcoming.

Althea looked up at her father. "When we were at the silk merchants." She turned to mother. "He said that he knew you and your cousin Michaela when you were my age."

The Master Athenan snapped her head in Aneurin's direction. "My Lord?" There was only one Michaela that she knew and as far as she was aware, they were not related.

"Althea – go and say hello to your brothers," Liam instructed. The tone of his wife's voice was dangerous. He did not want their daughter around if things became sticky.

"Okay." The little girl jumped off of her mother's lap and dashed out the door which her father closed behind her.

Her gaze pinning the Wuhern to his chair, Oriana demanded an explanation from her master. "Would you care to explain what you know of this?" He shifted in his chair. "Who is this Andrion? Why does he think Michaela and I are related?"

"Why the curiosity about Althea's necklace?" added Liam, leaning against the door he had closed.

Aneurin sighed. "The necklace belonged to my mother. Andrion is my brother." He looked into Oriana's eyes. "Although you would know him better as 'The Dog'." He held up a hand to prevent her explosion. "The reason he suggested you and Michaela are related is because you are." The Wuhern need not have worried about an explosion as Oriana was too shocked to even say a word. "Andrion visited me prior to your wedding. He informed me that the two of you were related. When I enquired as to how he knew this I was told that…" Aneurin paused as he tried to frame his words. "You are both daughters of his granddaughters."

Oriana went white. Liam leaped across the room, but she waved him away. The room was silent as the Athenan absorbed all the Wuhern had said.

Concern evident on his face, Liam watched as his wife assimilated the information. He could almost see the pieces of a puzzle he had not even realised existed, fall into place. The silence continued. Liam could almost hear the wax dripping from the time candle as they waited for Oriana to speak.

"This explains so much." She looked over at the Wuhern. "Now I understand why Isorren was sent to join the guards. He told me 'The Dog' had given him instructions. He also said his boss was responsible for Michaela and me joining the Order." She stopped, a thought suddenly occurring to her. "Michaela knows!" she accused Aneurin. "That is why you sent her away six years ago. Why she only has fleeting visits home!" The Wuhern nodded. It was safer not to say anything. "You didn't want her to tell me. Were you going to tell me at all?" she demanded.

"It was not time." Aneurin looked out of the window. "I would not have thought now was the time either, but the Twins seem to have other ideas."

Oriana gave him a fierce look. She was not happy with him at all. "Can she come home now?" said the Athenan, referring to her cousin.

The Wuhern shook his head. "Unfortunately no, not permanently at least," he replied. "She is actually doing rather important work for me, which will be essential to you when you are Wuhern, my dear."

Oriana went to reply, but all that came out of her mouth was a gasp of what sounded to the men suspiciously like pain. They gazes flew to her face except her attention was focused lower. She looked up at her husband, disbelief on her face. "I think the little one wants to make its entrance." Oriana watched as her words sunk in. Liam went white. "Send for the midwife." She sent the instruction in the direction of the Wuhern. "Liam, please help me to our rooms."

℘

"Congratulations my dear. You now have a full set," said Aneurin. Osten had left several minutes earlier to attend to a problem.

Although she was still unhappy with him, Oriana was unable to scowl due to her pleasure in her new born daughter. Instead she ignored her boss and addressed her husband. "Can we stop now?"

Liam grinned and went to answer but was interrupted before he could frame his reply.

"Mama?" said a small voice from the direction of the door. The adults parted to reveal Althea and Caelan nervously peaking in.

Oriana smiled. "Come here and meet you new little sister." Both children raced over to the bed. Liam lifted them on to it.

"She's so little," remarked Caelan. He slid a hand over toward the baby who waved hers and found his forefinger, grabbing hold and causing him to giggle.

"What is her name?" asked Althea as she watched her siblings.

"Jenifer," her mother told them. "Jenifer Eavan."

Happy that all was well with his apprentice, and knowing it would be a few days before she was willing to talk to him, Aneurin slipped quietly out of the room, closing the door behind him.

"All right you two, time for bed," said Liam after a short while.

Althea nodded and slipped off of the bed, surprising both her parents. "Come Caelan." She held out her hand to her brother. "We can tell Edain in the morning," she suggested when he would have complained. Leaving Oriana and Liam in shock, Althea took Caelan's hand, helped him from the bed and led him from the room. At the door she stopped. "Good night Mama, Papa and Jenifer," she said, echoed by her brother. Then she reached up, opened the door and headed toward the nursery.

Chapter Twenty Nine

Twentieth day of Jasper Moon, year 2983,
Royal Palace, Irskin, Astiria

The rain was falling as Claire stood staring out of her window. The weather that night was reflecting her mood. She was worried about her youngest son. Varian had slowly become a silent and sullen boy since his abduction eight years earlier. It had been a subtle thing, but her once cheeky and adventurous little boy was now a loner who would let no one in. She sometimes wondered if the only reason it had taken so long for her to realise what was happening was because of the presence of Phillip in their life.

"Darling?" Jaymes stood in the doorway. "What is wrong?"

Claire turned toward her husband. "It is Varian," she replied, tearfully. "We have to do something Jaymes. He is not our son anymore."

The King wrapped his arms around his Queen. "Surely you are over reacting."

Claire leaned into her husbands chest. "No. That young man is not our son. He has changed since the abduction."

"Boys change as they grow up. It is a natural part of life," he insisted.

She shook her head. "Not like this. Binjaymen and Josep didn't change like this." She took a moment to wipe her eyes, before looking up into his. "I think we are going to have to send him to the Order of the Twins."

Jaymes looked at her in surprise. "Are you sure? After our experiences with the Order of Wyman, I am shocked that you would suggest such a thing."

"I know, I know, but the Order of the Twins has a reputation as healers of both body and mind," she said. "I truly think Varian needs such healing." Claire wiped her eyes again. "He is not the happy, carefree person he was before the abduction. He hardly speaks to anyone, even Binjaymen or Phillip. These are not the normal changes of a growing boy."

"If you are sure, then I shall invite Wuhern Andjo to the palace to discuss the possibility," conceded Jaymes. He did not like to see his wife so upset.

Over the years they had watched as their children grew up, married and in the case of their daughters, moved away. Apart from Varian, the palace now housed Josep and his family. So far their eldest son had been blessed with two sons of his own and was now awaiting the birth of a third child which everyone hoped would be a girl.

Claire nodded into his chest. "Yes. I think we really must."

"Then I shall send the note in the morning."

◆

"Your Highness?"

Varian looked up from his book to find a footman standing in the doorway of the library. "Yes?"

"Your Highness, his Majesty requests your presence in his office," the man told him.

"Thank you. Please inform his Majesty I shall be there in a moment," said the young man, dismissing the servant. Once the man left, Varian marked the page he had been reading and placed the book on the table, before standing and heading toward his father's office. It was only a short distance away and in moments he was walking into the room, surprised by not only the number of people it contained, but also by the people themselves.

"Varian, thank you for coming," said his father. "Please have a seat and I shall introduce you to our guest."

The Prince did as he was instructed whilst taking in the expressions and moods of the people before him. His father was nervous, not an emotion that usually showed itself on the king. Behind his father stood his mother. She was pale, as though she was frightened, and showing more nerves than her husband. The third person in the room was an older man. He wore the robes of a priest of the Order of the Twins but they were more ornate than any Varian had seen previously. No emotion showed on the man, although there was an air of calm emanating from him.

"Varian, I'd like to introduce you to Wuhern Andjo of the Order of the Twins," said Jaymes. "He is here at your Mother and my request. We have decided your education requires something the tutors here at the Palace can not provide and it is unnecessary for you to have the training your brothers had. Instead, we feel you would be better off if you were to become a novice in the Order of the Twins," he informed his son.

"Do I get any choice in the matter?" asked Varian, petulantly.

"No," replied Claire from behind her husband. "You will have the choice whether or not to become a full member of the Order when you reach the required level of study to take full vows. At that point you may decide what you will do next. Your father and I have made this decision based on your behaviour and attitude over the past few months," she told the young man.

"This isn't fair!" he complained. As far as he was concerned, he had done nothing wrong, why should he be punished.

"This is not a punishment, your Highness," said the Wuhern, speaking for the first time since Varian had entered the room. "Think of it as a new lesson to be learnt. I promise you that we, like your parents, only have your best interests at heart."

Jaymes gave Varian a stern look. "Life isn't meant to be fair, Varian. As we speak Uriahl is packing your things. You may go and pack any items you consider to be of personal value to you," he instructed. "I expect you to stay at the College of the Twins and do as you are required by the Order. If I hear so much as a rumour that you have left, I will have Binjaymen on your tail before you can say 'boo' and he will be under orders to return you to the College kicking and screaming if necessary."

"Fine!" Varian stood and stormed out of the room.

♦

College of the Twins, Irskin, Astiria

"Welcome young Varian. Please remove your clothes and lie on the bench," said Master Grempal, gesturing at the table in front of him.

"Excuse me?!"

"Remove your clothes and lie on the bench," repeated Grempal. "It is a simple enough instruction. I can not asses your power centres properly if you are fully clothed. You may leave your loin cloth on for decency," he explained before stepping into the other room to gather some supplies.

"Gee thanks." Varian did as instructed.

Once he was settled on the bench, Master Grempal returned to the room and placed the supplies on a table. He lifted a large clear crystal from amongst them and brought it over to the young prince. Holding it at roughly ten centimetres above the boy, he slowly ran it over the length of him. "My goodness!" exclaimed the Master Athenan in surprise.

"What?"

"I have never seen anything like this in all my years!"

"What?" repeated Varian.

"What have you been doing to yourself boy? Your throat centre is blocked completely. The third eye has slowed to a crawl. The only normal looking centre is the heart and even that isn't healthy. Something must be done about this!" Before Varian could say word, the Master Athenan returned to the table and after removing several crystals he brought them back to the prince. "Please do not move," he told the boy as he placed them at various points down the centre of his body..

"How long do I have to stay like this?" Varian asked petulantly.

Master Grempal looked down his nose at the boy. "Until your power centres are cleared and healthy once more. I shall check on you at regular intervals, and be aware I shall know if you have moved so much as a millimetre," he told the prince as he walked to the door.

"So what am I to do in the mean time?"

"Think about your life as it was, as it is and as it will be," and with that Master Grempal walked out of the room.

◆

"Well Grempal? How does the boy look?" asked Andjo as the Master Athenan entered his office.

Grempal collapsed in a chair opposite his Wuhern before he answered. "I have him doing a complete cleansing," he said, running a hand through his long hair.

"A complete cleansing?" The Wuhern was shocked.

"Yes," Grempal nodded to emphasize his point. "I have never seen anything like it. Not one of his power centres was healthy. He could be there for quite some time, and I fully expect to have to change the crystals at some point."

"Is it really that bad?"

"Oh yes!" the Master was vehement about it. "Master Yaj would have had a fit if he had seen something like this. What did they do to the poor boy over at the palace?"

Andjo looked out of his window for a moment, considering. "I am not sure the palace is at fault here," he replied, turning back to his healer. "He was kidnapped about eight years ago. He escaped with the help of his brother Binjaymen, but it still affected him," he explained, choosing his words carefully.

The Master gaped at his boss. "Well! I would have thought the palace healers would have taken better care of him. Don't they know anything? They should have been able to prevent this!" Grempal was aghast at what he considered a serious case of malpractice by his colleagues in the healing profession.

"Obviously not as much as they should. I shall have a word with the King as soon as can be arranged. Their teaching structure must be investigated. Even a raw novice knows how to prevent this sort of situation." Andjo shook his head. "The son of a king should not be allowed to get into the state you have described. If the mental and emotional health of the child of a kingdom's ruler is not of importance to the best healers in the kingdom, then there is a major problem in the profession!"

♦

Varian looked around what was to be his bedroom for the next four years. It was smaller than his old room at the palace and it did not have its own bathing room. His only consolation was he did not have to share the room with anyone else. He sighed as he began to unpack his belongings.

He had spent half the day lying on a bench, half naked, with a dozen or so crystals resting on him. It was not something he particularly enjoyed, but it had given him the opportunity to consider what the next few years were going to be like.

He did not expect that he would miss family. Jay hardly spent any time at home these days. He was always off on some diplomatic mission or another for their father. Josep was too busy with his own family and taking over more of the reigns of running the kingdom. Jirrelle now lived in Demesa with her husband and his family. Shrialla had moved to Trimid when she married one of the Trimidian princes, and Marryam now lived in Quandar with her husband Warren. Phillip, or Pip as he still preferred to be called, was also hardly at the palace. He now spent most of his time getting to know his duchy. At the age of sixteen, Pip had begun to take responsibility for his reward.

As Varian unpacked he came across the tracings he made as a child in Demesa. He looked at them, intrigued. "Perhaps some good might come out of this enforced study," he said out loud. "I may learn to decipher these." He placed them on the bookshelf he had been provided. Varian continued to empty out his bag until he found the crystal shard he had been permitted to take by the knome priest. "I had forgotten about that," he murmured as he picked it up. He fossicked in his pack until he located a piece of leather string. Someone had fitted a gold loop and clasp to the crystal, enabling Varian to thread a leather cord through the top and wear it around his neck.

A knock sounded on the door. "Yes?" Varian called.

It opened to show a young Athenan, clearly having achieved the position only recently. "Novice Varian, welcome to the Order of the Twins. I am Athenan Tancred and I am your mentor for the next six months," the young man told him. "I am responsible for making sure you know where you are going, what your chores are and what lessons you should be in at any given time."

"Chores?" Varian stared at Tancred in disbelief. He had never done chores in his life, at least not of the sort he suspected the Athenan meant.

Tancred nodded. "Everyone in the Order is expected to help with various chores. We are a religious order and therefore do not have servants."

A sceptical expression crossed Varian's face. "You can't mean to tell me that even Wuhern Andjo does chores," he scoffed.

The Athenan gave him a look of pity at his lack of understanding. "Of course he does. What do you think his position is all about? He has the biggest chore of all – running the Order."

"That is not what I meant and you know it," Varian said angrily. He did not appreciate being pitied, and he really didn't like it when someone purposely misunderstood something which he said.

Tancred gave him another pitying look. "Lord Andjo does his fare share of domestic chores," he informed the boy. "I have done my chores alongside him several times in the last three months since I came to Astiria."

The mention of not being a native caught Varian's attention. He had detected something different in the man's speech, although he had refrained from making a comment about it. "Where are you from?" he asked, accepting the opening the Athenan provided him.

"Zialp," replied Tancred. Varian mentally kicked himself. He should have realised as soon as he saw the Athenan. The Zialpan features were very distinctive. Very pale skin, white blonde hair, pale blue eyes, whilst body size depended on which part of the country one came from. Very few Zialpans had different features and those that did usually had a non-Zialpan ancestor somewhere in their family history. "Wuhern Belalie sent me here to broaden my knowledge and my skills," the Athenan informed the boy before him. "I am not here to talk about me." His tone brooked no argument. "It is time to introduce you to the College and its rules." With that, the Athenan waved a hand in the direction of the hallway. It had an authoritative air to it that had Varian deciding against rebellion.

♦

Twenty eighth day of Jasper Moon, year 2983,
Royal Palace, Irskin, Astiria

Jaymes stood at the fireplace in his office, staring into the flames. It had been a week since he sent his youngest son away. The time had not lessened the guilt he felt over this action. Josep and Claire both remonstrated him for this, saying that it was the only thing he could do, yet he could not change his feelings. Even the letter he held in his hand made no difference to the emotions coursing through him. If anything, they made him feel slightly worse.

Wuhern Andjo had written to tell him Varian was settling in well. Even after a few days, the boy was excelling in his classes and had begun to make friends amongst the other novices. The Wuhern had been rather scathing of the Royal Healers in his report. He explained the situation that had been discovered by his healer. It was obvious to the King, it should have been prevented. As a father, it was distressing to feel as though you had failed your child, no matter what the situation. His only consolation was he could rightfully claim the strain of ruling a kingdom had hampered his ability to notice it.

Jaymes had already called the Royal Healers into his office. They were now well aware of their error. The King had informed them of his plan to have an outside investigator visit their facilities in the future to ensure new measures be put in place for the prevention of another such incident.

He continued to stare at the flames as he pondered the issue of what he told his wife. Jaymes knew he should let Claire read the missive from the Wuhern. It would engage the temper she was very careful to keep in check. A sad smile graced the King's face at the thought. It often surprised him when Claire let fly. She was such a calm woman most of the time. When her temper was given full reign he suspected it could strip the skin off a man without her even touching him. Though he had yet to see it, Jaymes suspected Varian may have inherited it from his mother.

The King moved back to his desk, opened a drawer and slid the letter inside. The decision made, he left the room to inform his wife of their son's improvement.

◆

Chapter Thirty

Third day Beryl Moon, Year 2988
Temple of the Twins, Athos, Westecroft

Oriana, Duchess of Carmichael, stared at the missive in her hand. "What is the old coot up to?" she asked the air. She and her family had been in Athos for six weeks. Liam had brought the family to the capital at the end of the mourning period for his father so the King and Queen could officially invest him in the title of Duke of Carmichael. Oriana was there publicly as the representative of the Order of the Twins.

Her relationship to Liam was not common knowledge and the monarchs were happy to keep it that way. As she was his wife she did not need to be invested with her title, which meant she could be in the capital as heir to the Wuhernship of the Order of the Twins and no one would suspect a thing. Liam was staying at the Palace, while Oriana and their children were residing at the Temple. This prevented the children from letting slip their mother was a Master Athenan, and kept up the pretence Liam had come to Athos and left his family at home.

"What is who up to?" asked Michaela walking in the door. She had just arrived home from a trip to Pella, and upon hearing that Oriana was in residence at the Temple, had taken it into her head to visit her cousin whilst she had the chance.

Oriana looked up from the paper in surprise. "Mick!" She stood and stepped away from her desk before racing across the room to give the other woman a hug. "When did you get in?"

"Ungerbunggerfunger," came the muffled response from the vacinity of Oriana's shoulder.

"Oops! Sorry." The Athenan released her cousin.

"Half an hour ago," Michaela told her. "Valeigh told me you were here." She looked back at Oriana's desk. "So, what was all that about?" she asked, pointing to the paper resting on a stack of books.

"Master Aneurin wants me to court Prince Rhawn and Princess Tarianne to the Order." Oriana looked at her friend. "Do you have any idea what that is about?"

Michaela shook her head. "No, but it wouldn't be a bad idea." She thought about it for a moment. "I have heard rumours Ignatz is interested in having Prince Rhawn join his Order."

The other Athenan blinked in surprise. "Really?" Her colleague nodded. "Why would he want that?"

Michaela shrugged. "Maybe because Queen Haileigh is the Wuhern of Demesa as well as its monarch?" she suggested. "He could be trying to take over the country?"

"That is ridiculous," scoffed Oriana. "If Ignatz wanted to do that he could have taken over the Empire of Trimid. I've lost count of the number of Randon Princes there are in Trimid. Heck, I can't even keep up with the current count of Princes generally."

"Who knows," said Michaela. "Are you going to be around for dinner?"

Oriana shook her head. "Their Majesties have invited me to join them this evening for an intimate dinner of fifty in honour of their Royal Highnesses successful completion of their schooling."

"Fifty? Intimate?" Michaela was flabbergasted.

The Duchess of Carmichael grinned. "One day I will arrange for you to attend one of their larger functions," she suggested. "There are usually in excess of six hundred people in attendance."

Michaela put her hands up in surrender. "Please, no! Anything but that!" She glanced around the room. "I guess I should leave you to get ready."

"You could always go and visit your cousins," said Oriana. "Liam and I brought them along and I know they will be thrilled to see their 'Aunty' Miki."

The Athenan gave her cousin a puzzled look. "They are here?"

Oriana nodded. "Yes. They are staying here with me whilst Liam is residing at the Palace."

Michaela blinked. "You are a strange, strange person Oriana." She shook her head. "Why?"

"This from the woman who is best described as Aneurin's lackey," responded Oriana. "You know more about what his nibs is up to and he was the one that suggested this arrangement."

"Oh."

"Go and see the children," the Athenan told her friend. "They are in a suite two doors down to the right. I will talk to you tomorrow."

⚘

The Palace, Athos, Westecroft

"Your Royal Highness." Oriana curtseyed before Princess Tarianne. "May I congratulate you on your achievements."

"Thank you Master Oriana," replied Tarianne, inclining her head in acknowledgement. The princess, like her twin, was similar in height to Oriana. Subsequently the two women were able to look each other in the eye whilst talking, without either one suffering from neck strain.

Taking after her mother, Tarianne was graced with long, flowing, golden blonde hair. Tonight she had it braided and twisted upon her head and held in place by a number of diamond-studded pins. A small coronet of plaited gold circled her head, resting comfortably in the middle of her brow. The princess' green eyes were highlighted with a small amount of make-up and she had reddened her lips with one of the glosses which were currently popular in the city. All of this, coupled with the scarlet gown she was wearing, presented a picture that had caused several young courtiers to pass out at the sight of her.

"Have you had a chance to consider what you will do now?" inquired the Master Athenan. "Will you study further? Get married?"

Tarianne considered the woman in front of her before responding. "I have yet to firmly decide my future path," she told her. Something about the other woman's manner suggested that she was after certain information, although Tarianne could not figure out what it was. "I have planted some seeds and am waiting to see what fruit they bear. On the subject of marriage, I feel that at this stage I am a touch too young to consider that option." The princess threw a cheeky grin at Oriana. "But I shall enjoy investigating the potentials in the mean time."

Oriana returned Tarianne's grin. "I understand perfectly, your Highness." She paused a moment, considering her words. "Tell me, if you don't mind, do you know what your brother's plans are?"

The young woman showed no surprise at the query. She realised this is what she had been waiting for. "I believe he is still considering his choices," she told the representative of the Order of the Twins. "Lord Ignatz has been speaking with him of late, however when I last spoke with Rhawn on the subject he mentioned he was still undecided." The princess watched as, despite her best efforts, a slight expression of glee appeared on the other woman's face.

"It is good to see his Highness does not make rash decisions," responded Oriana. "It bodes well for Westecroft that their future king shows such wisdom on the topic of his future." She winced as she realised how much like her mentor she sounded. On one as young as Oriana was, it came across as rather pompous.

Her royal training behind her, Tarianne was able to hide her amusement at the Master Athenan. Spying her brother out of the corner of her eye, the princess made a hand movement behind her back to get his attention and bring him over to her. Within moments he was by her side.

"Tari, who is this beautiful woman you are talking to?" enquired the prince as he joined them. Rhawn gave Oriana a flirtatious smile as he asked his sister the question.

Tarianne rolled her eyes at Oriana. "Rhawn, may I have the honour of introducing Master Athenan Oriana of the Order of the Twins. Lady Oriana, my rather irritating brother, Prince Rhawn."

Oriana bobbed a curtsey. "Your Highness."

"Lady Oriana." Rhawn bowed slightly and raised her hand to kiss it. "It is a pleasure to meet you," he told her. "I know we have met before, however I am afraid I was too young to remember you."

"That is perfectly fine, your Highness," replied Oriana. "It has been some years, and unfortunately we have not managed to cross paths since."

"So what were you lovely ladies talking about when I interrupted?" the prince asked.

"Strangely enough, you," said his twin, rather disgusted with her brother's manner.

"Me? How delightful!" Rhawn's tone was patently patronising. "Dare I ask what aspect of my good self you were discussing?"

An evil grin filled Tarianne's face. "Actually, Lady Oriana was wondering what you are going to do with yourself now you have finished all your studies." She watched with glee as the Master Athenan's face paled slightly. Before Oriana could respond, the princess stepped away from her brother and caught the closest courtier in conversation, leaving the other woman to deal with the prince's reaction alone.

Rhawn's expression sobered and the cheeky boy disappeared. "It is a tough decision to make," he told his companion, taking pity on her. "I am looking at many different avenues."

Oriana swallowed and regained her bearings before responding. "That is probably the best move to make. Your sister tells me you have been speaking with Lord Ignatz of the Order of Wyman?"

"Yes. He seems to feel I would make a good priest."

"Lord Aneurin once told me many nobles make good priests to the Gods as they are raised from birth to lead and look after," suggested Oriana as she cringed at the idea of the young man in front of her joining an Order with the reputation the Order of Wyman had. It did not fit with her picture of the prince.

Rhawn considered her words. "Lord Aneurin is wise. There is probably something to his observation. I had never really considered myself the religious type," he informed her. "However, since speaking with Lord Ignatz, I have been giving the Gods a lot more investigation than I had previously done." A movement behind Oriana suddenly caught his attention. Something was happening at the Dias where the King and Queen were residing. "What made you join the Order of the Twins, if I may ask?"

"There were many reasons," replied Oriana. "Some of them were purely selfish, others were not and I found that even the selfish ones were acceptable by the Twins."

Just then they were interrupted as the Duke of Carmichael appeared at Oriana's side. "Excuse me your Highness, Lady Oriana," said Liam, bowing to both the people in front of him. "The king requests your presence in the antechamber at once."

Oriana gave her husband an enquiring look. "Me? Or his Highness?" she asked.

"Both of you," was his curt response. Oriana blinked at his tone. As she fell in step beside the prince and followed the Duke to the antechamber she assessed his body language. Liam was upset. His posture was stiff to the point of being rock solid. She had only seen him like this once before and that was when he had found out about his father's passing. She was about to ask him what was wrong when they arrived. Liam opened the door and waited for them to enter. Inside the King, Queen and Princess Tarianne were waiting.

"Your Majesties, your Highness." Oriana curtsied.

"Father, Mother," said Rhawn. "You wished to see us?"

Carlyle, King of Westecroft, had a sombre expression on his face. "Lady Oriana, please have a seat." He gestured to a chair before him. He waited until she had followed his instruction before he continued. "It is with profound sorrow, I must inform you, Lord Aneurin has passed over."

Oriana shook her head. "No." Liam stepped up behind his wife.

"A messenger arrived ten minutes ago with the news. I am so sorry to be the bearer of such sad tidings." The King bowed his head in sorrow as he handed his wife a handkerchief.

"No. NO! That is not possible." Oriana went white as the news slowly sunk in.

"Master Athenan Michaela is organising your belongings so you can return to the College of the Twins for the funeral," Liam informed her quietly.

"No, no, no, no, no, NO!"

Chapter Thirty-One

Tenth day Peridot Moon, Year 2988
College of the Twins, Westecroft

Michaela looked at the sky and sighed. The day had dawned surprisingly clear for such a sad occasion. As she stood on the parapet watching the sun rise above the trees, Michaela wondered how Oriana would survive the day. Her cousin had been an absolute wreck since receiving the news of Wuhern Aneurin's death. Not that Michaela herself had been much better. The Wuhern had been the closest thing to a father that either woman had had. However, as Aneurin's heir, Oriana was now responsible for the running of the Westecroftan branch of the Order of the Twins. At the completion of today's funeral Oriana would be officially sworn in as Wuhern. The ordination ceremony was to be as elaborate and as long as the funeral itself and dignitaries from across the world had arrived to witness both events.

Michaela turned her head to glance in the direction of the village. Their Majesties, the King and Queen of Westecroft and their daughter Tarianne were staying with Liam and the children at the manor. Prince Rhawn had chosen to stay in Athos in his father's absence, or so they had been told. Michaela suspected that there was another reason, but she was not in a position to do anything about her suspicions.

The other Wuherns were staying in their rooms at the College. The representatives of the northern kings were staying with other aristocratic families in the neighbourhood, whilst Athenans and Masters who had come for the funeral and could not fit into the College were staying in the village, either at the inn or with whomever they could convince to put them up. Many nobles had made the trip too, and were staying wherever they could find accommodation. It was going to be one incredible day.

"Aunty Michaela?" came a voice from behind her. Michaela turned to see Althea standing at the top of the stairs. "Are you alright?" the girl asked.

Michaela smiled sadly. "I'm fine sweetheart. What are you doing here so early?"

"Father came over to check on Mother, so I came with him," Althea told her, walking over to join Michaela. "I couldn't handle being around all those people that have taken over our home any longer." She shrugged. "So I thought I would see if I could be useful over here."

Michaela raised an eyebrow, which caused Althea to blink at the gesture that was one she saw frequently on her mother. "And what exactly are you doing to be useful at the moment?" she inquired, crossing her arms and tipping her head to one side.

The girl mimicked the older woman's posture. "Talking to you," she replied impishly.

Michaela laughed. Shaking her head she gathered Althea up in a hug. "What would I do without you sprout?"

"You don't want to know," said Althea, grinning.

Michaela rolled her eyes. "Okay shrimp. Let's get this show on the road."

♌

As with Oriana and Liam's wedding, flags fluttered in the breeze and people filled the grounds of the College of the Twins, Westecroft. Oriana stood at her window, looking out at the sight. This was the last time she would use the room in which she stood. By the end of the day she would officially take possession of the rooms of Wuhern of the Order of the Twins. It was something she was dreading as it meant, truly meant that Aneurin was gone.

The past few weeks since she had been told of his passing had been a blur. Oriana could not recall the drive home. She could not even remember leaving the palace to return to the Temple. The entire Order was mourning the loss of the old Wuhern. Aneurin had touched the lives of so many people, something that was reflected by the crowds of people waiting to farewell him.

Liam walked into the room to the sight of his wife wearing nothing but a cotton shift and long cotton pants, her feet were bare and she was staring out of her window. "Um....Oriana? Shouldn't you be getting dressed?" he asked. "The ceremony starts in less than half an hour."

Oriana turned away from the window to face him. "This is what I am wearing," she told him. "As I am to be ordained as Wuhern after the ceremony I must wear the traditional garb of the incoming Wuhern."

Liam blinked. "And this traditional garb is undergarments?"

One of very few smiles to have graced her face recently appeared. "No Liam," she said, shaking her head. "The material is considerably thicker than that of undergarments. It is to represent the clothes which the first member of the Order of the Twins was wearing when the Twins accepted him to Their following and charged him with the task of preparing those who would come," Oriana explained as her husband crossed the room to join her by the window. "They won't look quite so clean by the end of the ordination."

"Okay....I don't think I want to know why," said Liam, a look of resigned confusion on his face.

Oriana patted his arm condescendingly. "Don't worry dear. You'll understand by the end of the day."

Before Liam could reply appropriately there was a knock on the doorframe. They both turned toward the sound. "Action time Oriana," announced Haileigh, Queen and Wuhern of Demesa from the doorway. "Sorry Liam, but you have to go and join Carlyle and Demetria. Don't worry about Oriana here. I'll look after her," she reassured the man.

Liam grinned. "Now I really am worried." He placed a kiss on Oriana's forehead. "It will be fine," he told her before giving her a quick hug and leaving.

"He's right you know," said Haileigh once Liam had left the room. "It will be fine." She leaned against the doorframe as Oriana gave her room one last glance before making her way over to join the Queen of Demesa. "I know it hurts, but he would not have chosen you if you were not up to the task."

Oriana sighed. "That doesn't mean I have to like it."

𝒵

The crowd stirred restlessly, waiting, anticipating. Due to the amount of people who had come to farewell the late Wuhern, the ceremonies were being held in the fields to the north of the actual College, past the small forest of trees which ranged around the main compound providing a natural screen from the outside world.

From somewhere in the distance came the sound of a drumbeat, just one long note. The noise of the crowd subsided, waiting, as surely this was a sign that the funeral had started. Moments passed, then another beat rang out, long and low. The next beat came sooner and louder, followed by another and then another, get progressively louder as they went. All heads turned, searching for the source of the beats. Their patience was soon rewarded.

Suddenly, in an opening in the trees, appeared a lone drummer. Slowly, methodically, he beat on the drum as he made his way into the clearing and field. So close to the people now, the sound was reminiscent of a war drum beating in time to the marching of troops. Then a flute joined the drum, lifting high, flying like a bird, complimenting, yet contrasting. A second, lower flute joined the melody, then a third, meshing, melding and chasing. The new musicians appeared out of the woods, like the drummer moving slowly, steadily toward the front of the crowd and the waiting platform on which the ceremony would be performed prior to the Wuhern's body returning to the College to be interred in the catacombs of the Temple with his predecessors.

Behind the flautists came a procession of acolytes, their pale green uniforms forming a pale snake as they made their way along the path between the guests towards the space left between the royal visitors and the rest of the attendees. After the acolytes came the Athenans. Their darker green uniforms making them almost invisible against the trees until they were well past the edge. The Masters followed the Athenans, their gold edged robes rippling in the sunlight. They proceeded past the gathered mass and up onto the platform, making a wall on its furthest edge.

Lord Aneurin, late Wuhern of Westcroft passed through the trees in simple, but elegantly carved, wooden coffin carried by his contemporaries. Oren and Quenmir stood at the head of the coffin, Andjo and Etheline came next, with the end of the coffin held by Rochelle and Belalie. Oriana followed the coffin, escorted by Michaela and Haileigh on either side of her. When they reached the platform the coffin was placed onto a long low table. The Wuherns of the Order of the Twins formed a semi-circle around the coffin and Michaela and Oriana stepped back to join their fellow Masters. Oriana in the centre of the row, very noticeable in her colourless garments. Once they were all in place the music swelled to a crescendo then slid to a halt.

Oren, Wuhern of Quandar, stepped forward, out of the semi-circle, closer to the coffin and addressed the crowd. "Your Royal Majesties, Highnesses, my Lords and Ladies and all of you gathered here today to farewell Aneurin, I welcome you and I thank you, on behalf of the Order of the Twins for the respect you pay to our dear and departed friend." He placed a hand on the coffin. "Aneurin was well loved by many, as is evidenced by your attendance here today. He touched many lives and we are grateful to the Gods for gifting us with him."

Oren now stepped back into the half circle of Wuherns. "Each one of us here today has personally benefited from the wisdom of Aneurin." He gestured to the other Wuherns and the Masters behind him, though he could have easily been meaning the gathered crowd also. "It is now time to say goodbye and thank you to the man we once knew and welcome in his place his chosen heir." The curve of Wuherns split to reveal Oriana, standing amongst her fellow Masters. Now she stepped forward to join the Wuherns. Quenmir, Wuhern of Trimid, standing on Oriana's left, took one hand, whilst Oren clasped the other. They stepped forward, taking Oriana with them.

"Before you stands Oriana, Master Athenan of the Order of the Twins, chosen by Aneurin take his place in guiding the Order of the Twins in Westecroft forward into whatever future may await it," said Quenmir. He turned slightly to face the line of Masters. "Do you, Master Athenans of the Order of the Twins, agree with your late Wuhern's decision?" He asked. "Will you accept her as your leader from this day forth?" It was not so much an actual question as it was a part of the ritual of both the funeral of a Wuhern and the ordination of his or her successor.

"Is she worthy?" The line responded in one voice. "Let her prove herself."

Oren faced the crowd more squarely. "Do you, Athenans of the Order of the Twins, accept the decision of your late Wuhern?" He asked the green uniformed group in the audience. "Will you accept her orders without quarrel or qualm from this day forth?"

As one voice they responded. "Is she strong?" They asked. "Let her prove herself."

Quenmir looked over to the acolytes, almost glowing in their light green garb. "Do you, acolytes of the Order of the Twins, concur with your late Wuhern's decision? Will you accept her teachings from this day forth?"

Like the previous respondents they answered in chorus. "Is she wise? Let her prove herself."

Finally Oren turned to his colleagues. "My friends, what say you? As Wuherns of the Order of the Twins, are you in agreement with Aneurin? Is Oriana the right person to take on this role, this job, this task?"

"Does she know compassion?" They asked in return. "Let her prove herself."

"Very well." Oren turned to Oriana. "You have heard the words of those of the Order of the Twins," he told her. "You must prove yourself worthy, strong, wise and compassionate enough to fulfill the position of Wuhern before you will be acknowledged. Do you accept this challenge? Will you face tests to prove these traits? Will you succeed?"

Oriana squared her shoulders. "I accept the challenge," she told the Wuhern. "I will face any test you give me and I will do everything in my power to succeed, to prove myself worthy, strong, wise and compassionate enough to be the person that Lord Aneurin thought me, that I may fulfill his dream and take the Order of the Twins in Westecroft into what ever the future may hold."

Oren nodded. "So be it!" He turned back to the crowd. "I ask for volunteers. I ask for a Wuhern, a Master Athenan, an Athenan and an Acolyte to witness the tests that Oriana shall now face." One person from amongst each rank stepped forward. They had been chosen long before this moment, waiting only for the call. "Take the applicant to the Temple," Oren instructed. "Witness her tests, and return only when she has passed them and proven that she is the right person to take on the role and responsibility of Wuhern."

Belalie, Wuhern of Zialp took Oriana's hand and lead her from the stage, they were joined by the other witnesses as they made their way from the platform and back into the College grounds to the Temple. Once they had left the gathering Quenmir turned his attention back to the crowd. "Let us continue the ceremony to celebrate the passing of our friend Aneurin. In time we shall know if Oriana, Master Athenan will be the new Wuhern, but now is for Aneurin."

ℒ

Five people entered the Temple of the Twins. All furniture except the altar had been removed from the ceremonial space, leaving an empty floor. On the floor was a mosaic circle of interlocking gold and silver representing the Twins twenty metres in diameter. At the quarter points of the circle, inside the gold and silver were four discs – one of malachite, one of garnet, one of lapis lazuli and one of moonstone. At the centre of the circle was another disc this one of amethyst. Between the discs was a mosaic story of the cycle of life and the seasons.

The first four people each stopped on one of the four cross point discs. The last person followed them into the circle but stopped on the centre disc. The Wuhern of Zialp lifted her arms to a horizontal position. "I call on the Spirits of Earth to protect all in this circle," she cried, and green light spread around her and out to halfway between her and the two people either side of her.

To her left stood Master Athenan Venci. He followed the example of Belalie and spread his arms out. "I call upon the Spirits of Air to protect all within this circle." His voice echoing in vaulted room. Shimmering white light came from his being, meshing with the green light surrounding the Wuhern, both of them arching over the group slightly.

Next to Venci and opposite Belalie stood Ziljana, a recently ordained Athenan. She mimicked the other two, opening her arms. "I call upon the Spirits of Fire to protect those inside this circle," she said, strong and sure. Red light appeared around her, blending seamlessly with the green and leaving only a quarter of the circle open.

Last in the circle was Azir, an Acolyte entering his final year before committing to the Order. He extended his arms and repeated the words he had spent a week studying so as to not make a mistake, "I call to the Spirits of Water to protect all who stand within this circle." Blue light misted into being about him merging with the green to his left and the red to his right, completing the circle and forming a perfect half sphere above the ground, the other half continuing beneath the group.

As one they spoke, "Spirits of the Elements, Lady Thayis and Lord Theron, before you stands Oriana, Master Athenan and servant to the Twins, to be tried and tested, to prove that she is worthy, strong, wise and compassionate enough to take on the role of Wuhern. We ask that you assess her strengths and weaknesses and judge her. We stand here as witnesses and await results of your examination." In perfect synchronization their arms dropped back to their sides, silence fell and all in the room waited.

$\mathcal{Q}$

Sixth day, Citrine Moon, year 2989

The room was vast. Over a mile in length and two miles wide, its walls were lined with bookshelves all the way to the roof, which was a mile above the floor and supported by huge stone columns. Two mezzanines interrupted the lines of bookshelves, with several staircases allowing for access. In the centre of the floor were many large tables, each covered with piles of books. At the largest of these sat a human man of middle years and a dragon of indiscriminate age.

The human, ensconced in a throne like chair with lots of padding, looked forlorn. His age showing in the lines on his face, sat staring at the open book before him without seeing a word.

"Don't be so negative Nimitz," scolded the dragon. "All is not lost. There is still plenty of time to set things right."

Nimitz gave his companion an assessing look. "Arist... What have you not told me?" he demanded of the dragon.

Arist gave a very human like shrug of his shoulders. "Nothing you should not have figured out on your own." He sighed as the man glared at him. "The Third has gone to the knomes," the dragon told him. "He will be looked after by them until he is ready to re-enter the world. Oryien has agreed to assign a couple of Gardeners to keep an eye on him when he re-emerges."

Nimitz blinked in surprise. "Really? That is a rather unusual move on His part."

Arist nodded his head in agreement before continuing. "The merfolk have the Fifth well in hand. The reports I have indicate that he is very close to the First in abilities at this stage. Queen Haileigh has everything under control with regards the Fourth and Aneurin set up the support network for the Sixth before he passed on," the dragon informed his friend.

"This helps us how?" Asked Nimitz. "All twelve need to be in agreement in order for Her to be released. So far only six have surfaced and we have lost one of those to the other side!" The last little bit of the sentence came out rather shrill. Nimitz' eyes were a touch wide.

Arist gave the human a pitying look. "All Twelve are in existence, even if they have not surfaced. The youngest is only seven at the moment. We have at least another seven years to fix the problem."

Nimitz scowled at the dragon. "That is if the other side don't get to the rest first."

*